WEAVING FATE

THE OMEGA PROPHECY II

NORA ASH

Illustrated by
NATASHA SNOW DESIGNS

ABOUT THE AUTHOR

Nora Ash writes thrilling romance and sexy paranormal fantasy.

Visit her website to learn more about her upcoming books.

WWW.NORA-ASH.COM

ANNABEL

"What do they mean, *pay with the same blood?* Are they going to kill them? They can't do that!"

Trud cut my panicked tirade short, grabbing me gently by my shoulders and halting my pacing in the upturned kitchen.

"We're not going to let anyone hurt Magni," she said.

"That's great, but what about Saga and his brothers?" I bit, shooting Modi a glare. I realized it wasn't the siblings' fault that their mother betrayed my mates, but right then, I needed an outlet. "Your brother's made it plenty clear he's more than happy to see them dead!"

Modi turned toward me, his blue eyes flashing, but when he opened his mouth—undoubtedly to retaliate —Trud shook her head at him before refocusing on me.

"Loki's sons are scum, it's true, but you're mated to

one of them. If he dies, you die. And if you die, so does our brother."

She seemed to be speaking as much to me as she was Modi, judging from his dark look in her direction.

"I'll find Dad," she continued. "The Valkyries will be taking them to Valhalla to stand trial in front of Odin. Without Thor's presence, I fear it will be too easy for the other gods to turn against our half-blooded brother and the traitor's spawn."

"I'm sure Dad would be the first to roast those three trolls next to Sæhrímnir," Modi muttered.

"Perhaps, but not at Magni's expense," Trud said, giving him a hard stare. "I'm going to go look for Dad. I'll meet you at Valhalla. I don't have to tell you to take care of your brother's omega while I'm gone, do I?"

Modi pursed his lips, and I got the distinct impression she'd insulted his honor somehow. "No, sister. You don't have to remind me to fulfill my obligations to my blood; I know my duties to my brother's mate. She will be under my care and protection. Now *go*."

Ah, there it was. For a moment, I'd forgotten I was a commodity in alphas' eyes, not a sentient being with my own agency.

I shot him an annoyed look, but decided against making a fuss—this time. There were more important things at stake than my need to assert myself, and I did need someone to guide me to Valhalla. Somehow I doubted a human would be left to wander on her own in the realm of the gods.

Trud gave me what was probably meant to be a reassuring smile. Then she walked out the door, leaving me with her brother.

The redheaded god shook his head, and I was pretty sure I heard him mutter, *"Fucking Magni,"* under his breath. Then he looked at me and heaved a deep sigh.

"All right then, omega. Let us prepare for Valhalla."

"My name's Annabel," I said. "How do we prepare for Valhalla? Is there a ritual, or—"

"Of course there's not a ritual—I'm the son of Thor. I come and go in all of Asgard as I please," he said, giving me a look as if he suspected I was slow. "Do they teach you nothing in Midgard? But one does not waltz into the house of Odin without a shirt, hmm?"

He indicated his very broad, very naked torso, and I flushed despite myself. Thor's legitimate son was a bit of a dick, but he was also extremely well-built.

"Well... get dressed, then," I said, looking away to avoid giving the impression I might have been ogling him. "I have two mates to save, and I'm not about to wait around while you try on pretty shirts."

Modi barked a laugh, slapping me on the back hard enough to make me stumble a step before I caught myself.

"I see my brother likes them feisty. All right, little omega. Wait here—I'll try not to take all day."

~

MODI DID, in fact, not take very long to get dressed. He came down after maybe five minutes, wearing a linen tunic and animal hide leggings with his sword hanging off a plain leather belt. Yet despite the simple outfit, he still emanated a near-regal presence with his arrow-straight posture and smooth strides.

He exuded all the confidence of a god—which kind of made sense, I supposed. He *was* a god. But so was Magni.

My thoughts turned to my redheaded mate's anger at Sif's reaction to our presence, and the old wounds I'd felt in our bond from his life in this house. Magni was formidable, a god among alphas in his own right—but he didn't carry himself the same way his brother did.

They may have looked alike, may have carried the same divine blood in their veins, but it was becoming increasingly obvious that even gods were affected by how much love they'd known.

I thought about what Bjarni had said on our trip to Udgaard—how Magni'd betrayed his mother's kin to gain access to Asgard, only to be seen as a second-class citizen due to his Jotunn lineage. Had he ever known love?

"We won't let anything happen to your mate," Modi rumbled, the way he glanced at my face making me aware my emotions were showing in my features. "Either of them," he reluctantly added.

"I don't understand why they were taken in the first

place," I said, grateful for the distraction. "Even if Loki betrayed Asgard, why take it out on his sons?"

Modi snorted, placing a hand on my spine as he led me out the door of Trudheim. The once-busy yard seemed devoid of life now.

"Has Magni truly allowed that scum to twist your mind, omega? They're not innocents, whatever they may have tried to portray to make you agree to this insane arrangement."

"Wasn't a whole lot of agreement from my side," I muttered. "What do you mean, they're not innocent?"

Modi sighed, free hand twitching on the pommel of his sword as if the mere mention of the Lokissons made him itch for battle. "I mean that they've taken up swords against the gods more than once. They align with the Jotunn whores who birthed them, not the Aesir. I myself have met them in battle. They'd see Asgard burned to the ground, if they had their way."

"Seems to me they'd rather hide out in the human world and wait for Ragnarök to do its thing than fight gods—or Jotunns," I said, reminded of how they'd tried to squirrel me away on their farm in Iceland.

"Perhaps—it's not a shock that Loki's spawn would turn cowards in the end," Modi said. "But cowardice does not absolve them of the crimes of their past."

"I mean..." The rush of offense his words stirred in me surprised me. The Lokissons were definitely still on my shit-list for how they'd gone about kidnapping me, but... "Is what you're doing so much better?"

"Beg your pardon?" Modi turned to face me, both russet eyebrows meeting his hairline.

"You're, what, planning to go off and fight that prick Surtr and his army? What good's that going to do? As far as I understand from all the prophecies floating around these days, the gods are destined to die. You're literally just going off to fight for no reason when you could be trying to save not only your own family, but the humans too. I don't think what the Lokisson brothers are doing is any less *noble*."

Heat colored Modi's cheeks in bright red splotches, his eyes narrowing as he glared down at me. Grabbing my shoulder, he pulled me to a hard stop.

"You dare question my honor because I refuse to lower myself to this... this *arrangement* between you, my brother, and the three trolls? You, who spread your legs for the betrayer's son? You know nothing of *honor*, omega, and you will not speak again on matters you don't understand."

Great. It seemed Magni didn't get his haughty views on an omega's place from strangers. I twisted my shoulder out of Modi's grip and gave him what I hoped was a withering stare.

"I don't care about your honor, Thorsson; I care about my parents surviving. My entire *species*. You're a freaking *god,* and you'd rather fight an unwinnable battle than even consider that Magni might be right. He took me to Verdandi, and she showed me the consequences of ignoring Mimir's prophecy.

"Do you think *I* wanted any part of this? That Saga or Magni wanted to share a mate with each other? We're doing what we have to to save the world. You don't want to be a part of that? Fine. We don't need you. But you don't get to play high and mighty when you don't have the balls to do what your brother or the *trolls* are trying to do."

I wasn't entirely sure where my anger came from. It wasn't like any of the four men who'd brought me here had set out with noble intentions—they'd all wanted to claim me for selfish reasons. But after everything—after Verdandi's warnings, after the trials to pass through to Asgard, and rescuing Magni in Freya's hall—I knew both Saga and Magni would help me save the world from destruction, and that Grim and Bjarni would follow where their brother led.

That this stranger, this golden son who'd been favored over my mate, looked down on his own brother for finally trying to do what was right? I was having exactly none of it.

"Now if it doesn't impede your precious honor," I sneered, "I'd like to try to get my mates back from whatever boorish Valkyrie thought she could grab them from me."

I spun to face the golden city towering on the mountain straight ahead on the path before Modi could even respond. I managed to stomp several yards down the path before gravel crunched behind me and the redheaded god fell in by my side.

"You're a nasty little thing." Despite his crass words, Modi's temper seemed to have settled in the wake of my own. In fact, he sounded mildly amused. "Loud-mouthed, abrasive... a discredit to omegas. My brother must truly have been desperate when he claimed you."

"Well, you're an overbearing dick. As far as gods go, you're pretty much a letdown too," I growled, annoyance and a surprising sensation of hurt fizzing in my veins.

It wasn't that I wanted to be a so-called *good omega*. As far as I was concerned, what men considered *good omegas* were women who'd been oppressed and culti-vated their whole lives to be demure and always bend to an alpha's will, disregarding her own wants and needs. It wasn't a life I wanted any part of.

But being told Magni must've been desperate to claim me? That hurt, even if I knew it to be true. Maybe even *because* I knew it was true.

I pressed a hand to my chest where his and Saga's bonds were humming agitatedly. This wasn't what I'd thought love would be like, in the few moments I'd spared it a thought while I was busy with my studies. This deep, aching incompleteness whenever my mates weren't with me was awful, like I'd somehow lost chunks of myself. There were gaping wounds left now, and only my mates could heal them.

Getting reminded that the only two people in the world who could make me stop aching wouldn't have picked me if they'd thought they had any other option? It straight-up sucked.

I shot Modi another glare before I refocused on the golden city ahead. Reluctant or not, they were *mine*, and no arrogant god-son or uppity Valkyrie was going to keep me from returning them to my side where they belonged.

2

ANNABEL

The trek up the mountain was tough, but I found that my desperation to be reunited with Saga and Magni kept my strides fast and even as I climbed the winding path.

Soon large halls and towers topped with gilded roofs sprung up beside us, getting more ornately decorated as we rose. Large reliefs depicting tales of battles adorned the rough-hewn walls, and despite my eagerness to find my mates, the historian in me couldn't contain herself.

When I came to one that was surrounded by runes, I paused to squint at the ancient writing. "Is this...?"

"The story of Arngrim the Beserker?" Modi asked. "Yes. When he is not fighting or feasting in Valhalla, he resides here."

I was vaguely aware my mouth was hanging open. I'd read about a number of old Norse heroes during my studies, and the realization that they lived on here was baffling. But then again, in a world where gods were alive, why not long-dead heroes?

I touched the part of the carving depicting a long-haired, smaller figure. "Eyfure? His wife?"

"You know your stories," Modi said. "Yes, the omega princess he won the right to claim after defeating two chieftains."

"Is she here too?"

Modi chuckled. "An omega among the warriors of Valhalla? No. I suspect she's in Hel."

I knew the old Vikings saw death differently than many religions did today and that Hel wasn't synonymous with hell, but the thought that a pair-bonded couple would be forced apart in the afterlife seemed so cruel.

I pressed a hand to my chest, wondering if the emptiness would vanish upon death, and turned away from the relief. It was not something I particularly wished to dwell on right now.

"Most noble warriors go to Valhalla," Modi said as we continued the climb. Judging from the gentleness in his tone, I suspected I hadn't managed to hide my anguish on Arngrim's and Eyfure's behalves. "It's the greatest honor. Any wife would wish nothing more for her mate."

I stopped myself from asking him how he'd have any inkling what a mated omega would want. Asshat or not, I needed as much of his support as I could get in rescuing my mates from whatever fate the Valkyries had planned for them.

Then something he'd said made me frown. *"Most noble warriors go to Valhalla? I thought it was all?"*

"Some go to Folkvangr," Modi explained. "Freya's house. You must have seen them when you visited."

"There was no one when we were there. Just Freya and her cats," I said, glancing at him.

He frowned. "No, that can't be right. Freya wouldn't deploy them without consulting with the other gods. You must be mistaken—she must have taken you to some other place."

I opened my mouth to protest, but just then we rounded the final corner and Valhalla finally rose up in front of me.

My jaw sagged as I stared up at the structure. It stretched even farther toward the sky than Udgard, its supporting beams seemingly made up of massive spears. At the front, two wolves the size of corn-fed bulls rested on each side of the gates wide enough for twenty men to walk through shoulder-to-shoulder. From what I could make out of the roof, it looked like...

"Golden shields?"

Modi followed my gaze. "Yes. And the birds circling—"

"Talking ravens?"

"Huginn and Munin," he said. "The Allfather's messengers."

"Saga and his brothers have some as well. They're

kinda rude." I squinted at movement far up on the roof where a huge tree stretched its branches toward the sun. "Wait, is that... Is that a *goat?*"

A light press against my lower back was all the answer I got this time as Modi ushered me toward the entrance.

"Shouldn't we wait for Trud?" I asked, eying the closer wolf when it raised its head at our approach. "And your dad?"

"They'll meet us inside," Modi said. "Let's go find Magni and see if we can learn something useful while we wait."

The inside of Valhalla was as jaw-dropping as the outside, if not more so. I'd thought Udgard's hall was huge, but this was on an entirely different scale.

Tables stretched for hundreds of yards, about half of them occupied with boisterous men singing, shouting, and eating. Winged women in fitted armor walked among them, refilling their horns and plates. A massive hearth burned in the center of the hall, a roasted pig the size of a truck slowly rotating over the fire.

Modi led me along the tables, nodding when someone shouted his name, but never stopping. A few spotted me by his side and offered crude suggestions followed by thunderous laughter.

"Maybe you should've let them bring their wives," I muttered to my self-appointed guard.

Modi waved a hand. "Love distracts from battle. Any

other urges they have, the Valkyries will tend as they see fit."

"Sounds delightful." I glared at a wild-bearded man making kissy noises at me as we passed. "Christ, you'd think they hadn't seen a woman in eons."

"They're used to fierce Valkyries who'll put them in their place if need be, or powerful goddesses. They haven't seen a soft little human girl in a thousand years." Modi nodded across two tables where a Valkyrie had smacked a warrior who'd gotten handsy across the face with her tray. "But so long as you stay by my side, you'll be safe."

I stuck extra-close to Modi as we continued through the hall. Only when we passed the hearth was I able to see the other end, and the sight that met me made my heart clench.

Raised up high was a platform with an empty throne. In front of it several Valkyries stood with their backs turned to the hall, and between them I could just make out four kneeling figures.

"What are they doing?" I asked, my pace picking up without my conscious thought.

"Waiting for Odin," Modi said as he placed a hand on my shoulder, ensuring I didn't pull too far ahead. "Ah—there he is."

From a gilded entryway to the side of the platform, a figure appeared. He looked tall, even from a distance, with a regal posture and long, flowing white hair and beard. On each of his shoulders sat a black bird—

Huginn and Munin, I assumed—and he carried a wooden staff in one hand. If there'd ever been a way I'd imagined the wise Allfather of the gods, this would be it.

He didn't speak as he made his way across the platform. Modi rushed me forward, and we made it to the stairs leading up to the platform just as Odin sat on the throne.

"Now, what do we have here?" he said, his voice quiet yet echoing through the grand hall as he looked at the four men kneeling before him. I sensed the noise behind us dying down, the rowdy Vikings turning their attention to the Allfather.

"We found these fugitives in Trudheim," the head Valkyrie said, nudging Bjarni with her boot. He growled, but stayed on his knees.

Shimmering ropes were wrapped around his and the others' wrists, I noticed when we finally made it to the top of the platform. I moved to rush to them, but Modi kept a grip on my shoulder, restraining.

"Wait," he murmured, bending so his lips brushed against my ear. "You won't help them by causing a scene."

"Thor's halfblooded son gave them passage into Valhalla, breaking our sacred laws," the Valkyrie continued. "We have brought them to you, Allfather, so that you may judge them for their crimes."

"Crimes?" Magni growled. "It is my right as an Asa to grant guests of my home safe passage."

Odin looked at the kneeling alphas. He only had one eye, the other socket covered by a leather patch, and I remembered how Magni had said he'd given one to Mimir.

"*Guests,* young grandson?" the Allfather asked, fixing his stare on Magni. "Every citizen of Asgard knows Loki's sons are not welcome here, yet you grant them safe passage? Into *my* kingdom?"

Magni grimaced, a fleeting look he quickly wiped from his features in favor of stoicism. "I had to pass through Jotunheim and was gravely injured. The Lokissons came to my aid, and in return, I promised them my protection while they remained in Asgard."

"It was foolish of you to make promises that are not yours to keep," Odin replied as his one-eyed gaze swept from Magni to the three brothers. "Loki betrayed us all, and as a result, Ragnarök is upon us. The traitor hides behind his foul magic while the worlds are coming to an end, and you sneak his Jotunn bastards in behind our walls?

"I was not pleased when your father insisted we open Asgard for you—the winds advised me that one day your allegiance may return to the Jotunns who bore you. And here you are, on the cusp of Ragnarök itself, showing your true colors at last."

"I will never align myself with the Jotunns," Magni growled. "I passed the test you set for me, earning my spot in Asgard. And I have not betrayed you."

"Yet here you are, harboring three of our enemies. You killed your own family for a place among the gods."

This time, Odin's voice didn't project through the great hall. It only resonated among the gathered Valkyries and halfgods on the dais.

"You brought the traitor's sons into our midst, breaking your sacred vow to always protect Asgard. I sentence the four of you to death for treason."

3

____

MAGNI

"No!"

Annabel's scream cut through my stupor and I jerked my head to the left. She was fighting tooth and nail in Modi's bulky arms—whether to get to me and Saga or to claw Odin's face off, I didn't know, because her expression was caught somewhere between anguish and murderous rage.

"Don't you dare put your hands on them, you senile piece of shi—"

Modi clamped a big hand across her mouth, shock plain on his face that the human omega had dared speak to the Allfather so crassly. He was growling orders to hush into her ear, but she was having exactly none of it.

I caught Saga's eye and saw the fierce look of pride and the curve of his lip as our mate tossed her head back, catching Modi in the nose in her desperate attempt to come to our aid. We'd both expected our fated omega to be meek and subservient, but she was wild as a thunderstorm over an open sea.

"What's this about?" Odin turned his eye to Modi and his bucking captive, head tilting to one side. "What is the meaning of bringing an untamed pet to Valhalla, grandson? If you can't keep your servants quiet, they have no place here."

"She's not a fucking pet, she's my mate!" Saga growled, jerking on the chain looped around his torso, but the Valkyrie holding on to the other end didn't give.

"And mine!" I snapped, the instinct to assert my claim rearing up before I could think better of it.

A murmur rose from the fallen warriors behind us and Odin's eye widened in shock, but before anyone could speak, a clap of thunder rolled through the great hall.

"*Where's my son?*"

Thor had come.

He didn't take long to arrive on the dais, hurtling into view like a bad-tempered bolt of lightning. Nostrils flared and cracks of energy practically sparking off his skin, he stared at me and the three alphas by my side for several long seconds before he turned his focus to Odin.

"Why do you have my son tied up and on his knees like a criminal?"

Odin's mouth pinched at the corner—my father's lack of manners had all days been a thorn in his side.

"Your *son* dragged three of the traitor's sons into Asgard. He has been found guilty of treason."

"*Treason?*" Thor blustered. "You tried *my son* for treason? Because he keeps Jotunn company? Do I have to remind you about your own Jotunn associations?"

He turned to the Valkyrie who had a hold of my chains. "Unchain him immediately, or so help me, I'm going to blast your wings off so thoroughly your asshole will be on fire for the next five months!"

Odin glared at him. "Yes, *your son*. You know the rules—and so does he. Any association with Loki carries the penalty of death. This is not a small matter. The betrayer has doomed us all, and Magni claims to share a mate with one of these... worms. Whatever his allegiance to them, clearly it is deep."

Thor blinked, and I steeled myself. "A *mate?* What's this nonsense? My son's never claimed an omega, and he'd certainly never *share* one, least of all with Loki's bastards!"

"Actually, Father..." I breathed in deeply, wishing Trud had had the chance to explain everything to him. Clearly she hadn't, but if Freya's warning about a possible traitor within the walls of Asgard was right, we needed to keep our cards as close to our chests as possible. It was bad enough I'd announced in front of the entirety of Valhalla that Saga and I shared a mate.

"Her name is Annabel." I nodded in the direction of my mate wrapped up in Modi's arms. She'd stopped fighting him now that Thor had intervened, but he still had a hand clasped over her mouth. Knowing her lip, it was probably a wise choice.

My father stared at me again for a series of long, *long* seconds. Then he turned his head toward Annabel. An incredulous snort escaped him.

"A human?" Both his red eyebrows lifted when he returned his gaze to me. "You mated a *human?* Are you *insane?* Did your mother beat the sense out of you when you were a babe? A worthless human cunt ensnared Thor's son?"

"Don't speak about her like that!" Saga snarled.

Shame filled me that he'd spoken up for our mate when I hadn't. I'd spent most of my life trying to please my father, but Saga's anger and the scent of his aggression bolstered me. I let out the snarl that'd stuck in my throat, baring my teeth at my father in warning.

"She is *mine.* You will address her with respect," I ground out.

But whatever reaction I'd expected from standing up to my father, he seemed to not hear me. His eyes widened as he stared at Saga, realization dawning in his blue eyes.

"It's true," he croaked. "You *share* her? With *him?*"

"Yes," I said. "It's a long story, and it has nothing to do with why the winged cunts burst into Trudheim and arrested me for upholding one of our most sacred laws."

Thor stared at me, his jaw working hard, and I could already tell he wasn't gonna let it go despite our less-than-ideal surroundings. That was just how he was—bullheaded, single-minded, and completely incapable of accepting anything less than perfection from his sons.

Sharing a mate with one of Loki's sons? Yeah, that was about as far from perfect as it got, in his mind.

"Dad." My sister's soft voice broke the tension. Trud, having apparently not managed to keep up with Thor's pace, appeared from the stairs and crossed the dais swiftly, placing her hand on our father's arm.

She didn't say anything else, but she didn't have to. She'd always had a way with our father that neither Magni nor I could replicate.

Father sighed deeply, looking from Trud back to Odin. "My son's right. Free passage is a founding law in Asgard. You will release him at once."

"And his guests," Trud said, nudging his arm. His only response was a tightening of his jaw, but it didn't matter—Odin had heard her too.

The Allfather narrowed his one eye. "This is Ragnarök! I will not allow those who wish to end us waltz freely around in my realm!"

"You won't be executing my blood, either," Thor growled, resting a hand on Mjölner, the hammer on his belt.

"A compromise!" Trud broke in, stepping in front of us with a swish of her robes and managing a respectful bow without losing the gentle power radiating from her.

"A compromise?" Odin repeated, his eyebrows raising. The gesture moved his eyepatch, underlining its grim presence on his somber face. "A *compromise?* This is the end of the world, child, and you want to strike a *compromise* with Loki's spawn?"

"Treason is their father's crime. Not theirs," Trud said, gaze darting to Annabel for a moment before she looked back to the Allfather. "Loki is the one who betrayed us. Would Saga have claimed a human mate if he was trying to bring about Ragnarök? She wouldn't survive it, and so neither would he."

"That's true," Thor said, looking back at Annabel with a frown. "Why would he claim a human if he was planning on killing her?"

"We don't know their plans," Odin said, glaring at Saga. "They could have found a way to keep her safe with the Jotunns."

"Or we're not fucking traitors," Saga growled. "You fucking Aesirs—always so high and mighty, always so quick to assume you're the only ones who could possibly have anything to lose. If we'd wanted an end to the world, we wouldn't have sought refuge in Asgard from Surtr's army.

"We brought our mate here to keep her safe among the gods, among Magni's supposed kin. Is it a wonder that the humans have abandoned their faith in you when you have so little interest in them that all you can think of to stop the end of the world is to kill the children of the supposed betrayer? Nothing will be gained by our death—Ragnarök is still here. Incompetence will be your only legacy."

I'd spent so long hating the Lokissons, despising them for what they were—for the Jotunn heritage they so proudly embraced while I'd done everything I could to distance myself from that part of my lineage. But as I watched Saga now, saw how he carefully chose his words like a warrior chooses his strikes to fell his enemy, pride swelled in my gut.

We'd both claimed Annabel in a bid to save our families, but through her, we'd become kin. When he took her alongside me, when he helped her save my life, I'd felt him as keenly as I had her. His magic, his desperation, his cock... and the warmth of his spirit.

We were brothers now, kindred in our need to keep Annabel safe and protected, and right now, my kindred brother was fighting with all he had. On his knees in front of the Allfather, he fought with clever words to save all of us once again.

I knew then that even if I could find a way to do so, I would never break his bond with Annabel. He was a worthy mate—a worthy brother. Sharing her with him was how it was always meant to be.

"Let us prove to you that we have no ill intent toward Asgard and its inhabitants," I broke in. "Set us a challenge, Allfather. We have nothing to hide from the gods."

Except we did. I caught Annabel's gaze, her eyes widening in a meaningful stare, and I remembered

Freya's warning. There was still a betrayer in Asgard, perhaps hiding in the great hall below. The less we revealed about our bond and Mimir's prophecy, the better.

"A challenge?" Odin repeated, rubbing his chin as he looked to Thor.

"That would be a fair compromise," Thor agreed. "Let them prove their worth."

"Very well." Odin leaned back in his seat, his focus moving to one of the ravens on his shoulder. It cawed and leaned in, whispering in his ear. The other—Munin, so far as I could tell—nipped at his beard to get his attention before whispering in his other ear.

The Allfather hummed and nodded, straightening up before looking at the four of us again.

"You shall have one chance to prove your innocence, young Jotunns. Bring me the traitor. Bring him to me in chains and on his knees. Trade his life for your own.

"Bring me Loki. That is your challenge."

4

———

BJARNI

Well, shit.

I exchanged a look with Grim on my right and knew his tight jaw reflected my own grinding of teeth.

Give Loki to this pompous ass? If the Allfather thought we'd sell out our own dad, he'd truly gone senile like Annabel had shouted before Modi shut her up. Of course, it didn't much matter what we agreed to, so long as the old fool let us leave unharmed.

Coming to Asgard had been a mistake. There were Jotunn healers we could have persuaded with coin to care for Magni's injuries, and there were more places in the nine realms to hide from Surtr than Asgard. There'd been bad blood between us and these Aesir pricks for eons, but going so far as to have us executed for our father's supposed crimes? That was a new development.

But I supposed it's what happened when your dad was accused of bringing around the literal end of the world.

"If that is what you require as proof of our innocence, then we will bring you Loki," Saga said, and he sounded so sincere I'd have believed him if I hadn't known him as well as I did. "Our loyalty lies with my mate and her kin, not our father."

"Well, it sounds like that's all sorted, then," Thor said, slapping Modi's shoulder. "Go untie your brother, and then prepare yourself for traveling—even with those three worms, he's gonna need you help capturing that sly bastard."

"Not so fast," Odin said, rising from his throne. "I am not inclined to simply trust your words, sons of Loki."

"You claim my son is dishonorable?" Thor boomed. "You may not trust Loki's sons, but you will trust mine, or so help me—"

"Dad!" Trud hissed. "You're not helping!"

It'd been a long time since I saw Thor's daughter. When we were younger, I'd tried to fool around with her, but these days, the urge to bend her over and defile her with my Jotunn dick was gone.

Instead I glanced at the dark-haired woman wrapped in Modi's arms and felt a spasm in my chest at her furious expression behind his palm. She'd gone to bat for us—or had tried to. I didn't know her well, but I knew she was strong. Fierce. And she was supposed to be mine.

"I will allow *one* of you to go," Odin said. "The three others will remain here as collateral. Bring Loki to me, and your brothers will live. Break your word..."

He didn't need to finish the sentence. We all knew what would happen.

"Magni will go," Thor growled. "He and Modi will bring you the betrayer."

"And how do you suppose he'll get close to our father?" Saga asked, the sardonic note clear even to me. "Who do you think'll have more luck luring the God of Trickery, your son or his own? *I* will go."

"You will not." Odin stared down at him, the threat of his power looming around him like a billowing cape. "You're mated. Your familiar ties may not be as strong as they once were."

I snorted before I could stop myself—clearly this old prick knew nothing of the power of blood. Yeah, Annabel was Saga's first priority now, but she was also *ours*. And neither of us would ever betray each other, even if it were to keep her safe. There'd always be another way.

My snort made Odin's single eye land on me. "You. You will go."

"No, I will," Grim said, speaking for the first time since we'd been captured by the Valkyries.

"I have made my decision," Odin replied, his disturbing gaze unwavering. "Bjarni Lokisson, your task is to bring your father to me. Do this, and your brothers shall live. Fail, and they will pay the price of his treason. You have three weeks until the moon grows full."

"And my son?" Thor asked.

"He stays here with the Jotunns he aligned himself with the moment he decided to share the omega with one of them. That is final."

Odin shot the redheaded god a look so loaded, the protest that had undoubtedly been about to burst out died on his lips.

The god-king glanced at the Valkyries behind us. "Keep our *guests* secure, but comfortable."

I stared after him as he left the same way he'd entered, his two ravens squawking from their perch as the weight of the duty he'd placed on my shoulders settled. I alone was responsible for my brothers' lives.

Throughout the ages, it had always been the three of us, each of us protecting the others as best we could. But where I'd had more of my mother's brawn than my brothers, they'd been gifted with more of our father's brains. I'd relied on them to outwit our enemies when necessary and work magic I had little to no grasp of.

Now it was all down to me, and I was pretty certain that I wouldn't be able to just bash in some skulls to fix this.

Hopefully our father would be able to formulate a plan—assuming I could find him.

"Get up," the winged bitch behind me sneered, pressing the butt of her spear against my lower back.

I growled as I stood, but she ignored me as she sliced the ropes off my wrists. My brothers and Magni weren't so lucky—a few other Valkyries shoved them toward the same door Odin had disappeared through, their hands still tied behind their backs.

"Mmph!"

The muted shriek made me look to Annabel, who'd gone wild in Modi's arms once more. She bucked and clawed, her eyes wide and fearful as she stared after the three alphas being led away.

"Let go of her," I said, clasping a hand around Modi's wrist.

He bared his teeth at me in an instinctive reaction to an enemy alpha's touch, but released the thrashing omega so swiftly it was obvious he was only too thrilled to let her go. It might have something to do with the blood trickling from his nostril where she'd head-butted him.

"Come," I said, reaching out to clasp my hand in Annabel's when she stumbled out of Modi's grasp. "I'll take you to them before I leave."

She didn't respond, only shot me a look so full of rage and terror it made my gut clench. She might not be my mate yet, but that expression made me want to move mountains to ensure her happiness. It wasn't just my brothers' lives in my hands now—it was hers as well.

Thor, Modi, and Trud followed us as we made our way after the Valkyries through the many winding halls deep in Valhalla's bowels. I'd never been to Valhalla before, but the carved beams, gilded artwork, and high ceilings were exactly like my father had described.

He'd often talked about the glory of Valhalla when he came to visit us as we grew up, describing its beauty and the power that lay within its walls. So far the rather unflattering descriptions of the god-king that resided within were also holding up.

THE VALKYRIES LED my brothers and Magni to the third floor of a tower and waited for everyone to enter before they locked the door behind us. A small trap door opened at the top, revealing one of the winged cunts' faces.

"Let us know when you're ready to leave," she said, her eyes resting on Thor. I supposed Annabel and I barely existed, so far as the Valkyries were concerned.

Not that the omega seemed to notice—the moment I released her hand, she hurled herself forward, wrapping her arms around both her mates' necks.

Thor rumbled an annoyed agreement before turning to Magni. "It's quite a mess you've gotten yourself tangled in. What were you thinking, bonding with a human? And *sharing* her with Loki's offspring?"

"I was thinking of our bloodline's survival," Magni answered as he lifted his head from Annabel's, though without releasing his fierce grip on her. "She is the omega in Mimir's prophecy."

"Which prophecy?" Thor snapped. "That bodiless crackpot spews his nonsense every other day. Tell me you didn't mate some human whore to fulfill one of his stupid prophecies! Ragnarök is here! We've got better things to worry about than whatever mead-fueled fantasy he's thought up this time!"

The snarl that ripped through the room and echoed off its rounded walls was instant and followed by the stench of mixed alpha aggressions, but Annabel stopped both her mates from barreling forward with a firm hand on their shoulders. She fixed the God of Thunder with a glare.

"I don't know why think you can call me a whore, nor do I understand why you're yelling at your son for trying to stop Ragnarök and save humankind. The literal end of the world's here, and we're trying to stop it. The prophecy is real."

Thor looked at her for half a second before he returned his focus to Magni. "Let me be very frank: I don't care about your so-called mate, and I don't care about your Jotunn friends. My only concern is that Odin gives up his ridiculous notion that you've switched allegiance so you can come fulfill your destiny by mine and Modi's sides as we fight the hordes of Jotunheim. *That* is your destiny. This human omega means nothing in the grand scheme of things. You, a god, do.

"Modi will travel with your *friend* here to ensure Loki is brought back to face his judgement. The end."

"You absolute piece of—" Saga's snarl was cut short when Thor rapped his knuckles against the wooden door. It swung open immediately, and the God of Thunder disappeared through it before my brother could finish his insult.

"—shit!" Saga roared at the once-again closed door.

5

MODI

"Your father's a dick," the feral omega growled at my brother.

"I know," he sighed, pressing his cheek against her dark hair in an achingly gentle gesture. "It doesn't matter. My fate is to be by your side, Annabel. Always."

I resisted the urge to roll my eyes. They said newly mated alphas were always overemotional right after claiming an omega, and my brother sure seemed to fit that stereotype.

In all the centuries we'd known each other, Magni had been fierce, cunning—strong. But now, as he clutched the human girl to his chest, unbothered by Saga Lokisson's presence, he looked... vulnerable. Weak.

As I watched the three of them, it was clear that this omega had changed him forever. And Saga too. Where once they'd been unyielding steel and muscle, there was now a soft spot that could end them both in the blink of an eye.

Magni was insane if he thought I'd ever join this hopeless love triangle.

"So. We need a plan," Trud said, looking from me to Bjarni. "No offense, but you two aren't a match for Loki, and I'm not about to lose my brother and new sister."

"You leave our father to us. We don't need no Asa's help," Bjarni growled, his tone raising my hackles. I'd always been protective of Trud, even if she rarely appreciated it.

"Sure, why don't we let a bumbling fool with meat for brains try to out-trick the God of Mischief?" I said, narrowing my eyes at the blond giant. "Nothing could possibly go wrong with that plan."

"You're not helping," Trud hissed at me, as Bjarni snarled in my direction, his muscles clenching. "Neither of you are equipped for this. Not without help. Loki is too clever."

"We won't need wit to convince him to help us—he's our father. All we have to do is find him," Bjarni said. I didn't miss his brothers exchanging a look behind his back. *Interesting.* What did they know that he didn't?

"He may be your father, but he's not going to surrender voluntarily. Plus how do you plan to find him when Odin's been searching for him for months with no luck? You need someone with magic to assist you," Trud said, crossing her arms over her chest in a way I knew all too well. She had a finite amount of patience for explaining concepts she found straightforward. It'd caused more than a few arguments over the centuries.

"I have plenty of magic," I said, arching an eyebrow as I summoned a bolt of electricity to let it dance between my fingertips. "As you well know."

My sister rolled her eyes so hard it was a miracle they didn't become lodged at the back of her skull. "Yes, and while it's great that you're a master at blowing things up, that's not the kind of magic we need. To find Loki and convince him to come with you, you need intuition. Guile. Stealth."

I narrowed my eyes. "Oh, we do, do we? And I suppose you know just the goddess to bring, huh?"

Trud shot me a bright smile. "As a matter of fact, I do. I'll be coming with you, because let's be honest—between the two of you, you have far too much muscle and not nearly enough brains to pull something like this off."

I growled half-heartedly at my sister's dig. I wasn't fond of basically being called stupid in front of a bunch of Jotunn scum, but the offended look on Bjarni's face was almost worth it.

"No, you need to stay here."

To my utter surprise, the words came from the omega. I blinked, surprised the puny human thought it wise to interrupt, let alone tell a goddess "no." But then again, said puny human had also headbutted me and bitten my hand. Clearly whatever wildling had birthed her hadn't raised her to respect her gods.

"I do?" Even Trud, who'd been way too excited since Magni declared the little thing his "mate," sounded startled.

"I..." Annabel frowned, her brown gaze seemingly locked on the wooden door. "I think *I* have to go. You need to stay here. You need to help Saga, Grim, and Magni figure out who's behind this."

"Did you have another vision, sweetling?" Saga asked.

"A *vision?*" I didn't realize I'd voiced my contemptuous thought out loud until I noticed Bjarni's glare. "She is just a human—"

"A human with power," Trud interrupted me, her blue eyes focusing on Annabel. "What did you see, my sister?"

"It... It wasn't a vision, I don't think... It was more of a... feeling." The omega looked up at Trud, capturing her gaze with an intensity that surprised me. "It has to be me. But they need you here. Asgard needs you."

"*No.*" This time, the denial came from Magni, his voice so dark it took me a second to recognize it. "You're going *nowhere,* Annabel. You're *never* leaving my side again."

"Magni, I have to. To save you," she whispered, raising her hand to his bearded cheek. After how feral she'd seemed so far, it surprised me to see such tenderness, and it warmed my disposition toward her... a *little.*

"You don't. I won't let you. Trud is a very capable sorceress and much more experienced than you. Your place is here, with me."

"And *me,*" Saga said, but even though his tone was salty, there was no hiding the jealousy in his eyes as he stared at the two. It dawned on me that this fucked-up union of theirs probably wasn't entirely peaceful.

Annabel tipped her head to lean against her Jotunn mate's shoulder without releasing Magni's face. "I don't want to leave either of you, but this is something I have to do. It has to be me."

"Why?" Saga demanded. "Why does it have to be you? The Asa can defend herself. You are ours to protect, Annabel."

"I don't know why," she said, furrowing her brow. "Why did it have to be me you mated? Why did the Norn weave *my* thread into this mess? I don't know—and neither do you. But I feel it in my bones, Saga. I *have* to go. If I don't..."

She shuddered. "Verdandi showed me what will happen if I don't follow my fate, and I'm not going to let that happen. I'm not going to let everyone die—least of all you two. We'll find Loki. You will have to search for Mimir here while we're away."

"Wait... Mimir?" I interrupted. "Why are you looking for Mimir here?"

"He wasn't in his well. Some dark creature was," Magni said, finally releasing his grip on the omega to rub his arm. "The Norn told us to find him."

"Verdandi?" I opened my mouth to suggest my brother needed to stop listening to hermits with too much free time on their hands, but Trud cut me off with another *look.*

"If Mimir's not in his well, he should be somewhere here in Valhalla," she said, before taking in a deep breath as she refocused on the omega. "I've seen you, sister—you are touched by Fate, and if Fate now calls for you to follow my brother and the Jotunn in search of Loki, then that's what has to happen. I will stay here and help them search for Mimir."

"Thank you," the omega said. She reached out for Trud, but Saga instantly wrapped himself around her tighter, constricting both her arms against her body.

"Annabel, no. Please, no."

The desperate plea in his voice shocked me to the core. He sounded so... vulnerable. The idea that one of Loki's sons would allow himself to be seen like this by me, an enemy, made just an inkling of pity worm its way into my chest.

"Saga," she whispered, pressing her forehead to his chest. She didn't say anything else, but the emotions playing across the Jotunn alpha's face spoke louder than words could have: fear, sorrow... and finally, acceptance.

"Damn that fucking Norn!" he hissed as he nuzzled against the top of her head.

"If it wasn't for her, we'd never have met," the omega reminded him. "Wouldn't that be worse?"

"Yes," he sighed. "It would. There's nothing without

you, sweetling. I wouldn't care if the world burns. I... love you."

I cleared my throat and looked away, embarrassed for the once-fierce alpha who'd clearly suffered a lobotomy along with his mating. The dark-haired Jotunn with the mismatched eyes looked just as uncomfortable as I felt and was also doing his best to pretend like he wasn't there—but Bjarni stared at the omega, longing and envy plain on his big, stupid face.

Gods, that idiot *wanted* to be part of their sick little love triangle? Well, he had all days been the dumb one of the bunch. Even the Fenris wolf was smarter than him.

"Well, if we're gonna find that slimy father of yours, we best get going," I said before the omega could respond to Saga's declaration. *If* she was going to answer. The way she'd lowered those long, dark lashes to avoid looking at his face suggested she wasn't too sure.

Which was apparently fortunate, because Magni looked like he'd just swallowed a spider, the way he stared at her and Saga. I guessed he hadn't shared any tender words of love with his omega yet. Good on him.

"Trud, let's go home and pack. And I suppose we'll have to find something for the Jotunn as well. He might not be the sharpest arrow in Loki's quiver, but with a bit of luck, the old fox will be more willing to come out of hiding if we're dragging one of his sons along."

I turned to face Magni. "Fear not, brother mine. We will bring Loki back and set you free."

A moment's silence followed my words. Then the little omega huffed and straightened from the cocoon between her two alphas. "Excuse me? Didn't you hear me? *I'm* going. Not Trud—she needs to stay here."

I smothered an eye-roll and leveled her with a stare. It seemed I'd have to train this female since my brother and Saga hadn't gotten around to yet.

"No, you won't. Touched by Fate or not, you are a human. This is a matter for gods. *You* will be staying here where your mates can take care of you. I'm not dragging an omega into the wilderness to search for the God of Mischief, nor am I going to cater to your whims and fancies like my dear brother has seemingly gotten you accustomed to."

6

ANNABEL

The only silver lining about leaving my mates was knowing that the grumpy redheaded god stomping ahead of me was possibly as miserable as I was, though for vastly different reasons.

Modi was a huge dick, end of discussion. He was your typical alpha, convinced he alone knew how to save the day, and with very set opinions on what an omega's role was. Especially a human omega, it seemed.

I guessed it would be hard not to develop a superiority complex when you were a literal god, but good gravy, did I want to smack his stupid face whenever he emphasized the word "human" while listing all the reasons why I needed to stay home and let him and his sister take care of this mess.

As if I *wanted* to leave Magni and Saga behind.

I rubbed at my ribs where my two ties squirmed for every step I took, increasing the distance between us.

Every newly awakened omega instinct in my body screamed at me to turn around and run until I was once again wrapped up in their embrace, safe in the arms of the two men who'd shown me that the only place I'd ever feel whole again was between them.

But I couldn't. Not if I wanted them to live.

I didn't understand much about my new powers, but the sensation echoing through my entire being had been clear: I had to go. It had to be me. Even if doing so meant leaving my mates behind.

"I'll get you home to them soon, I promise," Bjarni rumbled, his bear-sized hand patting my feathered shoulder as he looked at my fist pressed against my ribs.

Weakly I smiled up at him. Unlike Modi, he'd taken up pace by my side, allowing Magni's brother to take the lead so he could keep me company.

"I hope so. This sucks."

"Not so long ago, you were moaning about how much you hated both Saga and Magni," the blond giant teased. "Pretty sure you were hoping to find a way to get rid of both of them."

"Yes, funny how being torn apart from the inside makes a girl change her mind," I replied, though without malice.

Out of all the stupid alphas I'd been saddled with, Bjarni was the easiest to like. He was gentle and sweet, and he didn't try to boss me around every other second.

And he seemed to actually care if I liked him or not. As much as my heart panged with longing for Magni and Saga, I couldn't exactly say they'd gone out of their way to endear themselves to me. They hadn't seen the need.

I smiled a little more warmly, remembering the hot cocoa with little dots of marshmallows Bjarni'd made me back on their farm. It felt like decades ago.

He breathed in deeply and squeezed my shoulder. "You can make a man forget the end of the world is here when you smile like that, sweetie."

I flushed and batted his hand off with a snort. "You just had to go and ruin it, you cheesy goof," I chided, refocusing on Modi's figure up ahead. "This is no time for flirting."

"Saga told me to take care of you," he hummed, seemingly unconcerned with my brush-off or heated cheeks. "And when your next heat comes, I will claim you for my own. I figure it'd be nice if I can tell you I love you afterwards without having you squirming to avoid answering me, hmm?"

This time, the flood of heat to my cheeks came from an entirely different type of embarrassment, and I straightened my back and increased my pace, not wanting to dwell on the images his suggestion conjured up. I'd learned the hard way that once my heat struck, I didn't have much of a choice in who I let mount me. So far, realizing I was an omega hadn't been super fun.

Bjarni chuckled behind me, but he let me put a bit of distance between us—yet another difference between him and my mates.

"This is odd."

I looked up as Modi came to a halt, his head swaying from one side to the other as he took in the view of the lush valley sprawling out along the gravelly path we'd been following.

"Hmm?" Bjarni rumbled behind me.

"I've never seen Folkvangr so... quiet," Modi answered, twisting around to frown at Bjarni. "You said you passed through here when you first entered Asgard, right? Where were the warriors?"

I bit my lip to stop the bubble of annoyance from spilling out in a snarky comment. I'd told the idiot that there weren't any warriors in Folkvangr when we came through, but he'd dismissed me. Apparently he'd even take the word of his sworn enemy over a *human omega*.

But as much as I wanted to remind him that I'd fucking told him so, I was trying to conserve the amount of bullshit I called him on. He might be an insufferable jerk, but he was still one of the two men tasked with helping me save my mates. Ideally I wouldn't piss him off to the point he'd tell us to sort it out ourselves before we'd even left Asgard.

"Yeah, no warriors. Figured Odin had called on them, now that Ragnarök is here. That not the case?" Bjarni said, crossing the distance to Modi's vantage point in a few long strides. "Yup, looks pretty much like it did when we got here."

I made my way to them and peered around Bjarni's shoulder. Freya's temple-like home stretched toward the sky in the valley below. The only difference from when we first visited was that the setting sun was now drawing long, dark shadows around the structure and the surrounding woodland.

"No. Her warriors aren't in Valhalla," Modi mumbled, his frown deepening. "It seems the good goddess may have a few more questions to answer than I'd first thought. Come."

He led us farther down the path and into the valley surrounding the splendorous Folkvangr. Everything looked exactly as it had when we'd first arrived in Asgard, except...

"Where are the birds?" I asked, tilting my head to stare up at the silent trees. "And the insects? Everything is... quiet."

Neither alpha answered me, but both looked around, shoulders tensing when they found the same lack of life as I had. Without a word, they both slid their weapons free from their belts.

"Stay between us, Annabel," Bjarni murmured, his free hand coming to rest on my shoulder once more.

"So, this isn't... natural, right?" I pressed. "Something's going on?"

"Perhaps." It was Modi this time, his distracted tone reflecting his focus being on the building ahead. "We won't know until we speak with Freya. Let's move on."

. . .

NOTHING JUMPED out at us as we made our way to the beautiful temple, but the sense of foreboding itching up the back of my neck increased for every step—and judging from the way the warriors flanking me moved, I wasn't the only one.

Bjarni stuck to my ass like glue, grunting at every gust of wind rustling the leaves and swaying the grass, and Modi tensed every few seconds, whipping his head from side to side as he scanned our surroundings until we finally entered Folkvangr.

"*Freya?*" the redheaded god boomed. "Reveal yourself, woman!"

I arched an eyebrow at his less than respectful way of addressing the goddess—maybe his surly demeanor had less to do with me being a human than I'd originally thought. Maybe Thor's legitimate son was just your run-of-the-mill sexist prick.

Fab.

"Freya?" I called out, keeping my tone infinitely more polite. "Please, goddess. We need your guidance."

Modi snorted by my side. "Please, don't give her a big head—she gets difficult if she knows you need something from her."

I shot him a glare out the corner of my eye. "She was trying to help us—somehow I doubt she's gonna play games when it's about the goddamn end of the world. *Freya!*"

A low howling through the wooden pillars holding up the temple roof was the only response.

I shuddered despite my leather outfit, but in defiance of the niggling at the back of my skull that wanted to get out of the eerie structure and away from the deathly quiet valley, I continued deeper.

The great hall where Saga and I had saved Magni lay blanketed in shadow, no fires lighting up the altar this time.

"It's so cold," I mumbled, the chilly pressure weighing down on us from the high ceilings making me unwilling to raise my voice. "Something's wrong. I can feel it."

"Even I can feel it, sweetie," Bjarni rumbled behind me, his free hand coming to rest on my shoulder. "Something's happened here. And it ain't good."

"She's not here." Modi, who'd gone off to one of the side halls while we explored the great hall, came out from between two pillars opposite the altar. His forehead was locked in a deep frown. "No one is, not even a single servant. This is... unlike her."

"Are there any clues where she might have gone? A note? Anything?" I asked, idly rubbing my hand against the altar. It was smooth under my palm, and cold like the rest of Folkvangr. The furs we'd slept on were nowhere in sight.

"Doubtful," Modi grunted. "The energy here... I don't think she left of her own will."

"Someone kidnapped the Goddess of Love?" Bjarni asked, arching an eyebrow. "Why? She harms no one."

"Maybe because she knew something was wrong in

Asgard," I reminded him. "If someone found out she knew there was a traitor…"

"I suppose," he relented, his brows knitting into a frown to match Modi's. "Well, shit."

"We need to find her," Modi said, and to my utter surprise, he looked expectantly at me. "Get on with it, then."

"Uh… What do you expect me to do about it?" I asked.

He arched an eyebrow. "Isn't this why you're here? Trud would be able to sense something helpful—either Freya's whereabouts, or a clue to who the fuck's taken her. You insisted you had to come instead, so get on with it."

"Oh. Right." Well, shit. He did have a point. Sort of.

I gave him an ungrateful glance before closing my eyes. I wasn't exactly comfortable with the magic inside of me yet, but I'd felt it enough to know it was there and that it was powerful.

Bjarni might be strong as an ox, and Modi might be able to shoot lighting with his fingertips—but I was the one with premonitions. I was the one touched by Fate. I was the one who was going to figure out what the hell happened to Freya.

Hopefully.

I breathed slowly, reaching inside myself for that golden light I'd come to know as my magic, but only a faint flicker met me. I strained, trying to force it up to meet me, gritting my teeth and putting my full willpower into it.

"Annabel, stop." Bjarni's voice seemed to come from far away and was followed by warmth clasping around the back of my neck, shaking me none too gently.

I opened my eyes with a gasp, unfocused eyes finding Bjarni's gray-blue. He was crouched in front of me, and it took me a moment to realize that all that was keeping me remotely upright was his grasp on my neck. His sword lay on the floor next to us, making me suspect he'd had to discard it quickly to make sure I didn't faceplant into the stone altar.

Growling, he touched his free hand to my nose. His fingers came back bloody. "You pushed too hard."

"Pushed too hard? All she needs to do is a damn locator spell," Modi snorted from somewhere behind me. "This was a mistake. She's not strong enough. We're going back to get Trud, end of discussion."

Bjarni straightened to his full height, bringing me up with him. "I've seen this woman bring your brother back from the brink of death. Trust me, she is plenty strong enough—but she needs guidance. If we go back, we'll lose half a day, if not more, and time's not on our side."

"Guidance?" Modi growled. "I'm not a fucking teacher, and last I checked, you had as much spark as a mountain troll. Better to lose half a day than take an inexperienced omega cunt into the wilderness!"

"Watch how you talk about my future mate!" Bjarni

snarled, flexing his right hand as if searching for his sword.

"Guys, can we not?" I snapped. "Bjarni's right, I need... help. Saga guided me during the trials, and when I healed Magni." I bit my lip as unwanted images of exactly how Saga had helped me came flooding back. I looked up at Modi. "Can you do the same?"

He grimaced, and I could sense his urge to protest about my presence bubbling right underneath the surface, but for whatever reason, he kept it back this time. Lips flattened into a line of displeasure, he ground out, "What do you need?"

"I'm not sure. Saga... he reached inside of me somehow and guided my magic," I explained, trying to recall what the non-sexual aspect had felt like.

"Hmm," Modi grunted, and before I could blink, his hand came down on my shoulder and *power* zinged through my bones like a bolt of lightning.

I straightened with a yelp, my vision turning pure white—and then in a blaze of heat I was pushed forward at barreling speeds, thundering through tight pink tunnels and throbbing organs until finally, a warm golden glow surrounded me.

Impatience washed over me—not my own emotions, I dimly realized. Modi was here with me. Inside of me.

Crackles snapped around me—irritation. He was waiting for me to call my magic.

I did, not wanting to test him. This was nothing like

Saga's gentle guidance—it was like riding a fucking thunderstorm inside my own head. A short-tempered thunderstorm.

My magic came more willingly this time, but it still seemed sluggish, as if I was trying to wring water from the muddy bottom of a well.

Where is she?

I let the question echo through the golden light until it tremored through my entire being—and then everything went gray.

"Don't search for me, little one."

I blinked at the sweet, familiar voice echoing all around me.

"Freya?" I muttered, twisting around to see her. "Where are you?"

"Lost," was the infuriatingly unhelpful answer.

"Who took you? We'll find you."

"You don't have time. And where I am, no human can follow. Ragnarök is more important, child. Was Mimir in Valhalla? Did he..." Her voice faded to a whisper, her words eluding me.

"We didn't find Mimir. You're breaking up," I called, feeling all kinds of dumb for sounding like this was some sort of driving-through-a-tunnel-on-a-cell-phone situation.

"...don't have much time. Your energy's fading. You need to let your mates tend to you, or your power will be drained. You're still weak after healing Thor's son. Don't waste your

time in Folkvangr. Go. Save the world, omega. Only you six can do it."

"Wait!" I cried, because this time the fading of her voice seemed permanent, the gray mist emptier, as if I was the only thing there now. "You can't go. We need help. We have to find Loki, and—"

My voice died when what she'd said finally took root.

"Wait... what do you mean, *'let my mates tend to me'*?"

Only silence met me. Silence, and a distinct sense of foreboding.

"You can't be serious. Freya! Come back!"

"Enough!" This time the voice that rang through the mist seemed to come from all around me, and it was distinctly more aggressive—and followed by a hard shaking. *"I said—enough!"*

The mist evaporated in a burst of lightning and scattered around me in twinkling flakes. I blinked dazedly at Modi baring his teeth in my face as the world slowly racked back into focus.

"You're bleeding all over the place. What kind of a seer are you?" he growled as he wiped none too gently at my face and nose. His hand came back red. "I knew taking a human on this journey was a folly."

"Well, if you wanna argue with the Norns, be my guest," Bjarni said as he shoved him out of the way, wrapping an arm around me so he could ease me to the floor. "There we go, nice and easy now."

The floor was cool under my palms as I steadied

myself against it, but thankfully my leather pants shielded my butt from the chill. I was still feeling kinda dazed from whatever I'd just done, and I was grateful to not have to try to keep my balance.

"Well?" Modi pressed. "Did you find our wayward goddess?"

"I spoke with her," I said, but was interrupted when Bjarni promptly pressed two fingers around my nose and tilted my head backwards.

"Whant are ynou dnoing?" I protested, batting weakly at his hand. "Staph int."

"Don't be difficult," he hummed, unconcerned with my efforts to shoo him. "The sooner we get this nose-bleed taken care of, the sooner you can tell us what Freya had to say."

I bared my teeth at him in irritation, but since my lower face was blocked by his ginormous hand anyway, my annoyance went fully ignored.

In Bjarni's defense, his nose-pinching did stop it from bleeding within a few minutes.

"There," he said, releasing my nostrils to give my thigh a light pat. "Now, you say you spoke with Freya?"

Modi, who'd been impatiently pacing between us and the altar while my nose got it together, stopped abruptly by my side, arms folded across his massive chest. "Be quick about it, omega."

I glared at him. "Well, as I was about to say—she says there's no time to look for her. That humans can't go where she is anyway. And basically that our only focus should be to stop Ragnarök. And that it *has* to be us. No one else."

So if a certain Mister *Lightning Fingers* could stop trying to send me back...

Modi gave me an incredulous look. "Really? That's it? Nothing helpful whatsoever?"

"No, the connection wasn't holding any longer," I said, trying not to feel like a complete failure despite the irritated god. "I... my energy is kinda... burned out, she said. After healing Magni."

"Burned out?" Modi threw both arms to the sides. "*Burned out?* Then what the fuck did she suggest we do? Build a campfire and watch you sleep for a few days? Bjarni, even you must be able to see that this isn't going to work. If we're not back in Asgard with Loki in tow before the moon is full, both of us will lose our brothers!"

"Njal's prick," Bjarni muttered, rubbing his beard with fingers still speckled with my blood. "He has a point, sweetie. Finding my father isn't about stopping Ragnarök. If we take you back, we'll still be able to fulfill Mimir's prophecy once Saga, Grim, and that redheaded idiot are safe. Maybe it's better if we do. Let you rest?"

He was being sweet; I dimly recognized that. Trying to gentle me into going back, and largely out of concern for my wellbeing, it seemed. But a flood of panic instantly washed away all rational thought as the same sensation of urgency set in as it had when we'd discussed finding Loki back in Valhalla.

It *had* to be me. I didn't know why, or even how I knew that—I just knew that something horrible would happen if I didn't. Something that made the sore bonds in my chest quiver and ache with desperate foreboding.

"I don't have to go back," I blurted, clutching Bjarni's arm. "Please, don't, I—I don't need to rest to regain my energy."

"What do you mean?" he asked at the same time as Modi said, "How, then?"

"I..." I drew in a deep breath, steeling myself to say what I needed to. This had to be done. It was the only way.

"One of you needs to have sex with me."

7

BJARNI

"I beg your pardon?"

The sheer shock in Modi's voice made a rumble of laughter work its way up my chest. Annabel's suggestion was a surprise to me too, but definitely a delightful one. Modi sounded wholly less thrilled.

"Freya said... Well, she said I had to let my mates tend to me to restore my energy, but they're not here. And I can't go back before we find Loki. Not even... Not even for this. So one of you will have to do it."

There was steely determination in Annabel's voice, as well as a slight wobble. She wasn't keen, that much was obvious.

I reached out to stroke a hand over her cheek and saw the vulnerability in her eyes. No mated omega liked submitting to another alpha, but Annabel wasn't going to turn around and let Trud take her place. Not even for this, as she'd said.

Whatever had her so determined to search for Loki, at this moment, I understood that it was everything to her. She was right—she *had* to come.

"You are my brother's mate!" Modi snapped. "Under no circumstances am I bedding you!"

"Not a problem," I hummed, offering Annabel a smile when she paled under Modi's outrage. "Sniffling little godlings don't know how to please an omega anyway, hmm? I'll bed you anytime you ask me, sweetie. As much and as often as you like."

"It's not about what I want, Bjarni," she bit, lowering her dark lashes to avoid looking at me—but she kept clutching my arm, as if she needed something solid to anchor herself with. "I... I need to find Loki. I need to save Saga and Magni."

"I know," I said softly, pressing my hand against her cheek until she tilted her head to rest against my touch. It made my skin prickle—such a tiny submission, yet such a big step for the little omega who'd been bonded twice against her will. "But if you ask me for this, I will bring you pleasure. I've wanted you from the moment I laid eyes on you."

"Are you serious? You're going to screw your own brother's omega?" Modi spat. "Even for a Jotunn, that's repugnant."

I rolled my eyes and looked at him over my shoulder. "She will be mine as well soon enough. But until then, she still needs tending. If this is what she asks, this is what I'll provide. You can throw a tantrum about what needs to happen if you like, but it *is* happening. She's staying with us, she's helping us find Loki—and for that to happen, she needs her magic to work properly.

"Stay and watch if you need the pointers, or go kick rocks—I don't care—but either way, stuff a sock in it. Your yapping could wilt even the hardest of dicks."

Modi opened his mouth, rosy splotches of anger coloring his cheeks as he gaped at me. I halfway expected him to jump me, and I tensed my muscles in preparation, but instead he just glared, eyes like the darkest of thunderclouds.

"Screw the human whore if you so desire," he gritted. "If Magni is happy to share her with your brother, why not you too? Why not the rest of Jotunheim? But if she hasn't gotten her magic back once your knot's tied in her simpering cunt, I'm going back for Trud with or without you."

I shook my head as he stomped out of the great hall. Whether it was pride or sheer arrogance that had him acting such a fool, I wasn't sure, but his loss was my gain.

"I'm not doing this for pleasure! Why doesn't he understand?"

Annabel's growl made my focus return to her, just in time to see her wipe a few tears off her cheeks. She'd let go of my arm and folded hers around her midriff in a protective gesture.

"Sweetie." I cupped her face between both hands, bringing her chocolate gaze up to mine. "He's an Asa prick, and he doesn't get it. It doesn't matter. I'm here, and I'll take care of you. Always."

"I'm not a whore."

I smiled. She sounded so petulant it was almost sweet. "I'm aware."

"I'm only doing what I have to so we can save them," she insisted.

"I know. You don't have to convince me, Annabel. I understand. You were Fated to me a thousand years ago —I've waited many lifetimes for you. Modi doesn't get it, but you don't need him. You have me."

I leaned forward from my kneeling position and placed a chaste kiss on her lips. "Now let me help you, hmm?"

She stared at me for a long moment, her dark eyes searching mine. Then she closed them and nodded.

"Okay."

It was only a whisper, but it sent a shiver of exhilaration through my body. I'd fantasized *a lot* about fucking Annabel since she came of age and her parents sent us a picture of her, sometimes even trying to imagine what it'd be like to be with my Fated mate while bedding some local girl back in Iceland.

But then she'd finally come, it had finally been time

to take her—and that prick Magni had gotten in the way.

She should have been mine already, should have been familiar with my touch and not trembled as I slid my hands from her face down to her shoulders to caress her arms. She was scared, I realized. Only sheer determination kept her still for me.

It hurt my heart to know my mate-to-be feared our physical union—but it also awakened the hunter in me. I might not be able to put a claiming mark on her tender neck this time, but when we were done, she would be mine in every other sense of the word.

"I'm never going to hurt you," I whispered as I leaned in to brush my lips against the shell of her ear. "Sweet Annabel. So delicate. So terrified. And yet every inch as strong as dwarven steel."

I flicked her lobe with my tongue and trailed lower to bury my teeth in the side of her neck, wrapping one arm around her to quell any chance she might jerk away.

Annabelle expelled a trembling breath, her body stiff in my grip—but she didn't try to move away. I took it as encouragement.

Soft kisses along her jawline made her breathe faster, and when I finally reached her lips, they were swollen and ripe for me.

I tested her with a gentle kiss first, unable to hold back a groan of desire as my cock rose hard and fast between my thighs. *Gods*, I'd ached for her since her scent first wafted through our farm back home. Sweet, deep, lush— and it'd only strengthened since she'd gotten mated and her biology finally fully succumbed to its true nature.

"I'm gonna make you ache so deliciously," I rasped before deepening our kiss, slipping my tongue in between her lips when she sucked in a startled little breath. Warm, wet heat enveloped me, short-circuiting any and all connection to my brain. She filled my senses, drowning me in scent, touch, taste, and I lost myself.

I kissed her with every ounce of pent-up longing, pushing her onto her back with my much bigger body. The soft press of her shape against me made me growl, every cell throbbing as if on fire. The heat from where her thighs were spread around my hips made me gasp and rip at her leather armor, mindless to finally sink inside of her. My omega.

Fuck, yes.

She pawed at me as I pulled her pants down her thighs with a harsh tug, fueling the raging need in my blood for every bite of her blunt nails. She needed me as much as I needed her, needed to stretch for my big cock and cry out as I pounded her wet little cunt until she accepted me as her alpha, until she—

"*Fucking ow!*" I pulled back, releasing Annabel's leather pants to bring a hand to my bleeding lip. She *bit* me!

Hot, dark fury rose along my spine, blackness

tinging at the edges of my vision. Every alpha instinct embedded in my DNA thundered to flip the feisty omega over and force her into submission. She thought she could *bite* me? *Hurt* me?

"Bjarni." It was a broken whisper filled with dread. "Please. Please don't. Not like this."

Something twisted in my chest at that sound—at her pleas.

The darkness faded from my vision, and I saw her spread out underneath me, dark hair fanning on the cold stone floor. Her lips were flushed rosy from my rough kiss, trembling—and not from desire.

She'd experienced forceful mating before. That was how both Saga and Magni had claimed her, and her unwilling submission was forever etched into their bonds. That wasn't how I wanted us to be. That wasn't how *I* was.

I hadn't expected how harshly—how fully—my alpha instincts would kick in with her.

I raised up on my elbows, allowing for some space between our bodies even if my skin ached to press against her, and studied her scared face.

"I'm sorry," I rasped. "This isn't how it's supposed to be. The need... it's stronger than I expected. You're longing for them, and this goes against every instinct you've got. I understand. I... I'll control it."

"No," she frowned, her hands softening against my shoulders where she'd pushed to get me off. "It doesn't... It doesn't feel wrong. To be with you. I just..."

"Don't want another alpha to force you to submit," I finished for her, bowing my head to rest it against her own. "Shit, Annabel. You fucking *sing* to me. But I'll show you, it doesn't have to be rough. Not always."

She moved one hand from my shoulder to the back of my head, cupping it. "I'd like that," she whispered.

I inhaled deeply, soaking in her gentle embrace, and tried to focus on her hand in my hair instead of her lush thighs bracketing my hips. This woman... How Grim could have any doubt she was ours, I'd never understand. Simply touching her, I felt the ghostly caress of Fate shiver down my spine, mixing with a longing so deep it took my breath away.

It took longer than it should have to withdraw from the hungry claws of my more violent instincts, the urge to flip her to her knees and rut her like a beast tearing at the edges of my resolve for every shuddering breath of her scent that filled my nostrils. Only the knowledge that I wanted to do better for her, be better, allowed me to eventually roll to my back, ensuring she followed so I could shield her from the cold stone with my body.

The weight of her small frame against my chest felt so perfect, like she was made to fit against me. I rumbled a chuckle, earning me a curious glance from Annabel. I couldn't blame her—seconds ago, I'd been about to maul her.

"I find it amusing—that some Norn weaves two threads together and then here you are, in my arms. My perfect match. In about the worst circumstances imaginable," I added, lifting my free hand to touch her cheek.

"I'm glad *someone* finds it funny," she flatly replied. "I'd personally like to slap that Norn. If she wasn't so damn scary..."

The last bit she mumbled, pulling another laugh from me. "Don't go slapping any Norns, you hear?" I drew a finger along her jawline, a small bolt of glee sparking in my still-heated blood when her breath shuddered in response. "If she hurt you, I'd have to kill her. And I also find them fucking terrifying."

"I didn't think alphas ever admitted to feeling fear. Especially not the godly kind," she said, a small smile twitching the corner of her lip. It was fucking adorable, and I pressed a kiss to it, lingering for just a moment.

"Hmm," I hummed, distracted by the taste of her lips. I wasn't nearly as good at banter as my brothers on the best of days, and right now, most of my blood supply had relocated south of my navel.

Instead of answering, I drew my hand down along her side, caressing her breast and the curve of her hip before dragging my fingertips back up along the same path.

Her breath hitched again, her body tensing against mine. She was still afraid, but now it was mixed with arousal. Her omega instincts were warring against themselves.

I kissed her again, parting her lips with my own so my tongue could explore the wet cavern of her mouth.

Instantly blood thundered in my ears as my instincts roared to take charge, but I kept control this time—mostly. My hand dipped between her legs of its own accord.

She gasped into my mouth, squeezing her thighs around my touch, but I kept my fingers light on her mound, brushing the rough fur there until she relaxed, her focus returning to our kiss.

Gradually I worked my fingertips lower, eventually letting one slip down her cleft. She jerked in response, and I smiled against her lips at the familiar little bulb I grazed. She might be scared, she might miss her mates, she may only have offered her body to bring forth the power we needed to find Loki... but her clit was throbbing, begging for my touch.

"Little omega," I whispered, finally pulling back from her mouth so I could take in her flushed cheeks and dark eyes. I greedily swallowed every gasp, every tremor on her pretty face as I let my fingertips dance along her little nub, rubbing on the hood covering it and occasionally teasing her with a direct touch to the tender bundle of nerves protruding farther and farther the more I stimulated her.

Soon her hips rocked with my motions, the tension in her body shifting as her nature forced her to chase what I was offering. She squeezed her eyes tight, breath coming in sharp little pants, fingers digging into my shoulder and arm, almost as if she didn't know if she wanted to push me away or press me closer.

"Please... Please!" she gasped, nails biting into my skin. I pressed in harder, wrapped my free arm tighter around her so she couldn't escape, and rubbed her rough and fast right where she'd feel it the most.

She shrieked, head flying back and then forward, smacking against my face. I barely noticed the pain when my lip split open, the roar in my veins deafening me to anything but Annabel's keens as she came hard on my fingers, fighting me every inch of the way.

"Bjarni! Fuck! Goddamn, shit!" Her body arched, tensing so hard she shook as curses flew from her lips. I kept flicking her spasming clit until the tension drained from her muscles and she collapsed back onto my chest, panting for air as if she'd just run ten miles.

"Oh my God," she murmured drunkenly against my chest.

I knew it wasn't what she meant. But hearing her call me a god? *Her* god?

She grunted when I rolled her off my shoulder so she landed on the rough floor, and shrieked when I grabbed the pants caught halfway down her thighs and tugged so roughly she jerked along as I pulled them from her, boots and all, leaving her lower half bared. Finally.

With a growl I had no control over, I fell between her legs, wrapped my arms around her thighs so she couldn't deny me access, and buried my mouth in her core.

The onslaught of sensation that closed in around

me took my breath away. I gasped, inhaling her scent deep into my lungs, dragging it in as if my life depended on it.

And right then? It fucking did. I knew with every ounce of my being that if I didn't drink my fill of her honeyed cunt right goddamn then, I'd die.

She mewled when I dragged my tongue up through her cleft, splitting her open and tasting the juices I'd manipulated from her with my fingers. It was maddening.

Blind with need to feel her gush for me again, I found her clit and wrapped my lips tightly around it, sucking it with a hunger I'd never known the likes of.

"Bjarni! No, no!" she hollered, trying to wriggle her hips out of my grasp. Too soon—she was too sensitive after her first orgasm for such direct stimulation.

Tough shit, sweetie.

I held her tight, forcing her to experience every deep draw on her throbbing clit, making my entire body hum to the same tune. I'd never forcefully penetrate her, but I was still an alpha. Every instinct I had screamed for dominance, and so I sucked her clit while she cried for me to stop, thrashing against my grip, sucked it as she sobbed and her body slowly softened, sucked it until she finally surrendered to the pleasure and began to grind against my face.

She barely registered when I released her left thigh to slip a finger up inside of her, but she sure did notice when I hooked it, finding her G-spot.

"Bjarni!" she gasped, then went rigid, jerking once, twice...

Her hands in my hair tugged harshly, and then warm liquid spilled against my chin, wetting my beard as the sweetest moan rang in my ears.

I'd never been this hard in my entire life.

I rose to my knees between her thighs, her hands falling limply from my head to her sides as she looked up at me through hooded lids. We didn't speak—we didn't need to. She kept her gaze locked on mine while I freed my throbbing cock from the confines of my leather pants, never breaking eye contact as I fell on top of her, catching my weight on one elbow.

And then I brought my cock to her slick, open pussy.

The first brush of her lips over my throbbing cockhead sent shivers up my spine. It turned to a full-body shudder when I pressed in farther and she spread open like a flower, her folds wrapping around me as I speared her opening.

"Shit!" she mewled, hands flying to my stomach the second her tunnel stretched in preparation to finally take me.

I'd fucked enough women to recognize the worry in her eyes as she stared up at me, a plea to stop moments from spilling from her lips. I was bigger than even my brothers, and it had taken a lot of coaxing of the beta girls I'd bedded while living in exile in Midgard before they enjoyed this part.

But Annabel was an omega. She was built for me.

I grabbed her protesting hands, trapping them above her head by her wrists. And then I pushed in. Fully.

Hot. Tight. Perfect.

"*Fuck!* Anna! Annabel!" I was barely aware of my own roar, my senses full of nothing but the tight, wet grip she had on my dick. Every nerve in my body sang out of tune, my blood thundering like Thor himself had taken up residence in my veins.

This was it. This was what I'd waited for all my life. Her and her perfect little cunt.

The second I released her wrists, she was beating at my shoulders, her mouth forming angry words I couldn't comprehend while her cunt sucked on me, but I read her true feelings plain as day.

She fucking loved how I felt inside of her. Loved the stretch, loved the submission.

"*Omega,*" I growled, because right then, that was what she was. She was also Annabel, she was Fate's weapon, she was a little human lost in a world unknown. But in that moment, all that mattered was that she was an omega. *My* omega.

She whimpered, stilling her hands and flattening her palms against me. I bent my head for hers and she met me in a searing kiss.

She took my first thrust with a rough groan, her face still screwed up in pain sharply contradicted by the rhythmic pulses from her core. I peppered her lips, cheeks, and jaw with kisses, gasping encouragements into her ears for every roll of my hips, squeezing my eyes shut to the blinding flashes of pure bliss rocking through me every time I bottomed out in her.

Soon she reached for my face, pulling me down to return my kisses. Her legs wound around mine, heels digging into my hamstrings as she urged me deeper. Her moans spilled liberally from her lips, nothing but pleasure echoing in them now, and I wanted nothing more than to keep hearing them forever. But the tension low in my shaft spoke of the impending end to this, my first union with the woman who would be mine.

I groaned in protest and tried to hold it back, but it was no use. Annabel's slick sounds, mewls, and whimpers and that unending, tight squeeze sent me hurling toward the edge, and there was nothing I or any known deity could do to stop it.

Cursing, I thrust a hand between our bodies, finding Annabel's clit with my thumb. I pressed in and rubbed —and Annabel lost it.

She screamed, pushing herself up against me, clutching onto me as if I was the only thing that kept her tethered to this world.

The flutter of muscles clasping me tight as she came for me was my final undoing.

Blackness took my vision as pleasure unlike anything that should have existed gripped me by the throat. I ceased to exist in that moment, and all that was left of what I'd once been was raw nerves and the unwavering knowledge that this was it.

She was it.

My Annabel.

She cried out underneath me, weakly pawing at me again as my knot molded her trembling flesh, forcing her to stretch and open as it hooked behind her pelvic bone. It hurt her, *I* hurt her, and I was so sorry to cause her pain and yet not sorry at all. Because this? This was how we were meant to be. Tied together in flesh, tied together in soul.

Mindlessly I buried my mouth in her neck, desperate to complete our bond and mark her as mine for all to see. But as my teeth dug into her skin, I knew it was wrong. It wasn't the right time. I needed her heat to truly make her mine.

"Shit! Fuck!" I snarled, smacking my free hand against the stone floor. "Godsdamnit!"

She whimpered underneath me, hazy eyes darting to my face. Fear shone through, her instincts flaring at the presence of an angry alpha while she was at her most vulnerable, and I instantly tampered down my disappointment.

"Shh, shh, you're all right," I crooned, slipping my arm underneath her so I could roll us over and ensuring she could lay on me instead of the hard floor.

She winced and whined at the movement, and I swallowed a groan as it caused my knot to tug on our tie, pressing in harder against her clit until she shuddered in climax once more.

"No more," she rasped once her pussy's hard spasms on my knot eased again. "Please. No more."

I kissed her brow and released her nub of nerves, moving my hand to her round ass instead.

"I wish you'd been the one to claim me first," she whispered, her voice hollow. It wasn't a compliment. It was pain. Longing.

It was harder than I'd thought it would be to force a purr from my chest, but I did it. For her.

The girl who should've been mine.

8

—

ANNABEL

I meant it.

I wished Bjarni had been the one to claim me —the only one. And the thought wracked me with guilt and tore at my chest where my bonds to Magni and Saga were linked.

I loved them. Stars help me, I did. But it wasn't love alone. It was fear and anguish and fury as well, and everything in between, and I resented them for how they'd forced their claim on me even if I understood why. Even if I could forgive them, because Fate had fucked us all over, and I'd do anything to save my family too. I *was* doing everything to save them.

But Bjarni...

I lifted my head to look up at his bearded face. His eyes were closed, the arm not wrapped securely around my back resting against his forehead while he purred to comfort me. He was... so much simpler. Kinder.

He was still every inch an alpha, and he'd been rough when he took me, but there'd been so much consideration in his touches too, so much gentleness and awe. Worship.

In another life, if he'd been just a man, I could imagine falling in love with him. He was everything a woman could want from her mate: strong, gentle, loyal. Beautiful as fuck. A generous lover.

And all I could feel now as I lay tied to him, his seed still slicking my inner walls... was emptiness.

Despite how fully he stretched me, how his presence inside me anchored me to him more intimately than I could put into words, I only longed for the two men who'd claimed me already.

I didn't love Bjarni. I couldn't. There wasn't room inside of me for any more of that anguished, burning, all-consuming *thing* filling my chest.

I hadn't realized before—hadn't had time to think, to process everything that'd happened to me since that cave back in Iceland—but a human omega was not built to withstand more than one claim. I'd always thought it wasn't done because alphas were jealous, possessive creatures who'd never dream of sharing unless the literal end of the world was here. But now? Now I understood.

Fate might have five mates in store for me, but I was barely holding on with two. I wasn't *me* anymore; I was one being split in two, in danger of coming apart at the seams. The only thing that kept me together was knowing that if I didn't complete my mission, Magni and Saga would die, and I'd cease to exist.

I hadn't fully understood it before, but as I lay in silence and listened to the alpha's soothing purr, I finally found the quietude I needed to grasp my future.

If I were to take more mates—if I were to care this much for three more men—there would be nothing left of me. No lungs to breathe, no heart to beat; just shredded tissue and a broken mind.

Which meant that while I'd have to accept their claims to stop Ragnarök, I could never love Bjarni. Nor Modi. Nor Grim.

"Are you done with this lewd ritual? Can we get on with saving our brothers?"

Modi's voice broke through the great room, shocking me out of the daze Bjarni's purr had eventually lulled me into despite my morose thoughts.

The alpha underneath me tensed, his purr halting. "Odin's tits, let a man's knot go down before you barge in demanding results, hmm? We're still tied."

I looked over my shoulder just in time to see Modi roll his eyes and level us with a disgusted look. "And your dick's a magic-blocker? Evening's almost upon us. *Find me Loki.*"

It was almost refreshing, the way Modi could make me feel like a straight-up harlot. Being around the Lokissons and Magni, I'd pretty much gotten the impression that nothing could be considered depraved in the eyes of the Norse gods. Case in point: the last time we'd visited Folkvangr.

However, Modi's obvious disgust with how I'd gone about replenishing my power was palpable, and it went a long way to push my sadness to the backburner, making room for mortification instead.

Awesome.

I tried a little wiggle, wincing when Bjarni's knot held tight, keeping me locked securely in place.

Bjarni grunted and slid his hand to my ass to hold me still. "Settle down, sweetie. You'll hurt yourself."

His easy composure only made my humiliation at being observed in such an intimate situation deepen, but he was right—I wasn't going anywhere, no matter how much I wanted to regain just a smidgen of dignity. And pants.

Instead I breathed in deeply and closed my eyes, sinking inward.

It was surprisingly easy this time, the golden light rising to greet me within just a few breaths. It felt different than when Modi had guided me. Clearer. Stronger.

Freya's advice had shown true, just like when she'd told me how to heal Magni.

Show me Loki.

It was a silent command, and I half-expected nothing to happen, but then the world tilted, the golden light opening like a vortex underneath me—and I fell.

Or I would have, if a harsh tug between my legs didn't yank me back.

I whimpered and flailed, looking for purchase, but strong bands of iron seemed to close around my torso, taking the pressure off and holding me up, and a soothing rumble vibrated from all sides.

Below me the vortex still yawned, spreading ever wider, and I squinted as something blue and green appeared in the opening.

Was that... *Earth?*

It zoomed in closer, giving me a nauseating sense of vertigo as we seemed to barrel toward the North American continent. Specks of lights grew larger into cities, the vortex taking us west over the Rockies and down, down, down, until the twinkle directly below expanded into millions of lights, and suddenly, there was the snow-covered ground.

The world jerked and shifted again, zooming along streets, weaving through traffic at breakneck speeds, until finally it stopped in front of the peeling green door of what looked like a butcher shop. On the floor, two ravens were picking at a piece of frozen, raw meat half-buried in the snow.

"Arni? Magga?" I said, more startled that I could recognize the Lokissons' talking ravens than at their presence in what I was pretty sure was Seattle.

They both looked up from their food then and into the vortex.

Magga cocked her head, giving me an inquisitive

look. Then she squawked a sharp bark of laughter. *"Oh, Loki is going to love this."*

A hard jerk sent the world spinning before I could ask what she meant. Slowly, like I was moving through water, the green door opened for me and I passed through, rings shimmering in the air around me as I did.

And then I was inside, and there he was: Loki.

It wasn't the first time I'd seen him. I remembered him from Saga's trial. Yet staring at the man sitting in a wingback armchair with a book in his hand, it was clear he'd taken on a more human appearance. A sort of disguise, I guessed.

He was a tall man, with hair as dark as Grim's and features that reminded me of all three of his sons. The otherworldly glow he'd had during Saga's trial was missing, and the thought that maybe my mates and their brothers were also in human disguises made me blink. Did they also have divine forms I hadn't seen?

Loki's head jerked up, pulling me from my musings. He frowned and lifted his hand, and a shimmer spread around it.

In response, the golden vortex that had brought me here swirled around me, blurring out the image of the god.

It felt like I was sucked through time and space by my navel until finally I blinked my eyes open to stare at Bjarni.

"You all right, sweetie?" he rumbled.

I nodded dazedly, only then realizing he'd wrapped both arms around me. "You stopped me from falling?"

"Falling?" he snorted. "I stopped you from splitting my lip open again and ripping yourself apart on my knot. Maybe wait with magic tricks until we're not tied next time, hmm?"

He glanced darkly to his side, and when I followed his gaze, I saw Modi standing by the altar, arms folded across his wide chest.

"He's in Seattle," I said, turning back to Bjarni. "Magga and Arni are with him."

"Huh," he said. "So that's why they haven't come back yet. Father must have told them to stay by his side."

"Seattle?" Modi said, wrinkling his nose. "Is that in Midgard?"

"The New World," Bjarni answered, checking me over for any injuries I may have sustained during my little magic experiment.

"Fuck," Modi sighed. "Bifrost will land us in... What do the humans call it nowadays? *Norge?* We don't have time to find passage on a boat to the New World."

"A *boat?*" I repeated, momentarily stunned out of my discomfort by the realization that Modi had zero clue when it came to humanity's recent progress. "How long has it been since you were on Earth?"

"A few centuries," he said, frowning at me. "Why? Are your boats faster now?"

9

ANNABEL

Bifrost glowed multihued against the night sky, the darkness surrounding us doing nothing to dim the otherworldly bridge.

I stared in wonder as we approached the golden tower spiraling up at its end, feeling another touch of awe at the splendor that was Asgard. Given everything I'd gone through since leaving Iceland, it was sometimes hard to remember how mind-breaking it was to be traipsing around in freaking *Asgard*, home of the gods, the need for survival outshining the wonders surrounding me.

But Bifrost? Bifrost made my breath catch in my throat with its sheer beauty.

Legend had it that the rainbow connected Asgard with the human world—and seeing as we were about to use it to travel to Norway, it seemed legend was right on this one.

"We can't use that nifty map of yours?" I murmured to Bjarni as we walked a few paces behind Modi. "Might get us closer to Seattle."

He shook his head. "No portals showed up within Asgard. And, no offense to your mate, but I don't particularly trust his brother with our family secrets."

I was pretty sure there was plenty of offense to be had, should I have been so inclined, but I couldn't exactly fault him. The way the brothers acted around each other, it was obvious any current truce was tentative.

When we got to the tower, Modi stopped by the closed port. "Heimdall!" he called, voice booming.

"Heimdall?" I asked.

"The guardian of Bifrost," Bjarni rumbled. "And a real prick."

Modi grunted, and I arched both eyebrows. If these two agreed...

We waited several minutes before the clanking of a deadbolt opening sounded from behind the port and it swung open, revealing a pale-skinned alpha with a tumble of golden curls falling over his broad shoulders.

He looked at our small party, lip curling in disgust at the sight of Bjarni. "What is this, Thorsson? A human omega and the spawn of the betrayer? Am I to take it you have brought me a sacrifice?"

"Not exactly. We require passage to Midgard. It is an urgent matter. Please step aside," Modi said, voice calm but full of command.

Heimdall didn't move. "*I*, and only I, am responsible for alerting Asgard of the Jotunns' coming, and therefore *I* decide who gets to pass. I am not letting that halfblood use Bifrost on the word of a godling who still lives in his father's shadow. Now get your daddy to come vouch for you, or go home. Get!"

From the clench of Modi's hands and the splotches forming on his cheeks, Heimdall had apparently hit a sore spot, and I grimaced, instinctively reaching for Modi's arm to calm him down. He didn't so much as look in my direction when my fingers brushed against him, choosing instead to glare daggers at the guardian.

"Step. Aside," Modi repeated, this time with an unmistakable threat rumbling through each syllable. "Now."

"You're guarding Asgard from an invasion of Jotunns, but refuse to let us *out* of Asgard because I'm half-Jotunn? Excellent logic. Best do as the kid says," Bjarni said, touching his hand to the blade at his side. "We're in a rush."

Heimdall narrowed his eyes. "Don't give me a reason, Lokisson. I'd love nothing more than present your despicable father with your head on a pike."

Great. Fucking alphas. Muscles? Check. Conflict resolution skills? Zero.

I smothered an eyeroll and stepped forward, sidestepping Bjarni's attempt at pulling me back in line. With my best smile, I stopped in front of Heimdall.

"I'm so sorry for my companions. They're stressed

with the importance of our task. Odin has requested that we bring him Loki, and with Ragnarök looming, it's a matter of some urgency," I said, smoothly placing my hand on his forearm. "But that doesn't excuse our rudeness—you're the guardian of Bifrost, and you deserve our utmost respect. I, for one, appreciate you not letting just anybody through to my world."

Heimdall looked at my hand on his arm, and for a moment I thought he'd take offense to a mere human having the audacity to touch him. But then the set of his shoulders softened ever so slightly, and when he looked at my face, his nostrils twitched—scenting for any promise of heat, probably. So damn predictable.

"Odin ordered this... quest? A godling, a human, and a Jotunn, tasked with bringing back the Betrayer?"

I forced my smile to stay in place and scooted in a little closer, ignoring Bjarni's low growl.

"Shut up," Modi murmured behind me, silencing Bjarni, and I thanked the stars at least one of them had enough brain cells left to catch on to my plan.

"He did. I don't know how we're going to..." I trailed off, lip quivering for emphasis before I looked up at him with wide eyes, making myself seem as small as vulnerable as I could—the picture of a weak little omega. "We *have* to find him. Somehow we have to, or innocents will die for his crimes. Please, sir, can you help us? We must get to Midgard tonight. We don't have much time, and only you can help us get there. Please."

The golden-haired god hesitated for a moment, his

pale eyes falling from my eyes to my lips, then rising to the two alphas behind me.

"Does the omega speak the truth?" he asked, voice still curt, but his scent was no longer rife with aggression.

"She does," Modi said, and I imagined it had taken quite a bit for him to swallow his anger. "On my father's honor, her words are true."

Heimdall breathed in a deep sigh, eyes darting to me once more before he nodded. "Then this one time, I shall let you pass. But do not bring this half-blood to my door again, Thor's son."

"Thank you," I gushed before either of my alpha companions could ruin Heimdall's goodwill with more posturing. "A million times thank you, Great Guardian. You have done for us what no one else could."

Heimdall bowed his head in acknowledgement of my flattery and opened the port to its full width. As he turned, he slipped his hand to my hip.

"Come, little human. The splendor of Bifrost awaits."

Bifrost was indeed splendid. Heimdall's boasting about how he could see "one hundred leagues," however far that was, and hear the grass grow, and how the big horn—named Gjallarhorn, because of course his trumpet had a name—atop the tower would sound through all the realms when the Jotunns approached... was less splendid.

But I kind of had it coming, given how I'd buttered him up, so I smiled and fawned as he let us through to the great rainbow bridge, where I promptly lost the ability to care about the god by my side.

It was wide—at least sixty feet—and cut through the night with its bright ribbons of color. But where from the ground it had looked like it curved against the night sky, from its glowing foot it arched into the celestial sphere itself. Stars twinkled in the distance, and where the bridge dipped from view, a swirling galaxy embraced it.

"Is that... the Milky Way?" I breathed.

"That is what you humans have named it, yes," Heimdall said, pulling me closer to his strong body. "This bridge is not without its dangers for one such as you, little omega. Perchance you might stay behind while your companions carry out their task? I shall offer to be your caretaker myself while they are away, if you so desire."

Alphas. I cringed, wetting my lips while I searched for a gentle letdown.

"Sorry, the girl's coming with us," Bjarni said, snaking his huge hand around my waist and effectively yanking me from Heimdall's grip and into his own. "Her mates have placed her in our care. Come along, Annabel. No time to waste on idle chitchat."

"Mates?" Heimdall's obvious surprise made me

surreptitiously push my braid out of the way, revealing both claiming marks on my neck as I offered him a final parting smile.

"Plural?!"

"Goodbye, Heimdall. And thank you again for your help." I gave him a wave before Bjarni pulled me onto the bridge and away from the guardian, his arms wrapped possessively around me.

I SPENT the first two hours of our trek on Bifrost staring openmouthed at the universe above, below, and around us. Stars shimmered in the inky blackness, planets swirling around them, colored in reds, blues, and grays.

And through it all, Bifrost lit our way with its Technicolor beauty, allowing me to see the vastness gaping below our feet through its semi-transparency.

It was the sort of experience no human could ever hope to have, and yet here I was, flanked by two gods as they walked me through the wonders of the universe.

But even the beauty of Bifrost gets kind of monotonous after several hours of hiking.

"How much longer? My legs are killing me, and I'm *hungry.*"

I was fully aware how much I sounded like a petulant toddler. I also didn't care. We'd been walking since forever, and though it was impossible to tell time in whichever dimension we were currently in, I knew it was edging into *humans-should-be-sleeping* o'clock.

The ache in my chest intensified for every step, not yet as soul-breaking as when Magni had swept me through the portal, but that could easily change once we set foot in the human realm.

"I'm sorry, sweetie," Bjarni said, immediately coming to a halt as he eased his pack off one shoulder so he could reach into it. "I should have fed you after we fucked. Sometimes I forget you're just a human and need a bit more care."

The sparkle in his eye as he handed me what looked like a cloth-wrapped sandwich told me that he thought he was complimenting me.

I was too exhausted to complain about being called *"just a human,"* so I took the offered food with a mumbled "thank you." Compared to my two companions, my human shortcomings were becoming pretty clear. Neither alpha looked like they were the least bit tired from our long day—or in Bjarni's case, the sex that'd definitely drained my muscles of energy, even as it had refilled my magic reserves.

"We're not stopping until we reach Midgard," Modi said, and when I looked up at him, sandwich already halfway inside my mouth, he had a distinct no-nonsense frown on his face.

"You insisted you come, and so come you will. I will not let you slow us down—my brother's life is on the line, and in case you've forgotten, the Jotunns are marching on Asgard. I have duties back home, and I *will not* let a petulant omega slow down my return." Modi placed his hands on his hips, widening his already intimidating span as he glowered down at me. "Get moving."

If I'd been alone with the redheaded god, I'm pretty certain my first instinct to his commanding presence would have been intense fear, followed by immediate obedience. But I wasn't.

Bjarni was a sweetheart, and a formidable fighter, and as much as my time with the Lokissons had been fraught with uncertainty and danger, I knew without a shadow of a doubt that he'd back me against this haughty bastard any time. So instead of cowering at Modi's words, I glared right back. And then I plopped down on my ass on Bifrost, crossed my legs, and took an enormous bite from the sandwich.

The redhead's pale skin turned blotchy and red with anger at my open challenge, his blue eyes narrowing to slits as I held his gaze. "Get. Up."

"The girl needs to eat," Bjarni rumbled, his tone much more unconcerned than I'd expected in the face of Modi's aggression. "And rest. She won't be doing any magic tricks if she's passed out from exhaustion."

Modi continued to stare at me, and I got the distinct impression he was considering if he could somehow use my magic while I was passed out. But then he sighed, and a jolt of victory fizzed in my gut when he bit out, *"Fine."*

What I wasn't expecting was for him to grab me under my armpits the next second and swing me over his shoulder, the joint colliding with the singular bite of sandwich that'd made it into my stomach.

"G-*hngh*—what!" I groan-yelped, narrowly catching the rest of my sandwich before it fell. "Let me down!"

He locked his other arm across my hamstrings, keeping me from kicking him in the gut, and grunted, "Let's go," in Bjarni's general direction.

Fucking alphas! Always with the goddamn manhandling!

"Seriously? What the fuck?" I snarled, beating at Modi's back with my sandwich-free hand. "This is not rest! This is goddamn kidnapping! Put me down!"

Modi ignored me, his strides long and steady. Bjarni fell in next to me, bag once again slung over his back, not looking the least bit upset about my current predicament.

"Do something!" I snapped at him.

"Like what? I'd be happy to carry you myself, if you'd like." The gleam in his eyes as he let his gaze sweep over my upturned ass was decidedly lecherous. "But he is right—we have limited time, and this way, you get to rest."

I glared up at him. This was almost as bad as when Magni had dragged me up Verdandi's mountain like a sack of potatoes.

At least I was wearing pants this time. But I wasn't the same woman anymore, either. I wasn't a scared, helpless human girl lost in a strange land at the mercy of strangers. I had power. I had agency.

I had goddamn dignity.

Closing my eyes, I reached inside for the golden light, not entirely certain *what* I was going to do, but damn sure it was going to make Modi put me down instant-fucking-taneously.

But before the shimmering magic so much as connected with my mind, a sharp *zing* zapped my ass, making me scream and drop my focus, my eyes popping open with a start.

"*Ow!* What the hell?!" I shrieked, reaching back to rub at my sore rump. My muscles there spasmed as if they'd been electrocuted.

"The next time you try to use your magic against me, little human, it'll be significantly more painful for you," Modi gruffed, clenching my hamstring harder when I squirmed. "You may be touched by Fate, but I have centuries upon centuries of experience on you. And the blood of the thunder god in my veins."

He'd lightning-bolted my ass! He'd fucking *lightning-bolted* my ass!

I hung over his shoulder in stunned silence for several seconds while the humiliation and sheer audacity sunk in. And then, just like that, whatever grip I'd had on myself despite everything that'd led to this moment vanished into thin air.

"You goddamn piece of *shit*, I swear to fucking god, I'm gonna *murder* you!" I shrieked, throwing the sandwich at Bjarni's stupid, laughing face before I started beating at Modi's back with both fists

Modi scoffed. And then he kept walking as if he didn't have a furious human over his shoulders, not even flinching at my continued assault.

Enraged, I screamed and swung at him until I didn't have the energy any longer. But in the end, it didn't do a thing except drain me of my already flagging strength.

After a good half hour, I hung limply in his grip, exhausted and miserable, but resigned to my fate.

"Are you quite done?" Modi's haughty tone made me grit my teeth, but I didn't have it in me to bite at him. Instead I remained silent.

The air cracked somewhere close to my ass, the unmistakable sound of electricity sparking. "I asked: Are you done?"

I gasped in a breath of air, eyes widening in outrage and shock. He wouldn't!

But yeah, he would. He'd already proven as much. And he'd thoroughly won the battle of wills that followed.

Stupid goddam power-tripping alpha!

"Yes." I was going for terse, but my throat was raw from screaming, so it came out as a broken whisper.

"Good." He relaxed his hold on my hamstrings, only to pull on my legs so I slid down and into his arms, bridal-style.

I blinked up at him, suspicious of the motives behind this more comfortable position, but he didn't so much as look at me. Instead, he glanced at Bjarni.

"Feed her."

Bjarni arched an eyebrow at the command, but his features softened when he looked at me. "You done throwing away perfectly good food?"

I glared at him. He was *so* not forgiven for just standing by while Modi asserted his dominance over me.

The blond giant cracked a half-smile and swung his backpack off one shoulder to rummage through it for more food. "How about I take that as a yes, hmm? Here you go, sweetie."

It was a sandwich identical to the one I'd tossed at him before. I ate it in silence, wincing with every swallow. He gave me a leather jug of water to wash it down with too, followed by a golden apple that turned out to be so sweet and delicious I couldn't hold back a hum of appreciation at the first bite. Even my aching mate-bonds seemed slightly less painful while I ate it.

"Is that...?" Modi began as he stared at the apple between my lips.

"Mmhm," he confirmed with a relaxed rumble.

"She is *mortal!*" For the first time since he'd picked me up, Modi stopped, and abruptly so. His fury was palpable.

"She's the mate of gods," Bjarni said with a shrug. "Do you wish for your brother to have a mortal lifespan?"

Modi blinked, redness rising in his cheeks. "I... Of course not! But—they're sacred!"

Bjarni snorted. "Not *that* sacred. How do you think

my brothers and I haven't aged all these years we've been in exile?"

The redheaded god stared at him. "Loki," he whispered, his voice low and angry.

"Mostly," Bjarni agreed. "Idunn has a weakness for flattery."

"Idunn?" I croaked I remembered some of the more obscure texts I'd read on Norse mythology. "The goddess of youth? You gave me one of her apples? Am I... *immortal?*"

"Well, you shouldn't age, so long as you eat an apple once a year," Bjarni said. "Idunn wasn't sure about the effects on a human. Made me swear I'd never offer one to a human to find out. Of course, I didn't give it to you specifically to find out what would happen."

He looked very pleased with himself, but I was still too busy processing having just eaten a fruit that would potentially keep me alive for eternity to praise him for his wit.

Besides, if we didn't manage to stop Ragnarök, no one was going to live for that much longer. Not even the gods.

Eventually even the concept of immortality drifted to the back of my mind as exhaustion and the rocking motion of Modi's gait lulled me to sleep.

10

MODI

My kidneys still ached as we made our way off Bifrost and into Midgard, high on a windswept mountainside in the land I knew as *Norge*.

Bjarni insisted we call it Norway, reminding me how Annabel spoke English and so should we when we were around her. I didn't care enough to argue, even if a spiteful part of me wanted to take every opportunity to make the feral little omega as uncomfortable as possible.

She wasn't particularly strong, but during her tantrum as she hung over my shoulder screaming like a banshee, she'd had impeccable aim. I grimaced and shifted the sleeping girl in my arms, momentarily considering placing her back over my shoulder so I could rub my back where bruises from her tiny fists were undoubtedly blooming. But that would mean placing her sweetly perfumed nethers within scenting range once more.

"Want me to take her?" Bjarni asked. "You've carried her for hours, and the trek down this mountain isn't gonna be easy with this storm."

I glanced from the howling snowstorm around us to his bearded face already covered in flakes of snow, entertaining an errant thought that I should have let mine grow too.

"No. You're carrying our supplies. I'll carry the human—at least until we find civilization."

Under normal circumstances I'd have suggested we make camp and wait out the storm, but this was Ragnarök. There would be no respite until the world had ended.

For a moment the blond man's eyes narrowed, his face growing taut as if he were going to protest. Surprisingly anger rose in my gut, making me clutch the woman in my arms tighter without meaning to.

We stood in silence for a long, drawn-out breath, until finally my brain kicked back into gear as I realized what the Hel I was doing.

Idiot!

I practically thrust the sleeping female at Bjarni, ripping his weighty backpack off his shoulders in the same movement. She mumbled at the rough pass, moving weakly in protest, but the other alpha cooed and cuddled her in his arms as if she were an oversized baby until she settled down again.

"Pass me one of the blankets," he said, not looking up from her sleeping face. "I don't want her to get cold while we descend."

This—this right here was why I'd never taken a mate.

I dug out the blanket from the backpack and tossed it at Annabel, letting him figure out how to wrap her up himself.

Weak and demanding as omegas were, the real problem with them was how they affected otherwise sane, battle-hardened warriors. I'd fought Bjarni more than once, and he was a formidable foe, powerful, strong, and commanding. Yet now he was fucking *swaddling* a grown-ass woman, doing his very best not to disturb her sleep, *purring* like some absurdly overgrown cat tending to his kitten.

Not to mention how my own brother had lowered himself to mate a human and *share her* with our sworn enemies, all because of that sweet call from her cunt.

Sure, he'd claimed it was about some noble quest to save our family, but the moment he introduced her, I knew the truth. She might be human, but her scent was ensnaring on a level unlike any omega I'd experienced before. I was as much an alpha as my stupid brother—I knew exactly what had drawn him to her, despite the ridiculousness of such a low match. I felt it tug on me too, that delicious urge to give in to primitive instincts interwoven with my very DNA.

That was the danger of omegas—they could take a

loyal, dedicated, honorable man and twist him until he was nothing but a slave to her cunt.

I'd seen firsthand what damage a honeyed snatch could do, and I was still young when I swore I'd never answer an omega's call.

I'd stuck to that oath right up until Magni needed me to protect his ill-gotten mate, and I would continue once I ensured she was safely by his side once more.

Regardless of how much my muscles twitched at how Bjarni embraced her.

It was only natural, I assured myself. She was my brother's mate, and it was my task to protect her. Seeing her fondled by another alpha was bound to aggravate every defensive instinct in my body.

"Doesn't it bother you?" I asked as I began our descent, my voice more acrid than I'd planned. "Doting on a woman who doesn't carry your mark?"

"I'll mark her soon enough," Bjarni said with a shrug as he followed, his steps more careful now he was carrying the omega. "I've waited for her for a thousand years. She's here now—why would I not care for her just because my claim has yet to mark her neck? She was mine from the moment she was born."

He sounded so completely at ease, as if there was nothing wrong with this entire, insane prophecy they were all yammering about. As if sharing a mate with his brothers—and *my* brother—wasn't a problem at all.

"And the fact that she already carries two mate claims is just fine and dandy? Or that on top of the alphas who've already taken her, she'll happily welcome you *and* that cold brother of yours between her thighs, and who knows how many more?"

I continued as I ducked under a fir branch laden with snow, holding it aside for him so he could pass without dropping Annabel. "It doesn't strike you as a strange idea that Ragnarök itself, which was foretold before either of us were in existence, can be averted by a little human girl—so long as she ties five gods to her side? Not to mention no one has heard of this prophecy before now. *Why* are you blindly okay with this insanity?"

He was quiet for a little while, and I wasn't entirely sure if he was trying to control his temper or considering his answer.

Finally, he said, "I don't know why you're happy to believe our entire world and everyone we love is doomed, but not that there might be a way to stop it. You felt her magic when you guided her to Freya. Have you met many mortals with such power? I've been in Midgard for centuries. I have met no one like Annabel.

"I love my brothers more than life itself. I would die for them. Why would it be odd that I'd share my woman with them too? Magni I could have done without, but who am I to argue with a Norn?

"Fates or no, from the first moment I smelled this omega, I knew she was mine. What I don't get is why it bothers you this fucking much. If you don't feel the pull, then regardless of what Magni wants, you're not her fifth. Once we've freed our brothers from Valhalla, you can return to fight the Jotunn army with your beloved daddy and leave Mimir's prophecy to us."

I gritted my teeth against a particularly vicious gust of freezing wind, the chill in the air doing much to cool the heat rising in my cheeks. I wanted to snarl at him that my brother's fate was very much my concern, that none of them had felt any more fucking pull to the human girl than they would any other omega—

But I didn't. He was right. And what did I care? Magni had already mated her. There was no coming back from that.

I loved my brother, and I too would die for him like Bjarni would for his blood, but he'd chosen how he'd live his last days: hunting down a crackpot prophecy, chained to a woman who welcomed his enemies into her snatch.

I didn't answer. There really wasn't anything to say. My only job was to bring Loki back to Odin and ensure Magni's mate didn't die in the process. That was all I needed to care about.

11

ANNABEL

It wasn't until we got to Oslo, Norway's bustling capital, that it dawned on me we had an unexpected problem on our hands.

And not before some kid stopped in the waist-high snow along the pavement we were walking down and pointed at us, eyes alight with wonder as he chirped happily at his less-enthusiastic looking mother.

Up until then it'd been too bitterly cold for me to give much thought to the *hows* of our plan, my sole focus being on getting on a plane to Seattle ASAP.

"Uh... guys?" I said, ducking into a narrow alley to shield us from the relentless wind digging into every exposed part of my skin. Both alphas followed, Modi with an irritated scowl. If he wasn't careful, his face would permanently lock up in that expression.

"We've got to change outfits," I said once they boxed

me in from both sides, shielding me from any stray winds blowing into the alley.

"You want to go shopping?" It was a credit to Bjarni's mild temperament that he only sounded gently puzzled at what he clearly saw as some sort of womanly desire for pretties in the midst of our life-and-death quest.

I rolled my eyes nonetheless. "No, I don't *want* to go shopping, but in case you haven't noticed, we all look like we just stepped out of a Viking reenactment. There is no way any sane airline is gonna let us board a plane like this—especially not when they realize your weapons aren't made of Styrofoam. Also, we need money for the tickets. And for passports! Oh, lord, what on earth are we gonna do about passports?"

I couldn't believe I hadn't thought about that part. If one was to travel without magic portals and transdimensional rainbows, one needed traveling documents.

And a credit card. Mine were still back in Iceland, and I had a fairly good idea that neither god had thought of such mundane necessities either.

"Oh my god, what are we gonna do?" I hid my face in my hands, trying my best not to let hopelessness overwhelm me. If we ended up failing Saga and Magni over something as ridiculous as this...

"What is she talking about?" Modi rumbled from somewhere above me.

"Travel papers," Bjarni said, his voice as calm as ever as he pulled me into his body and rubbed my back.

"And coin for clothes that'll let us blend in, plus the fare."

"*Humans,*" Modi muttered, and something about his tone made me pretty sure he had a good eye-roll. I lowered my hands to glare up at him.

"I've got coin," he said, touching a hand to the leather purse on his belt. "Enough to buy us any papers and clothes we may need."

"Yeah? Is that Norwegian Krona, or American dollars?" I bit.

"It's gold," he said, an arrogant eyebrow creeping up on his forehead at my lip. "I've yet to see a human turn down gold coins."

I stared at him for a long moment. Then I turned to look at Bjarni. "How long has it been since this guy was on Earth?"

The blond alpha chuckled and lifted his chin at Modi. "Things have changed a bit down here. Regular traders don't accept silver or gold. We need access to the local currency, and travel papers take a long time to procure. Unless you have a little *völve* handy, of course." His gaze shifted back down to me as he gave me a wink.

"A what now?"

"A witch. Or a human girl touched by Fate and blessed with magic so strong she can stop the end of the world," he said, his voice pitching lower as his gaze turned heated. "With a little help, of course."

I stared at him. "I'm sorry, are you suggesting *I*

somehow pull three passports and several grand out of my ass?"

"Well. Not your ass," he said, a wicked grin spreading on his annoyingly handsome face. "I'm sure Modi can guide your magic, should you need it. And I'm more than happy to provide any top-up of power you may require."

Echoes of what it'd been like the last time he helped me *reenergize* flickered before my mind's eye, and my mate-bonds ached as the memory of the hopelessness I'd felt afterward set in. I opened my mouth to tell him exactly where he could stick his *top-up,* but Modi interrupted before I could even get a word in.

"We didn't just drag you over Bifrost and down the mountains to listen to you complain. How is your strength? Can you provide these travel documents, or do you need another rutting?"

The redhead's voice was harsh, but he did have a point. With a final stare at him, I closed my eyes and called on the golden magic within. It rose willingly enough—not as powerfully as right after Bjarni had tended to me, but it still filled me with a strength that seemed to hum through my bones.

I released my grip on it and let it settle back into the depths of my being. "I'm fine. But I don't know how to whip up passports and money out of the blue."

"I'll guide you. But we need some paper," Modi said, looking around the alley. "Ah, that should do."

I raised an eyebrow as he walked to the nearest

dumpster and pulled out some scraps of what looked like burger wrappings without flinching. When he handed them to me, I did my best not to grimace. If Asgard's mighty son of Thor could handle a little dumpster diving without whining, so could I.

Once I'd accepted the trash, Modi rubbed his palms together before wrapping one hand around the back of my neck. "Call your magic. Envision what we need."

"I... don't know how exactly a passport looks," I said, frowning. "The gist of it, sure, but there are so many details—"

"You don't need anything but a general idea," Modi snapped. He dug his fingers into my tendons a little tighter. *"Focus."*

"Well, excuse me for checking," I grumbled before I closed my eyes to once again call on my magic.

Modi's presence was like electricity sparking in every cell of my bloodstream, but it was gentler than last time. He pushed me forward at a calmer speed this time, wrapping golden ribbons around the image of a passport with my face I conjured. His presence tugged on mine, swathing me in a warmth that made even the chill of the Fimbulwinter fade from my consciousness.

"Like this." It was a low rumble, more of a sensation than a sound, but it had Modi's trademark impatience layered within. *"You've got to connect closer with your magic."*

I tried my best to do as he instructed, but I didn't understand what he meant by closer. As a result, the golden light within me rose in a sharp wave, the careful threads Modi had pulled from it washed away in an instant.

"*Odin's beard!*" Impatience turned to frustration. "*Like* this!"

The heat around me intensified, and suddenly red light wrapped around the gold and I *felt* him.

I'd felt him before too—his presence; his impatience; his strength as he'd guided me; but not like this. This was... intimate. This was his essence inside of me, his innermost core opened for me.

Curious, I followed the flow of red magic back to its source, and there he was. Warmth glowed against me as bright as the sun and as gentle as the softest caress. It radiated all around me, swept me up, and hugged me close in the most tender of embraces. And finally, I understood.

It was *him*. Modi's very spirit.

"*What in Hel's name are you doing?*" The not-a-voice echoed with anger, and something shoved at me, pushing me away from the light and back into myself.

It was such a shock my eyes snapped open, taking me back to the alley in Oslo between the alphas, one of whom was breathing rapidly, his chest heaving as if he'd just come off a battlefield.

"W-What was that?" I croaked, staring wide-eyed at Modi's furious face. "Was that... Did I see... *you*?"

"Don't *ever* do that again!" he snarled, teeth bared and eyes wild. "Ever!"

"What happened?" Bjarni's voice was calm, but he placed a warning hand on Modi's shoulder, bracing him.

If Modi registered his enemy's touch, he didn't show it. He only stared down at me, and in the depths of his blue eyes I saw the pure shock he was hiding behind his anger. He hadn't known that could happen. If he had, I was absolutely certain he'd have never bared his innermost self, least of all to me.

"Nothing," I said without taking my eyes off Modi, the overbearing alpha with a core as soft and gentle as a summer breeze. "I had a little... hiccup. Let's try again. For Magni."

He didn't move for a long breath. But then he wrapped his hand back around my neck, and I closed my eyes just as his magic barreled through my veins.

I gritted my teeth as he forced my power to obey his command, no longer showing me what to do. It was still unbearably intimate, his presence inside of me, his aggression forcing my innermost to submit, but I didn't fight him. I'd glimpsed something that, should the world know what I'd seen, he'd be done for. There was no room for softness in Asgard, least of all for the thunder god's son. And right now, he had to assert his dominance over me to ensure I knew my place.

Had he been any other alpha, he'd have pushed me to my knees and fucked me until I begged for mercy, so a little magical ravaging? I'd take it, and be grateful too.

It was as if he sensed my submission, because at my

lack of fight his presence in me became less painful. The red light bending my golden magic exerted less pressure, its roughness easing with every passing breath.

By the end he eased out of me almost gently, the sensation as his presence withdrew almost one of loss.

He released the back of my neck and I opened my eyes once more.

Three blue passports and a credit card lay in my hands where the junk food wrappers had been before.

"You okay, sweetie?" Bjarni rumbled behind me, the press of his strong body comforting as he supported my weight. Only then did I feel my lightheadedness and weakened knees. "You're shaking."

"Her magic is low," Modi answered for me, drawing my attention back to his face. "I won't deny she is powerful, but she burns out fast. Too fast."

"Luckily we know how to fix that," Bjarni said, unconcerned with the tension in the air between me and Modi. He brushed his lips against the top of my head, and once again I thought how easy my life could have been if he'd been the only alpha woven with my own life thread.

Staring up at Modi, I wondered what it would be like if he truly was my fifth like Magni seemed to take for granted.

There was gentleness in both Saga and Magni, that much I knew from the tender connection we shared, but I also understood that it was reserved for me. To the rest of the world they were your typical alphas—rough, domineering, and ruthless.

Modi... Modi was different. The anger still flickering in his blue eyes as he glared down at me ran deep, and it wasn't grounded in run-of-the-mill sexism as I'd first assumed. What kind of damage had been done to him before he built his shield of arrogance and fury around that soft core?

I pressed in closer against Bjarni, closing my eyes to steady my mind as much as my weakened body. For now, it didn't matter—only Saga and Magni's lives did.

"Let's get moving," I said, straightening with a determined breath. "We've got to get some appropriate clothes and then get on that plane."

12

MODI

Human garments had changed a lot since I last visited Earth.

I hadn't noticed how the humans had stared at us when we entered the large settlement of Oslo; my focus had been on shielding the omega from the harsh weather and not getting run over by the metal carriages that seemed to be everywhere.

It was only when we entered an establishment carrying articles of clothing and the female shopkeeper stared open-mouthed at the three of us that I begrudgingly had to agree with Annabel's point. We needed new garments in order to blend in.

I glanced at my brother's mate out the corner of my eye and scowled at the way my gut clenched. I could still feel the shiver of sensation in the very core of my magic from where she'd touched me in her uninvited explorations. She'd violated my most inner self, watched me laid completely bare, and the knowledge that she might have seen all my secrets, all my shameful weaknesses, filled me with rage. I didn't know how much she'd observed, how much she'd understood, but that look in her eyes after...

A shiver traveled up my spine, and I gritted my teeth against the gentlest brush of pleasure in it.

No. Nothing about it had felt good!

Not even after, when she submitted so beautifully to my fury it had my dick throbbing as I forced her magic to bend for my will.

"Hi there!" Annabel's chirpy voice drew my attention from my once-again rising cock as she approached the girl behind the counter.

"Sorry for the crazy outfits—we were doing some Viking LARPing at a meet outside of town, and someone apparently thought it was funny to steal our clothes. Long story short, do you have anything that can fit those two?" She indicated me and Bjarni with a jut of her chin.

The shopkeeper smiled, a friendly expression crossing her features. "Americans?" she said, slipping into English with very little hesitation. "Yes, we have a good selection of alpha clothes, and something for you too. I'm sorry someone stole from you. That's not how we usually like to treat visitors."

"I'm sure it's just someone taking a prank a bit too far," Annabel said with a wave of her hand as she made her way to the racks of garments. "But with the weather as it is, it'd be nice not to miss our plane. Who knows when they're shutting down the airports? They haven't yet, right? We've been without Wi-Fi for a few days."

"Not yet, but they're talking about it. It's crazy—we never get such bad snowstorms so late in the season," the shopkeeper said before she turned her attention to me and Bjarni. "Do you two need some assistance?"

"Yes," I said, because it was becoming quite obvious I had no idea what was appropriate for this age. I barely understood half the words Annabel had used, but I got the gist that she was asking about how the weather might affect our travels.

I set my jaw, not looking forward to the roughened seas. At least I'd been assured the journey to the New World would be faster than the months it'd taken back when the humans first crossed.

The girl pulled several garments from the metal racks, eyeballing me as she picked each piece. Eventually she handed me a large pile. "Here. That should get you started."

"Thank you," I grunted, reaching for my belt instead of taking the clothes from her. When I dropped my leather trousers and stepped out of them, the shop girl turned beet-red, a choking noise coming from her throat.

"S-Sir—"

"Oh my God, you barbarian!" Annabel practically leapt in front of me from wherever she'd been looking for her own garments, shielding my legs from the other girl as she grabbed the clothes from her arms. "I'm so sorry! You—come here!"

The last bit was clearly directed at me, and I narrowed my eyes at being commanded by an omega, of all things. Before I could voice a reprimand, she'd grabbed me by the arm and was tugging me toward the back of the shop.

"What is *wrong* with you? You can't just drop your pants in front of a stranger!" Annabel hissed as she did her best to shove me into a small enclosure shielded by a curtain.

"It's her job to dress people," I said, reflexively closing my arms around the clothes she shoved at me before she ripped the curtain shut between us. "She's seen men in stages of undress before."

The omega muttered something that sounded like a curse. "Look, times have changed, okay? These days, you're expected to be a big boy and manage your own clothes shopping. And you're certainly not supposed to flash some poor girl working minimum wage! Just... try on what she got and let me know if you need a different size of anything. I think it's best if you don't try to talk to her again."

I scoffed at how ridiculous she was being over my bare legs, but whatever. She was more used to this era than I was.

I tried on multiple pieces of the foreign garments, eventually settling for a tight-fitting gray tunic with buttons all the way down the front, and some equally tight, stiff trousers in a blue fabric. There was a mirror in the enclosure, and as far as I could tell, I looked like a person with clothes.

"This will do," I said, ripping the curtain back open before grabbing for my sword I'd propped against one of the walls. "Go pick something out for yourself so we can board a ship."

Annabel didn't obey. Instead she looked me up and down, and when her eyes reached my crotch, her cheeks blushed a deep pink.

"Let me guess—zippers weren't a thing back in your day?"

"Zippers?" I asked, following her gaze to my crotch.

"For Chrissakes," she muttered, taking a step forward and reaching for me.

Something pulled deep in my gut, a sensation of suction that went straight to my balls as her dainty finger connected with the front of my trousers, pulling on the odd metal adornment there. She brushed over the linen fabric of my underwear in the process, and my cock reacted instantly, rising as if to reach for more of her warm touch.

"Oh my god!" she croaked, releasing the trousers as if she'd burned herself. "Why are you all like this?!"

I glanced to her from my bulge straining to burst through the now-closed zipper, but she'd already turned her back on me and was beating a hasty retreat to the other end of the shop.

For a woman who'd been claimed by two alphas and let a third mount her, she seemed awfully shy about the natural desires her touch provoked. *I* was the one with reason to resent my body's reaction, not her. She was an omega—a *human* omega. Divine alpha cock should inspire nothing but desire in her.

I inhaled before I could stop myself, testing the air for her pheromones. I wrinkled my nose at the onslaught of scents hitting my nostrils; hundreds of prior patrons to the shop, the girl serving it, and Bjarni. But also *her*.

I breathed in again, filtering out anything but Annabel. She smelled of warm honey and thyme, and just a hint of omega pussy.

I shivered, swallowing a groan when my cock thickened further. *Idiot.* The girl was right—I was exactly as dumb as every other single-minded alpha who couldn't keep it together when an omega looked their way.

I stared at her across the shop as she fussed with Bjarni's hair, wrapping it up in a bun and stroking at his beard to tame the wild strands. His eyes crinkled at the corners at her efforts, and he mumbled something to her that made her laugh, the pealing sound ricocheting around the shop.

Something sick and angry rose in my gut as I watched them together.

She wasn't his, yet none would have known it from the way he acted around her. He had no right to pet her cheek, no right to press a kiss to her shoulder when she turned away to find her own garments.

No right to look at her with such adoration and longing, I just *knew* he was thinking about the next time she'd need his essence to replenish her magic reserves.

And neither did I.

I clenched my fists until my knuckles cracked, the bite of my nails in my palms finally returning a modicum of sanity to my dazed mind.

Yeah, I got why my stupid brother thought her some prophesied *völve* worth sharing with even our enemies. I was no stranger to the call of an omega's cunt, but no one had ever drawn me like this girl did. The longer I spent in her company, the harder it was to keep my walls in place, even if I still found her intolerable.

If a man wasn't careful, that call could make him throw away his pride and convictions for just a taste of what lay between her thighs.

Perhaps I'd been wrong. Perhaps she wasn't a human, but an elf—a cleverly placed distraction to have Valhalla's sons squabbling amongst themselves while Ragnarök ravished our world.

I watched her closely as she came out from another dressing room in odd, modern garments, smiled at the shopkeeper, and paid for our clothes with the rectangular piece of plastic she'd insisted we create along with the passports. Then she returned to me, a careful smile in place as she approached—a silent plea for my obedience as she reached for my hair.

I sat still while she dragged her fingers over my scalp, ignoring the zings of pleasure at her touch while she fastened my hair into a similar style as she had Bjarni's. She might have a golden cunt, but I was prepared for her influence now. She would not trick me like she had my brother.

13

ANNABEL

Even with modern clothes and man-buns, Modi and Bjarni looked incredibly *Viking,* what with their huge frames, pale eyes, and red and blond hair. The fact that Modi refused to part with his sword didn't help matters.

"Please, you can't go into an airport with a weapon on your belt! You'll get us all arrested!" I groaned, turning to Bjarni for help. He'd packed his own sword away without fuss, even going into the airport to get us the necessary forms to check weapons as luggage, but seemed far too amused at my current predicament to interfere.

"A warrior never leaves his weapon behind in enemy territory," Modi growled, his blue gaze suspicious as he stared down at me, arms folded across his wide chest. "Do you *want* me to be trapped at sea, defenseless?"

I rolled my eyes, and not for the first time in the past twenty minutes.

"You're a god! You don't *need* a sword!" I hissed, keeping my voice low when I registered the puzzled looks from passersby. "Look, you'll get it back as soon as we land. It's a safety precaution—they don't let *anyone* board with anything that could be used as a weapon. Please, Modi, we *have* to get to Seattle, and if we don't get on the next plane, we might end up stranded here. They're not going to be able to keep the airports open much longer with this weather."

"She's right," Bjarni rumbled, finally stepping the fuck up to help me with the world's most stubborn god. "Amusing as it'd be to see you try to fight your way through security, we don't have time. You wanna save that brother of yours? You need to check your sword."

It was kind of infuriating how easily Modi relinquished his stand once Bjarni weighed in. Sure, they were mortal enemies, but apparently it was much easier to trust him than it was the human omega who'd actually been *born* in an era with air travel.

I kept my comments to myself, knowing all that mattered was to get all of us on that plane ASAP.

It turned out to be somewhat easier said than done.

Modi had kept it together quite well while we made our way through Oslo, despite what had to be a lot of new impressions coming at him at rapid speeds. However, when it came to making our way through the airport, things got kinda *tense*.

Bjarni went through security first and I followed him, but when it was Modi's turn, the metal detector went off and some beta male tried to take him off to the side to get patted down.

I could already see the sweat on the poor man's forehead as he indicated to Modi that he needed to spread his arms and widen his stance and only got a narrowed gaze in return.

"Please. Do as he asks—he's just doing his job," I called out.

Modi gave me a withering stare, but finally obeyed. Not that that put the airport employee at ease—he was shaking under Modi's glare as he went about patting him down, and his relief that there was nothing of concern on the alpha was visible in his shoulders as he finally waved the redheaded Viking through.

"Never have I heard of such absurd precautions for boarding a ship," Modi growled when he reached us, his attention darting from us to the many distractions. "They think I'd bother concealing a weapon when it is so easy to toss someone into the waves?"

Only then did it dawn on me that he still thought we were about to board a literal ship.

"Uh... you do realize we're going on a plane, right? As in flying? In an enclosed vessel? If you toss anyone outside, the whole thing is gonna come crashing down with us in it."

Modi's eyes widened for a moment as he looked

from me to Bjarni. "Truly? The humans have mastered flight?"

"Eh, *mastered* might be taking it a bit far," Bjarni said with a shrug. "But yes, most people cross continents with air travel these days. Unnatural, if you ask me, but faster than sailing."

The news that we would be traveling via air seemed to quiet Modi for a bit. I couldn't really blame him—if you'd just learned about the wonders of aerodynamics, it probably took a few moments to come to terms with it. Even if you were a god.

We wandered the airport, waiting for our plane to board. Both alphas seemed restless, their attention darting with every noise and their postures tense. I figured some food might help calm them down and brought them to the nearest burger place I could find.

For once, paying the eye-watering airport prices didn't make me bat an eyelid, though I did give a brief thought to where the magic balance on the card Modi had helped me create came from. And if there was a limit.

"*Eugh*," Bjarni grumbled as he bit into his burger, nose wrinkling in distaste. "One of the worst parts of the modern world—you've forgotten what real food is."

I arched an eyebrow at him. "Listen to you—Viking food critic of the year over there."

"He's right," Modi huffed, face screwed up in a similar display of distaste. "What is this? It tastes like... air and grease."

I didn't bother arguing with them. I happened to like my greasy air burgers, and it wasn't like there were any magic apple trees around.

Despite their comments, the burgers seemed to go down well enough, followed by all three portions of fries. *All* of them. I didn't get a single one.

"How much longer until it's time to board?" Bjarni asked as I came back from clearing our cheap plastic trays off the table.

"About... two hours," I said, checking the nearby clock he couldn't see from his seat across from me. "You guys wanna go hang out in the lobby and wait?"

He grimaced. "Nah, that just makes it worse. C'mon, let's go for a stroll."

"Worse?" I asked, moving with him when he grabbed my hand, tugging me along. Modi fell in on my other side, silent but close. The way they flanked me, it seemed they were prepared for any random passenger to burst into the shape of a mountain troll and charge at us.

"There're too many people around," Bjarni said, stroking his thumb over mine, though his focus stayed on our surroundings. "Too much noise. I don't know a single alpha who doesn't hate airports with every fiber of his being. Patrolling eases the discomfort a bit."

"Oh." It wasn't often I considered the downsides of being an alpha. They were big, dominating, and largely took whatever they wanted without much consequence. Most people *I* knew would have given their left kidney to have been born an alpha and live life on top of the food chain.

But looking from Bjarni to Modi, it became clear that not everything was so simple. They had a boatload of instincts the rest of us didn't have to deal with, and it was becoming obvious that said instincts were screaming at both men about this crowded, noisy place not being safe. There were too many people to easily determine who might be a threat.

Bjarni's hand in mine suddenly felt less like his usual urge to ensure my safety and more like he needed my touch to calm some of his unease. I squeezed his fingers, briefly wondering how many alphas suffered from anxiety. Not that any of them would ever cop to it.

When I looked to my right and caught Modi's tense frown, pity rose in my gut. Poor guy had to have it even worse than Bjarni—this was his first brush with the crowded reality of modern life, after all.

I hesitated for a moment, not sure if the gesture would be appreciated, but in the end decided I was so used to his dismissive attitude that one more rejection wouldn't hurt. So I reached out with my free hand and wound my fingers with his.

He jolted, blue eyes darting from our surroundings to our interlocked hands, then to my face. I was fully bracing for a scathing remark, but he just stared at me for a long moment before returning his focus to the people passing us, his hand closing tight around mine.

• • •

IT WAS ONLY when we boarded the plane to Chicago that I realized I'd made a mistake.

"You booked us in coach?" Bjarni said behind me as the three of us stood in the narrow hallway between the rows of seats, blocking the passengers who desperately wanted to pass, but didn't have the guts to get pushy with two huge alphas.

Two huge alphas who were going to have an awful time trying to fit into the distinctly beta-sized seats we'd been assigned.

"*Coach?*" he repeated with a shake of his head. "What have I ever done to you?"

"Apart from kidnapping me?" I said, eyebrow raised in challenge. But my snarkiness died pretty instantly because despite his exasperation, he only looked mildly annoyed.

"I'm sorry," I relented with a sigh. "I'm not used to being able to splurge on first-class, and I completely spaced. I'll ask the stewardess if we can upgrade."

We couldn't. We were far from the only ones realizing this flight was probably the last one out of Norway for a while, and every first-class seat had been booked.

I'm not entirely sure how my alpha companions managed to squeeze themselves into their tiny-by-comparison seats, but if I hadn't been smushed in between them, I'd have laughed at the spectacle they made.

Both men looked like overgrown toddlers, knees

halfway up to their ears in an attempt at fitting in their long legs, and their displeasure was painted across their faces and emanated from their chests in aggravated snarls as the plane rolled toward takeoff.

However, I *was* smushed between them, leaving me exactly zero room to expand my lungs enough to laugh.

Takeoff wasn't much better. Modi, who had the window seat, looked out at the engines in alarm when they powered up and yelped when the jet barreled down the runway and G-forces flung us back in our seats. I didn't have time to reach for his hand this time—he grabbed for mine and squeezed it so tight my bones protested.

"It's all right. It's just getting up to speed so we can take off," I murmured. "Doesn't Thor have a flying carriage or something? Something about some rams? This can't be that much worse than getting dragged through the skies by livestock."

He shot me an ungrateful look. "Nothing about Tanngrisnir and Tanngnjóstr is remotely comparable to this metal death trap. You do know that if we die, we're all going to Hel? Valhalla's ports are closed—not that there'd be anything honorable about plunging to our deaths encased in flaming wreckage."

I wheezed a chuckle—the most my poor ribs could expand. It seemed Thor's other son was quite dramatic when the mood struck.

"We won't be doing any plunging—and generally,

it's considered good manners not to talk about hell and fiery death whilst aboard an airplane. Look, we're already airborne. It'll be fine. Just try to get some sleep, it's a ten-hour flight."

"*Ten* hours in this herring barrel?" Modi growled, though his focus shifted to the window once more. "We should have gotten on a damned boat."

FIVE HOURS IN, I was ready to agree with him.

Whatever Ragnarök had done at ground level, it also seemed to add an unpleasant amount of turbulence to the air streams. More than one person had had to make use of the provided puke bags, and the stench of vomit permeating the air made me think I might need my own very soon.

Bjarni had spent the last two hours leaned forward with his face buried in his hands, forehead resting against the seat in front of him, and to my right Modi leaned against the window, his skin an ungodly shade of green. No one was getting any sleep, and even though I was pretty hungry after my fry-less burger in Oslo airport, I didn't dare touch the in-flight meal out of fear I'd hock it up on one of my already worn-out travel companions.

Things didn't improve when, from somewhere behind us, commotion erupted.

Bjarni jerked up, head swinging back to assess the

situation, but I didn't have the energy to investigate—at least not until a girl in the seat immediately behind us screamed shrilly, and Modi gasped and straightened, eyes glued to the window.

"What's happening?" Bjarni asked, voice gruff and commanding.

"Your brother has made his first appearance," Modi said flatly.

For a wild moment, I almost expected to see Saga flying next to the plane, Superman-style, and I halfway threw myself over Modi's lap to see out the window.

But it wasn't Saga that had the entire plane so worked up.

Far, far below us, gray fissures crested with white marked our location high above the Atlantic Ocean. And in the midst of the waves that looked flat from this height, a huge, snakelike body broke the surface in ribbons. I couldn't see a head, but from how enormous the bends of the body I *could* see were, I didn't want to.

"What... What is that?" I whispered, my throat constricting as I stared at something so huge and so alien, my mind refused to accept it.

"That is Jörmungandr, the Midgard Serpent," Modi said. "Bjarni's baby brother."

"*Brother?*" I croaked.

"Loki has sired many a monster." Bjarni's voice was dark, angrier than what I was used to from him. "Jörmungandr is no brother of mine, blood or no."

"He is one of the signs of Ragnarök," Modi said for

my benefit. "During the three years of the Fimbulwinter, he will rise from the depths and spray his acid into the skies and seas. Metal deathtrap or not, I suddenly find myself thankful we did not board a ship to the Americas."

I breathed deeply, trying to control my panic as the great beast below once again disappeared beneath the surface, leaving white rapids behind. I'd thought the snow was bad enough.

"What other signs are there?" I asked.

Bjarni closed a hand around my knee, undoubtedly in response to the quiver in my voice.

"Different prophecies have been spoken on the subject, and not all align. In Midgard, the lands will turn to ice and Fenrir's offspring will eat the sun and the moon, casting everything into darkness. Fenrir himself will run across the lands, gorging on human flesh, spreading death and destruction until he succeeds in killing Odin.

"The dragon Níðhöggr will gnaw at Yggdrasil's roots until the Earth quakes and fire spits from within, and along with the mighty ship Naglfar, he will carry Hel and her army of dead across the ocean to finally defeat the gods in battle. And then there will be nothing."

"Not '*nothing*,'" Modi said. "My brother and I are prophesied to live as a new land reveals itself. Two humans will survive, and they will bring life into the world."

I blinked, trying to take in everything the gods had

just shared about their understanding of the end of the world.

"You... I'm sorry, you think... You think two humans can repopulate the Earth? Are you nuts?" I shook my head. "Look, creationism has been disproven. It's impossible for humanity to survive with less than a few thousand individuals to replenish the stock, and *where* is this land supposed to come from? The poisoned seas?"

"Not all prophecies are worth the air it takes to speak them," Bjarni rumbled. "The Jotunn witch who bore Magni gave Thor that particular one, along with news that he'd fathered her son. There's no denying your mate's paternity, but not everyone believes her so-called prophecy."

"By 'everyone,' do you mean your own father?" Modi bit. "The one who sired Jörmungandr, Fenrir, *and* Hel, all three of whom will play their part in Ragnarök?"

He turned to me, anger splotching his cheeks. "There's a reason Odin wanted to execute those three. Loki *and* his offspring have an ugly tendency to get everyone killed."

I was pretty sure I was having an out-of-body experience, sitting between two gods arguing over how exactly the end of the world would come about while a scratchy speaker above us implored the panicked passengers to stay calm, and something about whale sightings.

"None of this matters," I said softly, reaching a hand

out to either side. Bjarni grabbed mine without thought, Modi more hesitantly. "We need to save Saga and Magni. What comes after that, we'll worry about then."

14

BJARNI

We took a train from Chicago to Seattle. Modi flat-out refused to get on another plane after we finally landed in O'Hare, and I wasn't about to start arguing.

I'd not flown a lot during my time in Midgard, but what little experience I had was enough for me to know that I strongly preferred both my feet on the ground, even if it was covered in snow.

The urgency of getting to my father had anxiety clenching at my gut, but when I looked down at Annabel who'd nestled up by my side, I regretted not insisting we stop and rest before continuing our journey. It'd been too many hours since any of us had gotten any rest, and we were all feeling it.

"Can you not take up *so* much space?" the little omega growled next to me as she squirmed to get comfortable in her seat. "I still have a crick in my neck from that godawful flight, and I just want to breathe! You're like a goddamn furnace."

"You allow her too much leeway," Modi said from his seat across from us. He stared disapprovingly at Annabel's irritated scowl. "No omega I've met has dared give an alpha this much lip."

"Maybe you're just not used to omegas who aren't afraid to tell you when they're tired of your shit," Annabel hissed.

I sighed, pulling her closer to me despite her squirming to put distance between us. "You, settle down and go to sleep. It's fucking freezing out there— be happy you've got an alpha to keep you warm. And *you.*" I leveled Modi with a stare. "Try to not antagonize an omega running on zero sleep and an entire plane of existence's separation from her mates, hmm? You're supposed to be better than that, right, *Thorsson?*"

Modi had the good grace to look away, heat I chose to read as embarrassment coloring his cheeks.

Annabel, on the other hand, huffed out an insult about *overbearing alphas*, but a few moments later she stopped squirming and settled against me. It didn't take long before her breathing turned slow and steady.

I leaned back in my seat with a sigh, wishing I too could catch some sleep. I looked across at Modi, noticing how his gaze rested on Annabel's sleeping form. Irritation fizzled in my chest, but I smothered it. Even a prick like Modi would find it hard to completely ignore the primitive yearnings this little omega provoked.

"I'll take first watch," I said, drawing his attention. When he realized I'd seen him staring at Annabel, he flushed again and narrowed his eyes defensively. As if I didn't know how impossible it was to keep your attention off her.

"You think I'll sleep while *you* keep watch over me?"

I arched an eyebrow. "It's a two-day ride. I don't know about you, but I'm gonna need some shuteye or I won't be worth a lick of salt. Pretty sure we can both agree it'd be dumb to kill each other before we've freed our brothers."

His lips flattened in resigned annoyance. "I guess I'll need my strength when we face Loki."

"For what? He's my father—he'll help us."

Modi stared at me incredulously. "You actually think we're just gonna walk in there, tell Loki that Odin wants him brought back in chains, and he'll voluntarily come along to get executed?"

"Of course not," I huffed. "But he *is* the God of Mischief. He'll come up with a plan, or some sort of illusion to avoid death. He'll come with us—he's not gonna let Saga and Grim die."

Modi was silent for a long time, his eyes never leaving mine. Finally he said, "You really believe that. You think Loki, the betrayer who brought about the literal end of the world, cares enough about anyone to risk his own skin? Have you had a hard look around at the other creatures you share blood with? Did he care when Narfi was murdered? Why would he care about you three when he doesn't for anything else he's fathered? Or mothered, for that matter."

I frowned. I'd never known my half-brother Narfi. Loki had only mentioned him once during a visit when we were young. He'd laughed as he'd told the story of how Odin sought to hurt him by having one of his children killed, yet the god-king still happily rode around on Sleipner, the eight-legged horse Loki had given birth to after some misadventure with a vengeful Jotunn.

But Narfi had died long before any of us were born. My father was never a warm man, but he'd ensured Grim, Saga, and I were well-cared-for as we grew up. He'd even visited us semi-regularly and gifted us Arni and Magga.

I glanced down at Annabel and breathed in deeply as my gaze dropped to her still-flat belly. One day she'd bear us children, and even now, I knew I'd lay down my own life for them without a moment's hesitation.

"You know very little about my father's motivations, Thorsson, but know this: He is not behind Ragnarök, whatever you've been told. He has gone out of his way to attempt to secure our survival, ensuring the omega fated to stop this madness was brought to us.

"What has *your* father done to see you through the end of the world? Nothing. His plans for you are to feed you to Sutr's army and watch you die. Don't worry about what *my* father will risk for his sons—worry about what will happen to your own family if we fail to stop Ragnarök."

Modi's stare turned hard, but he didn't argue. After a little while, he twisted in his seat and turned his shoulder to me, his eyelids closing.

It took nearly an hour, but eventually, his breathing slowed as he allowed himself to drift asleep, his sworn enemy watching over him as he did.

THE SKY WAS dark when we arrived in Seattle, yet the local time was just after noon.

I glanced up as we stepped out of the station, shielding Annabel from the howling wind flinging more icy snow at the already blanketed city. Above us the clouds were thick and gray, and I breathed a small sigh of relief. Miserable as the blizzard was, at least the sun had yet to be swallowed, plunging Midgard into darkness.

Which meant we still had some time.

"I've never seen the city this quiet," Annabel said as she stared at the abandoned streets thick with ever-amassing snow. "Looks like even the cafes and bars have closed down."

"You know this place?" Modi asked. He was taking it in with both eyebrows locked in a frown, mouth set in a grim line.

"My parents live a couple of hours west. They took

me here often when I was growing up," she said, her voice quieting. One look at her face and I knew what she was thinking.

"We don't have time to visit them, Annabel. Our task is too important for detours," I warned, pulling her in closer at the sadness in her brown eyes. "Maybe once this is all over."

Her obvious heartache made me want to promise her the stars. Unlike my brothers, I got why she still had love for the family who'd deceived her into coming to us.

But this was Ragnarök. Even if we did manage to find a way to stop it, the odds weren't in favor of her parents making it through.

"Maybe," she agreed, looking away from me. She knew too.

"Do you know the way to Loki's location?" Modi asked. Whether he was oblivious to Annabel's pain or trying to distract her from it, I didn't know.

"No," she said, frowning. "It was a green door next to a butcher's, but I didn't recognize the street."

"Then you'll need to search for it," he said, pulling off his right glove so he could reach for her nape.

She cringed as if she feared his touch, but didn't move away. When his fingers closed around her slim neck, she dug her fingers into my arm for support.

"I thought you said her power was too low to do more magic yet," I growled. "I'm sure I don't have to remind you what happens if you hurt her."

Modi leveled me with a stare. "You want to screw her in the street and get her juiced back up again? It might be hard for her to concentrate with hypothermia. Or maybe the piss-covered privy back inside is more to your taste? She is rested—she will have enough for a minor location search."

I bared my teeth at him, half in anger that he'd suggest I'd do anything to harm her, half in annoyance that he had a point.

"It's all right," Annabel said softly, squeezing my arm to get my hackles down again. "I've got enough. I can do this, especially with Modi's help."

Especially with Modi's help.

I let those bothersome words rumble around in my head while they did whatever it was they did together.

I'd never been bothered by my lack of magical inclination, even growing up with two brothers who were particularly skilled at it. I was strong, and an excellent fighter, and whenever I'd encountered a problem that required something other than brawn, Grim had been there to sort it out.

But right now, as I looked at Annabel and Modi standing so still, his fingers around her nape as if she were his, I understood that what they shared I could never be a part of.

It'd become obvious that Annabel was powerful— very, very powerful, despite her lack of experience with magic. Up until now, it'd only made me want to see her submit to me even more, like a good mate would for her alpha. But knowing that Modi, my enemy who didn't care one whit about her, shared that sacred power with her? That he could guide her and teach her how to use it?

That fucking sucked.

I'd never worried how I might connect with the omega I'd been destined to mate. I'd never been concerned I might not live up to what she wanted in a mate. Not even after meeting her, not even after knowing I'd love her, had I worried.

As I watched them now, I realized there was very little her and I could share in the same way she shared this with Modi.

I was a simple man with simple desires. I enjoyed fighting, eating, and fucking. I missed tending to my sheep and sharing food and laughter with my brothers at night.

Annabel was anything but simple.

While I knew I'd love her, perhaps she wouldn't love me. She'd have four other mates, after all, four alphas who would do their best to please her, who'd be able to share conversations about history and magic with her in ways I never could.

It was funny, if you had a dark sense of humor. A thousand years I'd waited for her, and never once had I considered what life would be like with a woman who might look at me and find me wanting. What she'd have liked in her mate, had she had a choice in the matter.

And yet now, after finally understanding that her

sole purpose in life wasn't to stay locked up in our farm, bearing us sons and giving us pleasure, one thing was certain: If Fate hadn't wanted it so, she'd likely never have chosen me.

Annabel staggered, pulling me out of my souring mood. She gasped and opened her eyes just as I caught her by the elbow, ensuring she stayed upright.

"I found it," she whispered, voice so raspy and weak my self-pity vanished in the blink of an eye, concern taking its place.

"You pushed too hard," I growled, gathering her up in my arms as her knees buckled. Glaring at Modi, I added, "*You* pushed her too hard!"

"She is fine," he said, dismissing my anger with a shake of his head. "She didn't touch her life-force. Now let's go."

ANNABEL LED us through the deserted city from the safety of my arms, guiding us down snow-covered streets for several miles until finally she told me to stop in front of a closed butcher shop.

"It's in there," she said, pointing at a peeling green door next to it.

Modi took a step toward it, raised his boot-clad foot, and kicked through the old wood. It splintered, leaving a large enough gap that he could reach through and open the door from the inside.

"After you," he said, waving me toward the opening. "As you said—he's *your* father."

I huffed, half-contemplating calling him a coward, but he did have a point. Loki never shied away from setting up traps meant to stop anyone from sneaking up on him.

I only hesitated for a moment before I handed Annabel to him, the displeasure of seeing her in his arms outweighed by my need to ensure she didn't get caught in any accidental crossfire.

The hallway was narrow, and the yellow paint on it peeled worse than the door. A musty smell permeated the air as I made my way through, bringing notes of decay and animal feces with it.

Was this really where my father had been hiding out?

"Loki?" I called into the quietude. "Father, it's me— Bjarni. I've come to seek your aid."

A familiar *squawk* greeted me faintly from behind a thin apartment door, and my heart leapt into my chest. Finally. We'd found him.

I grabbed the knob and twisted, and the door slid open without resistance.

It took my eyes a few moments to adjust to the low light in the small apartment. Heavy curtains covered the two windows in what turned out to be the main living room, but after a moment, I could see the space entirely.

On the left end was a small kitchenette with a door

leading into what looked like a moldy little bathroom. By the window next to it was a twin-sized bed, and to my right stood a velvet wingback armchair in front of a dead fireplace.

On the mantelpiece Arni sat, the only proof of life amongst the shadows.

When our eyes connected, the raven flapped his wings and squawked again, a cry which morphed into a voice more borrowed than mastered. "Took you long enough."

"Arni," I greeted, reaching out an arm in invitation. "Where's my father? And Magga?"

"Is that...?" Modi trailed off behind me. When I looked over my shoulder I saw Annabel supporting herself against his arm as he led her across the doorstep into the apartment.

"Is that one of Odin's ravens?" Modi finished, eyes wide with surprise.

"One of *our* ravens," I said, turning my attention back to Arni still perched on the mantelpiece. "They've been in our family for centuries. Come, winged friend. Tell me where my father is."

He shook out his feathers, but didn't obey the invitation. *Odd.* Both he and his sister loved to sit on me when they visited.

"Loki is gone. He left me with a message to you," the raven said. "He was very angry that you allowed the girl to look for him. He didn't wish to be found."

"This is an emergency," I said, frowning as Arni

shifted. He looked disheveled, as if he hadn't preened his feathers for a few days. "Odin has Saga and Grim locked up in Valhalla. Tell me where he is—we need to speak with him."

"He will allow your company for a short visit, but only yours. Your companions cannot follow. If they do, he will not be pleased," Arni said, his feathers rising once again before finally he took flight, landing on my shoulder with a small bump.

He was lighter than normal, I noted, my confusion turning to concern.

"Are you ill, old friend?" I asked, cooing softly at the bird as I reached into my pockets for some of the left-over scraps of what we'd bought on the train. "Here, have a bit of food."

"What do you mean, we can't follow?" Modi broke in. "What trickery does the traitor have up his sleeve that he will only see his son?"

"Loki doesn't trust them," Arni crowed between alien clicks and rolls of his tongue. "Don't bring them, or you will surely regret it. Swear an oath that you will seek him out on your own, and I will tell you the location."

"This is silly," I protested, frowning when he turned his beak away from the offered food. "I can't leave the omega behind. He of all people would understand that. He's gone to great lengths to get her to us, after all. Tell me where he is."

"An oath is the only way you will find him," Arni

insisted.

"Bjarni, it's okay." Annabel's voice was still so weak just the thought of leaving her behind had every primitive instinct in my gut roaring. "I... I need to rest anyway, and this is too important. Modi can protect me while you go speak with your father."

Modi can protect me.

Her words did little to calm the already grated emotions throbbing in my blood, but she was right— Modi *could* protect her. And this was too important. If I didn't speak with my father, everything was lost.

"I swear on my blood, I will seek Loki on my own," I said. "How long will it take to reach him?"

Arni clenched his talons deeper into my shoulder. "Two days," he said in another rasping, stolen voice—a mimicry of someone far more human. "I will lead you there."

"Two *days*?" I nearly refused. I looked back over my shoulder at Annabel, fear clawing at my gut.

"I'll be okay." Unsteadily she walked to my side and placed her hand on my chest. "Go. Bring him back."

There wasn't much we shared, her and I. But the urgency of our task was one such thing. I had to go. I was the only one who could. There was some small measure of comfort in that.

Cupping her cheek in one hand, I bent down and pressed my mouth to hers.

She inhaled softly the moment before our lips connected, but didn't resist the kiss. It was soft and sweet, and it filled me with the strength I needed to do what I had to.

"I'll go," I said, pulling back from her with a deep breath. "And when I come back, I'll make sure you've got all the power you need to continue."

15

MODI

Letting the Jotunn go off on his own went against every instinct I had. He might be a bumbling fool, but he was still the spawn of the betrayer. One never knew what the two of them would cook up on their own.

I glared at the omega slouched on the edge of the bed in the dismal apartment I'd been left to babysit her in. She was the reason Loki had seen us coming. A more experienced sorceress...

A more experienced sorceress would still not have been able to out-trick the God of Mischief.

My shoulders slumped and I rubbed at my skull, trying to ease the irritation prickling my skin. I loathed to admit it, but the human had been a surprising asset. From the strength of her magic to how she had handled Heimdall, I doubted even Trud could have done better. Or, if I was honest, half as well.

"Eat," I growled at her, irrational anger that she had proven me wrong bubbling in my veins.

She flinched at my harsh tone, the uneaten food I had broken into one of the closed shops on the street below to get her falling from her hand to the bed sheet. Her eyes widened with fear for a split-second before she managed to school her expression into an irritated scowl.

"God, why are you such a dick?"

Instant regret had me grimacing at the sinking feeling in my gut when realization finally clicked into place. Despite the front she put up, I scared her. Of course I did. I had been harsh with her after she broke through my inner barriers, and now here she was, alone and vulnerable with me, her powerful magic burned to ashes and no way of defending herself, should she need to.

It was a curious sensation. For the first time, I looked at her and felt pity rather than irritation. She was just a human girl swept up in a world she had no way of understanding, separated from the two alphas who had claimed her.

I crossed the floor and sat on the bed next to her, picking up the food and returning it to her. "You need to eat. It won't replenish your magic, but it will help your body recuperate from the strain."

My softer tone made her look up at me, gaze guarded as if she expected me to snap at her again. "I'm not hungry."

I opened my mouth to tell her tough, she was eating anyway, but the shine in her brown eyes had me frowning. Impulsively I reached out to touch her forehead with the back of my hand.

"You are burning up!"

Shit. Was she sick? I knew little of human ailments and even less about keeping a sick one alive.

"Yeah." The way she said it, dodging my gaze as if she was hiding something, made me narrow my eyes.

"I take it you have been feverish for some time?"

"A couple of hours," she muttered.

So she decided to get sick shortly after Bjarni left. Of-fucking-course.

"What do you need? Medicines?" I asked. "A human healer? What do you call them... a doctor?"

"No. I'll be fine," she said. "I just need to rest until Bjarni comes back."

I stared at her, suspicion still hot in my gut. She wasn't telling me something. Her forehead was locked in a frown, and she was worrying her bottom lip with her front teeth in an oddly vulnerable display I hadn't seen from her before.

But pressuring her probably wasn't the wisest course of action right now. Hopefully she would indeed be fine until Bjarni returned. He had spent much more time with humans over the last decades—he would be better at figuring out what to do with a sick omega.

. . .

Being trapped in the dingy apartment with nothing to do but wait quickly turned from an annoyance to torture.

I couldn't sleep. By the time morning rolled around, I was pacing back and forth between the bed and fireplace, my muscles straining as if preparing for battle.

I was Thor's son! I was born to fight, not wait around patiently for another alpha to return with the enemy we needed to capture!

I glanced at the dark-haired girl still curled up on the bed. She was looking worse, sweat pearling on her forehead and her cheeks flushed a deep pink.

Bjarni needed to get his ass back, stat.

Though as soon as I had the thought, reluctance rose in my throat, acrid on my tongue. If he walked in the door right now, I was pretty sure I would punch him in the face just to relieve some of my pent-up frustration.

I looked at Annabel again, wetting my dry lips. There had to be something I could do for her, some way I could alleviate her discomfort—

My thoughts came to an abrupt halt when her face screwed up in a tight grimace and she keeled over, clutching her midriff.

"Ooooh!" Her low, anguished whimper rang through the apartment like a bell, seizing every muscle in my body and rendering me rigid. A rush of emotions rampaged through my blood, heating it to the point of boiling: concern, battle lust, victory... *excitement.*

The throb from my fully hard cock finally clicked the pieces into place.

"You are in heat!" It was an accusation, but it came out as a throaty growl.

She turned her head to look at me, eyes still glazed, pink lips parted with her soft panting. She didn't respond, but she didn't need to.

I could have slapped myself. How had I not recognized the signs earlier? How hadn't *she*?

Anger flared, doing little to dampen my riled-up hormones. "You're in *heat!* Why the *fuck* didn't you say anything?"

"I... didn't know how fast it would come," she croaked. "Last time it was much slower. I'd hoped... I'd hoped Bjarni..."

She'd hoped Bjarni would be back in time to take care of her.

I stared at her, my fists clenching without my consent. Instincts I'd done my best to suppress since I presented as alpha roared at the idea of another man seeing her through her heat, but I gritted my teeth against them.

This was exactly why I had never wanted anything to do with omegas. She was my brother's *mate*, and here I was, hard and ready to screw her into oblivion as if I had any right to her sweetly-scented snatch.

I growled when I didn't stop myself from inhaling deeply at that thought, and the most delicate smell of omega heat touched my nostrils.

Stars above, she smelled like thyme and honey and *woman.*

"I... I don't think I'll be able to make it until he's back," she said. "You'll have to..."

She trailed off once again, but what she'd left unsaid hung thick between us. She wanted me to rut her through her heat.

"No." Despite the ache in my dick at the thought of bending her over and shoving myself inside of her, I knew I'd never be able to do that. If I did, if I surrendered to the instincts fighting to take control, I would be lost.

She was my brother's mate. I was not going to split our family apart, not for a piece of ass.

Her eyes widened at my denial. Not that I could blame her—I was pretty sure no alpha in history had turned down an offer to fuck an omega in heat.

"What do you mean, 'no'?" she croaked, outrage subsuming her shock. "I can't do this on my own!"

"You will have to," I growled, finally finding the will to look away from her pink lips. With strength I didn't know I possessed, I turned and walked to the wingback by the dead hearth, letting myself collapse into it. I had to grip the armrests to stay seated when she let out another whine.

"You can't be fucking serious!" It was a snarl this time. "I thought your brother was an asshole, but you—you're *useless!*"

I gritted my teeth, my temper even more volatile

than usual. But I knew she was just baiting me, wanting me to engage so she could lure me into abandoning the principles that had kept me going for all these years.

"I need you, and you're just going to sit there? What a horrible excuse for an alpha you are! No wonder Magni thinks you need his help to secure a mate!"

Hot, red anger sparked in my brain, and I snapped my head around to stare at her. She was crouched on the bed like a tigress ready to strike, eyes glazed with need and fury and blunt teeth bared in challenge.

"I do not need a mate, nor do I want one," I snapped at her. "You think if I fuck you, I will claim you like the other idiots vying for their spot in some power-hungry Norn's web? What you are begging for is a rough rutting —to be forced into submission and taken like the whore you are. You want sex—dirty, filthy, brutal sex— not *love*. And you don't give a shit if you tear apart my family in the process. Isn't that right, omega? So long as you get your cunt stuffed, to hell with my brother waiting for you back home!"

She was breathing hard as if my words only fueled her desire. "He wants you to," she said, voice rough and so filled with need my dick throbbed at the sound of it. "Magni wants you to mate me. But even if you didn't—do you really think he'd want you to let me suffer like this? Do you have any idea how much it hurts? How much I ache? You promised to care for me in his place!"

Annabel slid off the bed, approaching my chair. She

moved stiffly, her agonized pleas ringing true, but even so...

My eyes followed the sway of her hips, then wandered up her sweat-covered blouse that clung to her breasts tightly enough to allow her peaked nipples to show. Hazy thoughts of closing my mouth around one of those little buds made me grip the chair's arms tighter.

Fucking hormones!

When she sank to her knees in front of me, a picture-perfect image of submission, I nearly lost myself. Oh, how easy it would be... She was so willing—she *needed* me. And Magni...

She was right—he had asked me to care for her, to make sure she was well-tended. Wouldn't he rather *I* rutted her than Bjarni?

"Modi... Modi, please." She looked up at me, and instead of fury, desperation danced in her eyes. "I don't want this either. It's so... so *humiliating* to beg an alpha I barely know for sex. But it *hurts*. Please, it hurts."

The flash of pity I had felt for her last night returned. There was nothing but honesty in her gaze. Honesty and agony.

Shit.

She was further into her heat than I had thought. Most omegas in her situation would have stripped bare and attempted to pleasure themselves to alleviate the discomfort until an alpha could tend to them, and she hadn't yet. I had mistakenly assumed she was still in the early stages, that the process was dragging out.

She was not.

Her pupils were blown wide, her hands trembling as she placed them on my knees. "Please. I'll do anything. *Anything,* Alpha."

Alpha.

Though I knew little of Annabel, I did know that she was a proud woman, independent, and strong. The way she handled herself around alphas, even her own mates, it was obvious she would never fall into the submissive omega role.

Except now she was kneeling prettily in front of me, calling me *Alpha* as she pleaded for my help.

How humbling, how humiliating it must be for a woman like her to be rendered so helpless by her own biology.

"Annabel," I said, softer than I had ever addressed her before. "I cannot."

"Why?" It was a pitiful moan.

I took a deep breath, hesitating as I stared at the trembling omega. My own instincts were roaring for me to fucking *do* something, my cock aching for her. It would be so easy.

But...

"I don't want to father a child out of wedlock."

I had never told a soul. I had never shared this fear with anyone, and yet as Annabel stared silently up at me, her breathing still too fast but her gaze free of judgement, it all came spilling out like a boil that had finally burst.

"Magni... he was given a shitty lot. His mother was an omega. She was in heat when my father came across her. He rutted her through her heat, and then he left her. He was only forced to confess his infidelity when the omega showed up at Valhalla demanding restitution.

"My mother.... She forgave my father. But she never forgave Magni. When my father allowed him to move in with us to get him out of Jotunheim, my mother could not get past the daily reminder of her husband's betrayal. She treated him terribly. Still does. He will never admit it out loud, but he struggles with not feeling wanted to this day.

"I have seen his pain. I feel it in my gut every day since I learned of his existence. I cannot... I cannot do that to a child. I will not risk bringing a life into this world, especially not with Ragnarök at our doorstep."

Annabel stared at me in silence for a long breath, but I saw understanding break behind her glazed eyes. And... empathy.

Even in the depths of her own agony, she was capable of empathy.

"I can't believe the one time I actually think you're a half-decent person, it's because you leave me to suffer." Her attempt at joking cut off with a pained groan. She keeled over, her hands slipping from my knees to her abdomen as she panted hard. *"Oh, god!"*

Rich, sultry slick perfumed the air as she writhed on the floor in front of me, pulling a growl from my chest at the heady blow to my already barely contained instincts.

Gods, this was fucking torture! For both of us.

"Y-You need to leave," she whispered from her curled-up position on the floor, resigned to her fate. "We don't both have to suffer."

I stared at her for a long moment, instincts warring with reason. If I left, if I waited in the hallway, I could still ensure her safety without this constant onslaught of omega heat. Leaving her to suffer alone.

Magni's mate, abandoned and in pain, because I was too much of a coward to risk losing control of myself.

"*No,*" I growled, rough but restrained. With a push, I got to my feet, looming over her. "I will tend to you, Annabel."

ANNABEL

I stared up at Modi, not fully grasping what he'd said through the haze of pain pulsing through my abdomen in dull waves.

"W-What? You'll...?"

"There are... ways that do not require me to knot you," he said, and if I'd been capable of laughing, I would have at the determined set of his jaw. He looked like he was heading into battle.

"Anything," I whispered. "Anything to make it stop."

"Strip." It was a command, his alpha nature rolling off his tongue with that deep rumble.

I obeyed, my hands responding without needing input from my brain. It took longer than it normally would have as I trembled and fumbled with the fabric of my clothes.

He hovered over me, watching me as I slowly removed layer after layer, his face still stern, features carved from granite. He was every inch the stoic, controlled god, even if heat flamed in his blue eyes.

Goosebumps sprawled across every inch of my exposed flesh as I bared myself for him, humiliation mixing with relief at finally feeling the cool air against my skin.

This was nothing like it had been with Magni and Saga. They'd been all-in, wild and untamed in their need to fuck me. It had scared me at the time, but right then, I'd have given anything to have that same feral desire forced on me so I could fight and surrender and know it wasn't my choice.

Under Modi's silent gaze, there was no escaping the reality that this was all me. I was the one who'd begged him for relief—I was the kind of woman who'd spread her legs for an alpha who despised me, as long as it quenched this hellish heat.

I was an omega, and no amount of make-believe would change that.

Sweat trickled from my neck, chest, stomach, thighs, and back as I knelt naked in front of the man who'd promised to help me. My breath came in soft pants, the smoldering heat in my abdomen threatening another cramp as I stared at his raw masculinity.

He was exceedingly handsome with clean, angular features and long, red hair, but that wasn't what had my heat-addled attention. No, it was his body—his big, musclebound torso and his wide thighs promising so much strength it made my pussy weep to think about what it'd be like if he thrust himself inside of me. How good he could make me hurt.

I whimpered, reaching for his jeans, my heat once more sweeping away reason.

Finally he moved. Spurred by my attempts at freeing his cock, he shrugged out of his sweater, tossing it to the floor by my side. It brought with it a delicious scent of alpha, and I was momentarily distracted from my task as I stared up at his bared chest.

God, he was gorgeous. And so very *alpha*.

Agony seared my abdomen, forcing another rivulet of slick from my throbbing channel. I cried out, bracing myself against Modi's thighs, blind to anything but the pain.

Modi growled, a rich, delicious sound that somehow eased the pain, yet made my pussy shudder with another pulsing cramp.

Wild, raw *need* gripped my mind, erasing anything but my desperation for that thick cock pressing against his zipper. It was a mind-numbing relief—I no longer gave a shit that I'd humiliated myself in front of a man who didn't like me. All that mattered was that he fucked me. *Now*.

I tore at his jeans, somehow managing to pop the button and jerk the zipper down despite having lost all finer motor skills. A rough tug on the stiff, blue fabric, and *finally* his cock was free.

I gasped at the sight of it. I still wasn't used to the

size of alphas, but that breath only gave me a lungful of his heady scent.

"*God,*" I whimpered, sliding my hands up his powerful thighs as I leaned in to rub my face against his dick, lured by the tangy scent of his pre-cum.

"Yes," he growled, his hand landing in my hair as I rubbed my nose and cheeks against his weeping cockhead like a cat greeting her master. "I am your god. Worship me, omega, and I'll ease your suffering."

Non-heat-drugged me would have laughed in his face at the haughty command.

Heat-drugged me placed my lips on his bloated mushroom head and sucked.

He moaned in response, the sound rough and *oh*-so-good, his fingers winding tightly in my locks. "That's it. That's a good little omega whore. Suck my cock, Annabel. Fill your mouth with me—only me."

I obeyed, his crass words fueling my need. In that moment I only lived to please him, to worship his cock and take his knot.

I lapped at his head and teased the tip of my tongue against his slit, craving every drop of liquid he had to give. But no matter how hard I tried, I could only fit the tip of him in my mouth and frustration sparked in my blood. I needed to please him, needed him *inside* me—

"*Enough!*" Modi snarled, followed by a hard yank at my skull. He pulled me off his cock by my hair despite my high-pitched protests at the severed contact with what I craved most in this world.

I shrank back from the threat of his bared teeth, wincing when his hold on my hair stopped my retreat. But instead of following up with another reprimand, the alpha grabbed me, lifted me, and swung me over his shoulder.

The next minute, I was on my back on the bed.

Finally!

I keened, spreading my legs wide and tilting my hips in invitation.

"Yes, Alpha, please!"

He fell on top of me, burying his mouth in my neck. I bracketed his hips with my thighs, whimpering and babbling as he dragged his thick cock over my belly and through my split labia, coating it in my slick. For a wild, wonderful moment, the thick head of his cock caught on my flushed opening, and I tensed in anticipation of him penetrating me.

Only it never came.

Modi growled, teeth gripping my skin hard enough to pinch. He moved his hips farther down, trailing pre-cum down my thigh, his thick fingers finding my opening instead.

"N-No! Don't!" I cried out at the loss, only to grunt a curse the next moment. Modi didn't pause to tease me —he pushed three fingers up inside me, spreading my pussy wide, and immediately began pumping them in and out in a fast rhythm.

It wasn't what I'd wanted, but it was close—maybe close enough. The tight feeling of penetration zinged every nerve in my abdomen, and he smelled so *good*. Like rutting alpha—like man and musk and ozone.

I buried my nose in his hair and drank in his scent in greedy gulps, focusing on the rocking motion of his hand inside of me.

"More!" I whimpered, clutching at his wide shoulders and tensing my whole body to chase the high I knew he could give me. "Please, Modi, more!"

"I'll give you more, omega," he growled, raising his head to look down at me writhing. "Come for me, my little whore. Come on my fingers and I'll give you *more!*"

When he brought the heel of his hand to my clit and pressed down, I did.

Pleasure wracked through my pelvis, up my abdomen, and down my thighs. I clung to Modi and mewled as my pussy clenched on his fingers until the tremors released me.

I sagged into the bed underneath him, tired to the bone. I hadn't managed to sleep since the train, but already fire was licking low in my belly once more.

"You come so prettily, little whore," Modi said, his voice soft despite the rough edge. When I looked up into his eyes, they were all fire and *need*. "I could watch you gush for hours. Do you want that? Do you like driving me mad with that beautiful cunt? Another god brought to his knees for what lays between your thighs?"

I should have been angry at his denigration, but right then, it only stoked the smolder in my blood. I nodded feverishly, arching my pelvis as high as his still deeply lodged fingers would allow.

"Yes! I want you, Alpha. God, I want you!"

He growled in response, angrily even as desire flickered in his burning gaze. "Then you shall have me!"

He pulled back his fingers and I mewled, ready for him to thrust again, but instead they slipped from my sheath.

"No! No, no, no!" I clawed at his shoulders, furious that he'd deny me the only thing I needed. I bit him, uncaring of the consequences, drawing a snarl from deep in his chest.

Modi lifted off me, pushing himself back to his knees before he grabbed my hips and flipped me over.

Yes!

I knew what came next—every instinct in my body screamed for it and I scrambled to get on my knees, ass up and cheek pressed into the mattress as I shamelessly presented my pussy for him.

But instead of his thick cock, he pressed his fingers into my opening again. Only this time, the stretch was harsher.

I mewled in confusion, unsure what was happening.

"*Stay,*" he commanded. "I'm giving you what you need—your cunt filled until it hurts." And then he pushed in deeper, and I finally realized his intentions.

Broad knuckles caught in my swollen entrance and I gasped, hurtling forward to escape despite my pelvis throbbing for penetration.

Modi caught me by the hair and yanked, curving my back. "I said *stay!*" he barked, ignoring my whimper of protest.

Unbearable pressure against my vulnerable opening made me grit my teeth. Slowly but surely my pussy stretched for him, until—

"Oh! Oh my god, *ow!* Oh, *yes!* Fuck!" I cried out as my body swallowed his hand with a wet slurp, sensations of pain and mind-bending pleasure blending into wonderful, terrible unity.

It was a thicker penetration than even an alpha cock, but not as unbearable as a knot, even if the hardness of his bones made me shudder with every inch he pushed deeper.

When he closed his hand into an unyielding fist inside of me, dark spots danced before my eyes, and I knew he'd been right. This—this was what it would take to break my heat.

Spreading my thighs as wide as they would go, I submitted to the alpha who was going to save me from hell.

Modi snarled again, approvingly this time, and the sound made liquid trickle from my stuffed pussy.

"*Yes!*"

He pushed his fist deep in one long, smooth stroke, forcing a cry from me as he opened my pelvis.

"*F-uck!*"

It hurt, but it hurt *good.*

"More! Alpha, *more!*" I commanded even though he was the one in control.

Another snarl, and then he gave me exactly what I'd asked for.

His fist barreled through my clutching sheath fast and hard, his knuckles rubbing savagely against my G-spot and tender walls.

I shrieked with every thrust, clawing at the cheap bedding as I took his fist over and over again. The heat in my blood flamed, sweat dripping from my every pore, but all I cared about was that ruthless penetration.

If I hadn't been in heat, I would have hated every second, but I was. And I never wanted it to end.

I rubbed my clit to orgasm more times than I could count, and still Modi fucked me on his fist, never easing, never pausing while I wailed in pleasure and clamped down on him in climax.

He fisted me until my vision blurred and I no longer had the fortitude to stay on my knees, the fire that had given me strength finally dousing.

"No more." It was a raspy whimper as I trembled in the throes of my final orgasm, sprawled on the bed where my jellied muscles had given up on supporting me. Where seconds ago his fist had felt so good, now it was too big, the stretch of his knuckles too wide.

"Please, Modi. No more."

He paused, breathing heavily with his hand still pressed deep inside of me, and for a moment I thought he was going to ignore my plea.

Thankfully, mercifully, I was wrong.

Slowly he pulled his fist out of my still-trembling pussy, drawing a whimper from me as it popped from my stretched lips.

Heavy weight settled on my back, warm muscle encompassing me from all sides. His cock was hard and huge against the small of my back, his breath harsh in my ear, his skin too hot—but I accepted his closeness.

There wasn't peace in his embrace like there had been every other time I'd let an alpha mount me. He wasn't sated, and where I'd normally be feeling the afterglow, tied by a knot to my lover, now there was only emptiness.

It was a curious sensation—feeling this sore and exhausted from a multitude of orgasms, and yet completely unsatisfied. He'd calmed my heat, and I knew if he kept fisting me when it flared again, eventually he'd break it. But it would be nothing like when Magni and then Saga had taken me through my first heat.

Pain flared from my mate bonds at the thought of them, and I closed my eyes to stem the tears threatening to spill over. I was ungrateful, and I knew it. Modi had given me more than I could have expected, considering his reasons for denying me in the first place. Especially with how little he thought of me.

He'd called me a whore while he prepared me, and I was pretty sure he'd meant it. He didn't like me, hated me for what I was and what it did to him and his brother, and where his harshness had been a turn-on while my heat was at its worst, right now it didn't feel good at all.

I shifted underneath him to put some distance between us, the closeness suddenly unbearable.

Modi growled, the sound so rough and frightening I froze, my heart skipping a beat.

"M-Modi?" I asked. "What are you doing?"

"*Stay.*" It was a perfect imitation of when he'd commanded me to stay put for his fist, but this time the order was followed by a nearly violent nuzzle against my neck and shoulders. He breathed me in, humming in appreciation, followed by a few flicks of his tongue against my nape.

Oh.

His instincts still had him wrapped in the craze of hormones, his lack of release keeping him suspended in the primal stage of a rutting male.

I bit my lip, knowing what I had to do.

"Let me... Let me help you like you helped me," I said, flushing as the words left my lips. I'd been more than happy to suck him off while I'd been high on my heat, but the current lull in my hormones made me all too aware of what I was offering.

He'd certainly not think me any less of a whore after this.

Modi scraped his teeth against my nape before he pulled back, lifting off me for a moment.

I began to turn to face him, but he pushed me back

down with a large hand between my shoulder blades, pinning me in place.

My breath caught in my throat as he spread my thighs with his knees. I wasn't ready for his fist again, but a tingle of excitement stirred low in my abdomen at being forced into position.

"No," I whispered, though I wasn't sure I meant it. "Not again. Not yet."

"*Yes.*" The hand he wasn't using to keep me pinned came up to rub against my swollen labia, thick fingertips finding my clit.

I mewled at the contact, fire licking through my pelvis in response, melting my resistance as slick dripped from my opening, showing my alpha I was ready for him.

Modi growled in appreciation of my offering and dipped a finger into my heated depths. I clutched around him, at the same time reluctant and eager for his fist to follow, but after a few pumps of that single finger, he pulled his hand from me and raised up high on his knees.

"W-What are you doing?" I breathed.

I got my answer in the next second.

His big cock rested in the crack of my ass, hot and throbbing against my skin as he pressed back down over me, his heavy body taking the place of his hand in keeping me pinned. Then, in one smooth move, he shifted his hips, letting his bloated cockhead find my opening.

"Oh! *Oh!*" My eyes popped wide when realization dawned. In the next second, Modi pushed past my parted labia and deep into my pussy, his hard length bottoming out.

I screamed, arching into him and shuddering. "Yes! Modi, *yes!*"

It was nothing like his fist.

He was big, his girth stretching my sore muscles past the point of pleasure, but it was perfect. *This* was what I'd craved, this was how I was meant to be—stretched open on an alpha's cock, a vessel for his lust.

But the alpha didn't fuck me. He held still inside of me, the tip of his cock pressed against my fluttering cervix, his body quaking against mine.

"Annabel." His voice broke on my name. "I.... *fuck*, I have never... You feel... Stars above, Anna!"

Only then did the true implication of his refusal to risk bringing a life into existence dawn on me.

I was his first.

I made him break his vow.

"Modi," I murmured, caught between my desperation for him to rut me through my rising heat and guilt at what we'd done. "Modi, pull out. You don't—you don't have to do this. We can—"

My voice drowned in a roar so furious it raised every single hair on my body.

"*Never!*" It was a snarl so primal I didn't even recognize his voice. Whatever had kept him still, my attempt to stop him broke it in two.

Harshly he snapped his hips, barreling through my trembling depths with punishing strength.

"I will never—"

Another thrust that had me gripping at the sheets and gritting my teeth.

"Ever—"

And another.

"Stop! Your cunt is mine, omega. *Mine!*"

With that, he found his rhythm. He pistoned in and out of my clinging sheath, his hips drumming against my upturned ass, making my pussy sing with syrupy smacks.

I screamed underneath him, every thought fleeing my mind as hormone-addled madness descended in full.

Nothing mattered but his thick cock. Nothing mattered but *him*.

I chanted his name and heard mine growled in response. His hands were everywhere, stroking, rubbing, fueling the fires in my blood like his cock fueled my orgasms.

He pulled me up to sit on his thighs and clutched my body to his so he could grope my breasts and rub my clit.

He pulled me to the end of the bed and fucked me with my ass hanging over the edge.

He kissed my shoulders and bit my neck and all the while, he cried out my name as if it were a prayer.

I was too exhausted to move and bordering on unconsciousness when he gave me my final climax.

My pussy spasmed weakly on his pumping cock, drawing a cry from my dry throat as pleasure washed over me in a blessed wave of relief. The pain of too much penetration faded into the background as Modi's moan of completion rang through the room.

He clamped his strong hands down on my hips, keeping me in place, and then... then came the stretch.

I whimpered in protest, but was too weak to even try to escape—not that Modi would have let me.

He forced his knot through my straining labia with a growl that vibrated into my bones, making my pelvis yawn wide before it snapped into place, tying us together. Warmth flooded my cervix and he moaned again, rocking gently as his seed bathed my battered pussy.

I panted hard, too exhausted to climax again despite how his knot ground on my G-spot and filled me painfully, perfectly right.

Modi wrapped his arms around me, pulling me in tight while his orgasm shuddered through us both. "Anna. Anna," he moaned into my ear, the wonder in his sex-roughened voice so very different from how he'd spoken to me before.

I closed my eyes, too exhausted to think about it. Too exhausted to do anything but breathe as the alpha filled me with his essence.

I'd almost lost the battle against unconsciousness

when Modi closed his teeth around the back of my neck and bit down, breaking the skin.

I shrieked, my eyes flying open at the pain, shock following like a wash of acid.

"Modi! Modi! What are you doing?!"

But I knew what he was doing. I felt it deep in my bones and in the core of my being when Modi, son of Thor, brother of Magni, claimed me for his own.

17

BJARNI

I was pretty sure I was walking in circles.

"Can't you just take the direct route? We don't have time for this," I growled at Arni, who was perched on a branch ahead of me.

"Your father gives instructions. I follow," he squawked. "This is the route we must take if you wish for an audience."

"An *audience*," I spat. "I'm his son. Why is he making this so difficult? He must know things are dire if I am here to see him."

"He doesn't trust your companions. And he is displeased that you failed him," Arni said, flapping his wings and then taking off so he could land on my shoulder. He thumped against my coat, scrambling to not fall off, not nearly as elegant as he normally flew.

"*Failed* him?" I asked, gobsmacked. "How? We

procured the omega and she is going to stop Ragnarök! What the fuck else does he expect?"

"You let Thor's bastard claim her, compromising your father's plans," Arni said, nibbling at my earlobe when I growled a curse.

"If my father has an issue with how things are getting done, maybe he needs to start doing things for himself!" I glared at the bird on my shoulder. "I thought you were *our* messenger. Aren't you supposed to be on *my* side?"

Arni gave me a measured look. "Have *you* tried denying your father, boy? Tail feathers take forever to grow back. Now quit your whining and keep walking. We'll be there soon enough."

I sighed. He had a point—in fact, I was mildly surprised the poor bird wasn't plucked bald after we had him deliver the news about Magni's interference.

I reached up to scratch at his head before I continued through the knee-high snow, knowing there was no alternative. If my father had decided to play games for me to prove my determination to reach him, then so be it. He was Saga and Grim's only hope, and I would rather die a thousand deaths than let Odin send them to Hel.

MY FATHER'S new hiding spot turned out to be an old cottage deep in the woods.

Light shone through the windows, casting a warm

glow on the drifts of snow surrounding it, and for a moment I was overwhelmed with memories of my mother's cozy house in Jotunheim.

Loki hadn't shared our home, but he'd visited when we were still children, often bringing presents. I hadn't seen him in... decades now. He'd come to see us at the farm in Iceland once, after we were exiled, but that was many years ago. Our communication usually went through Arni and Magga.

I reached up to pet Arni, who'd grown quieter the closer we got to our destination.

"Is he in there? Or is this another red herring, hmm?" I asked, nudging his beak.

"He's in there," the raven confirmed.

Finally.

I breathed in a sigh of relief and went to approach the cottage, but Arni stopped me.

"Wait."

I turned my head to arch an eyebrow at him in question.

The raven hesitated for a moment, then shook out its dulled feathers. "Be careful, boy. Ragnarök is here. No one is unmarked, not even the God of Mischief."

I frowned. "What do you mean? Speak clearly."

Instead of answering, he gave a squawk and set off from my shoulder, flying toward the roof of the cottage where he dove down the smoking chimney, disappearing from view.

I sighed. Messengers of gods they might be, but

they'd all days had a penchant for dramatics over clarity. And marked or not, I had a task to fulfill.

I strode across the snow-covered clearing and paused in front of the door, rapping my gloved knuckles against it. Loki might be my father, but Arni was right—he *was* the God of Mischief, and only the dumbest of fools walked through his front door uninvited.

"Enter, son."

That voice. I smiled even as the power of it shivered through my bones. I'd found my father. He would help us through this.

I opened the door and stepped inside a small, low-ceilinged room with rough planks for flooring and wooden beams supporting the ceiling. And there he sat, with Arni and Magga on his shoulders, one leg slung over the arm of a chair, straddling the old piece of furniture in an arrogant mockery of the god-king himself.

My smile widened. "Father, it's good to see you. You look well."

"Bjarni," he greeted me, his voice frosty.

I sighed. "Arni said you were angry."

"Angry?" Loki's voice was deceptively calm, and I swallowed a grimace. I knew that tone. When I was a kid, a beating had usually followed.

"Why would I be angry?" he continued. "I task my sons with the survival of our family, set them a simple task—mate a human omega and keep her safe—and the next I hear, only Saga has managed to complete the task and the omega is also bonded to Thor's bastard. Why would that make me *angry?*"

He pushed off the chair, coming to his feet as his voice grew rough with his fury. Both ravens on his shoulders squawked and flapped, clearly eager to retreat from the furious god, but they stayed put nonetheless. A binding spell, I suspected.

"Father, let Arni and Magga go," I said, trying to intervene on their behalves. Arni was right—it took them forever to grow their tail feathers back, and they were a pitiful sight in the meantime. "They're not to blame for what happened, and if you'd let me explain—"

"If you didn't want them to shoulder blame, you wouldn't have sent either with news of your shortcomings!" Loki snarled. "Their task was to watch over you and ensure you fulfilled my plans, and they failed!"

"We didn't fail, Father, not in the scheme of things. Saga mated the omega, and Grim and I will too on her next heat. She is powerful, and she is determined to stop Ragnarök. Isn't that what you wanted? Your plans will still come to fruition—we just had a little, ah, hiccup along the way," I said, hoping to soothe his flaring temper.

I failed.

"Don't presume to know my plans, boy," Loki said, his eyes narrow as he stared me down. "You allowed a stranger to search for me! You risked my life! And then, by all the stars in the sky, you brought Modi Thorsson to *hunt* for me! You were never my brightest child, but I would have hoped you'd be smart enough not to bring the enemy to my doorstep!"

"I wouldn't have, had the situation not been dire," I replied. "You know I'd never do anything to put you at risk, but Saga and Grim—they're in trouble. We need you."

"*You* need *me?*" He spat the words out, so much venom in his voice I took a step back. "After you failed me and brought an enemy to my door? Son, I did not bring you here to *help* you. I brought you so that you may know my disappointment and see your punishment with your own eyes."

I blinked. "Father... we don't have time for petty squabbles. Grim and Saga might die at Odin's hand. He will execute them for treason in your stead. Whatever punishment you wish to award me I will accept, but please—help me save my brothers first."

Loki's nostrils flared, and where I'd hoped to see reason bloom in his dark eyes, only renewed anger festered.

"You wish for me to step in the way of Odin's vengeance? You want me to *die,* son? If I come within a hundred leagues of Valhalla, he will execute *me.* Your brothers have gotten themselves into this mess—at least Grim should be smart enough to get them out again.

"In the meantime, *you* will mate the omega and *you* will make certain she is kept from Thor's bastard. Use her powers to ensure our bloodline lives—and keep her in line. We can't risk her expending her magic trying to save the whole world, let alone Thor. Prophecy or no."

I stared at my father for the longest moment, words refusing to form in my dazed mind. He still looked exactly like the man who'd come to visit us when we were children—who'd whispered the secrets of Valhalla in our ears and told of us our glorious destinies—tall, dark, mysterious, and beautiful in his divinity.

I'd always thought he loved us, that his cold mannerisms were just who he was, but he still felt... *something* beneath the surface. Because I'd loved *him*. He was my father.

It was only now, as I stood before him desperate for his help, that I understood. We were pawns to him, chess pieces he controlled to ensure his own goals.

He would never risk his own life to save my brothers. They were expendable.

I was expendable.

"Father..." I whispered hoarsely.

"Quiet!" he hissed. Dark magic rose around his body. On his shoulders, Arni and Magga's squawks rose to shrill screams. "This is your punishment, son. Fail me again and it will be your brothers'—or your children's, should you sire any with the omega before our paths cross again."

The magic flickered, turning into flames as they fully engulfed his body. His eyes shone bright white, making me squint to see.

I wished I hadn't.

Flames licked up his shoulders and set fire to the birds trapped there. Their agonized cries tore through my chest and I roared, lurching to save them.

Invisible bonds kept me in place, howling with rage and sorrow as the two ravens who'd watched over me all my life died screaming in the dark fire.

When there was nothing left of them but ashes, the fire died as swiftly as it had started, my father's eyes darkening once more.

"Do not seek me out again until Ragnarök is over," he said, his voice calmer now, though still laced with anger. "And do not fail me again, Bjarni."

Power grabbed my body and *pushed,* and I flew through the air, through the walls of the cabin and deep into the woods, landing on my back in the snow in a small clearing of trees.

I stared up at the darkening sky through the canopy high above, the silence of the forest overwhelming my senses. Grief and fury warred behind the wall of nothingness wrapping around my insides like a comforting blanket, but I was too numb to feel it.

Blessedly numb.

In the span of the past few minutes, so much had died.

My lifelong companions.

My belief that I was ever loved by the man who sired me.

My hope.

I lay in the snow for a long time before I found the strength to get to my feet. Back in Seattle, a woman was waiting for me. She needed me. My brothers needed *us*.

Even in the depths of nothingness, there was that. There was Annabel and Grim and Saga.

THE TREK back to Seattle was faster than the journey out, but it felt infinitely longer.

I kept expecting Arni to land on my shoulder and chatter some rudeness at me before he nipped my earlobe, kept peering to the sky in hopes that this was all just a horrible nightmare that I would wake up from any minute.

All that met me was solitude and snow.

Shortly after dawn, the numbness broke and grief took its place. I wished it'd been anger, but I wasn't so lucky.

Tears trickled silently down my face and into my beard, making me thankful for my loneliness. If anyone had seen one of Jotunheim's greatest warriors sobbing like a babe, my days would have been numbered. Weakness was the precursor to death, and right then I felt weaker than I'd ever thought possible.

The only thing that gave me the strength to keep walking was knowing that a few blocks away, Annabel was waiting for me.

18

ANNABEL

"Modi!"

I cried out my alpha's name as he penetrated my weeping sex once more, the agonizing new bond hooked behind my ribs flooding with pleasure, numbing the pain.

I'd lost count of how many times he'd mounted me since he'd put his claim on me, the times in between a hazy fog of hormonal madness and misery. We hadn't spoken—hadn't needed to. I felt his regret like an ice pick between my ribs whenever he wasn't buried inside of me, only the pleasure he found there overriding his anguish.

My heat refused to break, and as horrible as it was, I was grateful, because once it was over, there would be nothing to ease the torment.

Modi grunted behind me, his hands finding their

now-familiar place on my hips and yanking me back onto his thick dick.

At least this part didn't hurt any longer. He'd fucked me so many times my pussy swallowed him without protest. Even the knottings felt sort of good now.

I mewled, digging my fingers into the ripped mattress, closing my eyes as red-hot pleasure crawled through my pelvis and down my thighs. "Harder!"

"What in the ever-loving *fuck!*"

A roar that didn't belong to my lover ripped through my brain, seemingly coming from everywhere around me.

I opened my eyes, squeaking in shock when the hands on my hips and the dick inside me were ripped away, leaving me empty and cold as another roar shook the apartment.

Dazedly I looked over my shoulder, naked fear gripping my lungs at the sight.

Bjarni was there, only he looked nothing like the gentle giant I'd come to know.

His face was twisted in fury, red and almost unrecognizable, teeth bared as he stood over Modi where he'd flung him to the floor.

"*My* omega! You claimed *my* omega! *You,* who think she is so beneath you! You, who looked down on *me* for wanting her!"

He didn't wait for a reply. In the blink of an eye he'd lifted his foot and brought it down onto Modi's skull with a sickening *crack.*

I shrieked as agony flared in my chest, sharp and unbearable.

"Modi! Modi, Modi, no! Please, no!" I scrambled to get off the bed, all thoughts of heat and regret gone in that horrible, too-long moment when my mate lay still on the dirty floor.

"He's gonna live." Bjarni's voice was still a growl. He shoved Modi's limp body with a foot, and my new mate groaned softly but didn't stir otherwise.

Relief flooded my mind, anger taking the place of panic.

I bared my teeth at the man who'd hurt my mate, who'd stopped him from sating my desperate need. "You'll pay for that!"

My own voice was barely recognizable, hoarse from screaming and raw with primal fury. I grasped for the well of my magic, my reserves filled from uncounted mountings, determined to blast this prick into next week for what he'd done to Modi.

Only Bjarni had other ideas.

He narrowed his eyes in response to my bared teeth, and before I'd managed to summon my power, he crossed the space between us, grabbed me by the scruff of the neck, and shook until I lost my grasp on my magic.

"This is what you want, Annabel?" he snarled. "You want to *fight* me?"

"You hurt him!" I growled back, though whatever receptors he was pressing into had my body lax and compliant no matter how much I wanted to claw at him.

"You *hate* him!" he shouted, shaking me again hard enough to make my teeth clatter. "He took advantage of you while you were out of your mind with heat! But fine —if that's how you need it, that's how you're getting it!"

Roughly he threw me on the bed. I landed on my stomach, and before I managed to turn back around, he was on me.

The heavy press of his body kept me pinned to the mattress despite how frantically I fought to free myself. That undeniable tingle of excitement I'd come to know too well since Modi first took me crawled up my hamstrings and mixed with my anger.

Panting grunts in my ear had my heart pounding against my ribs and my ass arching up in invitation without my consent. He reached down to open his jeans, followed by the instant press of his hard alpha cock nestling in against my lips.

"No!" My protest was breathy, unconvincing even to my own ears. That aching tug behind my ribs thrashed in protest, but my body was still under the thrall of my heat. Mindlessly I spread my legs wider for the alpha whose mere presence promised to sate me.

"*Yes!*" Bjarni hissed, followed by a blazing stretch between my thighs that took my breath away. My pussy swallowed his cock with little resistance, my channel slick and eager, and he bottomed out inside of me with a pleasure-roughened groan.

"Gods! Annabel!" Despite the note of elation, of worship in his shout, Bjarni didn't pause to savor me this time. Where he'd been gentle and generous before, now...

Now he was anything but.

He grabbed my hips covered in finger-shaped bruises, the ache of being filled blending with the soreness in my exhausted body as he used his full strength to yank me down on his cock over and over again.

"This is how you like it, omega? Forced?" he gritted between harsh pants, thrusting his hips so hard and fast I couldn't even breathe to scream.

"You've been mine since you were born—*mine*. I've been patient, Annabel. So. Fucking. *Patient.* No more. I'm done. Done! From now on, you take my cock whenever I shove it into your pretty little cunt. You take it, and if you don't like it, I don't give a shit! You hear me? This is how you want your alpha to treat you? Then by the fucking gods, this is how I'll treat you!"

He was everywhere, filling me up and caging me in, his aggression painful and exactly what I craved on the most primal of levels. I cried for my injured mate, shrieked like I had for Modi before he'd claimed me and eased the thrashing bonds protesting the mounting from an alpha who wasn't mine.

Before, both with Bjarni and Modi, I'd been able to suffer through the wrongness of submitting to a man who wasn't my mate, knowing deep down it was the only way. But now, with Modi injured on the floor?

Surrendering my weeping core was still bliss—and it was torture.

Bjarni didn't give me a chance to fight my heat and come to Modi's aid. He kept me in place on my hands and knees, fucking me ever rougher no matter how much I screamed and cursed him.

In a way, I was grateful. My bonds may have protested at my submission, but this time it wasn't my choice—and in the end, all there was left for me to do was surrender my body and let Bjarni rut me through my heat.

His knot came with little warning.

One minute I was coming for the umpteenth time, my channel so oversexed it was more agony than bliss, and the next he roared like a wounded beast, the bottom of his already thick member swelling hard.

I whimpered but stayed put, tightening my fingers in the already shredded bedding, lost on endorphins and my traitorous body's need for that unyielding tie.

"*Mine!*" Bjarni clamped his teeth around my nape, tearing into my skin and ripping the sore flesh still scabbed from Modi's claim.

I shrieked, instincts making me fight it until his strong jaw dug into the pressure points meant to keep an omega compliant.

I collapsed onto the bed, my body boneless and my breathing haggard. It hurt worse than any of my previous claims, his bite half-covering the still-fresh wound from Modi's.

"*Bjarni.*" My throat was too tight to produce more than a hoarse croak. "Bjarni."

Ancient biology, older than humans—older than gods—penetrated my cells with every frantic pulse of my blood, forever altering my essence, my very DNA. His name turned sweet on my tongue as emotions that weren't my own flooded my system, bathing me in bone-deep satisfaction and raw ecstasy.

The giant alpha kept my neck locked in the grip of his jaw until his thick cock had deposited every drop of his seed deep in my body, thumbing my clit to wring another orgasm from my exhausted pussy.

Only when he had no more left to give did he release my neck and slide his hand from my clit to my hip. He peppered my shoulders with kisses, his beard tickling my skin as he murmured my name over and over.

Pleasure sang in my mind and in my chest, a sharp contrast to the unpleasant throb where Modi's bond was anchored. Behind that was the constant anguish from the mate bonds tying me to the men I'd left in Valhalla.

"Annabel." It was a soft rumble—so intimate it clutched at my quivering heart.

Love, raw and pure, welled up from that fresh bond dug deep into my chest.

Love.

Bjarni *loved* me, and as I lay tied to him by his knot

and this new bond, there was nothing either of us could do to hide that fact.

This was how a mating bond was supposed to work, only instead of elation, instead of comfort, his love only brought into sharp, agonizing distinction how my three other claimings had been nothing like this. How even in the arms of a man who loved me, I'd never be whole again.

I sobbed before I could stop myself, sorrow and hurt drowning out the pleasure of Bjarni's embrace.

"Annabel? Annabel!" Shock colored my alpha's voice and throbbed in our bond. He wound his arms underneath me, pulling me in tight against his chest. "Shh, please, don't cry. Please, please, don't cry."

And then... then our bond flooded with the worst sensation of them all: regret.

"I'm sorry. Sweetie, I'm so, so sorry," he whispered, voice trembling against my ear. "Oh, gods, what have I done?"

19

MODI

I was pulled from unconsciousness by the most unpleasant yank from something tender and unyielding anchored in my chest.

Groaning, I fought gravity to force my eyelids open. My vision was blurry and took a moment to refocus.

I stared up into a cracked ceiling, and I was lying on some form of hard surface.

A floor, Modi. If you're staring at a ceiling, it's probably a floor.

My nose throbbed, as did the rest of my head, and I groaned again, wanting nothing more than to sink back into sweet oblivion.

A woman's sobbing broke through the low hum in my ears, pushing away any and all thoughts of passing out as that awful thing in my chest spasmed again, shooting a bolt of adrenaline right to my brain.

"Annabel, please, *please* stop crying." A male voice laced with desperation mixed with the sobs.

Bjarni.

I bolted upright, cursing my vision momentarily blurred again. When it faded, my heart skipped several beats.

On the bed only a few feet from where I sat, Bjarni lay curled on top of a stained mattress as if he was protecting something precious. Or some*one.*

Bile rose in my throat when my hazy gaze landed on where his knot plugged a woman's yawning entrance wide, and finally everything came back to me in all-too-vivid detail.

Annabel.

My Annabel.

My sobbing, distraught Annabel whose distress alone had yanked me from the depths of unconsciousness.

Black rage slammed over my mind so instantaneously and completely that every ounce of fear and regret I'd experienced since claiming her vanished. Instinct alone got me to my feet faster than my concussed head would otherwise have allowed.

Without hesitation, I followed the momentum and threw myself on top of Bjarni, roaring like a beast, intent to *maim.*

"Get off her! Get off my *mate!*" My fists weren't as coordinated as they would normally have been, but I got a good few whacks in on the blond giant who'd penetrated my woman before he managed to rear up and throw me off.

I thudded to the floor, my shoulder impacting with the hard surface heavily enough to cause the floorboards to groan.

I was on my feet again in an instant, prepared to resume my attack, when Bjarni held up a hand.

"*Stop!*" he shouted. "We're fucking tied, you imbecile. You'll hurt her!"

Hurt her. *Hurt* her?

Those two words echoed in my throbbing head, pausing my already raised fist mid-air.

"Modi. Modi, stop."

That voice.

I stared at the bed, blind to anything but the girl twisting toward me underneath Bjarni's bulk.

He growled unhappily, but didn't move to stop me as I stumbled forward like a puppet on a string, that tight ache in my chest pulling me toward her. I fell to my knees by the side of the bed, reaching for her face.

"Annabel?" I murmured. The adrenaline in my blood was waning again and my vision was turning blurry once more. "Are you hurt?"

"No," she said, her voice soft despite its rasp. "I'm not hurt."

I frowned, the throb in my chest telling me an entirely different story. I pressed the hand not cupping her cheek to my ribs, rubbing them. "I..."

The silence between us seemed to stretch into eternity. The painful tugging in my chest was easier to manage now that I was close to her, but it still felt... wrong.

My bond to her, I thought, my dazed mind still having difficulties grasping at any one concept. It was my mating bond.

I rubbed at my ribs harder, my breathing turning ragged.

I'd claimed a mate.

A human, mortal mate. A woman I barely knew. My *brother's* woman.

Stars above, *why?*

I stared wide-eyed at Annabel, the sensation of being inside of her echoing in my dazed memories.

She had felt like home. Or so I had thought at the time, because she was the first woman I'd ever penetrated. I had not paused to think—I had acted on blissful instinct when I bit down on her neck, marking her as mine for eternity.

Who knew my lifelong, noble aspirations to never screw a woman would lead to mating the first one I stuck my dick into? Fucking priceless.

And stupid. So, *so* stupid.

I regretted it the moment my brain returned to a semi-functioning state and I realized that that gnawing, aching, tender new *thing* in my chest was a leash directly from my immortal soul to her mortal hands.

I'd claimed my brother's mate.

I'd claimed a *mate.*

I'd claimed a mate who belonged to three other men.

And I regretted it. Stars above, how I regretted it. But there was no going back. Mate claims were for life. Every alpha learned that at his mother's teat.

That now horrifically familiar void in my gut opened up again, sucking me down in a spiral of despair.

"Modi." It was a pained whisper, an achy spasm in my chest drawing back my attention to the girl on the bed in front of me. Her face was drawn and tears fell silently from her red-rimmed eyes as she looked at me —and I knew she felt every ounce of regret in me as keenly as I felt the turmoil in her.

But it wasn't just pain that radiated back at me from our bond this time. It was anger.

It took me a moment to realize that the sensation didn't originate from her—it came from Bjarni. I felt him through my connection with her. As if things were not messed up enough already.

"You ungrateful piece of shit," he growled, his voice low but still threatening. "*You* have regrets? You, who took her the moment I turned my back? You have some fucking nerve."

Of course. I felt his rage—he felt my emotions too.

My face burned. I was unsure if it was with anger or shame. I latched on to the anger nonetheless.

"Don't say another word, *Lokisson,* or I might forget your *connection* to the girl and toast your sorry ass," I hissed. It was an odd sensation, seeing him on top of the woman I had claimed—I wanted to tear him apart for claiming what was mine, but at the same time, that horrid bond in my chest shuddered at the thought of hurting him.

Hurting him would be hurting Annabel, and myself.

Gods be damned, this was a complicated nightmare!

"Guys. Please... Please don't." Annabel's hoarse voice snapped both our attention to her in the blink of an eye. "I can't... Everything is so messed up, and I can't contain it. I know this isn't what any of us wanted, but we didn't have a choice. The Norns saw to that. Please, can we just... focus on our task? This isn't going to get any easier with you two fighting, and we have a job to do."

A job. I had been so laser-focused on saving Magni's ass I had not cared about anything else—right up until I sank my teeth into Annabel's neck.

I blinked as I stared at her wan face, suddenly realizing that my entire world had shifted in more ways than one. I still loved my brother, sure, but all I could think about at her mention of *our task* was that, Loki or no, once my brother was free from Odin's righteous fury, Ragnarök was still here.

Annabel was still going to die.

Sick terror clenched my gut, followed by immediate, white-hot determination. *No.* I was Modí the Brave, son of Thor, slayer of Jotunns. I was never going to let that happen. I could not.

"We have to stop Ragnarök."

"I know," she said, wincing when Bjarni rolled them over and his coital tie pulled on her abused opening.

She looked so small in his arms, so... frail. Exhaustion painted every line of her face, bruises covering her skin from where he and I had held her in place while we took our pleasure from her mortal flesh.

She was the epitome of an omega: small, weak, and built to submit. Yet supposedly the Norns had decided that she would be the key to ending Ragnarök.

This tiny mortal.

Our bond flickered in my chest, pulling me from my musings. I frowned, rubbing at my ribs, but before I could process the alien sensation, Bjarni nuzzled at Annabel's messy hair and emitted a low rumbling noise.

A fucking *purr*. He was *purring* for her, soothing her frazzled mind and body as if he had no care in the world. As if this situation was in any way normal.

I had not purred for her after I took her.

I stared at them as the bond instantly relaxed and Annabel's eyelids fluttered, intense jealousy mixing with relief at the absence of tension in our connection. It was so easy for him—Hel, he would probably have claimed her even if he wasn't caught up in some ridiculous web of Fate and family obligations.

I could sense every tender emotion he felt as he stared in wonder down at the little thing in his arms. It was tinged with uncertainty and pain, but the soft, warm emotions were unmistakable.

Underneath all the bullshit, he cared for this human girl.

Annabel pressed her back closer to the blond alpha's body, her features easing with every rumble vibrating through his chest. When she put her hand on his arm in a display of gratitude, something in me snapped.

I moved without conscious thought, rage, jealousy, and *need* pulling me onto the bed. She did not open her eyelids when I slid down next to her, pressing my naked skin to her front. She shivered at the contact, but a small hum of appreciation escaped her throat.

At least she was getting jerked around by bullshit instinct too. I knew she did not care for me, did not even really like me, but she craved my nearness as much as I did hers.

Staring a challenge at Bjarni, I forced a loud purr from my chest as well, drowning out his low rumble.

The blond giant narrowed his eyes at me as he increased his volume, a touch of aggression to the tone.

Between us, Annabel sighed. *"Alphas,"* she muttered. But she kept her eyes closed, and soon she drifted off to sleep, sandwiched between the two gods who had given up their own fates for her.

20

Annabel slept for nearly twenty hours. I dozed in and out of consciousness while she rested, alternating with Modi. We didn't discuss staying awake to guard the omega between us. We took turns naturally. The schedule worked itself out.

I guessed that was one of the "perks" of sharing a bonded mate—there was another alpha to watch over her while I slept.

Of course I'd have happily traded the ability to sleep peacefully if it meant my Annabel belonged to me and me alone. Perhaps then she wouldn't have sobbed in my arms after I made her mine.

Agony twisted in my gut and I buried my face in her messy hair to calm the pain with a lungful of her scent. She hadn't wanted this—she'd confirmed as much when she'd said the Norns were behind our mating.

I couldn't even blame her—of course she didn't want this. No omega would want a bond with four alphas, four men who pulled her in four different directions, tore at what made her whole, and shattered any sense of individuality she may have had before.

I hadn't fully understood how fractured she was, how *broken*, until my bond hooked itself by her heart and I felt the depths of her despair.

I'd never thought I'd regret claiming Annabel, but I did. I'd fantasized of how I'd take her for so long, how I'd ensure she gasped my name with reverence, begged me to put my mark on her.

Seeing Modi on top of her had wiped away any such notions, leaving only the basest of instincts to *take*.

Just like every other alpha who'd claimed her against her will.

She could never love me like I loved her—and I'd spend eternity living with that knowledge intimately lodged behind my ribs.

Or at least until Odin killed Saga and Magni, and she, Modi, and I all died excruciating deaths alongside them.

Dread sank in past the misery. I'd failed her. I'd failed all of us. It had been my job to convince Loki to help us, and I'd been unable to.

The ache of my father's betrayal throbbed behind the numbness created by Arni and Magga's deaths, a nightmare that refused to wane in the light of day.

"Bjarni?" Annabel stirred, her sleepy murmur followed by a hand sliding to my hip. "What's wrong?"

My anguish must have woken her. I squashed down the thrill of her care. Of course she cared—my pain was hers.

"Nothing," I lied, reaching out to stroke her cheek. "Go back to sleep, sweetie."

"I've slept long enough," she muttered, straightening to a seated position. Her movement woke up Modi, whose eyelids fluttered, gaze zeroing in on her the moment he was conscious.

"Annabel?" His voice was thick with sleep.

"We need to get moving," she said. "Bjarni, did you reach Loki? Does he have a plan?"

"Are you strong enough to move?" Modi asked, frowning as he scanned her pale flesh, eyes resting on her many bruises. "We can afford a few days' rest, if you need it."

Such a different tune to what he'd sung before he'd stuck his knot in her. I snorted.

"I'm *fine.*" There was no patience in Annabel's voice as she withdrew from both of us to dangle her feet over the edge of the bed, stretching her legs experimentally. "We don't have time for this protective alpha routine. Bjarni?"

I glanced at Modi. His face tightened, turning stony at her rejection. *Poor sod.* He probably hated every instinctive urge clamoring to go overbearing alpha on the girl he'd had little patience for before mating her, and she wasn't having any of it.

"Loki isn't going to help us," I said. "We have to find a way to save them on our own."

"*What?*" Annabel's voice broke, either from outrage or shock—possibly both. "His own children are in danger! Did you explain to him that Saga and Grim might *die?*"

"I did. He doesn't care." It was hard to get the words out. My father—my *father*—didn't care whether we lived or died, so long as he was safe. "We will get nothing from him, so it's best we spend what time we have left finding another way to free our brothers."

"We don't need another way," Modi growled. "I never expected the traitor to risk his own neck—I came prepared to force his surrender. I suggest you get on board."

I stared at him. However grateful I was that he didn't take the opportunity to twist the knife of my father's refusal to help, after I'd so adamantly claimed he would, it was hard to hold back an eyeroll.

"He's the God of Mischief," I reminded him. "He's way too powerful for us to force him to do anything he doesn't want to—believe me."

A small, warm hand rested on my leg, sending a jolt of sensation to my ribs. When I looked back, Annabel's brown eyes locked with mine, glowing with intent.

"There is no other way, and you know it. He may be

the God of Mischief, but right now, he's what stands between us and the lives of those we love. He doesn't want to help? Fine. We don't give him a choice. One way or the other, he's going to get us your brothers back. That I promise you."

21

"The only way we stand a chance is if we take him by surprise."

I looked up at Bjarni as he paced in front of the makeshift board he'd made from scavenged pieces of paper and a broken chair. On it he'd drawn a rough layout of Loki's location, along with a few scribbled notes. As much as he thought his father wasn't going to be overcome by our ragtag little group, he'd committed to trying.

Possibly because we all knew that without Loki, we didn't stand a chance. He might be powerful, but it'd be infinitely easier to beat him than it would Odin and all the forces of Valhalla.

"How will we manage to surprise him?" Modi cut in. "He already knows we're here. He knows we want to bring him before Odin."

"He won't expect me to come back," Bjarni said, and

the bitter twinge in his voice made me look closer at him.

I hadn't taken any time to ponder what it had been like for him to go to his father and be denied. I'd been too wrapped up in my own misery at the painful new bonds thrashing in my chest like warring serpents.

I'd never considered that the pain I felt throbbing through me from Bjarni's tie was more than his regret over claiming me—I'd been too focused on the agony our connection caused us to think about what he'd endured.

Part of me wanted to go to him—to offer him what comfort I could.

I stayed seated on the floor.

There was too much there—too much turmoil, too much festering contagion—and I knew if I poked a hole in the fragile scab I'd managed to form since waking between my two new mates, it'd all come pouring out. The hurt, the resentment... the *regret*.

And I... I couldn't face it. Not now. Not when everything hinged on all of us keeping it together so we had at least a chance to save Saga, Magni, and Grim.

Once Saga and Magni were safe, there would be a time to deal with the bitter emptiness of confronting the fact that two of the men fated to be mine regretted their claims. Until then, I couldn't offer any more of myself to either man, no matter how much my stupid, frayed heart panged to ease the pain radiating through both newly carved bonds.

"The difficult part will be to sneak up on him without alerting him of our presence. And, of course, to capture him. My father is... very strong," Bjarni finished, his gaze flickering to Modi. "We'll need magic. But be cautious. He sensed Annabel searching for him."

Modi nodded, folding his massive arms over his wide chest. "I think that can be done. I can guide her power. Stealth is not my wheelhouse, but Anna's abilities should be able to conceal mine. The biggest problem will be to capture him and contain him until we reach Valhalla."

Anna.

I glanced at the redhead, forcing down the jab in my chest at that particular pet name. It was what my parents called me, my friends. It'd slipped from his lips so effortlessly I doubted he'd even noticed. I knew he felt anything but friendly toward me; our aching bond betrayed as much.

Can't think about that now.

There was no happy ending for me and Modi. There was no happy ending for any of us. I'd finally realized that when I'd awakened between him and Bjarni, every cell in my body throbbing with the ache in the four bonds splitting me into pieces.

There was a reason omegas didn't mate more than one alpha.

For a moment there, after Saga and Magni had united inside of me, I'd thought I'd be able to reconcile the two bonds. That perhaps once everything had settled down, I'd be able to find happiness with the five men destined to be mine.

But no woman was capable of holding five mating bonds within her, not even one blessed by Norns. In the end, there would only be pain.

It didn't matter. So long as we lived, so long as we stopped Ragnarök, my mates could resent me, could regret caving to Fate. I was strong enough to endure until we were all safe again.

I had to be.

"I don't suppose there's any way we can reach Thor and convince him to help?" I asked, looking at Modi. "I know he was adamant you bring Loki back, but is there a chance he'll come? It's *his* son's life on the line too."

A look I couldn't decipher flickered over Modi's features "No. He has tasked me with this. He is busy preparing to meet the Jotunn hordes, and nothing will deter him from his destiny. He has been preparing for that battle for a long time."

I blinked. What was it with gods making shitty parents?

The tiniest thread of a thought sparked and I pressed a hand to my abdomen, swallowing hard. Hopefully it wasn't all gods who'd abandon their offspring in their time of need.

It was insane, really—that I'd fucked multiple alphas while lost in heat, and the thought of pregnancy hadn't really entered my mind until then. I'd been lucky thus far, but who knew how long that would last?

How many gods does it take to knock up an omega?

Don't think about that now.

I forced down a hysterical urge to giggle—or cry. No one cared if I ended up pregnant, not with the end of the world looming. I shouldn't either.

Focus, Anna. Focus.

"Right. It's just us. Then we'll make it work. What're Loki's weaknesses?" I looked back to Bjarni. "Something we can exploit?"

The big alpha snorted. "Weaknesses? He has none."

"Everyone has a weakness," I said, rubbing my temples as I tried to conjure up any knowledge I had on the God of Mischief. "Does he have anything or anybody he cares about that we can leverage?"

Bjarni worked his jaw. When he answered, bitterness colored his voice. "No. He only cares for his own life."

"So he's selfish," I mumbled. "Self-serving. He will only cave if it's the best way to ensure his own survival."

"Pretty much," Bjarni said.

"Color me unsurprised," Modi muttered, earning a glare from the blond giant.

"Brute force it is, then," I said before the two of them could get at each other's throats. "Show him we are strong enough to kill him if he doesn't comply—and offer a carrot on the other end. He undoubtedly knows what plans Odin has for him. If we can somehow offer him an escape hatch once we reach Valhalla and your brothers are safe, he should be... persuadable to see things from our side."

"It's got merit," Modi said, and if I wasn't entirely mistaken, there was a drop of admiration in his voice. "But the question is how to convince him we *are* strong enough to kill him if he doesn't back down."

I looked from him to Bjarni. "Are we? Strong enough?"

"Perhaps," the blond said, his voice uncharacteristically somber. "There is one way in which we have and advantage: He has no allegiance with anyone but himself. He is alone. We... We are not. If the three of us combine our strengths, we might have a shot."

"Why did it take you two days to get here when the feather duster led you?" I grumbled as Bjarni turned off the road and walked toward the thick woods. "Even with a human in tow, it has been, what, sixteen hours? I presume your coward of a sire is hiding somewhere in the woods?"

Said human huffed behind me, but the irritation I felt in our bond at my words remained unvoiced. She was too exhausted from our sixteen-hour walk to argue. Not a terrible quality in a woman, in my opinion.

"His name was Arni," Bjarni said, his voice acrid. "I suspect Loki wanted to throw off any pursuers—he had us take the scenic route."

"*Arni?* Who names a raven *Eagle?*" I muttered.

"Was?" Annabel asked, her voice turning soft. She

pushed forward a couple of steps, placing a hand on Bjarni's arm. "His name *was* Arni?"

Bjarni hesitated, but his steps slowed, allowing the omega to keep pace. "Yes. Was," he finally bit out. "Loki saw Magni's claim on you as a failure of mine and my brothers. He killed Arni and Magga as punishment for our shortcomings, and as a reminder not to fail him again."

"Oh, no." Sorrow flickered in our bond, pulling uncomfortably on my instincts to step forward and comfort the girl. But before I could process the urge, she pressed her forehead against Bjarni's bicep and wrapped her arm around his back in an intimate gesture.

"I'm so sorry. They didn't deserve that."

Bjarni only responded with a grunt, but he pulled her closer against his side and kept her there as we entered the woods.

I followed them, fighting down the burn of jealousy as I stared at their backs.

It was just instincts—nothing but stupid, primitive *instincts* that had my body reacting as if Annabel were truly mine.

She was not.

What was between her and I was nothing but a Norn on a power trip deciding to weave our fates together, sprinkled with a healthy dose of hormones. Much as I loathed the thought, I could no longer deny that the prophecy they had blabbed about had to be true, at least to some extent. Why else would I have been compelled to bite down on her slender neck until her skin broke and the most ancient magic in existence bound us together? I certainly had not *wanted* to.

Sure, in that moment, while I was still dazed from the most pleasurable climax in my immortal life, my knot thick inside her tight heat and the scent of woman in my nostrils, it had seemed like the only choice. Like she was a piece of me and I would never survive being parted from her again.

Reality was... quite a lot less enjoyable.

I glared at the couple ahead of me. I had pushed down my confusion and pain when she had reminded me that this was the Norns' plan, that there was nothing we could do one way or the other, and that none of us had to like it. Her words rang true, and it made it infinitely easier to cope.

If I was destined not to die in glorious battle, but to instead sacrifice my sanity in an attempt to stop Ragnarök? Fine. I was willing to do that.

But it did not stop the gnawing in my gut as I watched Annabel quietly comfort her *other* mate. There was such an ease to it, as if they were two pieces of the same puzzle coming together without any of the jagged edges I felt in my own bond to her.

As if her speech about "none of us wanting this" only referred to *me*.

Just instincts. Just dumb, animal instincts.

My father was right—glory and honor were the

only things that mattered in the end. I would have that. I *would* bring Loki back to stand trial for treason, and I *would* stop Ragnarök. I was nothing but a means to an end for Annabel, and she was the same to me. What care did I have if the other alphas tied in our web of Fate wanted more from her than access to her powers?

I did not.

We stopped a little ways in, the hum of Annabel's exhaustion causing Bjarni and I to set up camp without exchanging a word. We did not have to—when it came to the omega's needs, we shared a direct link.

"Eat. It will help your body keep warm," I said, throwing some of the weirdly packaged stuff I had scavenged from the shops below the apartment at her. The moment we had stopped to make camp, she had dusted snow off a fallen log and plopped down, arms wrapped around her body and forehead resting against her knees.

She took the offered food—or that is at least what they called it—without protest this time, opening the packaging with a rattle of shaky fingers.

"We cannot risk making a fire if Loki's close," I said, feeling the need to explain why I was not doing more to keep her warm. *Stupid instincts.* "Bjarni will have our shelter ready in a moment."

"I know," she said, offering me a small smile between bites. "Thank you."

I grunted an acknowledgement and turned my back, taking a few steps to the outskirts of the small divot we had made our temporary home. Our enemy was close—my focus needed to be on him, not her.

"Annabel, the tent's up. It's time to sleep," Bjarni called from behind me.

She didn't answer, but I heard her get up from her tree trunk and head toward him. Heavy footfalls came my way, and I turned my head to nod at the blond alpha as he stopped by my side.

"I will take first watch," I said in response to his unasked question.

"Loki's hideout is about four hours from here, taking Annabel's pace into consideration," he answered. "We won't gain anything by approaching in the dark— for facing the God of Mischief, daylight is our friend. Wake me before dawn. Once you've slept, we'll head out."

I nodded again and he turned around and headed back to the tent. And Annabel.

I kept my focus on the quiet woods around us. Only the faintest sounds from the critters who awoke at night disturbed the peace, and even they were dampened by the thick cover of snow.

From the tent, I heard Annabel's voice. She was murmuring, her pitch soft. Comforting.

My gut knotted as I imagined her arms wrapped

around Bjarni, her dark hair tickling his skin as her gentle words soothed the loss of his familiars.

Just instincts.

There was silence again, save for a fox crossing a drift some yards away. It stopped to stare at me for a brief moment before it continued into the night.

Only when Bjarni's soft snoring reached me some minutes later and my muscles relaxed did I realize I had been tensed in anticipation of them having sex.

I was not entirely sure what I would have done if they had—whether I would have quietly seethed with the knowledge that it was his right as her mate to lay with her whenever he pleased, or if I'd have given in to the primitive instincts roaring at me to rip the imposter off *my* woman.

Perhaps I'd have taken his place between her thighs.

I ground my teeth, irritated at my cock already rising to half-mast at just the thought of pressing inside the omega again.

Just instincts.

I refocused my senses on the forest around us and my mind on the upcoming battle. The only thing I needed from Annabel was her power.

All that mattered was bringing Loki to Valhalla, and then—hopefully—putting an end to Ragnarök.

23

ANNABEL

It was such a peaceful scene. Heavy flakes of snow fell from the sky in unending but tranquil flurries, highlighting the thick, white blanket embracing the log cabin in its clearing. Smoke rose from the chimney and warm light glowed through the windows, a perfect postcard in the middle of the apocalypse.

Seasons greetings from the God of Mischief, killer of ravens.

Father of the fucking year.

I clenched my hands into fists, determination steeling me against the cold. I'd changed into the feathered outfit Verdandi had given me back in Jotunheim, partly for the added warmth and partly because it made me feel strong enough to take on what lay ahead.

In the sensation of the subtle leather against my skin lay a reminder of the power that had awakened in me since my paths crossed with my Norse gods. Plus I was pretty sure Verdandi had woven some sort of warming spell into the stitches—though not even a Norn's magic could fully negate the chill of the Fimbulwinter.

"Ready?" Modi's voice was a whisper, but I heard my own determination echoed in it.

"Ready," Bjarni ground out, and my heart gave an achy spasm for him. He'd lost so much, and his pain echoed in our bond. His lifelong friends, his father... and, as silly as it sounded to say of a centuries-old divine being, some of his innocence.

He wasn't as irreverent now, and I couldn't blame him. Being betrayed by your own parents came with a stain that wasn't easily forgotten.

I pushed away the thoughts of my own parents and how they'd never told me about my family's millennia-old debt. How they'd given me to the Lokissons as if I were nothing but some goods to trade. Now wasn't the time to dwell on that. Now was the time to collect what we'd come for.

Modi closed his hand around the back of my neck, and I focused on the well of golden magic rising up to greet him. Then he grabbed hold of it and *pushed.*

I raised my hand, allowing a beam of light to shoot from my palm and into the side of the cabin.

And just like that, the serene postcard was gone.

Cracks and screeches rung through the clearing as

wood and glass splintered with enough force to hurl the remains to all sides of the clearing.

Again Modi forced my power out, and the roof of the cabin landed in pieces on the far side.

"Loki!" Modi roared. "Betrayer of Asgard! We are here to bring you to your trial. Surrender!"

A shadow moved in the debris, followed by coughing.

I blinked as a long-limbed man stumbled through the wreckage, the dust from the crumbled cabin hiding his features until he stepped out into the snow and straightened up.

Loki.

I recognized his face from Saga's vision during our trials to enter Valhalla, divine beauty shining through despite the layer of dust covering his hair and clothes.

"Are you out of your mind?" His voice rung with authority, but was interrupted by a wheeze. He coughed again and glared at Bjarni. "You *betrayed* me? *Me?* I gave you *life!*"

My blond mate didn't respond. He stood silently by my side, his sword ready.

"Surrender!" Modi repeated. "You are outmatched. We are bringing you to Valhalla. It is up to you if you want to face Odin in one piece."

Loki laughed, a disbelieving sound that grated against my nerves. "*I'm* outmatched? And what do we have here? Two sniffling godlings and a human girl with a bit of juice? What ever will I *do?*"

I gritted my teeth. "We have more than enough strength to bring you to heel, Loki. Come with us willingly and we'll help you escape once Odin's released his prisoners."

The god's attention shifted to me, a chill running up my spine. There was so much *otherness* behind that gaze that it was impossible not to feel small and insignificant—and very, very human.

"So this is the prophesized omega I secured for my sons? Let's have a look at you, *daughter.*"

Loki bowed his head, but kept his eyes on mine through the dark, dusty strands of hair shadowing his face.

Another chill wrenched my spine, sending a jerk through my entire skeleton, and then darkness surrounded me from all sides, blinding my sight and numbing my other senses.

"Hmm. You are strong, little bird. Perhaps you even have enough power to trick Odin himself. But you're very raw, aren't you? Just an inexperienced little lamb attempting to intimidate the God of Mischief in a last-ditch effort to save the day.

"I'm sorry, my dear. I'd rather not risk my neck on the off-chance that you can get enough control of your magic in time to help me escape the god-king before my untimely beheading. You'll have to count me out of this little plan of yours."

A whooshing sound made me stumble forward,

followed by the sudden return of all my senses in one horrific kaleidoscope of sensation.

I blinked, my eyes adjusting to the brightness of the white-covered landscape. Only it wasn't like it'd been only moments ago.

Eerie déjà vu filled me as I stared at the snow-covered ground, dread following in its wake.

"We have to get out of here," I whispered, fear clenching my lungs too tight to speak any louder. *"Now!"*

"Annabel?" Modi asked, but his voice seemed to come from another plane.

"Run!" I shrieked. "For fuck's sake, run!"

But it was too late. The powdery snow trembled below our feet, and not ten yards away a humongous, snake-like monstrosity broke through the surface, hurtling into the air.

It came back to me in all too-vivid detail: the vision I'd had in Verdandi's cave—it was happening. It was happening now. I'd been wrong—it wasn't Saga and Magni I'd lose to it.

It was Modi and Bjarni.

I didn't think—the power rose from within me and out of my palms, crashing into the beast.

"Annabel!" Modi shook me, making my focus wobble. "Annabel, stop!"

I stared at the monster, Modi's touch strengthening me even as naked fear squeezed my lungs. My magic had done nothing to the wyrm, its gleaming scales unmarked.

Once again I pulled power from the depths of my being and hurled it at the monstrosity, saw the ball of golden energy collide with it—and leave not so much as a scuff.

"Run! Run, I can't stop it, run!" I shrieked, spinning around to reach for both men. I could lose them. They could die.

Two sets of large hands clasped my biceps, rooting me to the spot.

"Annabel, stop. Whatever you're seeing, it isn't real!" Bjarni shouted. "He's the God of Mischief—he's playing tricks on your mind."

Tricks.

I shuddered, my alpha's words finally penetrating my terror.

"Annabel," Modi said from my other side. "Come back to us—we need you. It is not too late to stop him."

I blinked again, looking over my shoulder. The wyrm was gone, but two singe-marks on the ground free of snow showed where I'd hurled my magic at nothing.

Pealing laughter sounded from the rubble of the house where Loki was halfway into some sort of feathery costume. His legs, which had been human the last time I checked, were now long and spindly like a bird's.

"If you have any desire to tangle with gods, little

omega, you need to get a lot better at deciphering between what's real and what's not," Loki mocked. And with that, he pulled the costume over his shoulders, leaving a heron where he'd stood.

I gaped at it as it took flight, my breath still coming in harsh gusts.

By my side, Modi growled and raised his hand. Blinding light split the air, and a bolt of lightning struck the heron. It shrieked and fell, a plume of smoke from its tail feathers following its path to the ground. It landed in the snow on the other side of the small clearing where the cottage had stood.

As one, Modi and Bjarni stalked toward it, bringing me stumbling along. It was only when Loki climbed out of his bird costume, sputtering snow and cursing, that it finally dawned on me exactly what had happened.

He'd penetrated my mind, found my worst nightmare... and made me believe he'd summoned it into reality.

He'd made me relive the horror of that vision—of knowing I would lose my mates.

Rage unlike anything I'd experienced rose from my gut and filled my limbs with leaden fury. Oh, was he going to *pay!*

I thrust both palms out and *threw* my magic at Loki, screaming with fury.

He managed to dodge at the last minute, darkness rising around him as he summoned his own magic.

"Don't make me hurt you, girl," he called out.

"You're still valuable to me, and to my blond oaf of a son."

His words only made me angrier. He didn't want to hurt me because he believed I was needed to secure his lineage—and to save his own hide from Ragnarök. He didn't care if his sons survived, so long as one of them stayed alive to tie me to his blood.

I fired another ball of energy at his stupid face, seething when his dark magic swallowed it up.

"Careful, Annabel. You have to conserve your magic," Modi cautioned. The warm press of his hand against my nape steadied me, his magic flowing into me, sparking along my veins.

Loki's dark magic swirled, and from it sprang two wolves the size of work horses. They snapped and snarled, bounding toward us with froth dangling from their maws.

"More trickery?" I asked my two companions.

"The kind of trickery that can tear your throat out," Bjarni growled. He clutched his sword and leapt forward, swinging it at the two beasts. His blade sliced through the first wolf's neck, cleaving the animal in two. It died with a haunting howl, its body disintegrating into a plume of smoke.

The other wolf snarled and threw itself at Modi. A sharp jab of pain lanced through my bond with the redheaded god, and I whirled just in time to see lightning strike, illuminating the wolf's ethereal body from within before it too became naught more than fog.

Blood dripped from a gash on Modi's cheek. He touched it with his free hand and cursed under his breath. "Damned trickster."

"Told you," Bjarni said.

Modi snarled, hurling his arm forward. A spinning bolt of lightning shot at Loki, but before it could impact, he flicked a finger at it and it turned into a burst of brightly colored butterflies.

Again the God of Mischief manipulated the dark energy around him. Beneath us the earth rumbled, and I squeaked and reached on instinct for both my mates just as vines sprouted up from the snow, wrapping tightly around our legs.

"I'm sorry, I just don't have time to teach you younglings how to wield magic properly," Loki called out with mock regret. "I've really got to get going. I'll see you on the other side of Ragnarök." He gave us a wave and turned to walk away without any sign of urgency.

"Come back here, you scoundrel! We are bringing you to justice for what you have done!" Modi barked.

If it had been a less serious situation, I might have mocked him for his choice of explicative. Once again he raised his free hand and called down a bolt of lightning, sending it into the vine wrapped around his trapped legs.

Black scorch marks were the only indications he'd even hit his target—the plant bound him as tightly as ever.

"Shit!" I muttered, reaching for my own magic.

Without having to ask, Modi guided me, and I sent a bolt of our combined energy directly into the unnatural vegetation keeping me trapped.

It swayed a little, but sprung back to form.

"Stop him—worry about getting free later!" Bjarni hissed to my right. He squeezed my hand. "Hurry, sweetie. If we lose sight of him, we're never catching up to him again."

He had a point.

"Guide me," I said to Modi.

The redhead's presence in me intensified as he took control of my flow of magic and *reached*. Loki, who'd gotten to the edge of the clearing while we fought his vines, stumbled as the snow beneath his feet wrapped up along his thighs before freezing to solid ice, locking him in place.

"Nice," Bjarni chuckled. "See how he likes it."

Loki twisted around to glare at us over his shoulder. "Careful—you're starting to make me mad. I might need you alive, but that doesn't mean I can't very easily make you wish for death."

"Ignore him," Modi mumbled. "Work on the vines. Quickly now."

"We're not going to beat him with magic," Bjarni said without taking his eyes off his father. "He's too experienced. If we're going to take him, it's gonna have to be with brute force."

"Brute force has a tendency not to work against experienced magic-users," Modi grumbled even as he directed my flow of energy at the vines. "Case in point —two gods and a Norn-blessed girl currently stuck in a damned bush!"

"I think he might have a point," I said, pointing at Bjarni's sword. "Give it to me."

My blond mate arched an eyebrow, but handed me his blade pommel-first.

Gently I placed my palm on the blade and called on my magic once more. Frankly I wasn't sure what I was doing, but even without Modi's guidance, my magic seemed to flow into the metal until it resonated with that well deep inside me.

I blinked my eyes open and handed it back to him. "Try it out."

Apparently trusting my abilities far more than I did, Bjarni grabbed his sword and swung it at the vines around his feet. They parted with a satisfying *slick* of his blade, the brambles falling to the ground. A few more swings, and he was free.

"We do not have time for you to free us too," Modi said, his voice urgent. I followed his gaze and saw Loki make quick work of the last block of ice still encompassing one of his feet. It looked like he was aiming a high-powered laser at it, the way it melted around his flesh.

"I've got this," Bjarni rumbled, raising his blade. His handsome face was locked in a fierce scowl. "Cover me."

He leapt across the clearing, his powerful legs carrying him faster than a regular human would be able to move. He roared a battle shout and the air vibrated around us all, raising the small hairs at the back of my neck.

More vines sprouted around his feet, but he slashed through them with a single swing of his sword, hardly slowing to do so.

Two more shadow-wolves leapt from Loki's fingertips, and then another two.

One died from lightning, the other from a ball of golden energy, and the two remaining from Bjarni's blade.

Loki bared his teeth at his son and raised both hands out straight, sending a shockwave through the air that shot Bjarni backward as if an invisible giant had kicked him in the gut. He landed on his ass by my side, gasping for breath.

"Damn!" Modi growled as I bent as best I could to ensure Bjarni wasn't injured.

"Just winded, sweetie," he panted. "Don't... waste your focus... on me. Focus... on my... asshole father."

I glanced at Loki, who'd finally managed to get free and was fleeing at full speed this time. Modi pulled bolts of lightning from the sky, but he only managed to slow the cowardly god by forcing him to raise his magic in protection or dodge the blasts.

We were never going to capture him this way.

Unless...

It came to me more as an instinctive pull rather than

a thought. My hand still clutching Modi's, I reached my other out to grab onto Bjarni too.

A current of awareness passed between us, not spurred by magic, but every bit as intense. And then, without giving any of us a moment to prepare, we became one.

All barriers of flesh and identity blurred and vanished, sweeping me into a warm, throbbing awareness. Anger, hurt, love, fear, desperation, longing—they were my emotions, and they were not. They belonged to all of us. I *felt* them—both of them—cocooning me from all sides, their consciousnesses shielding me.

And I felt their strength.

We were one.

My mind blinked back into reality, where I was once again staring into Bjarni's blue-gray eyes. Only now they glowed with a light that seemed to radiate from within him—from within all of us.

"*Go,*" I said.

Bjarni didn't pause. He barreled across the clearing once more. Loki shot more waves at him, making the air itself shudder, but this time my mate plowed through them as if they were no more than a mere breeze.

Wolves made from shadow sprung at him—five, seven, ten. He cleaved them all with his sword, and my arms felt the swing as if I were wielding the blade myself.

Loki ran, but he wasn't nearly fast enough. Bjarni

was on him before he could make it four steps, falling atop of him like a feral bear.

Loki attempted to evade him, his figure fading to mist, but electricity sparked from Bjarni's grip, lighting up the God of Mischief and jolting him back into flesh with a scream.

Finally he lay still, his long body sprawled in the snow beneath his son.

"I got you, you traitorous cunt," Bjarni growled, and I felt his rage as keenly as if it were my own. "God of Mischief? God of Cowards, is more like it. I hope you regret betraying your own blood before Odin takes your head."

24

ANNABEL

Modi showed me how to infuse my magic into a length of rope he pulled from the rucksack they'd carried with us from Asgard. It was tricky, my fingers fumbling on the twine and my vision blurring.

Now that the fight was over, the connection between the three of us that had flowed so freely seemed barely there, and I had to focus to keep my rapidly waning power connected with Bjarni so our prisoner didn't escape before we could tie him up.

"Just a little longer," the redhead said quietly when my hold on the rope slipped. He steadied me with his grip around my body as well as his presence within my magic.

His sparking power tightened around mine, pulling it into place rather than guiding it now. Not that I minded—with every second that passed, it became harder and harder to think of anything that wasn't sleep.

Blasted magical drawbacks. It seemed a real inconvenience that any use of it resulted in bone-deep exhaustion. If it weren't for Modi and Bjarni, I'd be well and truly fucked.

Well, I'd be fucked regardless, because *of course* sex was the only way to replenish my strength.

God, being an omega sucked.

"Why are you laughing?" Bjarni asked over his shoulder. It came out as a grunt, the only indication that he was expending any strength in holding down his father.

Was I? It took me a moment to realize that the jarring sound pounding in my ears wasn't my blood—it was the sound of my own deranged chuckling.

I swallowed, killing the inappropriate laugh to refocus on the rope. "Sorry, I'm... really tired."

Finally Modi managed to wrangle the dying embers of the golden light within me. The rope lit up, then faded, looking like any old measure of twine, but I could sense the dull throb of my powers radiating from it, even if what was left inside me was barely a flicker.

"There we are," Modi said, his magic sliding from mine and leaving me hollow. "That should keep you from attempting to slither away again before you have faced judgement for your ill-doings."

He handed the rope to Bjarni with one hand, keeping his other arm wrapped tightly around me—a gesture I was grateful for, because I was pretty sure I'd have faceplanted in the snow without his support.

"Foolish children," Loki growled as Bjarni tied his wrists behind his back. "You don't know what you're doing. *I'm* not responsible for this mess! I'm just the scapegoat—as usual."

"Yes, the true mark of a falsely accused man," Modi drawled. "Running away to hide until it is all over, all the while ensuring you and yours will survive the calamity. Well, I guess you get to be grateful that we are bringing you back so you can prove your innocence to the gods of Asgard."

"Frankly, Father, I no longer care much if you're innocent or not," Bjarni said, his voice rougher than Modi's as he sat up, yanking the dark-haired god to his knees. "You were going to leave my brothers to their fate after all your talk of the importance of our blood. You can hang, for all I care. Or burn. Or sit in a cage with ravens picking at your flesh—whatever Odin's got planned for you. You're already dead to me."

"Boys, boys." This time Loki's voice was gentler—smoother. "You're taking these unfortunate events *much* too personally. You wouldn't truly expect someone with my, ah, *history* with Asgard to willingly offer my neck, hmm? But clearly things have changed... I am willing to cooperate with you, if you vow to help me escape before Odin shortens me by a head."

"I think you forget that that was an offer we gave you *before* you were defeated and bound," I said, my voice raspier than I'd have liked. Even flanked by two powerful alphas, Loki clearly wasn't the type of being you wanted to display any sort of weakness to. "We don't need anything from you now that we can't *take*."

As if on cue, Loki turned to me, his dark eyes shrewd even as he molded his features into one of concern. "Is that true? You look so frail, my daughter. Your magic is all but gone. How are you going to stop Ragnarök from taking everyone you love if capturing me has nearly drained your life essence?"

"That's not for you to worry about," I gritted. I would stop it somehow, even though I knew he was right. I'd seen the World Serpent—only one of the heralds of Ragnarök—and deep down I knew I wasn't nearly powerful enough to take it on. Not even with my mates by my side.

Perhaps it'd been hubris all along. If the gods themselves weren't strong enough to stop Ragnarök, then what chance did I have, Norn-blessed or not?

The thought that had niggled at me since Verdandi's cave rose like a mountain in my chest, crushing what little strength I had. Was this all for naught? Were we doomed?

"I can help you," Loki said softly. "Thor's son can't show you how to truly reach your potential—he isn't experienced enough with the kind of power that lies within you. I am. I can teach you to control it."

"*Stop it!*" It was a roar so fierce it shook me out of the daze I hadn't even realized had settled around me. I looked up at Bjarni's rage-twisted face just as he pulled an arm back and socked Loki right in the nose.

Blood spattered, and a sickening crunch mixed with the god's pained wail as he tumbled into the snow, unable to break his fall.

"If I *ever* catch you using your powers on my mate again, I'll kill you myself!" my blond giant snarled. He glared down at Loki for a few seconds before he turned to me, his features softening at my confusion.

"Don't listen to him. His tongue is dipped in poison—he will deceive you first chance he gets."

I blinked, looking back at Loki as realization dawned. He'd manipulated my insecurities, twisted my fears until his suggestion seemed like the only solution. I had no doubt that if Bjarni hadn't intervened, I'd have fallen fully under his spell and accepted his offer.

Eyes narrowing, I glared at the God of Mischief. "Nice try."

He grimaced past the blood running down his face from his broken nose. "You kno' I'm righ'. You don' 'ave 'e streng' do save 'em."

It was a lot easier to ignore the chill of the god's words when he sounded like a fifth-grader with a cold. Looking away from him, I leaned into Modi.

"Let's make camp for the day. I have to rest. Tomorrow we bring this asshole to Valhalla and get your brothers back."

～

IT WASN'T JUST REST I needed—Modi and Bjarni knew
that as well as I did—but I wasn't about to admit what
else I required in front of Loki. Not that he wouldn't be
able to hear it, seeing as there was only a tent wall separating us.

"Here, sweetie. It's not the feast a warrior deserves
after taking down an enemy as magnificent as the God
of Mischief, but at least it's warm."

I looked up at Bjarni as he pushed through the tent
flap carrying two steaming bowls of something that
smelled delicious.

"A warrior, eh?" I said, eagerly grabbing one of the
bowls. It contained a meaty stew. Leave it to Bjarni to
conjure up a beautiful meal in the middle of the woods
during a blizzard.

"You're a warrior if I ever saw one, Annabel," he said
softly as he sat down in front of me with his own bowl,
legs crossed. "We could never have captured my father
if you hadn't been here. What you did today is no small
feat."

"I didn't do it alone," I reminded him, blowing on a
spoonful of stew. "*I* couldn't have done it without you
and Modi. I don't know what happened out there,
but..."

"But it wouldn't have happened without you," he
interrupted, blond eyebrows pulling into an uncharac-
teristic frown. "I don't really understand magic, but I do
know that *thing* came from you. Even the, *ugh,* connec-

tion between Modi and I ran through you. Through our bonds to you."

"You think?" I asked before finally shoveling the first spoonful of food into my mouth. It exploded in flavor and comforting warmth on my tongue, and I closed my eyes to savor it.

"I know. Our bond is the one thing that isn't complicated to me," he said, his voice still quiet. "Everything else around us, yes. But not this."

I opened my eyes again to look at him, the memory of his regret at claiming me flickering in my chest. "How can you say that when you wish you'd never created it?"

The words escaped me before I could bite them back, bitterness tingeing my voice. A stab of agony flared through that bond, and guilt instantly made me regret saying anything.

I shook my head. "I'm sorry. That wasn't fair. I don't blame you. Either of you. This wasn't what any of us wanted."

"It was what *I* wanted," he said, his voice rougher than I'd expected. He pressed his free hand to his heart. "I wanted our bond and everything that came with it. I wanted you to love me like I love you.

"Yes, I wish I'd never claimed you, because the agony of knowing that my mate hates our bond? Wouldn't have chosen me if she'd had a choice? Knowing you'll never love me? It's fucking unbearable!"

He threw the bowl to the ground with a clatter, stew

sloshing out to stain the fur bedding before burying his face in both hands with a groan.

"That's... *That's* why you regret claiming me?" I asked. "Because you think I wouldn't choose you willingly?"

"I *know* you wouldn't," he groaned without looking up. "I feel every ounce of your despair. You fucking *cried* after I claimed you. You told us that you wouldn't have done this if you'd had a choice."

"Bjarni..." I put down my own bowl of food and rolled up on my knees so I could touch his bicep. "I cried because your claim... it showed me how fucked up everything else is. It felt... so right. Like we're two pieces of a puzzle. And I... I feel *so much* for all four of you, I'm... I'm a part of all four of you, and it's tearing me to pieces.

"I didn't want Magni to claim me. I didn't want Saga to claim me. But they did, and it was painful—*is* painful. Like they forced their way into my heart, and it's rough and violent and I *miss* them. All the time, every second of every day, I feel incomplete without them. Like I'm missing two limbs.

"And then there is Modi. Modi..." I swallowed thickly, the pain of that bond still too raw to prod at. "Modi doesn't want this. He doesn't want *me*. With you, for a moment, it felt... so easy. So perfect. I was *happy*. And I finally understood what a mating bond is supposed to be like. It's supposed to be pleasure and love and comfort.

"I cried because I realized that I will never be whole like I was in that one moment with you. Because I can never be whole again. No, I wouldn't have chosen to be pulled apart by five alphas who are only with me because Fate has decreed it so. But... I would have chosen you."

He looked up at me then, the emotion in his eyes so intense it took my breath away. "Do you mean that? Had Ragnarök not been here, had no Norns interfered, would you still have been mine?"

I pushed down the anguish of imagining a world where three of my mates weren't a part of me and looked into my blond alpha's eyes. My sweet one, the one who went out of his way to comfort me, cook for me, dote on me, even with the world in turmoil and our bond in tatters. The one who loved me simply because he did.

"Yes, I would."

His eyes crinkled at the corners, a fine web of happiness amidst the anguish. With a rumbling grunt, he moved to clasp my nape in one big hand, pulling me up and in until our foreheads touched.

"That's enough. I don't need anything more than that."

"It feels so easy with you," I murmured, reaching up to wipe at the tears trickling down my cheeks. "I wish I could give you the same comfort you give me, but I am... so broken. I don't think I can give any of you much of anything, but I wish... I wish I could."

"You do," he said, moving to ghost his lips over my brow and pull me into his lap, enveloping me in warmth and woolly, hay-scented comfort. Even now, thousands of miles from his farm in Iceland, Bjarni smelled like the land he'd lived on and the air he'd breathed while he'd waited for Ragnarök.

And for me.

"I lost Arni and Magga. I lost my father. I thought I'd lost my brothers too. I would have, if it hadn't been for you. When I hold you like this, it's as if everything hurts a little less. As if there'll always be hope so long as you're with me. I love you, Annabel. And one day, when there is peace in your heart, you'll love me too."

"What if there'll never be peace?" I asked, looking up at him through my tears. I wanted so badly for him to make everything all right like my stupid instincts were clamoring for him to do. "What if I'll always be this broken *thing?*"

"You won't," he said, his soft voice taking on a core of steel. "This I swear to you, Annabel. I will help you find peace. I will be your comfort when everything's painful and complicated. You're not alone, my mate. I'm right here—and I'll make sure that by the end, you will know happiness."

I fell into him, pressing my lips to his with a desperation I hadn't known I possessed. I wanted everything he promised me, wanted to believe that he'd be able to keep his word.

He kissed me back with matching fervor, and in it I

found the truth: He would help me find a way out of the madness. Somehow, he would. My gentlest mate.

"Bjarni," I whimpered between kisses. "Bjarni..."

He undressed me, never separating our lips for more than a breath, large hands covering first my breasts and then sliding low, finding where they fit so perfectly on my hips.

His own clothes followed, a rumble of longing leaving his throat as I drew my hands up along his body to rest them on his thick pecs.

"You're beautiful," I whispered. Somehow along the way I'd forgotten what he was—an alpha god in his prime. Seeing him naked in front of me, there was no denying it. He was big and thickly muscled, blond fur soft under my palms as I took in every lean angle of his body and face.

He cracked a grin, eyes dark with hunger as they roamed over my bare form. "No one's called me *beautiful* before, sweetie. Handsome, yes. Mighty. *Big.* But nothing so soft and gentle as *beautiful*. You're the beautiful one, little omega, with your lush tits and those chocolate eyes of yours."

I sucked in a breath when he bent his head and took one of my nipples between his lips as if to underline his point.

"Mountains are beautiful. Storms. There's nothing soft of gentle about those." I gasped as he flicked his tongue over the sensitive bud and slipped one hand from my hips to my clit, thumbing the hood shielding it.

"I think you're beautiful. Don't tell me your masculinity is too fragile to take it as a compliment."

He grinned against my breast, the vibration drawing a moan from me before he popped his mouth off my nipple and pushed me down on my back on the furs. Looming over me high on his knees, he looked feral and fierce.

"Are you really daring your alpha to show you there's nothing *fragile* about his masculinity, mate?"

"Maybe," I breathed, excitement crawling up my inner thighs and right into my clit.

Bjarni's grin turned to a smirk, the look of a predator, and I bit my lip in anticipation. But when he fell on top of me, catching his weight on his arms, his expression softened.

"Don't push me, Annabel," he said, voice rough but resigned. "Your exhaustion is painted all over your face. I'll be gentle—this time."

Gratitude made me wrap my arms around his wide shoulders even as I pouted at him. He was right—I was worn to the bone, both from the magical exertion and the long walk to find Loki, as well as my heat and double-claiming before that.

Once upon a time, back when I'd thought I'd never be the kind of woman to spread her thighs for an alpha, sex had always been soft and gentle. I'd thought that was how I liked it—a slow build that never rent me of control.

Now I knew different. From the first time Magni had

been inside of me, I'd known my body craved rough, unyielding submission despite my mind's protests at the concept. In this moment, though, gentle sex sounded like chicken soup for my ovaries.

I stroked a hand along his shoulder to his jaw, pulling him into a deep kiss by his chin. He hummed with want, ravaging my mouth with his in the most languid, exquisite way.

I'd never known a kiss could be so undeniably laced with desire and yearning, yet so slow and gentle at the same time. I shouldn't have been surprised, though; Bjarni himself was sweet and gentle, yet entirely fueled by passion and instincts, and his kiss showed me with all possible clarity exactly what kind of man my newest mate was.

"Make love to me," I breathed.

"Gladly," he growled, the velvet gravel of it pebbling my nipples and making my clit throb.

He slid down my body, pressing kisses along my skin until he came to my flushed sex. Groaning, he sucked in a breath, scenting me.

"Gods, you smell so good," he rasped before he pressed in, splitting my labia with his tongue.

His clever lips found my clit the next second, and then he showed me how an alpha makes love.

"I wonder what Thor's going to say about both his sons sharing a mate with his least favorite god's offspring," Loki said, his tone conversational. The swelling had finally gone down enough that he was able to make himself understood—not that that was particularly a boon, as far as I was concerned.

"Does she moan as prettily when you're inside of her—or is it more of a grit-your-teeth-and-think-of-Valhalla deal with you?"

I shot him a glare, wishing with all I was that Bjarni would have managed to knock out his teeth while he was at it. "Quiet. Your cheap parlor tricks will not work on me."

"Sure. I guess we can just enjoy the peace and quiet, then." He gave me a meaningful look just as another of Annabel's broken moans momentarily drowned out the unmistakable sounds of flesh hitting flesh from within the tent.

I knew Bjarni would bed her when I offered to take first watch again. She needed it to replenish her magical reserves, and one of us had to help her with that. As much as my cock had begged me to swallow my pride and volunteer, I chose not to.

Last time I had taken her, I lost myself completely. I said words I never thought I would say, felt things I never thought I would feel. These were not sensations I wanted to repeat while Loki and Bjarni listened.

But that was before I felt the elation and relief from them both minutes before the sounds of sex began. Whatever had transpired between them, it had changed their connection significantly. Now where I had felt pain and confusion in my connection to them, there was hope. Joy.

Love.

None of which belonged to me.

"Jealousy" was too mild a word to cover the seething agony and fury bubbling in my blood as I was forced to sit and listen to Annabel give herself to another man like she never would give herself to me—and with none other than *Loki* as a captive audience to my suffering.

Just. Instincts.

"Do you *enjoy* listening to them? Is that it?" Loki continued after a long moment of silence save the sounds of sex from the tent. "No judgement—I've been known to indulge in a bit of voyeurism from time to time myself. It just surprises me, what with knowing your father. He's all days been all about the immediate gratification... less so the subtle pleasures. Or self-sacrifice. I didn't expect his proud son to be much different."

Fighting the urge to strangle him to release some of my pent-up misery, I got up to throw another log on the fire with more force than was necessary.

"You speak on what you do not know, *trickster god*," I growled. "If you wish to keep your teeth, maybe you shut your mouth."

Loki snorted, the sound somewhat distorted by a pained moan thanks to his broken nose. "I can't help but wonder *why* you chose to mate the girl. I don't have to do any *parlor tricks* to know you're not exactly keen—much unlike my son currently enjoying himself. It's not as if *your* father went out of his way to indebt her family a thousand years ago." His tone was sour. "I'm *dying* to know why you and your bastard brother decided to ruin my carefully laid plans."

"There is a prophecy. Supposedly we can stop Ragnarök by mating her," I said, avoiding his too-sharp eyes by staring into the fire. "What kind of gods would we be if we did not try to stop the end of the world?"

"Yes, how very heroic of you." Loki's voice was dripping with sarcasm. "You could be fighting the hordes of Jotunheim alongside your boneheaded father, but instead you're sat in Midgard listening to another man pleasuring your omega. I'm certain your sacrifice will go down in history, Thorsson."

I ground my teeth until the growl threatening to escape my throat was under control. I knew he was needling me—trying to get under my skin. Under different circumstances it would have been easier to resist his trickery, but my blood was already hot and itchy with pent-up frustration.

The sound of Annabel's keening climax did nothing to help.

"Perhaps the man willing to sacrifice his sons to save his own hide should not speak too loudly of heroism," I bit.

"Please. Where is *your* father, young one? Why isn't he here with you trying to drag me back to Asgard by my ear? *His* son also faces Odin's wrath, should you fail in this ridiculous quest of yours. I wager he's busy practicing his hammer throw and couldn't give two shits whether you succeed or not. Who cares if that bastard brother of yours lives, so long as Thor finds his glory in battle?"

Red-hot fury forced me to my feet. I glared down at him, hands fisted to contain my rage.

"You shut your mouth! My father is nothing like you! The moment he heard that Odin took Magni, he came and demanded his release! You would not have the balls to stand up to the Allfather. Thor does. He sent me because he knows I will get the job done!"

Loki's gaze was darkly triumphant, no doubt because he had finally succeeded in his attempts at getting to me. I was too pissed to care.

"Yes, I can see how much he stood up to Odin. I'm sure he blustered and blundered and threatened the old goat, and in the end, Odin shit his loincloth and immediately returned that half-Jotunn sibling of yours, right?

"Oh, wait... No. That's not what happened. Let me guess—Odin made his demands clear and Thor accepted, because deep down he doesn't care about you, and certainly not his bastard. He only cares that you make him look good.

"Who knows—maybe he sent you on this errand because two sons dead in battle against the mighty Loki is better than the embarrassment of all of Asgard knowing you're both fucking the same whore his enemy's spawn is soiling."

I moved before I could think, my fist connecting with his face with so much force his head bounced off the tree trunk he leaned against, and I felt the satisfying crunch of his cheekbone shattering against my knuckles.

Loki howled, the sound doing nothing to stop my rage—but the look of fresh blood splattering from his face did.

He may have been Loki, God of Mischief, betrayer of Asgard—and biggest fucking prick alive—but he was still my prisoner. My bound prisoner. I had more honor than to beat a defenseless man.

Disgusted with myself as much as with him, I bent to hogtie him, ignoring his protests at being yanked onto his stomach in the snow, face buried in a drift. He was a god—he would survive.

"I told you to shut your mouth, trickster god."

Only muffled sputtering answered me.

I stared down at him thrashing in his bonds, finding a certain satisfaction in knowing he was currently almost as miserable as I was.

But the longer I looked at him, the more my muscles itched to kick him until he stopped moving altogether. The things he had said about my father echoed in my head, as well as the things he had said about Annabel.

He had called her a soiled whore.

Murderous urges throbbed in my temples, but they mixed with something else—soft moans of pleasure and ragged breathing from the tent.

Something inside me snapped.

It did not matter that I knew my yearning for her was just instincts—that whether or not Bjarni screwed her from dusk until dawn, all I needed from her was her powers.

Right then, all that mattered was that Loki's spawn was fucking *my* omega, was spilling his seed inside of her uncontested.

I crossed the small camp in the blink of an eye, tore through the leather, and forced my way into the small shelter.

There was barely any room inside it, Bjarni's bulk filling most of the space as he rested on his knuckles over Annabel. She was lying flat on her stomach underneath him, head toward the opening and me, but too distracted with the knot my rival had shoved up her pussy to notice my presence.

Bjarni, on the other hand, looked up at my violent entry, breath coming out in heavy puffs as we locked eyes. I saw the question in his gaze, the evaluation of whether or not my rage presented a threat, and then the last thing I had expected to see: understanding.

"Give us a minute," he said, still panting. "I'm tied."

That fucking tie. All I wanted was to rip him off her and take his place in her velvety tight heat, but I knew doing so would hurt my mate. The thought alone made me sick, and I growled in frustration.

Annabel finally looked up then, her eyes dazed. "Modi?" she croaked, voice thick from her recent climax.

My name on her lips made me shudder. Gods, what sorcery had been encoded into my biology that one word from her had me quaking with longing?

"Modi, is... is something wrong?" she asked around a tight grimace, her breath hissing out in a curse when Bjarni shifted, his tie pulling on her undoubtedly well-fucked pussy.

I did not reply, the shiver traveling up my spine this time heated. I *liked* seeing her like this, and that realization was sudden and horrifying. Or it would have been horrifying if my dick had not redirected most of my blood supply, and with it, my ability to think.

As I stared from her swollen lips to where Bjarni

was so intimately connected with her, in our bond I *felt* how open and vulnerable she was, how completely conquered. How much *he* thrilled at the sensation of having her trapped on his dick, an alpha's pleasure weaving through the gentler emotions of his love for her.

I bared my teeth, impatience washing away the confusion of this new development. It did not matter why I liked seeing her knotted by him—all that mattered was that my dick was aching, and she had other ways of pleasuring me.

I grabbed her by the jaw and pulled her up, leaving her scrambling to support herself on her shaking arms. The moment she was at the right height, I freed my cock and slipped it between her soft lips, groaning with pleasure as wet heat enveloped me. She could not fit more than the tip in her mouth and her teeth scraped against my sensitive skin, but it had to do.

She sputtered once at the unexpected intrusion, but did not resist. After a moment she caught up and obediently formed a tight seal on my head, letting her tongue flick over my frenulum.

Such a good little omega.

She really was lovely, I dazedly thought as I stared into her eyes while she bobbed her head, doing her best to bring me relief despite how uncomfortably my girth stretched her jaw. I had half-expected her to fight me, to refuse me. The last time she did this, she had been high on hormones, her nature trying to coax me into giving in.

Now she had already had her orgasms. This time, the only reason she was sucking me was for my benefit.

I fisted her lush hair in both hands, throwing my head back as I dragged her down harder on my throbbing cock until her molars scraped my flesh.

"Good girl," I panted. "Such a good girl. Suck me. *Take* me."

She sputtered again, one hand coming up to press against my hip in protest. But before I found the strength to ease up on her, she let out a muffled whine, her hand falling back down.

I glanced down, my gaze falling on her pretty face screwed up in a grimace. Behind her, Bjarni was rocking his hips in short, sharp movements, grinding on her G-spot. He shot me a devious look across her naked body, then slipped one hand underneath her. I did not see what he did to her, but I did not need to.

Annabel's eyes flew wide, a scream muffled to choking sounds on my cock as she lurched forward, then fell back down, ass popping up and out. Whatever he was doing to her clit, it had her thoroughly captivated.

I grunted, angry he got to bring her pleasure, but grateful too. I was too desperate for release to make sure she enjoyed what I did, and some small part of me still capable of remorse knew I would hate myself after if she did not.

Abandoning all restraint in the knowledge that Bjarni would take care of Annabel, I tightened my grip in her hair and fucked her mouth rough and fast. Her teeth scraped on my head, wet gurgles bubbling around it, and *fuck,* it felt so good! *She* felt so good.

"Anna! Anna! Anna!" I chanted her name, eyes pinched shut, each thrust bringing me closer to climax

A great thunderclap rolled through my body, blinding white flashing before my eyes as my body finally released. I moaned brokenly and froze half-hunched over my mate, fingers trembling in the tangles of her hair while my semen flooded her mouth.

It took me a few moments to open my eyes, and I drew in a sharp breath at the look of beautiful, perfect Annabel swallowing hard to gulp down my essence, white froth and spit dripping from her lips around my still-bloated dick. Her face was a mask of post-orgasmic haze, wet eyes darting to mine as if needing to know how she pleased me.

"Annabel." Her name slipped from my lips as I caressed her face, something warm and tight and not wholly pleasant curling in my gut despite the relaxed state of my muscles.

Instincts.

She closed her eyes and pressed her cheek into my touch, finally releasing my dick with a small kiss to its crown.

"Better?" she rasped.

Yes. I felt better.

I moved as far away as the small tent allowed, which was not more than a few inches, trying to get my urges to purr and pet and *cuddle* under control.

Bjarni had no such reservations. He broke out in a soft purr of his own, wrapping his arms around her body and rolling them both to their sides so he could embrace the omega without smothering her.

"You're such a good girl," he crooned. "My sweetie. My brave mate."

I frowned. Hearing him call her a "good girl" like I had moments ago prodded at my need to display my rights to her.

It was an odd sensation—I should have been furious at seeing another alpha with my claimed omega, but now that my initial urges to fuck had been sated, anger was not among the emotions battling for dominance. The urge to stake my claim, though? That was very much alive.

He is her mate too.

The realization made me grit my teeth. Whatever fucked-up, twisted bond had been created by multiple alphas claiming the human girl, it soothed what possessive rage should have been in place at seeing my enemy with her. She belonged to both of us.

"Come lay with us," Annabel murmured, her voice syrupy in the afterglow. She reached for me, such an intimate gesture from a girl who had hated me right up until she needed my dick to calm her heat. "Your angsting is upsetting our bond and I need peace. Just for tonight."

I narrowed my eyes at her, unsure if she was mouthing off or just genuinely too exhausted to sugar-coat the request. "You seem perfectly content with what comfort Bjarni is providing."

"Modi," she sighed, somehow sounding both pleading and exasperated.

"Don't be such a dick," Bjarni rumbled, his tone wholly unconcerned as he rolled one of Annabel's nipples between his fingers. When she swatted at him, he chuckled and nipped at the back of her neck where our dual claims were still healing. "She got you off—least you can offer the lady is a cuddle."

My narrowed gaze landed on him, and he cracked a smirk at me so provoking I would have socked him if Annabel had not just sucked the anger right out of my dick.

But he had a point. I had taken my pleasure from her and given her none in return, whereas *he* had clearly provided her with more than one release of her own.

A fizzle of rivalry sparked in me and I slipped down in front of Annabel, sandwiching her between myself and the alpha still tied to her, one arm slung over her midriff to pull her torso toward me.

She chirped a happy little sound that made our bond throb, nuzzling her face against my chest.

I stared down at her messy hair, trying to rein in the

swell of possessive emotions bubbling from everywhere we touched. On some level it was a comfort that her instincts clearly screwed her over as much as mine did me, because the Annabel I had come to know was way too hardheaded to ask me for anything unless she was deep in hormonal insanity.

Bjarni's hand still playing with her breasts grazed against my skin, making my focus dart to him. Gods, it was so fucking *easy* for him. The lightness in their end of the bond still hummed vaguely through to me. It no longer even bothered him that I had staked a claim on the woman he loved, judging by his easy acceptance of my joining them and his taunt to get me to stay.

"I assume you ensured Loki isn't going anywhere?" he asked, his voice a quiet rumble as if trying to not disturb Annabel. A quick glance suggested it would take a lot more than a bit of talking to do so—her eyes were closed and her breathing slow and deep. She was moments from sleep.

He'd called him Loki—not his father.

I looked up at him, catching his gaze, and allowed myself a second's pity for the betrayal he had suffered at the hands of his own blood. I did not know what I would have done in his stead—something violent, no doubt.

Unbidden, Loki's words whispered through my mind. My own father had not come to help us bring back the God of Mischief, leaving Magni's fate in my hands.

But it was not the same. Thor had sent me because he knew I could do what was tasked of me.

You could not, though. Not without Annabel's magic and Bjarni's strength.

I slammed that door shut before Loki's poison festered further. All that mattered was that we had succeeded and Magni would be safe from Odin's retribution.

"He will not move until we want him to," I said.

"Good."

He trusted me, I realized. My enemy trusted that I had secured our captive. He'd entrusted his own brothers' lives to me.

Had the roles been reversed, would I have trusted him with Magni's life?

Yes. I would have. Ever since our powers had combined through our bond with Annabel, the knowledge that I could trust this man had taken root.

Fuck.

I looked back down at my mate, finding it impossible to grasp how one tiny human could change me so completely despite how furiously I'd fought against her.

I just needed her power. I did not need the comfort of her weight against my chest, did not need an ally in the man she had also ensnared with that sweetly-scented cunt of hers, did not need to bury my cock inside of her every time the thought of how perfectly she fit around me entered my head.

"You know," Bjarni said, "the less you fight it, the

less it hurts. You don't want this? Too bad, you chose it. Not even the Norns can force a mate claim."

I glared at him. I'd *chosen* this? Nothing about biting down on Annabel's neck and claiming her for all eternity had been a *choice*. In that moment, with her pussy clutching at my knot and the smell of her in my nostrils, there had been no other option, no other way.

But maybe he did have a point. Why was I fighting the instincts clamoring at me night and day? Why suffer through this self-flagellation and denial? Like it or not, Annabel was *mine*—my omega, my mate to enjoy as I pleased. That was my right. All my self-imposed abstinence had caused was misery and distraction. Loki had gotten under my skin largely because I had been so overcome with need for my omega.

Bjarni moved behind her, making my focus slide down Annabel's naked body to the apex of her thighs.

With a small grunt he pulled out of her pussy, making her moan in protest and shift uncomfortably between us. His knot had finally deflated, it seemed, leaving her used but empty, the scent from their union calling to me.

Why should I deny myself when her other mate did not?

26

ANNABEL

"*Anna.*"

My name, rough and demanding, stirred me from the edges of sleep.

I moaned, too exhausted to do much else when strong limbs tightened around me, bringing me back to my body.

A large hand slid from my hip to my ass, pressing me tight against a very male form, the hardness grinding into my pelvis unmistakable even in my groggy state.

"No," I whined, still too out of it to open my eyes—not that I needed to. Modi's scent was in my nostrils, our bond humming pleasantly in my chest where my breasts were pressed against his ribcage "*Sleep.*"

"You fuck him, you fuck me," he murmured in my ear, the unmistakable heat in his voice raising goosebumps along my neck despite myself. A press of a knee parted my legs, and I groaned another complaint when my thigh slid over his hip, opening me up.

"*Sleep,*" I repeated, trying to roll back and away from the handsy alpha, irritation rising as my consciousness was forced from the promise of sweet oblivion. I'd been thoroughly sated not moments ago, my only current desire being to rest. But my escape was blocked by another large, warm body—Bjarni.

"Sex, then sleep," my blond mate purred from behind me, his hands on my breasts tweaking, then lifting as his attention shifted. "Want to convince her? Or are you leaving the pleasuring to a worthier man?"

Even in my annoyed and exhausted state, it was impossible not to hear the challenge in Bjarni's words.

Instead of answering, Modi enveloped one of my nipples in a wet heat, making me squeak when he sucked it hard.

"*Modi,*" I protested, the zings of unwanted stimulation finally giving me the strength to raise my arms to push at his bulk. Not that it did any good, what with his mass being about the same as a medium-sized mountain. "Tomorrow, please—"

"You asked me to stay, *mate,*" he rasped against my breast, flicking my abused nipple with the tip of his tongue before switching his attention to my other breast.

I had.

It hadn't mattered that Bjarni and I had shared such a

private, intimate moment—when Modi had joined us, it felt natural. His cock in my mouth, his hands in my hair, the aching relief in our bond as he'd spilled himself between my lips; all I'd wanted was that moment's unity I'd felt while they were both inside of me to continue. To rest, safe in the knowledge that in this tiny space within the tent walls, for just a little while, everything was okay. Safe.

Modi slid his fingers down my stomach, locating my still-swollen clit. I moaned at the contact and jerked my hips back, but like with his mouth on my nipples, he was undeterred. He followed my movement, rubbing persistent but gentle circles around my tender pearl and feathering a fingertip directly over it now and again.

"Modi." I exhaled his name this time and bit my lip when the first tendrils of something other than over-stimulation flickered in my nerve endings. "Damn you both."

"Shh, little mate," Bjarni whispered huskily against my neck. Behind me his cock made a valiant effort at rising against my hamstrings, despite having just released every drop of his essence deep within me moments ago. "Relax. Enjoy. We only wish to serve you, hmm?"

That was a load of bullshit, and if I'd been more with it, I'd have called him out. Not all that long ago, he'd claimed he understood how exhausted I was. That exhaustion meant I was barely able to cling to consciousness—but my traitor of a body was starting to respond to my alphas' demands for more.

"Fine." My consent managed to convey an irritation that was rapidly drowning in Modi's caresses.

"That's the spirit," Bjarni chuckled, his teasing followed by the slide of his warm hand down my body. When he reached my thigh, he hiked it over his arm, lifting it off Modi's hip and back, opening me wider. "Show her how much you want her."

"I need no pointers from you, Lokisson," Modi growled against my breast. His hands went to my waist, and I instantly ached at the loss of his touch on my clit. But pointers or not, his intent became clear the next moment when he released my nipple with a final lap of his tongue and began kissing his way down my body, nipping at my skin and making anticipation bloom the closer he got.

When he placed a final kiss just above my pubis, I no longer had the patience to wait. With a whine, I wrapped my fingers in his long, red hair and pulled him down the final bit, gasping as his tongue flicked out to tease my throbbing clit.

"Yes," I moaned.

"See? There's no need to resist—you were made for sex, sweetie. Pleasure," Bjarni murmured in my ear.

It was impossible to argue when my body was tight with want despite my aching muscles and bone-deep exhaustion. I sucked in air in harsh pants, pressing my head back against his chest for some semblance of solidity amidst the onslaught of sensation.

Modi had skilled lips and a clever tongue, and I had the vague notion that while he may not have fucked a woman before me, he'd definitely practiced other sex acts. I wasn't prepared for the rush of jealousy that thought brought on, but I was too wrapped up in sensation to analyze why.

"Fuck me!" I spat, yanking hard on Modi's hair to move him farther up my body. "I want you inside me. Fill me, take me—prove you're mine!"

A growl vibrated through his chest and into my core. He rose up over me like a mountain; like the primeval god he embodied, face dark with hunger as he stared down at me. He wiped the glistening slick he'd pulled from me from his mouth with one hand and sank down on his left side in front of me, lining his much larger body up with mine.

"Modi," I whispered, the throb of arousal in our bond washing away the pain and allowing me to finally see him as the only thing that mattered: my mate.

My beautiful, powerful, tortured mate.

He grabbed me by the back of my neck and pressed my face into his chest.

"Anna."

My name on his lips was a raspy whisper overtaken by a moan when he pushed his hips forward, his cock pressing up inside of me, forcing me wide all the way to my cervix.

I whimpered at the sensation of being so full, but it didn't hurt. My body was still slick and limber from Bjarni, adapted to stretching for my alphas after my last claimings. It was only heat, pressure—pleasure.

He clutched my torso to his, Bjarni's grip on my thigh keeping my lower body pressed against my blond mate. Split between them both, an echo of the powerful magic that allowed us to take down Loki hummed in the bonds that tied us, a reminder that I wasn't a whole being—but right then, it didn't matter.

"Yes!"

Modi fucked me with rough, harsh thrusts, nothing like how Bjarni had taken me. He was all aggression, lust, and frustration, no tender love or whispered reassurances, and if it hadn't been for Bjarni's unwavering presence behind me, my aching heart would have broken at the sharp contrast.

But as Modi took possession of my pussy, Bjarni was right there with us, his breath coming hard and fast behind me as he jerked his cock against my thigh, his promise that he'd help me find peace fresh in my mind, allowing me to focus on nothing but the pleasure of being fucked like the omega I was in the very depths of my DNA.

When Modi's knot tied us, his movements shortening to grind on my G-spot, I let my climax wash away everything but the pure, blinding sensation of completion.

Heat filled my womb and painted my ass and thigh,

grunts of alpha pleasure filling my world. Darkness swarmed, my consciousness fleeting as my muscles released and I floated away in the knowledge that, at least for a little while, nothing evil would touch me. I was safe with them.

My mates.

27

ANNABEL

arkness gave way to gray light, allowing shadows to flicker into shapes of jagged rocks and a rough sea past an unfriendly beach. A battered rowboat tethered to an outcrop by a frayed rope only narrowly avoided the greedy waves crashing where land met sea.

A sense of urgency pushed me across the stony beach, stumbling for every step. That boat was my only hope!

Power knocked against my back, sending me forward with a scream. My knees knocked into jagged rocks, pain lancing through my kneecaps and palms, skin splitting. I bit my lip to try and contain the agony, focusing on the rowing boat once more. Crawling on bleeding hands and knees, I pushed forward, knowing I had to get to it. Had to.

Another wave of power, this time grabbing me around the waist, flipped me to my back, pressing me into the ground until I was pinned, immobile.

Above me a man with hair like powdered charcoal strode forward until he stopped by my feet. His pitch-black locks hid his features for a moment, but it didn't matter. I'd seen him a hundred times before, exactly like this.

He lifted his head, the long hair hiding his face whipping back, revealing ice-pale skin and mismatched eyes wild with fury.

Grim's face was drawn up in rage, teeth bared as he snarled, "There's no point in fighting me. You're already dead."

ADRENALINE SPIKED my heart-rate from the dead of sleep, propelling me up like a spring-assisted knife. I gasped for air as the darkness around me washed away the memory of the bleak beach, leaving only a woolen vision of Grim's furious face.

"Annabel?" My name rumbled from the darkness, two voices pulling me further into reality. Thickly muscled arms closed around my midriff as a hand clasped my shoulder, both making me aware of how chilled the air was in the small enclosure I'd woken up in.

Modi and Bjarni.

My stuttering heart eased its frantic pace the second my brain caught up. I was with two of my mates. I was safe.

"Sorry," I groaned, rubbing my face with both hands. "It was just a nightmare. Sorry."

"You sure? Not a vision?" Bjarni rumbled. His arms around me constricted for a moment.

I cracked a half-smile and patted his thigh on top of the furs, grateful despite myself for his ironclad belief in my newly found powers. "Yeah. I... I've had this one since I was a kid. Go back to sleep. Both of you."

Modi grunted behind me and slid one hand down my side, the gesture sweetly calming even if Bjarni was the one to pull me back down with him, nestling my head on his chest.

Modi was asleep again moments later, his deep breaths warm against the back of my skull, arm loose around my waist.

"Tell me about this nightmare," Bjarni rumbled, his voice heavy with sleep.

"There's not much to tell," I murmured, frowning as I tried to recall the details. Only Grim's face and that horrid sense of urgency lingered. Distractedly, I drew my fingers through his soft chest hair, pulling a hum of pleasure from the alpha in response. "I can never remember the details. Just your brother's face. He's always so... angry."

"You dream of Saga?" Bjarni asked.

"No. Grim." I sighed. "Seeing him the first time in the flesh was such a shock. But these dreams are nothing like the visions I've had since... since my magic was awakened."

"Hmm. I'm no scholar, but once we've reunited with my brothers, perhaps you should mention this to Grim.

He's the expert when it comes to magical phenomena. If you've dreamed of him since you were a child, he should be interested. Might even give him the ego boost he needs to stop sulking about having to claim you," he rumbled, amusement blending through his deep voice. "Give it a magical twist. That should warm his cold blood."

"Perhaps," I agreed, though the thought caused the lingering anxiety from the nightmare to clutch at my gut. Even non-nightmare Grim wasn't the most approachable guy to begin with. I wasn't entirely sure I wanted to tell him all about how he terrified me in my sleep.

"He'd never harm you, sweetie," Bjarni assured me, undoubtedly in response to the flicker of unease in our bond. With a deep sigh he sat back up again, easing my head into the bend of Modi's arm as he did.

"Right. I guess someone should go keep watch, and that useless mate of yours doesn't seem to be waking up anytime soon." Despite the bite in his words, there was no venom in them. "Your pussy's dangerous for a man's constitution, woman. There isn't much in the world that can bring two gods to their knees as efficiently as that sweet little snatch."

I huffed at his crudeness, but didn't deign to answer. It wasn't like I'd be running around doing cartwheels after last night.

Bjarni chuckled and patted my head before he

slipped out from underneath the covers. "Sleep well, my little mate."

I DIDN'T. Even with the heat from Modi's naked body wrapped around my back, the lack of Bjarni sandwiching me from the other side meant my teeth were clattering for most of the night.

When the darkness in the tent finally shifted to dull gray, I gave up and tried to wrestle free of Modi's grasp —something that proved pretty difficult.

"Stay," the redhead mumbled, tightening his arms around me.

"Modi, I need to pee," I protested, squirming uselessly against him. "Let go."

He didn't answer, and when I managed to twist around so I was facing him, it became obvious that he was still fast asleep.

"*Modi,*" I hissed, pushing at his pecs—the only movement I could manage, trapped as I was. "Modi!"

A rumbling grunt passed his full lips, one of his arms loosening its grip on me, and I thought I'd managed to wake him. Until that same hand traveled down to my ass and around, its goal becoming crystal clear the next second.

I jolted when he brushed against my pussy, fingers rubbing leisurely against my labia until they connected with my clit.

"Nope! No, absolutely not!" I squirmed harder, crossing my legs tightly. There was exactly no chance I was letting my horny octopus of a mate molest me while I was freezing my tits off in the middle of what had to be approaching zero degrees—and especially not with how sore I already was from his and Bjarni's joined efforts over the past few days.

And dammit, I really did have to pee!

My refusal was not received well. Modi's sleepy grunt turned to a threatening growl, his knee moving up to force my legs apart so he could continue his questing, still asleep.

"Dammit!" I growled when his cock swelled against me, jutting up against my labia in search of entry. "Why are all you alphas such rapey bastards, even in your sleep?"

Modi rumbled a soothing noise, his subconscious probably picking up on my reluctance, and slid his hand from my clit to my thigh, lining himself up.

I did the only thing I could think of to stop him, save from calling out to Bjarni—and to be frank, after last night I wasn't entirely sure which of us my blond mate would help in this particular situation—I reached down and grabbed his cock, diverting its trajectory.

Modi jolted hard, his eyes flying open with a hiss of expelled breath.

"Hel's tits!" He quickly released his grip on my body so he could wrest my hands free from his member. "Your fingers are pure ice!"

I let out a disbelieving snort. "Don't try and mount me in your sleep and maybe I won't have to ice your dick."

He frowned, eyes darting down our entangled bodies as if he hadn't picked up on what exactly was going on before now. Some of the indignation died in the blue depths. "Oh. I am... sorry."

An apology from a rapey alpha? Color me shocked.

"S'okay," I mumbled, pulling away. Somewhat more reluctantly this time, because the second I wasn't plastered against Modi's warm skin, my body temperature truly plummeted. "God, why is it so fucking cold?"

"It is the Fimbulwinter," Modi said as if speaking to a particularly slow child. He reached for me and pulled me back against his chest, capturing my hands in one of his palms this time. "Go back to sleep—it is still early, and we have a long day ahead."

I sighed, half-irritated at being manhandled into position against my will and half-tempted to obey. At least this way, half of me would be warm. "I have to pee."

Modi—eyes already closed again—made a noise of displeasure but released me without a fight.

I got into the clothes gifted to me by Verdandi as quickly as possible and sighed with relief as I exited the tent. Sure, it was still colder than an icebox, but the feathery garments held up against the howling blizzard much better than any human polar expedition outfit would have.

Bjarni was sitting by the small fire, his looming figure hunched on a log of tree as flurries of snow tumbled down around him. If it hadn't been for the hooting wind, he'd have made an idyllic picture. *Viking before Sunrise.*

I didn't see any sign of Loki, but I assumed since Bjarni was calm as could be that he was still around somewhere.

I hurried behind a tree, emptying my bladder as swiftly as possible before incurring any frostbites to tender parts, and then walked back to the fire.

"Morning," I told my blond mate as he turned toward me.

A small frown creased his forehead. "It's early still. You should try for some more sleep, sweetie."

I grimaced. "Eh, it's too cold. Whichever side of me isn't plastered against one of you two walking furnaces gets frosty. Besides, Modi's handsy in his sleep and I'm not in the mood."

Bjarni cracked a small grin and wrapped me in his arms. It was warm and comfortable, and I didn't resist as he dragged me onto his lap. "I'm sure it'd warm you up."

I rolled my eyes at him. "What happened to you barely tolerating him? If I remember right, you weren't best pleased the last time you found us together, and now here you are, trying to whore me out to him every chance you get."

"It's not really whoring when the man in your bed is

your mate," he said calmly, not biting at my provocation. "Guy's got issues. Your pussy seems to calm him down, at least for a little bit."

I narrowed my eyes. "And why do you care if he's calm or not?"

"'Cause I feel him too, through you. All his anger and uncertainty. Can't really do anything about that, so the next best thing is to get him to calm down and realize what a lucky bastard he is for getting to call you his." Bjarni gave me a smoldering look.

"Flattery will get you nothing," I teased, leaning in to kiss his cheek. He turned his head last moment, catching my lips with his.

The unexpected kiss heated my body from the inside, and I moaned softly into his mouth, clutching my fingers in his long, blond hair until he finally pulled away, leaving me panting.

"I promised I would help you find peace, Annabel," he said softly. "The only way to do that is to help your other idiot mate get his head out of his own ass. I might not be *thrilled* about Magni, but at least he's not such a ball of angst about all this, hmm?"

"I'm not sure there's any helping Modi," I said softly. "He doesn't want this, and I don't think anything can ever make him want it."

Bjarni scoffed. "Please. You think Fate forced him to put a claiming mark on you? That was all him, sweetie. He's just a bit thick. He'll come around once he gets over his fancy Asgardian upbringing and realizes he couldn't handle you on his own anyway."

"His fancy Asgardian upbringing?" I asked, eyebrows raised.

"You saw his dad's reaction to the news of Magni claiming a human girl, and *sharing* her with us filthy Jotunns, no less. And Magni's the bastard son—of Jotunn heritage himself. Thor's gonna birth a ram when he realizes his pure born's gotten himself entangled with the same human, and Modi knows it.

"He's been raised to be the noble, obedient son, always living up to expectations. Asgard's golden child. Pretty sure all that angst you can feel in your bond to him is him coming to grips with what he's been raised to be is nothing like what he actually is. There's no human mate for Thor's perfect son, no mercy for his enemies, and most especially no trading of glory on the battlefield for a place next to a woman who might just end up being more powerful than he.

"It'll take him a minute to learn to listen to his heart, not his father's voice at the back of his thick skull telling him who he's *supposed* to be."

"You seem to be getting a lot more from our bond than I am," I said, sighing at the thought of the agony I knew awaited once Modi woke up again and returned to his usual loathing of our connection.

"It's not so much the bond as it's experience with asshole gods who like to dominate their offspring," he said mildly, giving my nose a peck. "You hungry? I can start breakfast early."

"Sure. Thank you." I brushed my fingers through his beard and climbed off his lap, sad to lose his warmth, but thankful for his care and the words he'd shared. True or not, the possibility that maybe the pain in Modi's and my bond wouldn't be forever gave me just a smidgen of hope. And soon we'd be back in Asgard. Back with Magni and Saga.

"Speaking of asshole fathers—where's Loki?" I asked, glancing over my shoulder to see if I could spot him.

"Over there." Bjarni nodded in the direction of a large snowdrift.

I turned and squinted. "What? Where? I don't see—"

Reality struck like a bolt of lightning, and I squeaked and ran through the snow toward the drift. Frantically I dug at the white mass, shifting as much as I could with my hands.

"What did you do? Oh my god, what the fuck?!"

"*I* didn't do a thing," Bjarni drawled as he rummaged in the large rucksack for what he needed to make breakfast. "That was all Modi."

"And you've just sat here for how many hours?" I hissed as black hair finally emerged. I scraped at the snow, digging the God of Mischief's head free so I could turn him over. His face was blue and unmoving, purple bruising around his nose and cheekbone indicating broken bones.

"He's dead! We were meant to bring him back alive!"

"He's not," Bjarni rumbled. "He's a god—it takes a lot more than a bit of frostbite to kill one off. He'll thaw out if we leave him by the fire for an hour before we move on."

I stared down at what very much looked like a frozen corpse, right down to the frost in his black eyelashes. The temptation to leave him be danced at the back of my mind. This was the man who'd hurt my mate, who'd abandoned his own sons to their fate. Who'd killed innocent birds just to punish Bjarni. Who'd quite possibly brought about the end of the world.

But he was also our captive, and under our care. I got that Viking gods probably didn't care much about the Geneva Convention, but despite everything I still had too much humanity left to torture the bastard.

I reached inside myself, finding my magic glowing and plentiful. It came easily when I beckoned and wrapped around Loki's frozen form like a warm blanket.

"You shouldn't waste your energy on him," Bjarni said. "He's not worth a drop of your essence."

"We're better than this," I replied, voice not unlike my third-grade teacher, Mrs. Miller, who could make you sit straight and keep quiet with nothing more than a *look.* "He might be a prick, but we're not. And we will treat our prisoner with some dignity."

Bjarni grunted, sounding very much like he didn't think he was better than this, but at least he didn't argue.

I refocused on Loki, whose features were slowly turning white rather than blue. I tightened my magic around him, infusing his limbs with warmth until finally, his eyelids fluttered, and he drew in a raspy breath.

"Welcome back," I said.

He only winced in response and I sighed at the sight of the damages to his face. Now that his blood was circulating again, both his nose and cheekbone looked extra terrible.

"If you promise to watch your mouth, I'll try to heal that for you. But if you're only gonna provoke Modi and Bjarni again, I'm not going to bother. It's a lot of effort."

The trickster god didn't respond, but the one eye that wasn't swollen shut rolled toward me, measuring me.

I pushed down the shiver of unease at his attention and reached for my magic once more. I was no expert on how to use it, but I remembered how Saga had guided me when I'd healed Magni. I did the same now, Loki's injuries much more compliant than the infection that'd nearly taken my mate.

It didn't take long before his skin only showed the faintest yellow marks, as if his injuries were weeks old.

Pleased with myself, I rocked back on my heels and smiled down at him. "There you are, almost as good as new."

"Thank you," he said, his voice free from snark for the first time so far. "Now if you might also consider redoing my ties to a more dignified position...?

I snorted. "Sure. But just a word of warning—if you make an escape attempt because you think I'm some bleeding heart omega, you're going to be very disappointed. You'll spend the trip back to Asgard dragged face-down in the snow, and I'm not going to raise a finger to help you."

"I'm starting to understand that you're not a helpless little omega, human," he said, arching an eyebrow at me. "It seems I made a better bargain with your ancestors than I realized at the time."

"Hmm." I wasn't sure if it was flattery or not and decided it didn't matter either way. Careful to keep my full focus on him, I undid the hogtie Modi had strung him up with, only to redo his binds with his wrists tied snugly in front of him, the golden glow from the rope I'd infused the prior day making me feel pretty safe. I'd never been a Girl Scout, but my magic hummed when I tested the fibers, reassuring me of its strength.

"Is there enough breakfast to feed him too?" I asked over my shoulder.

"He doesn't need to eat," Bjarni growled.

I sighed. I understood why my mate was so angry

with his father, but starving him wasn't going to make what he'd done any easier to cope with.

"Bjarni. Please. Feed him."

The blond giant shot me a glare, but a few moments later he stomped over and dropped a wooden plate of fried bacon and beans by my side.

"Your breakfast is by the fire, once you're done with him," he said, turning away without so much as another look.

I heaved another sigh and placed the plate in Loki's bound hands. It wasn't going to be the most dignified way of eating for him, but so long as he propped the plate up on his knees, he'd manage. It was a fair few steps up from being literally frozen solid face-down in the snow.

"Thank you," Loki said, his voice gentle. "Daughter."

I narrowed my eyes at him. "Don't even try it. I'm not falling for your tricks again. I didn't ask for you—I asked for him. He's got a good heart, despite who sired him. I don't want him regretting anything once you're a head shorter and won't be capable of eating ever again."

His lips curled up in a wry smile. "I suppose that's fair. He always was surprisingly gentle—considering the mother I sired him on. Hard as nails, that Jotunn bitch. At least he got her fighting prowess."

"There's nothing wrong with being gentle," I said, eyes narrowing as a compulsive urge to defend my mate rose along my spine. "If more of you asshole gods considered it a boon, perhaps you wouldn't be so busy trying to bring about the end of the damn world.

"Why? Why are you doing it? Even if you survive, what's the point? To rule over a dark mass of nothing? Please, enlighten me."

This time, Loki was the one to sigh. "I told you—I have nothing to do with this."

"Several prophecies and a very pissed-off god-king suggest otherwise," I said. "And I saw one of your other *sons* on our way here—big, serpent-like. Enjoys devouring ships and laying waste to the world. Ring a bell?"

"As I'm sure you've learned by now, prophecies can be manipulated. And I am not responsible for my offspring's actions." He motioned with his plate toward Bjarni. "Clearly. Did you know Odin has one of them in his stables? His own steed came from my loins."

I blinked. "I'm sorry... are you saying Odin's *riding* one of your sons? Like... like a horse?"

Loki snorted. "Well, it isn't often people refer to Sleipner as a simple horse, but yes. Odin is more than happy to claim my spawn as a boon if it suits him. But if they're trouble? I'm apparently behind it."

"A horse? You fathered a *horse?*" I was still having a really hard time getting past the whole equine-son thing. "*And* a ginormous sea-serpent? I... I'm sorry, I know you're a god and there're different rules, but *how* do you even...? Never mind, I don't think I want to know."

"Ah. Mortal morals," he said, a small smirk pulling up the corner of his mouth. "I'm pleased they're not a hindrance when it comes to who you yourself share your body with. From the sounds of it, having multiple mates comes very, hmm, *natural* to you. Not a lot of human women would be able to enjoy themselves with more than one alpha. I admit, I expected this arrangement I established with your ancestors to be more of a burden than it appears it is."

A flush of embarrassment heated my face at the confirmation that he'd heard me with Modi and Bjarni.

"You know nothing about my mate bonds, and I'll thank you to not speak another word of them," I hissed. Angry that I'd let him get under my skin again, I stood and turned to leave.

"Annabel," he called.

I stopped and looked at him over my shoulder. Bound on the ground and surrounded by snow as he was, he still looked every inch a dark god, charcoal hair framing his eerily glowing face.

"I am not behind Ragnarök. I swear it on my own life. There's a traitor in Asgard."

I stared at him. There was absolute sincerity in his dark eyes. But he was the trickster god—how could I ever hope to determine if he was just manipulating me again?

"This sounds like something you should tell Odin once we get to Asgard," I said.

He chuffed a laugh through his nose. "If history has

proven anything, it's that Odin cares little for finding the truth if it means losing out on a chance to blame me for whatever threat is at Asgard's gates this time around. I fear your mates might be similarly afflicted, blinded by hatred and skewed perception. But *you.* You hold no such preconceived notions, hmm, little omega?"

I blinked. "Are you telling me everyone hates you for no good reason? After you've just manipulated me into thinking I would lose my mates? After you killed Arni and Magga? Told your own son he and his brothers are on their own?"

Loki grimaced. "I know I'm no conventional *hero.* I'm the God of Mischief, after all. But I have no reason to want to bring forth Ragnarök, and if you don't listen to me, all your efforts, all your sacrifice will be for naught. You might live—you might not. But your world will be gone. Your friends, your family. There is a traitor in Asgard. Left unchecked, they will succeed in their evil purpose."

"And you just happen to know who this traitor is?" I asked, eyebrows raised in mock-surprise. "How very convenient."

"I do not," he said, somewhat to my surprise. "But I know how to reveal them."

"Let me guess—for the low, low price of your freedom?" I folded my arms across my chest. "How come you haven't revealed this traitor on your own a bit sooner? Say, before the Fimbulwinter hit and that serpent son of yours started paddling around the Atlantic?"

"I've been unable to access Valhalla for many years now. And to be frank, so long as I could secure my own lineage, I wasn't too concerned. Obviously, that has changed now."

He held out his bound hands, a sardonic slant to his lips. "My offer is simple: once you have displayed my successful capture to the god-king and as a result my sons are free from his retribution, *you* will free me. Once you have done that, I will tell you how to reveal the traitor."

I arched an eyebrow at him. "And what guarantee will I have that you won't just take off without revealing a thing?"

Loki gazed over my shoulder toward the fire. When I twisted to follow his gaze, I saw Bjarni watching us like a hawk. A small bubble of warmth grew in my gut at the confirmation that he would always look out for me.

"I will tell you at a... more opportune time," Loki said lightly, his focus returning to the wooden plate hosting his rapidly cooling breakfast. "You can think on my offer until then. I can only hope that you will see the wisdom of my words."

28

The furs were empty by my side when I woke up again sometime after dawn. Empty and cold.

I caught myself stroking the skins where Annabel had slept, her scent still lingering. Hers and Bjarni's.

I wrinkled my nose, but the smell of alpha wasn't unpleasant. Perhaps because it was so thoroughly intertwined with my own and mixed with copious amounts of omega fluids.

Tentatively I prodded the bond connecting me to Annabel—and through her, Bjarni. It hummed peacefully in response, followed by an immediate tension.

Annabel. She felt me awaken. And where she had been calm, she was now anxious.

I swallowed a frustrated growl. What had I expected? That giving in to my instincts would have quelled the nightmare of confusion and pain between us?

Please, Modi. It was sex. Nothing more.

Just instincts.

THE SNOW WAS STILL TUMBLING from a gray sky in thick flakes when I exited the flimsy tent to take stock of the camp.

Bjarni and Annabel sat on the near side of the fire, her in his lap, undoubtedly to protect her from the cold trunk serving as a seat. They both looked at me when I appeared, Annabel's pretty face drawn with trepidation and Bjarni's relaxed.

On the other side someone had rebound Loki with his hands in front of his body, and had even shoved a mug of something hot and steamy into them.

"We are pampering the World Breaker now?" I asked as I strode toward Bjarni and Annabel. "I thought you had given up on the ties of blood after his betrayal."

"More names?" Loki asked, arcing a sardonic eyebrow over his mug. "I suppose World Breaker sounds better than The Betrayer. If you must."

"Don't look at me," Bjarni rumbled. "I'd have been happy to leave him frozen solid until we reach Valhalla. Our soft-hearted mate thought that would be too cruel. Something about being better than that."

I glanced down at Annabel and caught her gaze

before she managed to look away. Heat rose in her cheeks, a flicker of embarrassment stirring our bond. Not for what she had done for Loki—for what we had done last night.

Judging from how she was cozied up to Bjarni, it did not seem she had such reservations with him.

"Soft-hearted?" I repeated, breaking our eye contact as I stepped away and toward the fire where a plate of bacon and beans was warming. I might not be Bjarni Lokisson's biggest fan, but I had to hand it to the man— not many would be able to cook up such an inviting meal mid-Fimbulwinter, with only the sparsest of provisions available.

"Foolish, more likely. Do not fall for the trickster's words of pity. I do not want to have to hunt him down again because of your inability to do what is necessary. He has earned everything that is coming to him and more."

Annabel did not respond, but I felt the flicker of embarrassment turn to hurt, then anger. Bjarni only sighed.

Better. It was much easier to deal with the blasted bond when her end reflected nothing but that nasty temper of hers back at me. She was my reluctant mate —we had fucked, it felt good, and in the bright light of day there was no room for confusing emotions. Anger was easy. Painful, but familiar.

I would take anger over regret any day of the week.

THE TREK back to the human settlement of Seattle took longer than our journey out. The snow was thicker on the ground, making walking a slower, more arduous task, especially for Annabel.

Bjarni led our small group, Loki in tow with a firm grasp on the rope around his wrists. Annabel followed, leaving me to bring up the rear, carrying our tent and supplies.

To the little omega's credit, she did not complain as she struggled through the snow, and she was smart to stay directly behind Loki and his Jotunn son, but the snow was still deep and tricky. I watched her fight her way through the harsh terrain, her pace slowing gradually despite her best efforts, and gritted my teeth.

If she had been any less stubborn, I would have picked her up and slung her over the gear on my back to save her the struggle, but thanks to our little *moment* on Bifrost, I had a good inkling that it would not be well-received.

Not that I should have cared. She was slowing us down. I should have grabbed her, hoisted her over my shoulder, and ignored her displeasure. The end.

To Hel with the stupid bond aching in my chest at the thought of another harsh rejection from my bitter mate.

Just as I increased my stride to catch up with her,

Bjarni paused and turned, frowning when his gaze landed on Annabel.

"I'm sorry, sweetie—I should have realized you'd be struggling. Come, let me carry you."

"I can walk just fine," she replied, though there was a distinct lack of fire in her rebuttal.

Bjarni gave her a patient look. "Yes. You're a very capable woman. Now stop making a fuss, hmm? What kind of a mate would I be if I knowingly let you struggle?"

Yes, what kind of mate indeed?

I glared at him as he walked back to Annabel, pulling Loki along with him, and picked her up despite her token protests. He settled her against his chest, her legs wrapped around his waist and her arms around his neck, before he turned back around to resume the trek.

Acid seethed in my veins as I followed, but I pushed it down with an iron hand. It was bad enough he had shown me up without even trying—bad enough I was jealous at how warm and comfortable her weight would feel against him. I was not about to let either of them feel my petty envy in our blasted bond.

It was deep in the night when we finally made it to King Street Station. The large settlement of Seattle was as dead as it had been on our arrival, the only humans we spotted on our way through the white-blanketed streets through windows in the odd, tall houses lining them.

It was not a surprise then that the station also lay silent amidst the howling winds, but when I jogged up the stairs to open the door, they were locked.

Too eager to get out of the weather to be denied entry, I sent a bolt of lightning through the lock, melting it off so I could push through.

Darkness and the echo of the door slamming open was all that met us.

"Well, this isn't looking promising," Bjarni rumbled as he put Annabel down, looking around the large, silent room. "Did you spot anything outside? Anything about the service being disrupted?"

"All I saw was snow," I said.

"And that big sign saying all transport has been canceled on the orders of the governor," Loki said mildly. "Looks like we're staying in the great city of Seattle for the duration of this little blizzard."

"What sign?" Annabel snapped, her attention turning to the trickster god.

"He's lying," Bjarni growled, though I saw the flicker of unease in his eyes.

"By all means, go check if you don't believe me," Loki said, rubbing his hands together. "I'll just stay he —*uff!*"

His voice died on a huff when Bjarni yanked him along by the rope, heading back toward the doors.

"Watch her," he said to me. As if he needed to.

Annabel looked at me as silence spread once more, and I forced myself not to rub at my chest where our bond hummed out of tune. It was the first time we had been alone since I woke up with her in my arms in the tent, the tension between us thicker from a full day's separation.

"Are you hungry?" I asked, because leave it to my primitive alpha instincts to breach the gap. Right then, feeding her seemed like the best way to break the tension. Or maybe a nice fuck. Despite my own exhaustion from the long trek, my dick gave a spasm at that particular thought. *Gods dammit.*

"Too anxious. If Loki isn't lying, then... then we have no way of getting back to Norway and Bifrost. If the trains aren't running, then the planes definitely aren't either." She wrapped her arms around her body, looking so vulnerable I almost crossed the distance between us to wrap her up in my arms. "Modi, what are we gonna do? If we can't get back to Asgard. Odin's gonna..."

She did not finish that sentence, but she did not need to.

"We will find a way," I said. "If all else fails, I can call on Thor. Even the Fimbulwinter will not stop Tanngrisnir and Tanngnjóstr. He will come for us."

The frown on her forehead eased to a small crease, and she nodded. "Good. That's good." Then, giving me a hesitant smile, she asked, "Is that offer of food still open?"

Some of the tension in my gut eased. I swung the backpack over my shoulder and rummaged through it for some of our packed provisions. It was not a warm meal, but it was sustenance. I nearly purred when she, eyes closed from exhaustion, bit down on the sandwich I had provided, accepting my role as her alpha; her provider.

Idiot instincts.

The doors banged open behind us, and I spun around, ready to ward off an attack—but it was only Bjarni, dragging his father along by the golden rope.

"The trains won't be running until the snow lets up. The sign said all transport across the continent is halted —even ships. *Fuck!*" Bjarni spat, kicking a row of seats.

"It's okay—Modi has a way for us to get back," Annabel said, looking to me. "He can call his father."

"Uh... how about we just wait it out?" Loki asked, the grimace crossing his face more uneasy than I had seen him before.

I chuffed a derisive laugh. "What is the matter, trickster god? Not too keen on facing Thor, are we?"

"We're not waiting out the fucking Fimbulwinter," Bjarni growled. "If Thor can get us back to Valhalla in time, then that's what we're doing. Call on him—we can rest once we're in Asgard."

I nodded and undid my outer clothes to get at the ring adorning my right bicep, a birth gift from my father—my connection to him across all nine worlds. I had never had reason to use it before, but it had stayed with me from my first breath, a constant reassurance of my ties to my home.

Pressing my hand against it, I channeled the lightning in my blood, letting it sing through the gold until I felt the magic connection open.

Father, we are in need of your aid. We have captured Loki but are cut off from returning to Asgard.

I waited, the other end of the link lying dormant for a breath. Two. Three.

Father.

Another breath, and then I felt a *click* within the magic, felt a touch of consciousness before it died, leaving nothing but emptiness behind.

I expelled a harsh breath, my eyes snapping open.

He had... He had rejected me?

He'd heard my plea, and he'd... rejected me.

Brown eyes focused on mine, their depths the only thing keeping me grounded as the Earth itself seemed to fall from underneath my feet.

"Modi?" Annabel asked, concern evident in her voice. Gloved hands closed around my wrist, the chill of them slowly bringing me back to my body. "What's wrong? You feel..."

Our bond. She felt everything I did. I stared at her, knowing that the most intimate, the most painful moment of my life was laid bare to her—and through her to Bjarni, my enemy.

I breathed slow and deep, until my steel grip was back, forcing the depths of my despair down.

Finally, I freed my wrists of her grip and stepped back, unwilling to see the hope break in those pretty eyes.

"Thor is not coming," I said. "We are on our own."

I frowned. "What do you mean, he's not—"

Annabel's hand on my arm quieted me. She shook her head just in time for me to catch on to why our bond echoed with pain: *Modi.*

"Thor's not coming?" Loki repeated, the glee in his voice like nails on a chalkboard in the quiet hall. "How *peculiar.* Seems he's really not bothered about bringing the so-called *Betrayer* to justice. Could it truly be he's too busy knocking Jotunn skulls and drinking mead to save his little bastard?"

I glared at my father, but the smirk on his lips spoke all too clearly of his intentions. He wasn't just unbothered about needling Modi—he was actively trying to bring him misery.

Once upon a time I'd have laughed at such antics, delighted in my enemy's pain. But that was before a rope made of flesh and iron tied us together, making me feel every ounce of agony he did. Before I'd known for myself what pain came from your own father betraying you.

"I don't know how we're going to get back to Valhalla—but we will," the redhead said, the determination in his voice subverted by the despair ricocheting through the bond tying me to Annabel.

I breathed in deeply, and without looking at my father, undid my thick winter coat to reach for the hidden leather pouch I carried close to my chest. "I may have a solution."

Doubt mixed with curiosity was plain on his face when I pulled out the old map and knelt to spread it on the floor, smoothing the curled edges as I looked over it.

"Bjarni! No!" Loki jolted forward, reaching for the map. I jerked on the rope, sending him ass over teakettle without so much as a glance in his direction.

"What are you doing, boy? If the Aesir discover—"

"I don't give a flying crap," I rumbled. "Ragnarök is at our doorstep. Saga and Grim are in enemy hands. Modi can burn it if he wants, once we've put a stop to this mess. All I care about right now is getting to Asgard before my brothers are a head shorter, and all *you* should care about is how you're going to plead your case to the other gods once we get there. One more word out of you, and you'll spend the rest of this trek with a sock stuffed down your gullet. Got it?"

Loki gasped an insulted breath, but whatever biting

words he wanted to sling at me, he was wise enough to only mutter.

"What is this?" Modi asked as he bent by my side, brows knotted in a frown.

"It's a map of the nine worlds," I answered, pointing toward a small, swirling vortex I knew all too well. An unexpected pang of homesickness threatened to distract my focus. I forced it down. "This is a portal to Jotunheim. We can locate a path from Midgard back to Asgard using these portals."

Modi's frown deepened. "This is... this is a backdoor through the realms? The gods would never let such an artifact fall into Jotunn hands! How did you—"

"Does it really matter?" I asked him, eyebrow arched. "Not all magic in the nine world belongs to the Aesir, and Jotunn hands or no, this is our best shot at saving our brothers. Our *only* shot, unless you have any other bright ideas you've yet to share with the class."

He looked like he wanted to protest, undoubtedly pushed by eons of Asa superiority complex, but reason must have set in, because in the end he only nodded.

"This is Iceland," Annabel said as she crouched between us, her fingertips grazing the swirl of the portal near our farm. "How are we supposed to get there?"

I smoothed my hand across the map. The ink shimmered and flickered, then slid into new shapes and forms until it displayed a detailed map of North America. "Hopefully there'll be one not too far from us."

It was harder to spot the portals on this map thanks

to the vast size of the continent. I frowned and squinted at the map, hoping against hope that one would be close to Seattle.

"There," Annabel said, pointing to a small black ink smudge. Far up in Alberta, Canada.

"We won't make it there in time," I said softly. "We need something closer."

Silence fell again as the three of us stared at the map while Loki tapped his fingers impatiently against the floor, thankfully keeping his mouth shut.

"Is that one?" Modi finally asked after several minutes.

I followed his finger to a small smudge north-east of Portland, Oregon. My heart picked up speed as I caught the swirl in its center.

"Yes! It's..." I stopped myself, cursing under my breath.

"What?" Annabel asked.

"It leads to Niflheim. *Fuck!*"

"Niflheim?" she asked as Modi spat out a foul oath from her other side.

"The realm of fog and mist," Loki said, that damned smirk back in his voice. "Darkness and ice rule there. It's certainly no place to bring a vulnerable little human."

"What did I say about keeping your mouth shut?" I growled at my father.

"He is right," Modi said. "We cannot bring Annabel

there. It is not just ice and darkness that lurks in Niflheim."

"Are you joking right now?" our mate asked, a snarl in her voice that had no business coming from an omega. "If this is the only way we'll make it back in time, then this is the portal we're using. The human world's currently hosting an unending winter and a big fucking serpent planning on covering the world in acid. It's basically already ice-and-darkness time here. So, unless someone spots a better portal, let's *go*."

I exchanged a look with Modi. The girl had a point.

"Let's see where the next closest portal in Niflheim is located first. We have limited time, and with all this blasted snow it's going to take at least five to six days to make it down far enough into Oregon," I said, brushing my palm over the map once more.

It shimmered again, ink moving until the jagged edges of Niflheim lay in front of us.

"There's our spot," I mumbled, placing the pad of my index finger on the location we'd be arriving from. "Now where's the nearest portal out?"

It took the three of us a lot of scouring until finally Annabel prodded a black vortex several inches from my digit. "There. Where does that one lead?"

I squinted at the mark, then lit up in a grin as hope seeped through my veins. "Asgard! Stars be blessed, it's a portal to Asgard!

"How long will it take us to get there?" she asked. I

saw the same kind of wild longing on her pretty face as pounded in my heart. We were so close.

"About... three days?" Modi said, measuring the distance between Annabel's and my fingers with his hand before he looked to me for confirmation.

"All depending," I murmured, frowning at the flat map. "I've never been, though I hear the terrain is supposedly as rough as its inhabitants. But yes, I think three days is a reasonable estimate. That gets us back to Valhalla with only a single day to spare for any unforeseen circumstances along the way."

"Then it looks like it is our best bet," Modi said. "Let us rest and eat so we can head out in the morning with as much energy as possible. We are going to need it."

30

The trek to Oregon was tougher than our hike from Seattle to find Loki and back. Much, much tougher. The wind howled constantly, throwing icy snow in my face despite Modi and Bjarni doing their best to shield me from the elements by sandwiching me between the bulk of their bodies.

We walked for sixteen hours that first day, forcing our way through hip-deep snow—though again, the alphas took turns taking the lead, so they could flatten the path for my human self. They did everything to make the journey as easy as possible for me, and it made me feel absolutely useless when we still had to stop for the night because I physically couldn't move anymore.

"You should have said something," Bjarni rumbled as he slipped underneath the blankets and wrapped me up in his blessed warmth shortly after we made camp.

"All this is gonna be for nothing if you keel over dead from exhaustion."

"We're never going to make it if I can't even handle walking in my own damn world," I growled. "We're *so close,* Bjarni. But if we have to keep stopping because I'm not strong enough—"

He stopped me with a kiss. "Shush. You're human, Annabel. You've shown resilience above and beyond anything I could have dreamed, but you *are* human. It's not a weakness. Look at all that magic thrumming right underneath your skin. Your willpower. You brought the God of Mischief to heel. You're strong enough, sweetie. Stars, you're strong enough to stop even Ragnarök. Tomorrow, when you start to tire, Modi or I will carry you. And we will make it in time."

"I'll slow you down," I said, guilt clutching at my throat. "Without me—"

"Without you, we wouldn't have had a chance at capturing Loki. Stop this nonsense, Annabel. Do you expect to do everything on your own? Why do you think Fate planned five mates for you? If your fate is truly to stop Ragnarök, then ours is to lend you our strength when you need it."

"You make it sound so simple," I whispered.

"It *is* simple," he sighed, placing a peck on my forehead. "I don't understand why you're all angsting about it all the damn time. We're meant for each other. I feel it right through my bones every time I look at you. And I feel it when Modi, curse his stupid ass, touches you. I *saw* it when the three of us took down one of the most powerful gods in the world. So tomorrow, you will let your mates carry you when your body grows tired, and together we will make it back to Asgard in time to save my brothers."

It was a strange sensation, floating on the edge of consciousness and listening to his completely calm, rational explanation for something I'd struggled with ever since I fled from their farm so many weeks ago now. As if this whole, insane Norn-created mess was the most natural thing in the world. But my exhausted mind could only grasp onto the here and now, the physical problem.

"You need your strength. It's so much harder for you two—"

"Annabel. We're gods." Bjarni's otherwise so patient voice took on a stern note. "We've both faced far, far harder challenges in our immortal existence than dragging your sweet ass through some snow. Now, I will hear no more protest out of you. It's time to sleep, and so help me if you don't let us know the *second* you need to be carried tomorrow, I'll show you exactly how much strength I have left. Fimbulwinter or no."

I had a pretty good idea of how he was planning on showing me his strength, and I couldn't hold back an amused snort even as my eyelids slid closed, my body more than prepared to obey his command to sleep. "Why is it always about fucking with alphas?"

"*Sleep,*" he growled.

I did.

THE REST of the journey was still exhausting on a level I hadn't experienced before, but true to his promise, Modi and Bjarni carried me whenever my body refused to continue another step. I knew it slowed the pace they could have set on their own, but I soon realized that it was faster for us all than if I tried to force my legs forward after I'd run out of steam.

It was midday on the fifth day when we, deep into Mount Rainier National park, finally located the portal.

We found it deep between a forest of huge pines and thick undergrowth that ripped at our clothes, its dark expanse a sharp contrast to the blanket of white covering everything else.

"Finally," Bjarni sighed at the sight of it. He hadn't said anything, but I knew both my alphas were stressing at our tight timeline. "Let's not waste any time —come on."

"I really think you should reconsider," Loki said. He'd kept mostly quiet for the entirety of our journey, probably keeping Bjarni's threat of getting silenced with a dirty sock in fresh recollection. "Niflheim is no place for a human. You know this."

"I'm sure you are just dying with concern for our mate, and not in the least motivated by desire *not* to face

Odin's wrath," Modi said, not bothering to look at him as he eyed the portal.

"Yes, well, be that as it may, *my* survival is also relying on the human girl surviving," Loki said. "That part of the prophecy was clear. And if you get her killed in Niflheim, we're *all* screwed."

Bjarni spun toward him, eyes narrowed. "You *do* understand that if Saga or Magni dies, so does she, right? You do know how fundamental and inescapable the bond you were so keen on your sons to enter into is? Or was this grand plan of yours less contingent of the nitty-gritty details of how our lives would be forever altered, and more focused on how to save your own skin?"

Loki rolled his eyes. "Please, I have enough faith in Grim to know he'll find a way out, even if Saga and Thor's oaf of a bastard fail. If there'd been any real danger to them, *of course* I would have come to their aid."

"Of course," Bjarni bit.

"Ignore him," I murmured, placing a hand on Bjarni's bicep. "He's just trying to distract us. Let's go."

"I will go through first with Loki," Modi said. He was standing in front of the portal, letting his fingers skim over the void as he inspected it. "Make sure it is safe before you bring her through."

"No!" My shout rushed out of my throat before I could stop it. I lunged the few yards from Bjarni to

Modi, my heart hammering in my throat. I grasped on to his coat with both hands.

Modi stared down at where I had a hold of him, one eyebrow arched in clear bemusement at my reaction. "No?"

"I..." How did I explain to him how it'd felt like when Magni abducted me to Jotunheim through a portal and I'd thought I would die until Saga followed, gluing my soul back together? "We... We need to go together. At the same time."

"It's safer—" he started, but I cut him off before he had a chance to continue.

"*No.* If anything, it's safer if all three of us are there, should something dangerous be waiting for us. It took the three of us to catch *him,* remember?" I said, jerking my head toward Loki without releasing my grip on Modi's coat.

Modi sighed, an exasperated look passing over his handsome features, but he didn't pry my hands off him. "Annabel—"

"Girl has a point," Bjarni rumbled, his amusement obvious even without looking at him. "And if you make her use her magic to stay attached to you like a barnacle, she's gonna need a fuck the moment we hit Niflheim. Dunno about you, but it's almost been a week since I got off, and there's no chance in Hel I'm keeping watch while you top off her magic."

It was the first mention of the fact that that we hadn't had sex since before we'd left Seattle, and embarrassment heated my cheeks at Bjarni's bluntness. The journey had left me near-unconscious every night, and miraculously both alphas had decided it was more important that I recuperated my strength than satisfy them.

Modi grunted. "Fine. But you stay *behind* me. Got it?"

"Yeah. Got it," I said, relief making me smile up at him. "Thank you."

He only nodded and turned his focus back to the portal. "You're with me, Betrayer."

Loki sighed dramatically but trudged through the snow toward him and the portal—encouraged by the yank on his rope from Bjarni. He eyed the darkness and pressed his lips into a thin line. "I truly hate this place."

"Everyone does," Modi rumbled. "Forward."

Loki rolled his eyes again, shooting the redhead an ungrateful look. Then he stepped through, leaving nothing but the end of the rope in Bjarni's hand behind.

Bjarni grabbed my shoulder with his free hand and pushed, making me press up tight against Modi. I grabbed onto his waist as he turned around, effectively sandwiching me between his back and Bjarni's chest.

We stepped through as one, and I sucked in a breath as the sensation of falling rippled through my body, pulling me apart and putting me back together again before I could scream.

. . .

A COLD, clammy sensation clung to my face and seemed to bore into my lungs with every breath. I opened my eyes, blinking rapidly to try and regain my bearings.

For a long moment, everything seemed to be silent, gray nothingness. If it hadn't been for the comforting pressure from in front- and behind me, I'd have panicked at the absence of sight.

Only when a shadow moved in the gray nothingness a little bit ahead did I realize that the clammy chill was thick fog surrounding us from all sides.

"*Ugh*. You could have warned me that this portal of yours would land us in the middle of a swamp," Loki's voice sounded from the dark figure. He waved his bound hands, making the fog swirl around him enough that he became somewhat more visible. "Where's our exit, then?"

I shifted cautiously at his words, trying to make out the surface we were standing on, but it seemed to be frozen solid. A few dead tufts of grass crunched underneath my feet, but at least there was no snow.

"Three days east-northeast from here," Bjarni rumbled behind me.

"And where exactly is 'here'?" Loki said, forced patience dripping from every syllable. "Because it generally helps to know where you are when you're looking to find somewhere to go."

"We're at the portal. Don't really need to know

anything other than that," Bjarni said, irritation flickering in our bond as well as his voice.

"Just show him the map," Modi sighed. "Your brother, the cold one—there is a rumor he spawned from this world, right? Which would mean your dear father knows these lands better than most. Odin or no, I am pretty sure even the God of Mischief can see the benefit of spending as little time as possible in Niflheim."

"Is that why Grim's so cold?" I asked, distracted by the unexpected bit of gossip. "His mother is from here? What—what is she?" I frowned, remembering what *else* Loki had fathered. "Oh, God, she's... she's human-*ish*, right?"

"*Ish*," Loki agreed mildly, doing nothing to calm the wild images suddenly flying free in my imagination. "Ah, thank you."

The last bit was directed at Bjarni, who thrust the rolled-up map at him. It took him a bit of fumbling to smooth it out with his bound hands, but when he managed he crouched down to scrutinize the old parchment. Apparently, god eyes had less trouble with the thick fog than my human ones.

"Ah, so we're in *Sötunmarsken*," he said, drawing his finger to the right. "And the other portal is—*no!* No, are you *mad?*"

The change in Loki's tone was so immediate and volatile I took a step back. Bjarni's hand on my shoulder kept me from tripping over another lump of frozen grass and falling on my ass.

Loki rose up to his full height, his face twisted with horror visible through the gray nothingness as he stared at us. "You're taking us directly to Hvergelmir! *Hvergelmir!* Do you know what slumbers there? Do your puerile, foolish little minds not grasp the danger? You take us there, you take us to *Níðhöggr's* door, and you will cost us all our lives!"

In the little time I'd known Loki, I'd learned you could never trust his words. He was the God of Mischief, or trickery and betrayal. But right then, as I looked at the absolute terror on his otherwise so divine features, I knew into the marrow of my bones that this time—this time he wasn't acting.

He believed we were going to die.

31

MODI

"Nidhug?" Annabel asked, butchering the word completely, yet removing none of the chill just the sound of that name caused. "You've mentioned him before, right? Who's he again?"

"The Devourer," Loki said, his face as pale as the fog surrounding us. "Your foolish mates are planning on bringing us directly into his maw."

"I'm sorry, that's really not an explanation," she snapped. "Some of us aren't all that well-versed in mythology."

Loki turned to look at her. His eyes seemed dark as midnight as his gaze locked on her small form. "Perhaps that is the problem, human—you and your kind have forgotten what you once knew to be true. You have forsaken the old ways. Forsaken your old gods, your old fears."

Annabel only blinked once, then turned to Bjarni.

"Your dad is speaking in riddles. Could someone please tell me in plain English why this Nidhug is so bad the god of misery is shaking in his boots? What can *possibly* be worse than what we've already seen? Because I gotta tell you, that sea serpent we flew over on our way to America was kind of terrifying on an entirely new level."

"Mischief," Loki bit. "The God of *Mischief.*"

Bjarni ignored him. "Níðhöggr isn't *worse* than Jörmungandr, per se. He is a monster that dwells underneath Yggdrasil, gnawing at its roots and feasting on the flesh of murderers, adulterers, and oath breakers. He is a great dragon, foretold to break free of his prison and fly across the worlds to herald Ragnarök. He is the embodiment of earthquakes, volcanos and destruction.

"And yes—we have to pass very close by the well he resides in to get to the portal. So long as he is asleep, we'll be fine."

Annabel swallowed thickly. "Oh. Great. Another well-dweller. At least it's not like Ragnarök is already here and there's every chance he's awake and ready to rumble..."

"We do not have another choice," I said, though I couldn't fault the fear wavering in her voice. "It's this portal, or nothing."

I know," she said, her lips flattening in a determined line. "We've survived so far. We'll survive a little dragon-action, too."

"Well. Hopefully there won't be any dragon action,"

Bjarni rumbled. He did not bother pointing out that any action involving an awake Níðhöggr would most definitely end in a gruesome death. And not for the dragon.

"You're mad," Loki hissed. "I've gone along with this nonsense so far, but enough is enough! I won't end my life in the maws of Níðhöggr for this folly!"

NIFLHEIM WAS QUIET. I had only briefly accompanied my father here once when I was young, and the heavy press of the fog and chill of the air had stayed in my memories. But even then, it had not been this silent. In the absence of warmth and light, there had still been life, albeit hidden.

Hurried footfalls from the darkness, vermin and serpents slithering underfoot—we had even caught a glimpse of one of the mist-like Jotunns that inhabited this world, though it had disappeared the moment it saw us. Beasts had howled at night, sending goosebumps up my adolescent skin even as I had put on a brave front for my father. The world was cast in eeriness then as well, but it was still different now.

This time... there was nothing. Not a snake rattled the frozen grass, no beasts called out in the night. There was only deep, ominous silence and that ever-present mist clinging to our faces and threatening to cloy its way into our lungs for every breath.

Except from Loki's muffled curses through the sock Bjarni had stuffed in his mouth when he grew tired of listening to his protests.

The journey was physically easier than the trek we had overcome in Midgard to reach the portal there. Despite the frozen ground underneath our feet, there was no snow to wade through and no heavy inclines either.

Yet as we made camp at the end of the second day, the mental drain was undeniable. I saw it in Bjarni's drawn features and felt it in the tension in my bond to Annabel. She was stressed and anxious, the barbed hook in my chest aching worse than my own worry for the day ahead. If we had estimated correctly, tomorrow would be the day we passed by the great well of Hvergelmir—and passed through the final portal to Asgard.

If.

I glanced at Annabel, who had pulled Loki's gag from his mouth to offer him water and food. If Níðhöggr still slept, before midnight tomorrow we might reunite with mine and Bjarni's brothers. Annabel's other mates.

It was an odd sensation, thinking about my omega reuniting with the alphas she had been longing for since we left. I was not *jealous*. Watching Bjarni with her that one night had provoked my possessive urges, sure, but all it had really done was make me more desperate to penetrate her myself. The thought of

Magni and Saga fucking her? That didn't faze me either.

And yet... it wasn't *not* jealousy. I had seen her fierce, protective love for them back in Asgard when she tried to challenge the god-king himself. Felt her longing to be reunited with them. And I knew, once they were free and with us again, it would no longer just be Bjarni's bond to her that left me on the outside. An intruder looking in.

I pushed down the violent roil in my gut at that thought and went to sit by the small fire Bjarni had started, grabbing myself a plate of the stew bubbling over it. It did not matter how she felt for her other mates. What was between her and I was a business arrangement. Fate's insistence. Why should I care that from tomorrow she would have three other alphas to dote on her, rather than just one? Her magic would be just as powerful—perhaps even more so.

The four of us ate in silence, the sound of firewood crackling only interrupted by occasional slurping. Even in Niflheim, Bjarni managed to cook delicious meals.

Loki's voice shattered the quietude. "I am curious, Modi."

I grimaced—having him silenced for most of the day had been a blessing, but Annabel insisted we remove the gag to let him eat his meals in peace.

"Don't make me stuff that sock back in there before you've finished," Bjarni warned. "You're not getting fed again before breakfast."

"If Thor has betrayed you, which side will you and your brother fall on? His? Or your newfound friends'?" Loki continued, ignoring his son.

"The Hel are you talking about?" I growled, lowering my spoon to glare at him.

"Don't listen to him—he's fucking with your mind again," Bjarni warned before he sat down his bowl with a sigh. "Time for the sock, old man."

"I am just asking a simple question." Loki shrugged, turning his focus back to his food. "You could be right—he could have sent you to capture me rather than go himself because he has full faith in your abilities. Sure, he wouldn't have known how that handy little connection to your new mate works, but let us say that he *did*, in fact, trust his son to bring me back.

"What I find ever so curious is how he ignored your plea for help. I am *certain* he knows nothing of this map my foolish son chose to reveal to you. How did he expect you to make it back in time to save Magni? Unless—"

"*Do not!*" I snarled. Fury at the mere thought of what he was hinting at pounded in my temples, making the stew thick in my throat. I thrust the bowl to the ground, glaring at the asshole trickster attempting to smear my father's name.

"Unless he never meant for you to return with me," Loki finished, raising his gaze once more. His dark eyes bored into mine.

"I thought you didn't know who the traitor was?" Annabel said.

"I do not." Loki shrugged again. "I am merely speculating. I find it odd that a man as dedicated to *honor* and *family* as Thor wouldn't come to his son's aid when both his sons' fates are on the line. And, seeing as I have a vested interest in your survival, little human... I can't help but wonder where your redheaded mates' loyalties will fall. *If* Thor turns out to be something other than he pretends."

Bjarni, who had made it to Loki's side, sock in hand, hesitated. His brows locked in a frown as he glanced back at me over his shoulder.

"You cannot seriously be listening to this horseshit," I growled, shock and fury lancing up my spine. "My father is no traitor!"

"Well, no... maybe not," Annabel said, her voice soft. "But..."

"But *nothing*." Betrayal stabbed through as I swung around to glare at my mate. She had *seen* me. Back in Oslo, she had forced her way into my innermost, and yet she thought for even a second that Loki's words might be anything other than poison spewed to sow suspicion between us?

"You dare question my father's loyalties? You dare question *my* loyalties? *You?*"

"Calm down." Bjarni moved fluidly, his shoulders widening as he stepped between Annabel and me, though he kept his pose nonthreatening. "No one's taking his word for anything. But you've got to admit—it's odd that Thor didn't come for us when you called on him, no?"

"Thor has served Asgard for eternity. You will not smear his name in my presence," I hissed, leveling my glare at him.

When Annabel came to stand by his side, her hand on his bicep as she looked at me with her brows locked in a matching frown to his, I narrowed my eyes further. *Just look at them!* They were so completely in sync. The picture-perfect pairing. They looked so at ease together, so... *right.* If it was not for Fate, Annabel would likely still have let him claim her and to Hel with the rest of us.

To Hel with *me.*

She thought I was sired by a man capable of bringing around the end of the worlds. She thought I was capable of betraying *her.*

I turned around before my temper got the better of me, stomping into the fog. This time, the chilly dampness of it clinging to my skin was a blessing against the pounding of blood in my temples.

"Modi!" Annabel called after me.

I ignored her, lengthening my strides as I disappeared into the mist.

THEY LET me cool off for the better part of an hour before they came for me.

I knew they had found me before I heard their steps. That aching in my chest from my bond to Annabel eased incrementally the closer she came, and through her, I sensed Bjarni's presence.

"Not smart to leave Loki unattended in the midst of Niflheim," I said, not bothering to rise from the fallen log of tree I had been sitting on for the past half hour.

"Not smart to storm off into the fog on your own," Annabel countered.

I looked over my shoulder at her just in time to see the outline of Bjarni's hulking figure retreating back into the mist, leaving her in my care.

"I am a god. I can take care of myself."

"I know." She hesitated for a moment, then stepped closer, stopping just a few feet from me.

I turned back to stare into the nothingness.

"Modi…" Her hesitation was present in her voice too. "I didn't mean to upset you. Neither of us did."

I closed my eyes as the throbbing in my blood threatened to return. "You did not mean to *upset* me, human? Did you not hear me? *I am a god.*"

I got to my feet and strode past the tree trunk, invading her personal space. She was small, an omega of stature if not of temperament, and I loomed over her. It felt good.

"Fate or no, you do not possess the ability to *upset* me."

She rolled her eyes. *Rolled. Her. Eyes.* "Yeah. Sure. You're a fountain of Zen—the embodiment of divine calm. Can we cut the bullshit for just a moment? Please? This is important. Can you think of any plausible reason for Thor to ignore your call?"

This again. I bared my teeth at her. "I am warning you, *omega*, do not repeat Loki's poison again."

Annabel huffed, frustration playing across her pretty features. "Modi... I know it's going to be tough to consider, but... we know there's a traitor in Asgard."

"Yes. It is Loki," I said, eyes narrowed to slits. "Which is why we have got him trussed up and are dragging him all the way back to Asgard."

"No," she said. "The traitor is in Asgard, and Loki hasn't been for a very long time. I'm not saying he's a saint, but he isn't the traitor we're looking for. I think it's someone else."

"Someone like my father?"

Annabel grimaced. "I don't know. But I saw you when he didn't respond to your call. You know something's not right about it. I'm not saying we charge in and accuse the god of thunder of anything, but Modi... you gotta be prepared to at least consider the possibility. And... and *if* he is... the traitor... I need you to tell me you won't turn on us."

And there it was. She thought I was capable of *turning* on her. She had no concept of how profoundly she had changed my very DNA, my every waken thought and connection I had ever had—no idea how tightly I was bound to her.

Because she did not feel the same. Her innermost

was split between four alphas, and I... I was the one she would have chosen to deny, had Fate let her.

Rage descended on me, a scalding counterpoint to the frosty mist clinging to my skin. I snarled, only losing myself further to the embrace of violence when she shrank back in the face of my anger.

"You think I will *hurt* you, omega?" My voice was twisted, unrecognizable, but I did not care. There was nothing but the fury. The betrayal.

Instincts.

"You think I, Modi the Brave, son of Thor, will *hurt* you? I suppose you do. If you think my father capable of betraying all nine worlds, you must think me capable of every horrible thing your little human mind can conjure up.

"There is only one thing I can do to you, omega. One single thing I can force upon you. You think I am a piece of shit? No better than Loki the Betrayer? By the Allfather—I will show you exactly what I am!"

She yipped when I grabbed for her, her hands reflexively coming up to stop me. It was easy to ignore her human weakness—but the look in her wide eyes proved much more difficult. For one agonizing heartbeat, she stared at me with genuine fear—and every ounce of strength in my body crumbled into a pile of ash.

But then, as if she saw something in my eyes too, her look of terror faded, leaving vulnerability and understanding behind.

Pity. She pities you.

I bared my teeth, anger rising again. She did not fight me when I yanked her toward me this time, and it only angered me more. *Toothless.* She knew I was not going to force her, not truly. She knew I was incapable. She was allowing me to act her alpha, *pretending* to surrender.

I tossed her over the barrel of the tree trunk I had sat on, my focus mercifully shifting at the sight of her ass thrust up and out in her tight leathers. *This.* This was the easy part.

I yanked her trousers down, pulling them over her boots so I could step in between her legs.

She twisted her neck to look at me over her shoulder, her lips parted in soft pants. "Modi," she whispered. "It's okay."

"I do not need your permission!" I growled, though we both knew I was lying.

I pressed my palm up between her thighs, reveling in the full-body shiver that transferred from her soft flesh into mine. She was not as dry as I had expected, but she was not wet enough for me either. Another day I might have knelt behind her and sucked her clit into my mouth until her pussy gushed for me—but not today.

"You ask if I will betray you," I rasped, rubbing my palm against her lower lips with enough force to catch her still-hidden clit. "Maybe I will. Maybe the Norns have woven it into their vile net. It will not be my fault then, will it? We are all just caught up in Fate's game, no free will of our own. That is why you and I are tied together in the first place, little omega. Why fight what Fate has decided?"

She mewled in response, spreading her thighs for my palm. Moisture clung to my skin and I smiled wryly.

"My poor omega. So willful, yet so completely enslaved to every base instinct. I *could* take you against your will—and your body would only aid me. Do you feel as trapped as I do?"

I undid my pants and pulled out my achingly hard dick, pressing it up against her lower back as I leaned in over her, my hand still working her rapidly dampening sex.

"Modi," she moaned. "Don't care. You're *mine!* Just fucking fuck me!"

She was as needy as when her heat had made her crawl on her knees to suck my dick. My body panged with longing to spear her open, and I growled and bit down on her neck where the fresh scar from my claim shone bright pink.

She went lax underneath me, her soft flesh wonderfully compliant against mine as she whimpered softly. Wetness gushed from her pussy, soaking my hand. She may be far too mouthy and demanding, but at least her body knew how a good omega behaved.

I relaxed my jaw and pushed back up, holding my weight on one hand on the trunk while I shifted the other from her pussy to my cock. Wet, hot heat enveloped my cockhead, and I groaned, all thoughts vanishing at that first, blissful touch of her cunt.

"Modi-*oh!* Ow! Slow... Please, slow!" Annabel's voice hitched as I pushed up inside of her, hilting her to the balls. She was so blessedly tight—too tight. A week without penetration had allowed her slick tunnel to turn less pliable.

"You wanted to get fucked," I snarled. I pulled my hips back, only to thrust back into her tight flesh with the full force of my divine body. "Little omega... you will be *fucked.*"

She howled underneath me, rearing up in an instinctive bid to save her little pussy. I pressed a hand between her shoulder blades and pinned her to the trunk, grabbing her hip for leverage with the other, and fucked up into her again.

And again. Her reason for being was to quell my need, quell the flaming anger, the devastation, the choking sense of despair, and I was not going to let her escape before she had done her duty. She was *my* omega, my vessel, my reason for existing.

Fuck!

Furious that even now, even as I pummeled her body to the tune of her screams and the wet *thwacks* of my hips smacking against her pussy and ass, I could not release the knowledge that all I was, was for her. Centuries of existing, centuries of building my power, of gaining glory and might on the battlefield meant *nothing.* The only thing that would ever matter was this tiny, infuriating human and how tightly she had me wrapped around her will.

Oh, but by the stars, she felt... she felt like *life*. I snarled with pleasure into the fog, clutching at her hip, drowning myself in her for every full thrust into her tight heat. Right now, there was only *us*. One in flesh as well as spirit.

I took her for every ounce she had and gave her everything of myself in return. I fucked her until her whimpers and cries turned to passionate moans, I fucked her through one orgasm, and then another. I fucked her until her moans turned to whimpers once more, pleas to finish spilling from her lips.

Finally, some long minutes later, when my rage was a distant memory and pleasure rolled through my veins like thunder, did I surrender to her cunt's demands.

"Mate," I moaned. "Anna!"

It was all the warning she had before my knot swelled hard and fast. I pressed inside her fully and stilled, instincts making me keep a firm hold of my mate as the thickness in her entrance turned painful and she squirmed to escape. I kept her pinned, forced her to accept the harsh stretch, groaning her name over and over while shudders of pleasure from the depths of my being wracked my powerful body.

My seed spilled into her in pulses, filling her in rhythm with my heartbeats. Completing our union in the most ancient, most primal way nature had created. In that moment, we were nothing but a man and his mate. An alpha worshipping his omega how she was born to be worshipped.

I relaxed over Annabel's prone body, wrapping my arms around her torso to ward her from the cold mist.

She gasped at the movement, shifting restlessly underneath me, the pull from our tie no doubt unpleasant. I hummed soothingly against her ear and reached underneath her to rub her clit.

Annabel moaned softly, her body turning instantly pliable underneath me. "Purr," she whispered, her voice hoarse from her screams. "Purr for me, Modi."

It took maybe twenty minutes before my brain came back from orbit. When I came to my senses again, I was lying on top of Annabel, keeping just enough weight off that she could still breathe. My purr rumbled loudly through the nothingness, keeping the omega underneath me docile despite the uncomfortableness of the rough tree trunk she was pressed into.

I swallowed the rumble in my chest, cutting the sound off so instantaneously the silence following seemed deafening.

Annabel finally stirred. "Mm? Is something wrong?" Her voice was groggy.

"Shh," I hissed, straining my senses against the fog. No sound reached me, and my nostrils were full of nothing but the scent of our sex. I waited for a full minute in silence before I finally relaxed. No beasts had snuck up on us while we mated.

Stupid.

I had lost myself completely in her, to the point that I had stopped paying attention to our surroundings. We might not have seen a single sign of life on our journey through Niflheim so far, but I should still have kept my wits about me. What if something had attacked while I was knot-deep inside her? What if I had let someone hurt her?

Sick dread helped the last of my cock's swelling to subside. I pulled from her with a grunt of sensation, pushing myself to standing before I refastened my pants. "We need to get back."

"Sure. Not a problem. Just need my legs to start functioning again," Annabel muttered. She pushed against the fallen tree, groaning with the effort.

I hesitated for a moment, the weight of her and Bjarni's accusations coming back now that I was no longer buried inside of her. The agony of our frayed bond returned as a dull, now familiar throb in my chest.

She managed to get upright, a hiss of breath escaping her as she caught her own weight. She limped as she picked up and pulled on her trousers and made her way toward me, making up my mind.

"I have you," I said, the innate gruffness in my voice softened some by my recent climax. I did not wait for her to respond, scooping her into my arms without looking at her face.

"Thanks," she said. Her voice was still groggy, and when I began walking us back to our small camp, her head came in to rest against my chest. She did not speak a single word on the way back, but her weight in my arms was a warm, comfortable reminder of her presence. And of our most recent union.

I had never had many thoughts on what my mate would be like, should I ever choose one, but I had had a hazy idea of the family I would create with her: a warm, comforting unit with me as its head. I would protect them, provide for them... and in return, I would be bathed in their love and adoration, be cared for and know I would always have that safe base to call home.

Instead I shared a willful little human with three other alphas—instead of a family unit, I was a small piece of a puzzle. Instead of warmth and adoration, there was pain and confusion.

Still... I could not deny that when I was with her, *inside* of her, everything was bliss. Everything felt better, warmer, *safer* than I had ever imagined it could.

In those moments, I loved her.

ANNABEL WAS fast asleep when I walked into our small campsite. Bjarni looked up from the fire he had been staring at, eyebrows raised.

I tilted my head toward the tent before I headed in there. I laid Annabel on the furs and tucked her in, taking a moment to look at her relaxed features. She looked so young when she slept. Young and innocent.

It was hard to believe that this tiny human held the fate of the nine worlds in her hands. Her entire lifespan was barely more than a blink in comparison to my own, yet I could no longer deny it. I had felt her power run through me like a current. Felt Bjarni's strength within her, bolstering my own.

In the end, it did not matter how I felt about it. She was my fate.

I left her to sleep, leaving the tent to rejoin Bjarni by the campfire. Loki was fast asleep on the other side, snoring quietly.

"I see you spared him the sock," I said, giving the God of Mischief a bitter look before I reached for my abandoned bowl. The food in it was steaming—a kind gesture from Bjarni, I suspected.

Bjarni shrugged. "Not much point when he's sleeping. I suspect he already said what he wanted to, anyway."

I narrowed my eyes at the blond giant. "I suspect you are right."

The corner of Bjarni's mouth quirked up in a half-smile. "She didn't fuck the rage fully out of you, then?"

"It takes more than a bit of sex to forget someone accusing your father of treason. I would have thought you were familiar with the concept," I replied tartly.

Bjarni chuckled. "You could say that, yeah." He sighed and brushed his hand through his beard, the mirth leaving his eyes as he glanced at the still-snoring Loki. "He was never the best of fathers. Pretty much left us to our mother to raise, stopped by with presents now and then. Had a lot of expectations of us. It didn't stop me from loving him, y'know? Even now, knowing he'd abandon us without another thought just to save himself... even if it does turn out he's responsible for Ragnarök... He's still my father."

I grunted. Being sired by Loki had to be a pretty shitty lot. "At least you're not an eight-legged horse logging around some haughty god all day."

Bjarni snorted. "True. Could be worse. I could be splashing around the Atlantic, burping up shipping containers."

We sat in silence for a bit while I ate. It was hard to hold back a hum of appreciation as the stew passed my lips and danced on my tongue—fucking Annabel had left me pretty depleted, and for all his faults, this Lokisson was an excellent cook.

"What was it like growing up with Thor as your father?" he asked after a little while.

I arched an eyebrow at him, still chewing on a mouthful of stew.

His lip curled up in a half-smile again. "I was told a lot of stories about your sire as a kid—a lot of them probably not entirely true. I always wondered what it'd be like—growing up the golden son of Asgard's favored warrior. I suspect you're not unfamiliar with the burden of grand expectations."

I shrugged, refocusing on the stew. "I never minded. It is an honor to carry out my duties as Thor's heir."

"Your brother seems... of a somewhat different view," Bjarni said, his tone still casual. "Sure, he was all *'I am the son of Thor, you will respect my authority'* in the beginning, but I got the impression he has a more troubled relationship with your father."

Images I did not care to entertain came up—of Magni as an adolescent boy, recently arrived in Trudheim, sobbing in the training yard after a lesson from our father, wooden sword still dangling from his hand. Red stripes from Thor's belt coloring his pale skin.

I has been too young to realize how ashamed he had been and kept asking him why he was crying. He had eventually confessed that our father had told him his *"Jotunn ways"* were an abomination, and he would beat them out of him if he had to.

Magni had made me swear to keep that incident a secret, and I had. But my young eyes were open from then on, however much I wished they had not been. I saw the mistreatment my mother bestowed on him, and I saw Thor accept it. I saw Thor's pride when Magni excelled at combat, and his anger and disappointment when he did not.

And I saw Magni redirect our father's temper onto himself whenever I had failed, oftentimes letting me have the glory when an accomplishment belonged to us both. Thor liked to brag about us. He told tales of our prowess in the mead halls of Valhalla and offered our strength up in duels that we always won.

"My father is not the traitor," I said quietly, finally putting the bowl of stew aside. "He did not come when I called to him not because he wants us to fail, but *because* I failed. He gave me the task of bringing Loki back. If he has to come *rescue* me, then I am an embarrassment. Unworthy of a place by his side. And so is Magni. That is what you wanted to know, is it not? That was the purpose of this little bonding moment?"

Bjarni hummed a thoughtful tune. "In part."

"In part?" I glared at him, but my heart was not in it. Not truly. I was too tired and light from sex, and too... oddly *calm*. Telling Bjarni what I had never told another soul did not feel like divulging my secrets to an enemy. It felt like talking with a friend. Or a brother.

"You are my mate's mate. That makes you my family," he rumbled, stretching his long legs out toward the fire. "I feel you through Annabel, yet there's so much animosity in our blood. I'm not suggesting we mend fences the way Saga and Magni did, but maybe we can find other ways to see eye to eye. Seems we both have shitty fathers—that's something, eh?"

I chuffed an amused snort. "That is something."

Silence settled again, save Loki's soft snores and the crackle from the fire. I thought about what he had said —and what I had said. And about how resolute Magni had been in his idea that I share Annabel with him— and the Lokissons. How undeniably in love he was with the feral little thing. And her with him. With *all* of them.

Perhaps one day, she would love me, too. Maybe then the thought of giving her my heart would not fill me with gut-wrenching terror.

"How did they mend fences? Magni and Saga?" I asked, piercing the silence.

This time, the amused snort was Bjarni's. "You don't want to know. Trust me." He stretched and yawned. "Want first sleep?"

I darted a glance at the tent. The thought of pulling Annabel into me as sleep took me away was pleasant— and painful. A stab from where my bond hooked made me shake my head with a grimace. I wasn't ready to face the stark contrast between our connectedness during sex and the gaping chasm between us the rest of the time.

"No. It is your turn."

He nodded and threw another piece of scavenged wood on the fire before he got to his feet. "Night, then. Brother."

32

____

ANNABEL

I awoke nestled in the crook of Bjarni's arm. He was still fast asleep, sprawled out on his back as if the chill in the air didn't bother him in the least. Which it probably didn't, what with him being an alpha god and running at about a million degrees.

I curled up into him as tightly as I could, pressing my icy toes against his shins. Even though he'd clearly held me all night, my body temperature was still lower than ideal. Damn Fimbulwinter.

Bjarni groaned in protest, but obligingly rolled over so he could wrap me up in his grasp, enveloping me in all that delicious heat of his.

"Mmm. Thanks," I mumbled, rubbing my nose against his blond chest hair as my feet climbed higher up his legs.

He clamped his knees together around them, stopping their ascent before grunting sleepily into my hair. "Is it dawn?"

"Hard to tell when it's constantly gray outside," I said. "But I feel moderately less exhausted than I did when I fell asleep, so I guess?"

He sighed. "Ah. Modi let me have the night, then. I'd be grateful, but if we're passing Níðhöggr's well today, I'd have preferred him to be at least semi-rested."

Something heavy dropped in my gut, removing the pleasant vestiges of sleep from my mind. "Oh."

"I know, sweetie," he rumbled, patting my head. "He's just... not that bright when it comes to his feelings for you. Give him time. He'll get there in the end like the rest of us have."

I grimaced. "I'm pretty sure he has no interest in *feelings*." Apart from when he was fucking me. That was the only time there wasn't any barrier between us, the only time being with him felt good. Right.

"Well, you're not that bright about it, either," Bjarni said, a good-natured smile in his voice. He dipped his head to brush a kiss to my lips before he rolled out from underneath the furs covering us.

"I'm gonna get breakfast started. If all goes well, we'll be back in Asgard tonight. Once you're reunited with Saga and Magni, I suspect you're going to feel a whole lot better."

A jolt of excitement burned away my gloom. *Saga and Magni!* I'd done my best to push down my intense longing for my two first mates, but it'd been there like a gnawing, aching wound for every second of every day. The thought of finally being with them again, knowing that I was only hours away from pressing myself into their arms, went a long way to lighten my mood.

It lasted until a little while later when Bjarni called to me to come get my breakfast.

I pushed out from the tent, eager to get started with the day—until my gaze fell on Modi.

My redheaded mate sat with his own bowl of porridge and salted meat, a grim expression on his handsome features. Upon my exit from the tent, his eyes darted from the fire to me for just a sliver of a second. It was long enough for the agony in our bond to flare, my heart giving a dull spasm in response.

Last night I'd gone to him to try and soothe his pain. It was obvious he wasn't thrilled at the thought of his father betraying him—or the rest of the worlds. But I hadn't managed to do that. All I'd accomplished was a moment's respite. I'd allowed him to slake his anger between my thighs, but in the end, it changed nothing.

"Eat up, sweetie," Bjarni said, his large hand landing on my shoulder as he thrust a bowl of breakfast at me with the other. "It's going to be a long day. And challenging. We all need to keep our focus—passing Hvergelmir will require all of us to be alert at all times. *All* of us."

The last bit he said with a meaningful stare at his father, who once again had a sock stuck in his mouth. Seemed Loki had gotten mouthy again.

The dark-haired god only gave him a reproachful glare in response.

I nodded, pushing the pain of my damaged bond to Modi to the back of my mind as well as I could. By now, I was used to feeling broken. It was a constant, gnawing agony, the result of being torn into four jagged pieces. If we made it through the day, at least by the end of it I would be reunited with Magni and Saga. Then there would only be one source of pain left.

I sat down by the fire and looked at my two mates. "Okay. What's the plan?"

"It's at least eight hours to Hvergelmir," Modi said, apparently having also decided to pretend like last night hadn't happened. "Once we're close, we will know if Níðhöggr is awake. If he isn't, passage should be easy."

"If he is," Bjarni continued, "we will have to rely on your magic to keep us hidden. Once we've passed, it's less than half an hour to the portal."

I choked. "*My* magic? I don't know how—" My voice died when Bjarni raised his hand.

"You've proven time and time again that your strength and resilience is more than enough to carry us through. It won't be any different this time. Modi and I will be there to guide you. Now is not the time to doubt yourself, mate. We're on the final stretch."

I nodded. He was right. Whatever I had to do to get us back to Saga and Magni, I would find a way.

∼

THE NEARER we came to Nidhug's well, the lighter the fog became. It was so gradual, it wasn't before I noticed the huge, dark surface rising high on our right side that I realized how much easier it was to see my travel companions now.

"What's that?" I asked, staring at the dark thing. In all directions, it stretched far out of my field of vision, the mist hiding its true size, but the looming nature of it reminded me of a mountain range.

"One of Yggdrasil's roots," Modi answered. He was up front, leading us through the frozen wasteland for the past few hours. He and Bjarni still took turns, even though there was no snow to press down to ease my way here. "The World Tree gets much of its nourishment from the springs surrounding Hvergelmir."

"It looks like a mountain," I said, squinting to see it better through the mist. Now that I knew it was a root, I could sense that the surface of it was a different texture than I would have expected from something shaped from rock.

"It's big as one too," Bjarni rumbled from behind me. "We're getting close—if the fog is lifting, it means the heat from the springs is not too far."

"Or it means Níðhöggr is awake and spewing his fire into the air," Modi mumbled.

Muffled protestations came from behind Bjarni. Apparently Loki wasn't pleased with that suggestion.

"I agree," my blond mate said matter-of-factly. "Let's not jinx it, hmm?"

Modi only chuffed in response.

IT TOOK ONLY a couple more hours of walking until the mist was fully gone, revealing the landscape around us for the first time. But where it had been frozen and dead for the rest of our journey, here green sprouted from the ground, flowers, bushes and trees dotting the land in a kaleidoscope of colors.

I could now make out the full scope of the root guiding our path to the right, and it was a magnificent sight to behold. It was indeed as large as a mountain range, its form twisting and gnarly like the roots of an ancient oak. It stretched into the sky and deep into the horizon, far past where my eyes could see, a dark contrast to the lush greenery surrounding us.

"This is the only place of warmth and fertility in Niflheim," Modi said. He must have noticed my open-mouthed stare. "The springs fight back the icy grip of the rest of the realm."

"It should be teeming with life," I mumbled. "I mean... mammals. Birds. Why is it as quiet as the rest of this word?"

"Niflheim's inhabitants never come here," Bjarni said. "Nothing that wishes to live trespasses on Níðhöggr's domain. It's far odder that we have had no run-ins on the rest of our journey."

"Great. That's exactly what I needed to hear right now," I muttered. "Why—"

A rumble interrupted me. It seemed to come from above and below—the sky, the earth beneath our feet, the giant root disappearing into the distance.

Another rumble, and this time the ground swayed beneath us and made Yggdrasil's root tremor.

I gasped and stumbled forward, but managed to get my bearings by grabbing on to Modi's coat until the earth finally stilled again.

"W-What the hell was that?" I croaked, looking to my travel companions for an answer.

"That was Níðhöggr," Bjarni replied, his voice betraying the same grimness as was written across all three gods' features. "The dragon is awake."

33

"Awake? He's awake?" The quaking in Annabel's voice made me want to reach for her to offer what comfort I could, but Bjarni beat me to it.

"Yes." I scrubbed my face with both hands and looked toward the horizon where the steam from the springs surrounding Hvergelmir met the air. "Unfortunately."

"It's not a problem," Bjarni said, though the dark look on his face betrayed his true feelings on the subject. "Annabel will shield us and we will make it past."

Behind him, Loki's eyes went wide and muffled noises of outrage spilled past the sock still firmly wedged in his mouth. Bjarni gave him an annoyed glance.

"I suggest you quiet down, old man. We're not far

out now. A few more miles and he'll be able to hear you."

Loki let out a scream of rage—at least I assumed it was of rage, judging by how the veins in his neck and forehead bulged—but when Bjarni just snorted, he quieted with a murderous glare at his son.

"Yes," I said, looking back to my mate. Bjarni still had his arms around her, but this time it did not fill me with anger to see a display of how close they were—just sadness.

I pushed it away and focused on the task ahead. "Annabel, you will need to rise a shield now. I do not want to risk us getting too close. I know every extra minute will be a drain on your power, but I will lend you what strength I can. If he catches sight of us..."

I did not have to finish that sentence. Annabel nodded, her mouth drawn into a grim line. "Then we'll be crunchy and dipped in ketchup."

"What?"

She shook her head. "Never mind. Let's do this. Guide me."

I reached for her with my hand and magic, pushing my power inside of her not unlike how I had penetrated her last night.

She gasped in response, and I had to force down my body's reaction to the sound. *Not the time.*

Her golden light welled up around me, coming willingly when I called to it. I felt her consciousness brush against mine and shuddered with the pleasure of it.

Like sex.

I caught her thought—or the *feeling* of her thought—and the bubbling sensation of her amusement immediately after, along with a touch of embarrassment. Apparently she had not meant for me to hear that.

I pushed a brush of admonishment at her—ignoring my own thoughts desperately trying to turn in that direction as well. There was no denying the intimacy of taking control of her powers like this—of being *inside* her, touching her innermost—but we had a dragon to slip past, and a tight schedule to stick to.

If we were not in Valhalla by tomorrow evening at the latest...

With a force of will, I focused on our combined magic and lifted it up and away from our intermingled essences. When I opened my eyes, a golden shimmer caved around us, transparent apart from the odd sparkle of magic.

I looked back down at Annabel, a touch of pride in my gut. She was so strong. If she ever received true training, there was no telling how powerful she could become.

"How is it?" I asked, scanning her face for signs of strain. "Are you good?"

"Mm, I think so. For now." She gave me a small smile. "Not sure for how long, though."

"Let me know when you need support." I lifted my hand from her nape and let it hover for a moment by her cheek. I wanted to brush away the strand of hair clinging to her skin there, but I stopped myself.

Sighing, I pulled my hand to my side and turned to Bjarni. "All right. Forward."

THE CLOSER WE came to Hvergelmir, the more sulfur tainted the air. But it was not just the scent from the multiple hot springs surrounding the well that warned of our closeness to the only inhabitant in the region. Periodically the ground would tremble underneath our feet, and what had first sounded like distant thunder soon became distinguishable as animalistic roars.

"Sounds like he's in a bad mood," Bjarni murmured.

"Shh," I shushed, pointing out a shadow on the top of Yggdrasil's root. "So long as he stays up there, we should be able to slip by underneath him without being detected. How is the cover holding up, Anna?"

She nodded, but the sweat beading on her forehead told its own story. Gently I cradled the back of her neck and let a small part of my magic bolster her. She gave me a brief smile in response.

"I'm okay," she rasped, voice low. "Save your strength, Modi. If this doesn't go to plan..."

"It will," Bjarni assured from behind her, placing his rope-free hand on her lower back. "Okay, let's focus. See that thin strip of land below the root, by that large body of water to the left? That will take us past Hvergelmir.

We follow that past the well, it will lead us directly to the portal."

"And right past Níðhöggr," I mumbled. "But so long as he stays up on the rim... We will not get a better chance. Okay. It is time. Everyone—keep quiet. Not a word until we are at the portal. Move fast and light-footed. Ready?"

Annabel and Bjarni nodded solemnly—only Loki frantically shook his head, but even he kept his protests muted this time. When Bjarni gave his rope a yank, he followed along without further objections.

It did not take us long before we were close enough to get a better view of Níðhöggr. Even from so far below, he made a formidable figure.

I had never actually seen him before—when my father brought me to Niflheim, we had stayed in the colder regions—and the sight of him struck me with awe. He had to be at least the size of that carriage station we had arrived at in the settlement of Seattle, his scales inky black against the sky. When he roared, he extended his massive wingspan, casting a threatening shadow over the ground below as he sent a spire of flames into the sky.

A pang in my chest was followed by the acrid scent of my omega's fear. I reached back, instinctively looking to soothe Annabel, and bumped my fingers into Bjarni's.

A quick look over my shoulder confirmed he had reacted on the same instincts, our hands colliding on her shoulder. He gave me a wry smile and nodded, urging me to continue forward.

Right. Annabel's fear was natural, and slowing down to try and comfort her here would only prolong the danger.

I turned back to the path and led us forward.

We kept a good pace, and soon we reached the edge of the great well Hvergelmir. Annabel gasped from behind me, and I could not blame her. The great stone circle spanned several hundred yards across, sitting like a dark, yawning maw surrounded by steaming springs pooling around its outer walls. It was truly a wonder to behold.

A bone-chilling screech from high above tore us from our reverence. The ground shook, making Annabel stumble into my back, but it only lasted for a moment.

Then a chilling shadow spread above us, plunging us into darkness. The wind pressure that followed flattened us against the grass.

I forced my way back up to my knees and looked up. The sight that met me lodged my heart in my throat.

Níðhöggr was directly above us, gliding down from his perch atop the mighty root. Every beat of his terrible wings pressed another gust of wind down upon us, getting stronger the closer he came.

Annabel whimpered, and when I turned to look, she had both hands pressed against her mouth and tears of terror trickling from the corners of her eyes. I grasped her shoulder and let my power meld with hers, ensuring she did not drop the magical barrier.

From her other side, Bjarni leaned halfway over her, using his body to shield her from the terrible beast. I felt him through our bond, felt him push soothing calmness at her until she stopped trembling and gently nudged my presence from within her, resuming control just as the dragon landed on the edge of the mighty well.

A great thud made the ground shudder underneath us, screeching of claws against stones sending painful jabs through my brain. He roared again, shaking his great, serpentine head as if angry with something, but folded his wings in tight against his body. He had settled on the edge of the well less than thirty yards from us.

Time seemed to stand still. The four of us remained frozen, all of us staring at the great beast, trying to control our breathing as we watched him for any sign that he might have noticed us.

But Níðhöggr seemed oblivious to our presence. He scraped at the well with his claws, bending his long neck to gnaw at bark from the World Tree stuck in one of the gleaming talons. This close I could make out his every scale, and the subtle gleam of orange fire reflecting from within him in jagged lines along their seams. The thought struck me that no one who had survived to tell the tale had ever been this close to the great beast before.

Careful not to make a sound, I waved a hand at my companions. With or without my aid, Annabel would only be able to keep the shield up for so long before her powers ran dry. We could not wait here until Níðhöggr decided to take off again. So long as we moved carefully, we should be able to pass him.

Slowly, making sure to keep my sword pressed against my thigh to silence it, I got to my feet before turning to help up Annabel, then Bjarni and Loki as well. I pressed a finger to my lips, though at this point it was hardly necessary to remind anyone of the importance of silence, and caught Annabel's wide-eyed stare. She was clinging to Bjarni's free hand, but her eyes were glued to me, searching for reassurance and leadership.

I nodded, an unspoken promise that I would get her through this, and then returned my focus to the dragon and the path ahead.

One step at a time, we moved along the narrow strip of grass between the great root to our right and the well on our left. To my great relief, Níðhöggr did not so much as look in our direction.

We were going to make it.

We were almost past the beast when a soft touch of wind brushed like a lover's caress against my cheek, cooling the sweat of concentration beading there.

Just a few hundred more yards and the worst of the danger would be over.

A deep rumble to our left made my heart skip a beat. It was a low, rippling growl of anger and inquiry. I stared up at Níðhöggr, my blood turning to ice in my veins when he lifted his head, nostrils flaring.

He smells us.

The realization hit me like a ton of rocks, but I did not manage to move before he turned his head and stared straight at us.

The air trembled around him as he drew in breath and opened his maw. In its depths, an inferno swelled.

34

ANNABEL

"*Down!*" Modi's roar was followed by his hand grasping my nape, his power forcing its way into mine in the blink of an eye, our combined magic strengthening what had been nothing more than a cover into a shield.

He landed on top of me, covering half my body with his own. My other half was pressed underneath Bjarni as he also dove on top of me.

The next second fire blazed against us, splitting just above our heads and encircling us around Modi's and my combined shield. The grass ignited and turned to ash, forming a perfect circle around us.

I felt the fire as a heavy press, its intensity forcing my magic out in order to sustain the shield. I gritted my teeth and clung to my mates for strength, knowing that if I dropped it, we too would be nothing but ash on the ground.

The fire flamed around us in what felt like one long, eternal moment, then disappeared just as abruptly.

I gasped for breath as the pressure lifted off my magical shield, rolling to my back when both my mates sprung to their feet, swords drawn as they stared at the dragon.

"We have to run," I panted between breaths, scrambling to get up as well. "I can't hold off many more of that kind of attack. Not even with your help."

"It will not help," Modi said, his air coming out in harsh breaths as well. "We will not make it to the portal before he is through our defenses."

The dragon growled again, making every hair on my body stand on end. With a deep inhale, he sent another breath of fire at us.

"Then what do you suggest? *Fuck!*" I shouted to be heard over the roar of the flames, hooking my fingers into his and Bjarni's flesh to draw on their strength again.

I wasn't an experienced magic-user, and the few times I had used my powers had been nothing like this. This felt like I was physically trying to hold up a heavy iron shield while an enemy battered at it with the strength of a mountain.

He hesitated, my redheaded mate, his eyes flicking from Bjarni to me. Sorrow settled in the blue depths, followed by steadfast resolve. His hand came up to cup the back of my head, pulling me into his chest with enough strength to bruise my flesh where it met his.

"*Uff*, Modi, what are you—"

He cut off my protest with a searing kiss, his lips harsh and demanding against mine. A breath and he was gone, pulling away from me as I struggled to keep my focus on the shield rather than that bone-shattering kiss.

"You do not need me, Annabel. Remember that. It will hurt, but in the end, you will be okay. You have three other mates—mates you love. They will get you through it, I promise you. They will see you heal."

"What?" I wasn't following him at all. He was making little sense, and I looked past him to see the dragon descend from its perch on the giant well, lumbering toward us on all fours. Apparently it had decided that fire wasn't going to drive us out into the open, and I wasn't keen on finding out what other methods it had planned to get at its dinner.

"He's coming!"

But Modi didn't move. Instead he looked to Bjarni. "I am going to draw his attention. Once he is locked on me, you take our mate and our captive and run. Do not stop running until you are through that portal."

It was only then that it dawned on me what he was planning.

"No! Modi, what?!" I reached for him, but he stepped back and away from the protection of my magic, turning to face the dragon.

"Come get me then, you ugly lizard!" he bellowed.

The giant dragon turned its head, its window-sized

eyes focusing on him as he moved sideways, away from us.

"Bjarni!" I screeched, hysteria finally taking over. "He's going to die!"

Lightning slammed down from the sky, hitting the dragon's inky scales. A horrible sound, like metal scraping along concrete, echoed through the air. Ozone mixed with the smell of the charred grass, but Nidhug didn't have so much as a scratch. He swung fully around toward Modi, drawing in a lungful of air to ignite his horrible fire once more.

I reacted on instinct, slinging the magical shield protecting us outward. It wrapped around Modi in the last possible second, flames bending around him and leaving him unharmed.

"*Fuck!*" Bjarni cursed. "*Shit,* that goddamn fool!" He stared at me, eyes wide and pupils dilated. I recognized his battle lust descending, but behind it was panic.

"Sweetie—I'm going to need you to do whatever it was you did when we caught *him.*" He nodded at Loki, then pulled me in for my second desperate kiss, his beard brushing against my face as his lips danced over mine.

Then he handed me Loki's rope, stepped back, and turned toward Nidhug and Modi, drawing his sword.

"He's wrong," he said. "You need him." And he too charged at the train-station sized dragon, roaring a battle cry.

"Jesus fucking Christ!" Everything in me roiled as

my mates fought off against a creature they both knew couldn't be killed. "No, no, no!"

Bjarni sprinted across the grass and jumped, thrusting his blade at Nidhug's side. The metal screeched against his scale, a slightly duller tone than the lightning, sending Bjarni flying backwards from impact.

I reached out with my magic, tendrils of it melding with the bonds I shared with both men without my conscious input. It was like a puzzle piece snapping into place—that perfect connection I'd felt with them only once before. Their battle rage was mine, their bravery, their fury, and their desperation to ensure my survival.

I caught Bjarni before he hit the ground, mine and Modi's powers cushioning his fall. He immediately launched himself across the clearing again, sword drawn.

I tried to focus my magic into his blade, but caught the glow of fire out of the corner of my eye. In the last second, I changed direction and pulled the barrier up around Modi again, shielding him from the flames.

Pain lanced through my body. Nidhug caught Bjarni with one of its claws, smacking him into the ground and tearing a cut along his thigh.

I screamed, fear and fury blending into a desperate inferno as I shielded my blond mate from the dragon's wrath, too.

Sweat beaded on my brow and my pulse drummed

in my ears, muffling all other noise. My magic was draining. Fast.

Keep fighting!

I don't know whose command lanced through my mind, but it gave me another surge of energy. I roared a challenge and gathered my power, thrusting it outward with all my might. The golden ball of energy soared through the air and slammed into Nidhug's side with a low rumble.

The dragon staggered, and I had a moment's worth of elation. He *could* be defeated!

Snarling, he swung his enormous head around, his alien eyes locking on me. He flapped his wings, the gust of it pushing both me and Loki by my side to the ground before he opened his maw and shot a burst of fire at us.

No! No!

Sickening fear that didn't belong to me seized my body. From each side of the dragon, my mates shouted and beat at its impenetrable scales, lightning bolts bouncing off its flesh as they did everything in their power to take the beast's focus away from me.

Nidhug ignored them as if they were nothing more than annoying flies.

I managed to raise the shield before its fire hit, groaning with the effort of keeping it up as the power of the dragon beat down upon me.

Hands grabbed onto my shoulder and shook.

I hissed, looking behind me at Loki, who was shaking me hard enough to disturb my concentration.

"If I drop this fucking shield, we're both dead!" I growled between labored breaths.

"*Hmmmmnng!*" He released my shoulder, but held out his bound wrists, his dark eyes imploring as he gestured toward the still-fire-breathing dragon. Even without words, his plea was clear.

I stared at him, weighing my options. This was Loki, god of fucking everyone over. There was every chance he'd make a run for it the moment he was free, and I was in no state to stop him.

But... if we didn't get help, we would be dead in a very short time, anyway. I only had minutes left of my magic reserves.

I pulled the sock from his mouth and yanked at the tight knots tying his wrists together. My divided attention made the shield above us flicker, heat from the flames encasing us slipping through.

"Shit!" I pushed harder, forcing my magic out again, until the heat eased. Only when the flames relented did I return to Loki, franticly pulling at his rope.

"Go for his tendons!" Loki roared at my mates, who were still fighting to regain Nidhug's attention. "Quick!"

They moved as one, darting behind a hind leg each. They swung their swords in unison, hammering them in against the tendons above his heel.

The dragon snarled and turned his long neck toward them, whipping his tail like a weapon. They both sprang aside before he could hit them, and he turned to swing at them with his claws.

"Hurry," Loki breathed. "They aren't going to last long without your magic shielding them, and once they're dead, he's coming for us."

"Noble to the fucking end," I growled, pulling desperately at the knots. Whoever'd bound them—Bjarni, if memory served—had been overzealous in his execution. I had to grasp onto one of the flickering tendrils of my magic and shot a bolt into the rope to force the first knot apart. The rest came easier.

The rope fell to the ground by his feet and I stared up at the dark god, waiting for him to snap his fingers and disappear in a cloud of charcoal mist. Or possibly bats.

Another searing burst of pain along my back made me spin around to the horrifying vision of Modi falling to the ground, ruby liquid spraying from a long gash in his back. Nidhug pulled back his mighty claw dripping with my mate's lifeblood, readying his final strike.

"*Modi!*" I screamed, throwing everything I had at him.

My magic sliced through the air and burst against the dragon's leg, shoving him off course. He hissed and righted himself, but instead of coming for me, he opened his maw, focusing on my wounded mate lying gasping before him.

I tried to force another bolt of magic out, but all I

caught were a few embers that sparked in the air around me before fizzing into nothing.

Panting, I collapsed, my vision swimming. I had no more to give.

Modi. Modi. No.

A cool hand wrapped around my nape and shocks of power rushed through my body like voltage rushing through a depleted battery. I jerked and spasmed, the intensity forced through me too much for my body and mind.

"Meld with them. Now!"

Loki's command came with the strength of a hundred barking hounds, and I reacted on it without thought. I reached for my mates through our bonds, pulling them to me with everything I was.

His magic burst through me like an invasive ravishing, horrible yet powerful, unlike anything I'd experienced before. He fanned the embers of my own magic, and through me connected to my mates, pulling their strength into me.

Lightning flashed, the sky above the well turning black. Everything took on an ashen color, a living, breathing black-and-white image.

Lightning flashed again, this time striking the dragon. Another bolt struck his scales, the horrible screech of impact making my teeth smart.

Nidhug roared, swinging his huge body from Modi to us. When he breathed his fire, I was ready with the shield.

Bjarni ran around the giant beast's body while he was preoccupied with me and Loki, sword gleaming in his hand.

"Infuse his weapon!" Loki shouted over the roar of the fire. "He needs your power to penetrate the scales!"

I reached out, my consciousness entering Bjarni's through our bond. He welcomed me, warmth and love and fear of loss so intense it threatened to shatter my focus enveloping me. I pushed through and into his blood, down, down until I reached the metal of his sword. It hummed and sucked in every ounce of magic I pushed into the sharp steel.

I jolted back into my own body just in time to see Bjarni roll underneath the mighty beast and aim his sword straight up at its chest.

Another shattering bolt of lightning slammed into Nidhug's back, making him toss his head back with a roar, fire gathering in his throat.

But before he could aim it at us again, Bjarni thrust his sword up with all his strength, his muscles bulging as the tip sliced through the dragon's chest and sunk into its body all the way to the hilt.

Nidhug's roar died in a long, bone-chilling wail. It stumbled, reaching for the sword with its front claws. Bjarni rolled away and scrambled to his feet just as the dragon slumped to its side, its enormous body colliding with the ground sending a shockwave through the landscape.

I fell to my knees next to Loki, bracing my hands

against the singed grass to watch the dragon's death throes. The stone wall around the well shattered from his kicks, huge boulders flying into its depths with hollow clatters until finally Nidhug stilled.

Dead.

Victory brought me the rush I needed to scramble to my feet, my focus shifting from the defeat of an impossible foe to fear once more.

Modi was injured.

Spurred by adrenaline and fear, I ran across the battlefield toward his slumped figure lying on a small patch of green amidst a sea of ash and embers. The second I was by his side, I fell to my knees and grasped his face between my hands, my only thought to look into his eyes once more.

Modi groaned, his eyelids fluttering open. His blue gaze met mine, the pain in them undeniable.

"Oh, Modi!" I pressed my mouth to his, breathing in his scent, roaming my fingers over his shoulders, his hair and his jaw in search for confirmation that he was there, that he wouldn't leave me.

Only when his arms came up to rest around my body did I pull back, certain that yes, he was going to make it.

"You absolute twat!" I snarled, smacking my palm against his chest.

He coughed and groaned in protest.

"What the fuck did you think you were doing, charging in against a fucking *dragon* like that? Telling me that I don't need you? That we should run away and let you fucking *die?*" I hit him again.

"Anna," he mumbled, reaching up to capture my wrist before I could whack him a third time. "I could not... let you die."

"Why on Earth would you think *I* could let *you* die?" I snarled. "This stupid bond goes both ways!"

"No. Ours is... damaged." He coughed again, wincing as he did. "You will never love me.... like you do them. My fate... My fate is to die for you." Then his eyes widened a little. "You... you thwarted Fate! You were meant to run!"

I stared at him, mouth agape as the million insults I wanted to hurl at him fought to be the winner. This idiot alpha really believed that Fate had woven us together so that he could *die* for me?

Then the full impact of his words set in and sorrow flooded my chest. He thought I would never love him, and how could I blame him? I'd thought the same thing, wallowing in the pain and longing of my bonds to Saga and Magni. Even Bjarni... I'd thought I couldn't love him, when the truth was right there, staring me in the face.

I'd been so stupid. So goddamn, inexcusably stupid.

"I love you," I whispered, wiping at the tears that started trickling from the corners of my eyes. "You're every bit my mate, every bit a part of my soul. There is no difference in how much I need each one of you,

Modi. How could you think I would run and leave you to die? You're my *mate*. My life."

He stared up at me, the expression in his blue eyes inscrutable, but I felt the roil of his emotions in our bond. "How? How can you love me? I have felt your anguish since the day I put my mark on your neck. Your regret."

"As I have felt yours," I said softly, cupping his cheek with my now-damp hand. "Do you love me, Modi?"

His gaze didn't waver from mine as the silence stretched between us. Finally, he said, "I would die for you a thousand times over, Annabel. I did not choose to love you. Fate forced me to. But I cannot deny it. Not anymore."

I cracked a smile at the regretful notion to his confession of love. "That's what every girl wants to hear."

He snorted a laugh that devolved into another cough.

"I need to heal you," I said, frowning down at his bloodied body, my focus switching back to the present.

"You do not have the strength," he murmured, eyelids closing halfway. "I just need... to rest for a little while."

"We don't have time for rest." The rumble of Bjarni's voice made me look up. My blond mate stood behind me, the golden rope I'd untied from Loki's wrists in his hand, now looped more loosely around the dark god's neck. They both looked as exhausted as Modi and me.

"Help her," Bjarni said, nudging his father toward me before he slid the rope off his neck, though he stayed alert.

"Isn't it enough that I saved the day and killed the bloody dragon?" Loki muttered. But—somewhat to my surprise—he knelt by my side and put his hand on my nape. His magic filled me again, far less intense but still unpleasant.

I suppressed the shudder of his presence inside of me and grasped on to his offered power, directing it through my own before I let it spill into Modi's broken body.

Modi's injury was deep and ran the length of his spine, and it took me the better part of an hour to heal it enough so that he could sit up.

"That is enough, Anna," he said, grasping the hand I'd pushed against his chest and lifting it off, separating my magic from his wound.

I looked him over, squinting to focus on his face when white dots danced in front of my eyes.

"You have used too much of your energy, mate," he murmured, pressing my hand to his lips before he stroked my cheek. When our eyes met, the emotion I saw dancing in his made my heart stutter.

Fate might have forced it, but yes, he did love me. We'd both been such fools.

"*Her* energy?" Loki muttered, letting his hand fall

from my neck to the ground. His voice was raw, exhaustion painting every syllable.

I twisted to look up, catching Bjarni's gaze. I'd felt his steadfast presence throughout the healing process, his nearness strengthening me.

"Bjarni, I... I'm so sorry."

He cocked his head. "Don't be."

"No, I am. And I should be. I've been so wrapped up in my pain I didn't allow myself to feel anything else. I love you too. I should have been able to tell you that from the first moment."

He cracked a smile and reached down, pulling me to my feet and into his chest. "I know. Now come—we've slayed the dragon. It's time to save some damsels in distress, hmm?"

"I am so telling Saga you called him a damsel," Modi said, wincing as he pushed himself to his feet. "I am sure he will love it."

Three weeks.

It had been three weeks less a day since Bjarni left with the girl and Magni's brother, and all we had discovered in their absence was that Mimir wasn't in Valhalla and Freya had vanished from Folkvangr.

In the first few days, Magni's sister had proven herself a valuable ally. She'd asked questions I would never have been granted an answer to and lobbied for me, Magni, and Saga to receive some freedom to move around Valhalla during our captivity.

But on the fourth day, after discovering Freya's disappearance, she'd informed us that she would leave to search for her, certain that the wayward goddess was linked to the traitor she'd claimed resided in Valhalla and leaving us to search for clues on our own.

I shot my brother a look across the room. Not that he and Magni had been particularly helpful.

"She's still alive," Magni murmured as he slid down on the floor by Saga's side.

Saga nodded, clenching his jaw as he looked from the scroll in his hand up at the redhead. They shared a long look, one that made me uncomfortable every time I saw it.

It had become their mantra: "she is still alive." Those were some of the only words they'd spoken since Annabel had left Valhalla. Most of the time I wasn't entirely certain they even registered that I was around, or perhaps it was simply that they didn't care. They searched through old texts in a bid to discover Mimir's whereabouts, but I had the distinct impression they were only doing so because it was what the human omega needed.

When I looked at my brother, I knew in my gut that he would watch the world burn, and us along with it, so long as he found a way to keep Annabel safe through Ragnarök.

Worse was the knowledge that while he had turned his back on me, his bond to Thor's bastard seemed stronger than iron. They even fell asleep together each night, their mutual and pathetic need for comfort allowing them to seek it in one another.

I shuddered and focused on my own scroll. If this was life as a mated alpha, I was starting to suspect that death was preferable.

The bitter thought that perhaps Saga would now be more inclined to let me select that option than he had while we'd planned for Annabel's arrival to our farm wormed its way through my mind.

I rubbed at my forehead and stared out the window in our tower room. Not that there would be much of a choice one way or the other if Bjarni didn't return with our father before the moon rose tomorrow.

I tossed a scroll containing yet another of Mimir's more absurd prophecies to the floor, shooting a disgusted look at the two other alphas. Magni's hand covered Saga's, a silent, intimate gesture of support. The brother I'd grown up with would have never accepted such closeness with a man who was supposed to be our enemy, shared mating claim or not.

"There is nothing helpful in these records," I bit through clenched teeth. "No indication of where Mimir is, and certainly no help in discovering who this supposed traitor is. If there even is one." At this point, I was starting to think Freya was less reliable than we'd given her credit for. She was the goddess of love, after all—not intrigue. "Perhaps Ragnarök is simply here because it is time, and there is nothing we can do to stop it."

"You're wrong, little brother," Saga said, his voice surprisingly gentle. He looked up at me, possibly for the first time in days. His eyes were as dull as they'd been for the past three weeks, but the flicker of fire in them heartened me. "This isn't the time for everything to end.

Once you and Annabel are united, you will understand."

"Hel's beard!" I snarled, my patience shattering. "What *happened* to you, Saga? You used to be cunning, clever—an actual *god*, not... this empty shell of a being! Annabel is not the answer to everything! She is a human girl. That's all. A vessel, at most!

"Look at yourself. You're crumpled on the floor, incapable of so much as saving your own ass from the god-king. Waiting for a *woman* to come rescue you! I am not about to join you in this madness. You two enjoy your misery. I am going to find a way for us to escape."

I stormed out of the tower room, slamming the door behind me. There hadn't been any Valkyrie guards stationed outside of it for weeks, which was fortunate, seeing as I'd been shouting about staging an escape.

I scrubbed my face with both hands and inhaled deeply before I continued down the corridor. I was done following these harebrained schemes. Done with trying to sort out whatever Aesir mess had been stirred up in Asgard. This wasn't my home, and its inhabitants were not my people. I cared for exactly two people in this world.

Ensuring the survival of my brothers and me was all that mattered—and right now, the logical first step in that plan was for us to escape this fortress.

. . .

I walked undisturbed the entire way to the god-king's stables. Valhalla's servants had grown used to my presence, letting me pass mostly unnoticed. The iron ring lodged on my left index finger ensured my powers were inaccessible, rendering me harmless in the eyes of Odin and his kin, but even Asa magic could do little to dampen my innate ability to blend into the shadows.

The large wooden door was unguarded, making me hesitate for a moment, hand over the doorknob. One of Odin's most prized possessions was inside this room. He would never risk Sleipner being stolen—and I couldn't imagine him leaving a steed capable of flight unguarded while three captives resided within Valhalla's walls.

I let my hand drop to twist at the iron ring on my finger. Not for the first time, I wished I still had my connection to my magic. It felt like I'd lost an eye, my ability to sense treachery hindered. If there was a trap on the other side of that door, my magic could have warned me.

As if I'd spoken out loud, a metallic *clunk* of the handles being pushed down rung through the hallways. Hinges squeaked as the door swung open, but the space behind it revealed no one.

"Grim," an all-too-familiar voice said from within. "I have been expecting you. Please, come in. We have much to discuss."

36

ANNABEL

The trek up the mountain to Valhalla nearly broke me.

Just staying conscious had been difficult since before we'd passed through the portal into Asgard, and after just a few yards, my legs buckled.

Bjarni caught me before I faceplanted on the path and pulled me into his arms mid-stride. It seemed effortless, but I wasn't fooled—I felt his exhaustion in our bond.

"Put me down, Bjarni," I murmured, even as my head lolled in against his shoulder. "You're injured too. I'll walk."

"I'm not so injured I can't carry my mate," he rumbled. "Just a short while and we're there."

Despite my body's refusal to stay upright, a surge of adrenaline made my heart beat faster. Soon I would get to see Saga and Magni again, and the first, horrible step to stop Ragnarök would be over.

Hopefully they would have found Mimir, or at the very least know where he was. But first I was going to sleep. In a bed. With all my mates near me, and that awful, aching emptiness in my chest banished for good.

Loki hadn't said much since he'd helped me heal Modi—the fight with Nidhug had taken it out of him too. But now he walked behind Modi, golden rope around his wrists and head held high.

I'd been on the fence on whether or not I'd help the God of Mischief escape Valhalla, but after what he'd done for us in Niflheim, I didn't have much of a choice. He could have fled when I freed him, but he'd stayed and fought. He'd saved us. And yeah, it was probably for purely selfish reasons, since he believed he needed me and at least one of his sons alive, but the end result was the same.

I owed Loki a life debt.

The path to Valhalla was mostly empty, but the few Viking warriors, servants, and even a Valkyrie we passed on the way turned and stared, gasping whenever they spotted Loki.

"Been a while since you've visited the place, eh?" Bjarni said. He cracked a half-smile at his dad. "Seems you made quite an impression."

Loki ignored him. He kept his eyes on Valhalla's large port, the set of his jaw betraying his unease at our approach. Not that I could blame him, really. Whatever hand he'd played in bringing forth Ragnarök, walking toward your own beheading had to suck.

We were greeted by throngs of silent Valkyries lining the gate on either side. Wordlessly, one of them broke free and came to stand in front of us, hand outstretched toward Modi.

He hesitated. "Our agreement is with Odin. My brother and the two Lokissons are to be freed."

The blond woman nodded. "That is the agreement, son of Thor."

Modi drew in a deep breath, nodding as well. Then he handed her his end of Loki's rope. "Very well."

The Valkyrie's blue eyes roamed over Loki's face, her lip curling in distaste. With a yank, she turned around, forcing him to stumble forward as to not fall flat on his face.

"Sisters! With me!"

The gathered Valkyries crowded in around Loki, pushing us out of the way as they took up position around him. As one, they walked through the gates of Valhalla and into the great hall within.

"I guess we follow," Bjarni said.

Modi nodded. "It would seem that way. Magni... is close. And Saga." He rubbed his chest where our bonds were hooked.

I could feel them too, which I was pretty sure was the only reason I was still conscious. Adrenaline alone kept me awake, my instinctive knowledge of my other mates' nearness keeping me alert.

We crossed the threshold to the mighty fortress, following the throng of Valkyries leading Loki to the dais at the front. This time not a single Viking noticed my presence—everyone was staring at our prisoner in silence.

Odin sat at the front, raised up above the hall on his throne, his staff in one hand and a raven on each shoulder. As was true the last time I saw him, he looked every inch the god-king, but my gaze barely touched him because by his side stood Magni, Saga, and Grim.

They saw me at the same moment I did them. Magni and Saga jerked, both moving forward as one. They didn't bother with the stairs, leaping from the dais and rushing through the hall, jumping over benches, tables, and warriors alike, until finally, *finally*—

"Sweetling!"

"Annabel!"

Saga plucked me from Bjarni's arms, pulling me close as Magni grabbed my chin and pressed a deep kiss to my lips, slipping his tongue in between as he claimed my mouth for his.

His scorching lips nipped at my neck and hands roamed the length of my body, searching every millimeter of my skin for injuries.

"My mate," Saga groaned against my ear. "You're here."

I clutched at him, winding a hand into each of their long manes, holding them so wonderfully, perfectly close.

The hollowness I'd carried since we parted melted away as if it'd never been there, and for the first time, all four bonds hooked in my chest hummed peacefully from within.

"I love you both," I gasped in the short moment's breath I was allowed before Saga claimed my mouth from Magni. "I love you."

"I love you too," Magni rumbled in my ear. "I should never have let you leave without telling you."

"Should never have let you leave at all," Saga breathed in between desperate kisses. "Never again."

"It was fortunate that you did," Modi said from the other side of the cocoon of Magni's and Saga's bodies. "Without her, we would never have captured Loki. Or survived the journey home."

Warmth bathed my already humming heart. It meant so much to hear those words from Modi—the man who'd been adamant I was nothing but a burden when we first set out. But not anymore.

I broke away from Saga's kiss to give him an appreciative smile. He caught my gaze, and the tenderness and pride in it took my breath away.

Magni unwound one arm from my body and clasped a hand on his brother's shoulder. "Thank you both. For taking care of our mate and for bringing her back to us."

"She belongs to us too now," Bjarni said, just the barest of threats making its way to his voice. "Don't thank us for looking after our own mate."

"We felt you bond," Saga said. He pressed his forehead against the top of my scalp, drawing my scent in for a few breaths before he looked up to his brother and Modi, a frown marring his handsome face.

I rolled my eyes, irritation mixing with the bliss of finally being reunited with all my mates. "Can we not? This is definitely not the time for a territorial pissing contest."

"The girl is right," a dark rasp interjected. Grim appeared by Saga's side, his mismatched eyes only briefly touching mine before he focused on his brothers. "Our father is about to face judgement. Perhaps... *this*... can wait?"

I flushed, a touch of embarrassment wheedling its way through my exhausted euphoria, but when I dared a quick look around, exactly no one was looking in our direction. Loki had climbed the stairs to the dais. The Valkyries, except the blonde leading him, remained at the foot, taking up guard.

"Loki," Odin said, his voice filling the great hall even though he didn't shout. "I am so very pleased to see you decided to return to the home you betrayed."

"Your invitation was hard to refuse," Loki replied. Sarcasm dripped from every word as he held out his bound wrists.

The god-king only looked at him, his face impassive. "You have been found guilty of treason, God of Mischief. You have been found guilty of orchestrating

Ragnarök. Tomorrow you will face the consequences of your betrayal.

"At moonrise, you will look upon your brothers and sisters of Asgard one final time. It is my hope you will do so with remorse for the fate you have brought down upon us all. But regret or no, once the moon rises, you will be executed."

"Am I not even allowed to plead my defense?" Loki asked. "What is this mockery of justice, god-king? You would condemn an innocent man to death without granting him so much as a trial?"

Odin leaned forward on his throne. Even from way back where we stood, I saw the fury in his one eye as he stared at the dark god. "You had a trial, serpent-tongue. If you had been less of a coward, if you had remained in our realm, you could have pleaded your case then. But you fled—and so we had your trial in your absence. You are *guilty*, Loki. And tomorrow, you die."

He stood in a swirl of gray robes, his gaze landing on the head Valkyrie. "Take him to the cells below."

The great hall was silent as the grave until Odin disappeared through the doorway behind the throne. Then, as one, the thousands of warriors started shouting, some whooping, others chanting songs of victory. Above the long tables, enormous, gilded horns appeared, pouring mead into every cup.

"Let's go," Magni said, hoisting me into his arms. "We have much to discuss."

37

ANNABEL

Saga, Grim, and Magni led us back to the tower room they'd been locked in the first time we arrived at Valhalla, but it seemed they'd been granted more freedoms since. No guards were stationed in the hallway outside the door, and no one seemed to care how and where they moved.

Magni placed me on one of the wooden beds in the room. It smelled like him, and I hummed and leaned into him, my mind finally starting to relax. I'd been wiped out since our fight against Nidhug, but we hadn't had time to rest—or otherwise replenish my reserves. Being here, surrounded by all four of my mates, bathing in their scents and their nearness, was blissful relaxation.

The bed dipped as Saga sat on my other side and possessively wrapped his arms around my midriff as he pressed in close. But where before I would have expected jealousy to burn in our bond, now it was peaceful. He didn't mind that Magni had taken me to his bed. In fact, he didn't mind Magni's presence at all.

"You're friends?" I murmured, nuzzling against the blond alpha's scruffy stubble.

Magni hummed a noise of agreement.

"No wonder Father is not here to greet us," Modi mumbled. He knelt down on the floor in front of us, reaching out to touch my leg as if on instinct rather than conscious thought. "I am sure he is unimpressed."

Magni snorted. "That's one way of putting it. Though I don't think he knows nor cares. The whole mate-sharing thing was enough to earn his unwavering disapproval. He hasn't been back to Valhalla since you left. Trud said he's sulking back home."

Bjarni caught my eyes, one blond eyebrow edging up a half inch. I knew what he was thinking, but we both understood that now wasn't the time to revisit the whole "Thor might be the traitor" concept. There'd be plenty of time to worry about that later—after some sleep.

"Rest, sweetie," Bjarni said. He sat down by Modi's side, sliding a hand up my other leg in a calming gesture. "We'll catch up while you relax for a bit, hmm?"

I smiled sleepily at him. Out of all four men, he was the one I could always count on to pamper me—which he confirmed when he absentmindedly slipped my boot off and began pressing his fingers into the sole of my foot.

I slumped back against Magni and Saga with a happy sigh. The last thing I saw before my eyelids slid closed was Grim leaning against the wall across from the bed, arms folded over his chest and lips pressed into a thin line.

One day he was supposed to mate me too. I wondered if he was watching his brothers quietly bonding with men who had once been their enemies and if he resented me for uniting them. If he feared the devotion that came with a mating bond.

I drifted off to the rumbling sound of my four alphas' voices, soothed into the core of my soul.

Kisses along my jawline brought me back from the depths of sleep. I hovered on the edge of consciousness for a long while, my mind fighting to dip back into oblivion, but the lips against my skin were unyielding.

"*Mmph,*" I protested, but it was quickly swallowed in a deep kiss.

I groaned another protest into the mouth gently teasing my lips apart, but despite my desire to go back to sleep, I lifted my arms and wound them around my mate's shoulders.

Saga. I felt him in our bond, his happiness and desire, and recognized his scent as I breathed him in.

When he pulled back from our kiss, I cracked my eyelids open. Despite the darkness in the room, I saw the outline of his long hair and wide shoulders clear enough thanks to the moonlight streaming through the window.

"D'you mind? I'm trying to sleep here."

"Shh," Saga whispered, giving my lips a peck when I opened them to admonish him for shushing me. "You'll wake them."

I dared a glance to my side, noticing several big lumps in the darkness, some on the other beds, some on the floor.

"What time is it?"

"Late," he said, delving back to trail kisses along my jawline. Despite my still-exhausted state, heat bloomed everywhere his mouth touched. "But I couldn't wait any longer, sweetling. I've missed you too much. Missed your scent. Your taste. The way you feel underneath my palms."

He followed the last sentence up by stroking one large hand down the length of my body and up between my thigh, squeezing my vulva. It was then I realized they'd undressed me.

Without waiting for further permission, Saga pressed in against my clit, sending a zing of pleasure up my spine.

"I've missed you too," I murmured, breathier than I'd meant to. "But we can't just... Not while everyone's here. And I'm exhausted..."

"Sure we can." Saga sounded completely unfazed, save for the smoldering heat deep in his throat. He kept his hand pressed right up against my clit, working it slowly while his kisses turned to light nips down my throat. "So long as you're quiet while I make you milk my cock. I don't mind sharing your little cunt like I did on Freya's altar, but if you're too tired to take four knots tonight, I suggest you keep any noises to a minimum."

"You're incorrigible," I grumbled—but his fingers between my thighs were working. I spread my legs a little, allowing him better access, and breathed deeply at the intensifying pleasure.

"Just worried for my mate. Bjarni told us how there's only one way to help you get your energy back. My only desire is to serve my omega."

His words, his tone of voice... it was such a *Saga* thing to say, I couldn't hold back an amused snort. "How very selfless of you."

"Shh." Saga covered my mouth with his hand and looked to the floor. One of the guys—Bjarni—had stopped breathing quite as deeply, probably disturbed by my giggle. Saga kept his hand in place until my blond giant rolled over, his breathing deepening once more.

"We agreed to let you rest until morning," Saga whispered as he eased his palm off my mouth. I could *feel* his smirk in the darkness. "And we drew straws on who'd get to keep you in their bed. I may have cheated."

"Why am I not surprised?" I slipped my hands from

his shoulders down his torso until I could wrap my arms around his sides, pressing myself close to him. My heart thrummed, partly with awakened desire, but mostly with relief at his nearness.

"Don't cry, sweetling." His voice, silky soft and reverberating with tenderness, was followed by gentle kisses to my cheeks. Only then did I realize tears were trickling down them.

"I was so broken without you," I whispered.

He bumped my forehead gently with his, pressing his weight down on top of me until my heartbeat slowed, comforted by his nearness. For the longest time, all he did was breathe with me, his hand on my hip rather than between my legs.

"Bjarni and Modi told us of your bravery," he finally said. "How fiercely you fought. How powerful your magic is. How strong your spirit. I hated every minute we were apart, but I am proud of you for withstanding our separation. I am not sure I could have done the same, had I been the one who had to put distance between us."

"Yeah. You would have. Every one of you," I said, pressing my cheek to his. "There was no other choice. You would do anything to ensure my survival. I understand that now."

He hummed a small noise of agreement. "There is nothing I won't give for you, Annabel. Nothing."

I bit my lip, remembering Loki's judgement. "Your father…"

"He will find a way out," he said, a faint brush of pain touching his voice. "And if not, Bjarni told us what happened. I was... not too surprised. Our father has all days cared more about his own skin than ours. So, should he not manage to free himself, I am at peace with that. He would sacrifice us for his own life, and you—you are my family now. You and your mates."

"I'm going to help him," I said softly.

He pulled back, lifting up on one elbow. I felt his eyes scrutinize me, but he remained silent.

"He saved our lives. Nidhug would have killed us without him. So... I am going to repay him the favor. I have to."

"How?"

It was a simple question, but I had no answer. Instead, I brushed my fingertips through his soft hair to his jaw, pulling him back down for a kiss.

"I'll find a way," I murmured against his lips. "Tomorrow."

"Don't risk your life for his," Saga said, his exhale hot against mine. "Promise me."

"I promise," I said. "That would defeat the entire purpose of these past three weeks."

"It would," he agreed. And then he swallowed my breath in a searing kiss.

I spread my thighs again, but this time instead of using his hand to pleasure me, he broke free from our kiss to move down my body, nipping and licking my skin as he descended.

I gasped into the darkness when he captured first one nipple and then the other, sucking them both until they were stiff and aching. Then he delved lower, and I had to bite the back of my hand to keep myself quiet.

Saga placed teasing kisses on my vulva, trailing down to my inner thighs where he nipped and sucked until I wound my fingers through his long hair and pulled him up where I needed him.

His tongue flicked right over the tip of my clit peeking out from its hood, and my breath exploded out in a hiss of sensation, my thighs clamping shut around Saga's head on instinct.

He chuckled and grabbed my thighs, forcing them wide. And then, he descended on me like a starved man.

It took everything I had to hold back my moans and whimpers as Saga devoured my pussy, thrusting his tongue up inside of me and sucking my clit until it hurt. When I couldn't stand it anymore, he eased up on the stimulation, gently licking in circles around it until I stopped trying to shove him away—only to suck it back into his mouth the next second.

I came in a violent torrent of sensation exploding through my pelvis and into my brain. If Saga hadn't released one thigh to press a hand against my mouth, my scream would have ripped through the room as I bucked and writhed, lost to the waves of pleasure.

While I was still coming down from my orgasm, Saga sat up on his knees between my thighs. He wiped his mouth with one hand, then ranged over me and brushed his lips over mine—gently until my addled brain came back from orbit, then deeply.

I tasted myself on his lips, tangy and rich, and hummed in appreciation as I stroked down his back, enjoying the ripple of his muscles.

"You feel like battle and victory," he rasped, pulling back a little to look down at me again. Though I couldn't make out his eyes, I felt the burning intensity in them as he drank me In. "You're the one who conquered me. You won my heart, my devotion... my unending loyalty."

He reached between us, and I hissed a breath in when the thick head of his cock nudged between my splayed labia, finding my slickened entrance.

"But when I'm inside you—you yield to *me*."

With that he pushed in, seating his cock in its entirety in my core.

I whimpered and bit down on his shoulder to keep from crying out, the stretch of taking him bringing that now familiar mix of pleasure and pain I'd learned to love.

Once I was fully hilted, he paused, our breaths coming in equally harsh pants, mingling in the space between us. Nothing felt like this—like being one with him. It was physical, and it was emotional, our bond humming with completion we'd never experience when we weren't locked together in flesh.

"I will never want anything more than this," Saga whispered.

His first thrust made me bite back down on his shoulder, my fingers grasping for purchase against his back. He filled me so perfectly, forced my pussy so wonderfully wide, and I could do nothing but lay underneath him and take it.

He was right, in some ways. I would have his heart and his undivided devotion for the rest of eternity—but when we had sex, I would always be the one to surrender. He was alpha through and through, they all were, and I—Norn-blessed, fated to save the world, wielding magic so powerful I still didn't fully understand the extent of it—underneath them, I was only their omega. Born to submit.

He fucked me in long, hard thrusts, his breath harsh in my ear as he showed me his full power. I clung to him, clawed at his back and bit his shoulder from the intensity of taking him, and wound my legs around his to press myself up for more.

When my body started its climb toward my second peak, Saga thrust his hand down between us, finding my clit with experienced ease. I jerked at the contact and screamed into his shoulder when he began flicking the little bud hard and fast.

He grunted in my ear and pounded my pussy until my body bowed up and I flung my head back and *came.*

Saga clamped his hand not busy on my clit over my mouth, but not before my howl of pleasure burst out into the quiet room. A howl that swiftly turned to protest when the base of his already thick cock swelled, tormenting my sheath as he forced his growing knot in and out of my opening a few times before finally seating it behind my pelvic bone, right up against my G-spot.

I gritted my teeth and breathed through the hard expanse, shuddering as the pressure of his knot forced my climax to roll through my body in continual waves. There'd been a time when I'd hated everything about getting knotted, but now... It still hurt, it was still so forceful, but my body had gotten accustomed to the violent stretch. Where before I'd hated being forced to be so vulnerable and had found the experience humiliating, now it was something else. A proof of how deeply I trusted this man, how completely I surrendered myself to him.

Saga held me so perfectly tight to his hulking body while we both came, murmuring a mixture of filthy words and sweet confessions of love as he emptied himself inside of me. Only when we both had no more left to give did he release my mouth with his hand to plant a sweet kiss on my lips.

Breathing a happy sigh, I nuzzled against the side of his neck and relaxed into the mattress, fully planning on dozing off underneath him while he waited for his knot to ease.

"I distinctly remember us *all* agreeing not to disturb our mate until morning," a tart voice said from the darkness somewhere beyond Saga's embrace.

Bjarni.

"That's funny—so do I. In fact, I do believe *he* was the one to suggest it," Magni joined in.

I looked to my left, and past the bulky shape of Saga's arm caught sight of the outline of four male figures either sitting upright or standing. One of them —from the outline of his hair, I guessed Grim—moved away from the others and toward the door, followed by the sound of it opening and closing.

Saga smirked down at me. "Oh, sweetling. You've gone and woken them now. I did warn you what would happen if you didn't keep quiet while you milked my cock."

I grimaced, turning my focus to the three others. "Sorry."

Modi snorted. "It did not sound like you were too sorry just a moment ago."

"It didn't, did it?" There was a distinctly predatory note to Magni's voice. He got to his feet in a smooth movement, prowling closer to loom over the bed. "Looks like we were foolish to expect this little minx to need a full night's sleep before she gets her pretty cunt filled. Weren't we, pet?"

I groaned and hid my face in Saga's shoulder. "No, not foolish at all. I'm shattered, really, I am—"

Magni bent farther down over the bed, his fingers finding where Saga and I were connected. My blond mate jerked and hissed out a breath at the contact, quickly snapping his head around to glare over his shoulder.

"Oi!"

"Not so fun this way around, is it?" Magni said, a dark note of amusement in his voice. "If it wasn't for this fucking ring, I'd shock you to pop that knot out of her."

Saga growled a half-hearted threat, then hissed again when Magni moved his finger, slipping one digit in alongside Saga's knot. I let out a gasp at the extra stretch, clenching at Saga's shoulders and whimpering as Magni worked his finger against our melded flesh.

Whatever he was doing, it had distinctly different effects on Saga and me. Where my pussy slowly bloomed alive with the rhythm of his knuckle rubbing at my G-spot, Saga's knot subsided significantly faster than normal. After about five minutes, he let out a breath and reached back to shove Magni away.

"You'd be wise to remember that I'm not gonna allow this every time you want inside of her," Saga growled. "Next time, I'm snapping your wrist."

He pulled his hips back, making my breath hitch when his knot momentarily caught in the mouth of my pussy. Then he pulled free and sat back on his heels, brushing both hands up my splayed legs in a loving caress before he climbed off the bed, leaving me naked and open to the other alphas.

Magni climbed between my thighs, but when he

went to settle his hips, Modi grabbed his shoulder. Firmly.

"I love you, brother, but there is no chance you are going to fuck my mate while I simply watch."

Magni snarled. "It has been three weeks since I was last inside my woman, *brother*. No fucking power in the entire nine worlds is strong enough to stop me from taking her."

"Well, we know she can take two of us at once," Bjarni said, a distinct purr in his voice.

"No. No. Absolutely not." I winced at the thought of how I'd had to heal Magni's injuries. "Not unless one of you is literally fucking dying."

"How cute. You think you get a say, omega?" Magni teased, that edge of darkness in his voice raising goosebumps of excitement along my bared skin. "Grab some blankets. Make her a nest. She was happy enough to take Saga's dick while we were sleeping—she gets to satisfy all of us simultaneously."

"Wait, what—"

My protest died on a squeal when Magni grabbed me by the hips and pulled me up tight against his torso before he stood, carrying me with him. Around us, the other three alphas were tossing furs, pillows and blankets in a pile on the floor. By the single, small desk by the window, someone lit a candle, bathing the room in a warm glow that finally allowed me to see them fully. All bare skin and rolling muscle.

When they'd finished with the thick layer of soft

furnishings on the floor, Magni unceremoniously put me down in the middle of them, hiked my right thigh over his shoulder, lined up, and shoved himself inside of me.

My pussy, still warm and lubricated from Saga, opened for him with minimal pain, but the sensation of being filled in the span of a breath made me cry out and grab at his forearms to anchor myself.

"Fucking Hel, pet," Magni groaned, stilling with his hips pressed tight to my pussy and ass. "Oh, I missed you. I missed *this.*"

"I missed you too," I panted, my thoughts of anything but him momentarily vanished like mist on a hot summer's day. "Shit, that's—*oh!*"

Hot lips closing around my left nipple brought me back to reality with a sharp twang. Dazedly I clutched Bjarni to my chest, tangling my fingers in his messy hair, panting at the dual onslaught of stimulation. Stimulation that only increased when Saga laid down on my right side, popping my unattended nipple into his mouth with a deep suck.

"Fuck!"

"Your wish is my command," Magni grunted. He pulled his hips back, leaving just half his meaty length inside, only to thrust back the next second. And again.

I whimpered, and keened when someone—I wasn't sure if it was Saga or Bjarni—found my clit.

In a matter of moments, I lost myself in the stimulation of every erogenous zone on my body, until a strong hand closed around my jaw, tipping my head up and to the side. When I opened my eyes, Modi was staring down at me. He teased my lips with his thumb, pressing it into my mouth to the first knuckle.

"Suck," he commanded, voice rough as gravel.

I swirled my tongue around his fingertip and pulled hard on it with a deep suck, mirroring Saga's attentions to my right breast until Modi closed his eyes and hissed out a curse. He pulled his thumb from my lips, and the next second pushed his thick cock against them.

"Show me how well you can suck my cock, my little whore," he rasped.

I opened my mouth willingly, the ache in my jaw as he pushed the tip in as far as it would go numbed by the pleasure shaking my body in rhythm with my three other mates' stimulation.

Modi groaned at the touch of my tongue to his sensitive head. He buried a hand in my hair to keep me in place, his eyes raking over me. "Gods be damned, you feel so good, Anna!"

I moaned in response, flicking my tongue at his slit and earning another hiss of pleasure. Blindly I reached for Saga and Bjarni, grasping their cocks in each hand. Saga was still wet from our union but as hard as if he hadn't just spilled himself inside of me. I didn't have enough multitasking skills to stroke them as the Thorsson brothers fucked my pussy and mouth in a rough rhythm, but I didn't need to.

Bjarni growled with pleasure against my breast and

rolled his hips, fucking my hand with long, languid strokes.

Saga popped off my nipple and kissed his way up my throat and jaw until he got to my ear. "Look at you, Annabel," he whispered, his hot breath raising goosebumps along my neck. "One little human omega servicing four immortal alphas. How you would have blushed at the mere thought when I first met you. How ashamed you would have been as you rubbed your little clit to the thought of it, hiding alone in your bed.

"My beautiful, deviant mate. So far you've come. You want us all to seed that greedy little cunt of yours, don't you? I feel you in our bond, sweetling. You crave us as much we do you. Maybe you even want me to slide inside of you again, hmm? Fill your pussy alongside Magni—make it hurt like the first time I knotted you? Just keep touching my cock like that, and that's exactly what you'll get."

Despite the rush of desire at his dirty words and the flood of liquid bathing Magni's already soaking cock, I instantly released my grip on his thick dick. I had no illusions that they were going to stop before each of them had knotted me, and yeah, despite my initial protests, I wanted this as much as they did... but I also remembered what it'd been like to have two alphas inside of me.

Saga chuckled into my ear and nipped at my earlobe. "Wuss."

I didn't get a chance to answer—not that I could

have—because just then Magni wrapped an arm underneath my torso and pulled me up to rest against his thighs, popping my mouth off Modi's cock with a wet sound and Bjarni off my nipple and clit.

Growls of protest sounded around me, but the burn in Magni's eyes forced my full focus on him.

His beautiful face was strained with pleasure, and those forest green eyes pulled me in like a moth to the flame. There was so much love, so much devotion—so much despair in them.

"Annabel. My Annabel," he groaned. "I was lost without you, mate. *Fuck!* Fuck, you feel like *life* on my cock, pet. Never, ever leave again!"

"I won't," I moaned, his desperation pulling me closer to him, making me want to do anything, say anything to wipe away the pain I saw in his beautiful, haunted eyes. "I'm yours. I'll always be yours. You're my family. My everything."

Magni squeezed his eyes shut and crushed me to his thickly muscled chest, groaning as he thrust up inside me several more times before his knot swelled, forcing my pussy to stretch obscenely wide until it snapped shut behind the violent protrusion, locking us together.

The pressure on my G-spot and the feel of Magni's throbbing cock as he spilled his seed inside me sent me over the edge once more. I clung to him as tightly as he did me, pressing kisses to his neck, shoulders, and jaw. In my chest, our bond reverberated with the depth of his emotions: love, reverence, *home.*

We breathed together, shivering for every pulse of our bodies releasing in waves of pleasure.

Only when my pussy had wrung the last of his essence from his still-throbbing cock did my senses come back to the room—and the alphas still hungry for their taste of me.

Warm hands stroked up my back, soft lips framed by a scruffy beard kissing my shoulder and teasing at one of my claiming marks. *Bjarni.*

I hummed and leaned my head back against him, letting him catch my lips in a hungry kiss. His hands slid from my back to my breasts, wedging between Magni and me.

Modi knelt behind Magni, his hands slipping between our hips. I jerked when he flicked my clit, making Magni hiss as I clenched around him.

"You keep doing that, my knot's staying inside of her for the next hour," Magni moaned. He shifted his hips demonstratively, rubbing my G-spot with his hard knot tied in my still-trembling channel, making me mewl.

"Do not make me do what you did to the Jotunn, brother," Modi growled.

"Just... give it time," I gasped, wincing when Magni shifted again. "Come. Let me... Let me help you."

"You just wanna pump our cocks, don't you?" Bjarni purred in my ear. He shifted to my right, grabbing my hand from Magni's shoulder and brought it to his throbbing member.

Obediently I wrapped my fingers around it and gave

him a slow stroke all the way from the base to tip that had him hissing with pleasure. Immediately, another thick cock was pushed into my other hand. Modi moaned brokenly when I gave him a stroke in rhythm with Bjarni, wrapping an arm around my body and pulling me into him and away from Magni.

Magni growled, but it was somewhat unconvincing. "Careful. So long as she's stuck on my knot, she's mine."

Saga snorted. "I'd be careful with such statements. I hear a finger up the ass can settle a knot down right quick."

Magni shot him a death glare.

"Dunno about your brother, but I'm getting closer to giving it a go than I'd ever thought I would. *Fuck!*" Bjarni rumbled, his breath expelling in a burst when I rubbed my thumb over his swollen head, smearing the ample pre-cum pearling there.

"Just... give me a couple of minutes," Magni gasped. He pressed his forehead to my shoulder and wound his arms loosely around my midsection, breathing deeply.

I kept up a steady pace for Modi and Bjarni, massaging their cocks as well as I could with only one hand for each. The scent of sex was thick in my nostrils, and the feel of them in my hands and their low growls of desire forced my exhausted body to heat once more.

Magni groaned when my pussy trembled around him with awakening desire. "You're killing me, pet," he rasped. "Every time you tighten that slick cunt on me, you're adding minutes to my knot. Keep it up and I'll need to fuck you again before I let them have you."

"You do that, it won't just be my finger that goes up your asshole," Bjarni growled.

"I am with the Jotunn on this one, brother," Modi said, swallowing a groan as my thumb rubbed at his frenulum. "I would die for you, but if you do not pop that knot out of her in the next two minutes, you are getting a bolt of lightning where no one wants a zap."

Magni barked a half-laugh, half-growl. "Bunch of fucking pricks," he mumbled against my skin. "This is what you do to us, pet—turning brother against brother just for a taste of your cunt."

With another groan he pulled his hips back as far as he could go, making me whimper at the aching stretch of his knot battling my trembling channel. He reached between us and grabbed the bottom of his cock barely sticking out of me, squeezing it hard.

We both growled through it, the sensation less than pleasant—but it worked. After a few moments, he jerked his hips back again, this time managing to force his still semi-hard knot free with a wet pop.

"Shit, *ow!*" I released Bjarni's cock to smack Magni's chest.

"Blame them, pet. I would have happily stayed until it went down on its own," Magni panted, diving in for a stolen kiss before he dodged my next attempt to swipe at him, rolling up on his knees by my side.

Modi and Bjarni moved at once, but I still had a grip

on Modi's cock, so Bjarni managed to claim the spot between my thighs. He shot Modi a devilish smirk. "Too slow."

"I'm not a fucking amusement ride," I growled. My pussy still ached from Magni. I reached between my legs to rub at my agitated lips and grimaced at the wet mess left there.

"I beg to differ," Bjarni purred. He leaned in, and when I raised my arms to push him away, he grabbed my wrists and held them against his chest to kiss me. Deeply. When he pulled back, a smirk danced on his soft lips. "Definitely a rollercoaster."

I narrowed my eyes at him. "There speaks a man who wants to get off in his own palm."

A rumble of laughter echoed around the room. Even Bjarni grinned, but the gleam in his eyes was predatory.

"It's *so cute* when you pretend like you have a choice in how much and how hard your pussy gets pounded, sweetie."

"Adorable," Modi growled from behind me. He slid his hand around my hips, descending on my vulva. I jerked at his touch, but Bjarni kept my wrists trapped and my thighs spread around his hips. *Defenseless.*

Despite my soreness, something deeply biological made my pussy pulse in response to the complete vulnerability in my position between the two huge alphas.

Modi opened my labia with his left hand. Splitting his fingers apart, he drew them up until he got to my clitoris. It was swollen from arousal and peeking from underneath its protective hood, but Modi pressed the pads of his fingers on each side and pulled up, fully exposing the tender nub.

"There we go," he purred in my ear before he popped his right thumb and index finger into his mouth, wetting them. Then he brought them down to my throbbing clitoris, closing them firmly around the small stem. A shock of sensation made me jolt and arch back against his chest with a moan.

"Feels good, does it not?" he whispered.

I nodded a breathy agreement, the ache in my channel slowly fading to the background as he rubbed up and down my bundle of nerves, driving pleasure to the forefront of my mind again.

"If you are a good little omega and do not complain when your alphas demand you serve them, then this is how it will always feel, Anna."

Perhaps if I hadn't been so out of it from the prolonged stimulation of my entire body, I would have caught on to the dark tone to his voice. But I only breathed a hoarse "uh-huh," rolling my hips for more of his wonderful touch. The longer he stroked me, the harder it was to push back the promise of the orgasm building in my loins.

"A pity you are such a poorly behaved woman," he growled, squeezing the very tip of my clit hard enough to make me gasp, my eyes popping open from shock. And then—then came the lightning.

In reality, it was probably a very minor current, but when Modi sent a bold of electricity directly through my clitoris, it felt like my entire world shattered in blinding rapture.

It wasn't even pain. It was like the raw energy that built every atom of the universe shot right into my pelvis, short-circuiting my nervous system.

I *screamed*, bowing back hard, my head smacking into Modi's face, but I couldn't feel anything except for my clit alive with the very source of life itself. I came *hard*—at least, it felt like I came, but it could honestly have been seizures. My entire pelvis cramped, my gaping pussy contracting hard and rhythmically as every nerve ending in my body fired.

Modi only released my clit when white dots danced in front of my eyes and I had no more air left to scream.

I sagged in his arms, half-sobbing, half hysterically giggling.

"Any more objections to offering up your pussy?" Bjarni asked, arching an eyebrow at me.

Somehow, I managed to shake my head.

"Good." He released my wrists and grabbed my hips, flipping me onto my stomach. Another yank and I was on my knees, ass up and head pressed into the furs. The perfect image of omega submission.

Bjarni slid his hands from my hips to my ass, spreading my cheeks apart to reveal my pussy. He pulled my lips open and pressed his thick cockhead to my still-trembling opening, holding it there for a moment. Letting me anticipate the incoming stretch.

When he finally pushed in, it was so slow it was almost gentle.

I breathed through the sensation of the rim of his head popping past my entrance, clutching at the furs underneath me as he drove in smoothly, filling me to the brim.

"Bjarni!" I gasped out his name, whimpering when he hilted, his balls smacking up tight against me. He was *so big*. They all were, but Bjarni had an extra maybe quarter inch of girth, and I felt it all the way through my core.

"There's my good girl," he cooed. "Wrung out and aching from too much sex, and you still crave my dick. My knot. Let's show them how much of a woman you are. How much more you can take." With that, he wound one hand in my long hair and pulled me up on all four, holding me steady for his first thrust.

I grimaced at the pull on my roots mingling with the delicious ache of taking his cock, then moaned when he thrust in harder the second time.

Bjarni didn't stay gentle for long. Within five thrusts of his powerful hips, I was keening every time I was forced to take his pummeling cock, my pussy protesting with wet, rapid smacks. He rode me hard, keeping me locked in place to take his assault by the grip on my hair, pushing me toward a rapidly approaching climax.

"Come for me, Annabel," he growled, fucking me harder and faster still. "Come, or I'm gonna put your clit through so much worse than he did, I swear it!"

I whimpered something between a plea and a cry of excitement. I'd long since given up on trying to understand why lewd threats and humiliating submission got me so fucking good, and all I cared about at that moment was the roughness of his cock and the complete ecstasy of being *taken*.

My orgasm came from the very roots of my pelvis, forced forward by the brutality of his invasion. It rolled through my body like a thunderstorm, making me flex my hip and cry out his name as my pussy clamped tight on his girth before overworked muscles erupted in hard spasms, milking him.

Bjarni moaned a broken curse and froze with one hand still wound tight in my hair, the other locked on my breast and his pelvis pressed tight up against my ass. His knot barely hurt, swelling right into a perfect tie up against my G-spot before he spilled himself deep in my womb. Every pulse of his cock forced his knot harder against my frontal wall, and I spasmed with every one of them, the sensation prolonging my orgasm with aftershocks.

Halfway through, I had no more strength left. My arms gave up and I collapsed into the furs. Mercifully Bjarni followed me down, saving my poor pussy from getting yanked on his knot. He covered me fully with his big body, encapsulating me in an embrace that had my worn body relaxing.

"I love you," he murmured in my ear. A kiss followed. And another. "Always. Always."

"Love you too." It was barely a whisper, I was that wiped out from the sex, but I felt the tremor of tenderness in our bond keenly.

"Poor Annabel," he chuckled, nuzzling at the back of my head. "Don't worry—we'll work on your stamina."

"Prick," I groaned, earning me another chuckle.

"*Move.*" The dark snarl reverberated from somewhere on the other side of my cocoon, completely devoid of the playfulness that had been between my alphas up until now. "*Right. Now.*"

Through the pleasured hum of my three sated bonds, one still twanged with desire and *need*—Modi.

Bjarni shifted above me, and a sigh rushed through his wide chest. "I'm way too relaxed to fight you," he said. "And way too stuck. Guess you can zap me if you must, but keep your paws away from my ass."

The next second, he jerked violently on top of me, slapping his palm down hard next to my head as he growled a curse. The knot lodged inside of me shrank, allowing him to pull from me with a grumble.

Saga barked a laugh. "Not sure you chose right there, brother."

"I'll remember your preference for next time, *brother,*" Bjarni bit, his tone wholly less calm now. He gave me a final stroke up my thigh before he moved away, leaving me splayed on my stomach on the furs.

I knew what had to happen. Even if Modi hadn't been past all pretenses of control, there was no way I could deny him after allowing my other three mates to take me. Our understanding was still too tender, the ache in our bond still in fresh recollection, and so instead of curling up into a fetal position and pleading for mercy for my oversexed pussy, I looked over my shoulder through the mess of my hair for my fourth mate.

He was already towering behind me, his eyes dark and wild as he fell to his knees between my legs and grabbed my ass, clutching at my flesh.

"Modi," I whispered. "I want you to. I want you."

He didn't need permission—the moment he carved his mating claim into my neck, my body and my pleasure belonged to him. But I gave it to him anyway, because I knew, deep down, he craved it. He needed to know that he was wanted.

He grabbed my hip, his hands rough as he turned me to my back and hooked my legs over his arms, spreading me open in invitation.

I looked into his eyes as he guided his cock to my sodden folds and fucked up inside of me with a hard thrust, gasping with him when he was fully embraced by my wet heat.

He didn't pause to savor the moment; he was too far gone to have the capability. I clung to his shoulders as he screwed me rough, hard and thoroughly. No dirty words fell from his lips—only his harsh grunts, my own whimpers and the wet smacks of my pussy taking him all the way to the root over and over and over again filled the room.

When his knot finally swelled in my opening, my body obeyed his dominance and broke with him, the ache of our tie snapping in place behind my pelvic bone forcing me through a climax that drained the very last of my energy.

I collapsed underneath him, my arms and legs flopping to the floor in a decent starfish imitation. The last thing I saw before my consciousness fled the scene was the overwhelming love in Modi's eyes as he gazed down at me while his cock pulsed, coating my cervix with every last drop of his essence.

I fell asleep to his rumbling purr, knowing into the marrow of my bones that I was finally whole again. Whole, and loved completely and eternally.

38

ANNABEL

Wake up, Annabel.
Dawn is here. Wake up.

I GROANED IN PROTEST, my eyelids feeling like they weighed at least a ton. Each. When I finally managed to crack them open, the faintest of gray light met me. Gray light and silence, save the soothing sound of deeply breathing men.

My men.

I forced the muscles in my neck into action, twisting to search for whoever'd woken me up. Around me, all four of my mates lay sprawled, fast asleep. Or, more like around and on top of me.

On the journey here, I'd been grateful for Modi's

and Bjarni's body heat, but buried underneath four huge furnaces, things were a bit on the toasty side.

Gently so as to not disturb anyone, I tried to extricate my arm from where it was wrapped around Modi's neck.

He grunted, rolling halfway so my limb got trapped in the bend of his elbow.

"Modi," I whispered, poking him in the face—the only place I could reach now, since Bjarni had a hold of my other arm. "Let go."

Another grunt. Slowly he cracked an eyelid at me. "Hmm?"

"I gotta get up. C'mon, release."

He closed his eyes again, pushing in closer against me to rest his head against my ribs and underboob. "Stay."

"*Modi!*" I somehow managed to keep my hiss quiet enough not to wake anyone else—I hadn't tried to move my lower body yet, but from the throbbing from down yonder, I was very, *very* sure I didn't need anyone waking up and suggesting round two.

His eyes rolled open again, both of them this time.

"I gotta pee. Help me get up. Please?"

Modi sighed, rolling off me with a reluctant groan. He even lifted Bjarni's arm off me so I could sit up. When I did, and winced at the way my abdominal muscles spasmed in protest, he rumbled out a concerned note, his warm hand finding my stomach. "Does it hurt?"

Despite the drunken quality to his voice, I could see worry that I might be injured spark in his blue eyes.

"I'll be fine. Go back to sleep." I gave him a smile that I hoped wasn't too much of a grimace.

"Hmm." His eyelids were already sliding closed again, his head relaxing into the space in the furs where I'd lain. "Hurry back."

I stroked a hand up along his side instead of answering. It seemed to do the trick—within moments he was breathing deeply again.

It was easier to pull free from the tangle of Magni's and Saga's legs, except doing so engaged my core muscles a fair bit, and I had to bite my lip not to whimper as I freed myself.

We definitely had to come up with some sort of schedule. Or a rotation. Norn-blessed or not, my poor vagina was still very much human, and if my four brutes had plans on making these sorts of nights a regular occurrence, I was relatively certain she was gonna pack up shop and flee the premises.

Ow.

Somehow I managed to get to my feet and stagger out of the pile of alphas still sleeping peacefully. You'd think they were the ones that'd been fucked beyond their limits, with how zonked they all were.

I took a moment to look back at them, and my heart stuttered with a warm kind of happiness I couldn't put into words. I was finally whole. More than whole—their bonds in my chest filled me past overflowing. In the bleakest moments, I'd thought I'd sacrificed my sanity, my very essence to Fate. That being permanently hollow, broken, was my sacrifice for a chance to save the world and everything that lived in it.

I'd been so wrong.

Fate had gifted me my mates, not punished me with them.

Moving stiffly, I found my clothes and pulled them on, grimacing as I did. The second I got the chance, I was taking the longest, hottest bath known to man.

I gave my sleeping alphas a final lingering look before I quietly slipped out the door and made my way through Valhalla's halls.

THERE WERE no guards stationed by Loki's cell. I hadn't met a single soul on my way from the tower room, last night's celebrations seemingly having taken everyone out of commission.

I used my magic to gain access to the dungeon, pressing it through locks to click them open rather than melting them off.

The dark god sat on the bare floor, leaning against the rough stone wall with his legs outstretched, looking haughtily bored despite his dire circumstances.

"You came," he said. There was no surprise in his voice.

"You knew I would."

Loki inclined his head a fraction of an inch. "I saw

your sense of honor when I touched your mind. And your soft heart. You were unlikely to wish your mates' sire dead, even if they are currently somewhat disillusioned by my... ah, *motivations*. You understand the complicated devotion a child has to their parents—even if she feels betrayed by them. Don't you?"

I drew in a deep breath, pushing down the hurt still festering from what my mom and dad had done. *He* was behind the deal that had sealed my fate—a deal made centuries before either of my parents were alive.

"Do you want to waste time tormenting me? Because at some point, your guards are gonna wake up from their hangover, and soft heart or not, I'm not going to risk mine or my mates' lives for you."

His lips pulled into a wry smile. With smooth movement, he got to his feet and walked across the cell floor to the bars separating us. This close, his presence was intimidating—almost as if the dark energy I'd seen when I fought him seeped from his skin and reached out to me with chilling tendrils. His eyes were as dark as his hair, and their touch as he looked me up and down put every hair on my body on end.

"Perhaps if I had truly been interested in breaking apart the nine worlds and ruling over broken ruins as the dark and terrible king Odin seems to believe is my true goal, I would not have given you to my sons," he said, his voice raspy and silky all in one. "Such *devotion*. Such power. You would make a magnificent God-queen. A worthy mother of my spawn."

I grimaced. "Yeah, no thanks. I've seen one of your *spawn* swimming around the Atlantic. Not interested. Now, do you want out or not?"

His smile hiked up a millimeter. "I suppose I better. Can't give Odin the satisfaction of mounting my head on a pike, can we." He reached his hands out between the bars. "Remove the ring."

I looked at his hand, frowning at the iron band around his index finger. "What is it?"

"A band to suppress my magic," he said. "Odin favors them. I suspect Saga and Magni have worn one similar to this during their stay in Valhalla."

Now that he mentioned it, I did have a vague recollection of Magni having a metal band around one index finger.

"And it can just be popped right off? Seems a bit of a design flaw."

Loki chuckled. "Not so much. You'll need to put a bit of your magic behind it, my dear."

Hesitantly I closed my fingers around the ring. It felt... odd. It didn't hum with magic so much as it felt weirdly dead. Like an absence of sensation, though I could feel its physical presence easily enough.

I gave it an experimental pull and frowned when it seemed to just slip between the pads of my fingers as if coated in oil. I tried again, this time allowing a thread of my magic to weave through my arm and into my hand.

It came off as if it was nothing but a plain band.

"Huh," I mumbled, turning it between my fingertips

to look more thoroughly at it. Small runes were etched along the inside of the metal, but there were no other indicators of what it could do.

"Dwarven magic," Loki said, rubbing his finger before he reached out his palm for the ring.

"I think I best keep hold of this for now," I said, arching my eyebrows at him as I shoved it into my pocket.

Loki shot me an offended look. "If you remember, I saved you from becoming dragon food *and* healed Thor's golden son. You have no reason not to trust me."

I stared blankly at him. "None at all, you sweet, innocent lamb, you. Now do you need me for anything else, or can you magic yourself out of here?"

"Your hand, if you please," he said, reaching out his own again, palm up.

I hesitated only for a moment before I placed mine in his.

Instantly the same dark magic I'd felt when we fought Nidhug entered me. I suppressed a shudder and let the golden light inside me follow his darkness. It pooled into a tight point, contracting inward like a black hole inside of me—until it expanded outward in the blink of an eye.

Bright light flashed in the dungeon, and when I blinked my vision clear again, Loki stood on my side of the bars.

"W-What was that?" I asked, blinking several more times.

"Teleportation," he said, releasing my hand so he could dust off his clothing. "It's a shame I can't stick around any longer—that power source inside of you is quite extraordinary. I could have taught you all manners of delightful tricks. But alas, this is where I must take my leave."

"Bye, then," I said, quirking an eyebrow at him. "Don't worry about me, I'll be fine."

Loki, who'd been on his way toward the door, turned halfway around to me. "Of course you will. No one's going to suspect a little human omega to have the kind of power it takes to break out of Odin's prison. I meant what I said—you are the key to my own survival."

"But fuck the rest of the world, eh?" I may have been a little bitter. "You're going to run off and leave us to try and stop Ragnarök. You say I have so much power, but you—you're a god. We couldn't have defeated Nidhug without you."

That irritating smirk returned to his face. "You knew I would even before you decided to help me. I don't know why you're complaining now. Would you scold a cat for eating a mouse? It is it's nature, after all. And this is mine.

"But..." His voice turned thoughtful and he cocked his head. "I suppose I did promise you that I would help discover who the real traitor is. The being who is determined to bring about the end of the worlds."

"So you know who it is now?" I asked, some of my irritation drowning in a burst of adrenaline.

"I have my suspicions." The corner of Loki's mouth quirked up again. "But I do know how you can unmask them. Seek out Grim. Out of all my sons, he is the most powerful and the cleverest. Go now before your mates awaken, and you will learn the identity of the traitor."

I blinked. "Grim? Grim knows? Why wouldn't he tell us?"

"I didn't say that he did. I said that if you go to him, you will learn the traitor's identity. But you must make haste, or the opportunity will pass."

Loki nodded at me. "And now I really must bid you farewell daughter. I suspect it will be some time before we meet again."

I DIDN'T KNOW where to even begin to look for Grim. He'd slipped out when I'd woken everyone up mid-orgasm last night, leaving me with little to no clue as to his whereabouts.

I forced my still-sore muscles into a jog as I passed through hallway upon hallway, trying to guess where the hell a grumpy Lokisson would have gone to rest for the night. There was still not a living soul to be found anywhere, but that was bound to change any moment. If Loki were to be believed, speed was of the essence.

"Annabel."

The sound of my name lilting in a deep, raspy voice nearly made me jump out of my skin. I spun around toward the sound, drawing a breath of relief when I saw Grim poking his head out the opening of a beautifully carved door.

"I've been looking for you," I said, quickly moving back down the hallway to him.

He quirked an eyebrow at me. "I wasn't interested in seeing you have sex."

Heat filled my cheeks. Considering how depraved and voyeuristic my sex life had gotten, it was probably a miracle I could still feel shame about it.

But getting that disgusted look from cool, reserved Grim? Yeah, that was shame tightening my belly, all right.

Before I could stutter an apology, he moved back, opening the door farther. "I need to show you something before everyone gets up."

Adrenaline started pumping through my body again and I hurried through the door, squeezing past him into what looked to be some sort of library. From floor to ceiling, shelves with scrolls, leather bound books, and stone tablets lined the walls, and in the center were a handful of tables with unlit candles and a chair at each.

"Is this about the betrayer?" I whispered. "Have you discovered his identity?"

Grim frowned. "The betrayer? No. It's about Mimir. I found him."

"Oh! That's even better!" I took a half-step toward him to give him a hug, but stopped in my tracks when he leveled me with an icy stare. "Uh... well done. We should tell the others."

"No," he said, walking deeper into the library.

I followed. "No?"

He sighed and looked at me over his shoulder. A lock of black hair hid his amber eye from me, allowing only his blue one to meet mine. "Mimir is on another plane. The only way we can get there is through magic—powerful, ancient magic. Not the kind my brothers or *the others* possess. To bring them there...

"You and I have the kind of magic needed to travel across the planes. They would only hinder us."

"Oh." I frowned. "Are you sure? My magic is much stronger when I'm with them."

"I am certain. This is the only way we'll get to Mimir, but we have to go now. Whoever the betrayer is, if he discovers that we've located Mimir, he'll try to stop us."

"Okay." I'd really, *really* hoped for a few days' rest before we continued our mission to stop Ragnarök, but Grim was right—the less of a chance the betrayer had to learn of our plans the better. "I will wake the others and tell them."

Grim shook his head. "There is no time for that. They will argue endlessly to keep you here, wasting what head start we've got. We will only be gone for a few hours and will return before they realize you're gone. Please, Annabel. This is the only way."

The earnest plea from the man I was pretty sure was half ice block was impossible to ignore. I winced internally at the thought of shifting planes of existence without my mates—it didn't sound like it'd be any less painful than jumping between worlds.

But if Grim was right, if this was our best shot at finally getting to Mimir...

"Okay. How do we...?"

Grim stepped away from me and closed his eyes. When he opened them again, he reached out both arms and drew a shimmering silver circle in the air between us, big enough to fit a person through.

Apparently Loki had been wrong. Odin hadn't made his other captives wear the magic-suppressing ring.

"This will take us there," he said, holding out a hand toward me. It disappeared into nothingness when it entered the circle. "Come, Annabel."

I drew in a deep breath, and bracing for the expected pain from my bonds, I stepped through the circle.

ANNABEL

It took several moments before I could breathe again. The agony behind my ribs was blinding, and I lost track of time as I shuddered, hands pressed to where it felt like I was being torn asunder.

But slowly the pain eased to a dull, aching throb. That familiar agony I'd carried while I'd been parted from Saga and Magni for the past three weeks set in, only instead of two tears in the fabric of my mind, it was four.

"Sonuvabitch," I gasped once I could speak. "Mother of god."

"You will find sons of bitches and their mothers aplenty here, omega. And even gods," a dry voice sounded from beyond my misery. "But I suspect that is not why you have sought me out."

Slowly I raised my head to take in my surroundings, forcing my body to straighten from the fetal position I'd curled into the moment I stepped through Grim's magic circle.

I blinked, trying to clear my vision, but no matter how much I squeezed my eyes shut and opened them again, everything around me was rendered in stark black and white. There was not an ounce of color anywhere.

I was in a forest, I realized—or rather, in a clearing in a forest. It took me a moment to make out, the lack of color confusing to my ability to orient myself. Straight ahead of me, on a tree stump, sat a head.

When I only stared mutely at it, it arched its bushy eyebrows at me.

"Oh, what the fuck?" I croaked. "Grim? Grim, what the hell is this place?"

Movement made me look up. Grim stopped by my left side, his face inscrutable as he stared at the severed head.

"Mimir," he said, his voice low and devoid of emotion.

The head—*Mimir?*—flicked his eyes up to look at Grim. He looked at him for a long moment, then returned his gaze to me.

"Well, you are almost correct, omega. Your companion has brought you to Hel."

"You are Mimir?" I asked, pushing myself fully up on my knees. "We have come to ask for your help. I am... you prophesized a, uh, prophecy about... about me. Us."

"You are the omega who could have stopped Ragnarök," Mimir said. "The one whose fate was woven with five young godlings."

I frowned. "Uh...? '*Could* have?'"

"You are a mortal in the land of the dead," Mimir said solemnly. "Whatever you could have been and however your life thread was woven matters little now. You were lost the moment you stepped foot in this realm."

"W-What?" A horrible sucking sensation pulled at my gut. I heard the words, but no matter how much I tried, I couldn't make sense of them. "I don't... I don't understand..."

"No mortal who crosses into Hel can ever leave again," Grim said, his voice uncharacteristically soft. He looked down at me then, and in his eyes I saw the horrible, inconceivable truth. "You will remain here until the end of time. The prophecy is broken, and you, Annabel... You are dead."

It finally came together then, my mind sharpening to a pinpoint as sick despair clawed at my aching, constricting chest.

He had tricked me here. He had planned this.

Grim had betrayed us.

BETRAYING DESTINY
THE OMEGA PROPHECY III

THE STORY CONTINUES IN *BETRAYING DESTINY*

Betrayed and killed by the god destined to love her

He was meant to be her lover, but he would rather see the Omega dead than surrender to Fate's snare.

No one escapes the Realm of Death, but if Annabel doesn't find a way out, her mates will die along with her, and Ragnarök will leave nothing behind but darkness and ashes.

Her only hope is to win the heart of the god who killed her. But even if she can trick her way into his icy soul, can she ever love a man whose hatred for her reaches back to the moment of her birth?

~

READ BETRAYING DESTINY

~

GO TO *WWW.NORA-ASH.COM* TO GET YOUR COPY OF *THE OMEGA PROPHECY III*

CONNECT WITH NORA

Want to chat all things alpha? (and ruthlessly sexy book-boyfriends in general?)

❧

Join Nora's Reader's Group:

EMAIL:
www.nora-ash.com/newsletter

FACEBOOK:
https://www.facebook.com/groups/Yayromance/

ALSO BY NORA ASH

THE OMEGA PROPHECY

Ragnarök Rising

Weaving Fate

Betraying Destiny

DEMON'S MARK

Branded

Demon's Mark

Prince of Demons*

ALPHA TIES

Alpha

Feral

ANCIENT BLOOD

Origin

Wicked Soul

Debt of Bones*

DARKNESS

Into the Darkness

Hidden in Darkness

Shades of Darkness

Fires in the Darkness

MADE & BROKEN

Dangerous

Monster

Trouble